# SALVAGE

## MARTIN RODOREDA

ODYSSEY
BOOKS

Published by Odyssey Books in 2016



www.odysseybooks.com.au

A Cataloguing-in-Publication entry is available from the National Library of Australia

ISBN: 978-1-922200-62-4 (pbk)
ISBN: 978-1-922200-63-1 (ebook)

Cover artwork by Rachel Roberts (www.pencilpusher.biz)

*For Noah, Jacob and Thomas.*
*May your future be healthy and bright.*

# Chapter 1

The ruined building groaned ominously and Silver froze in place, holding her breath lest the hundreds of tonnes of twisted metal and broken concrete above her give way. Her heart thundered in her chest, and she counted the beats. Once, long ago, her dad told her that if you got to ten beats then you'd be all right. Within a few seconds, she had reached the number and the rubble above remained intact. She wondered briefly whether her dad's heart had ever reached ten beats as quickly as hers just had.

'You still with us, Sil?' The deep voice of her partner Coal sounded distant. She shifted slightly and raised her head to look around. Illuminated from the light built into the side of her gas mask, the air around her had taken on a smoky quality from the dust that had been disturbed. The beam of light revealed broken concrete, the twisted mess of metal reinforcing, and a few other odds and ends. She imagined she could taste the grit in her mouth, smell the mouldering damp of the place, and was thankful for the breathing filter. Apart from the metal, there was little here of value, and not much hope of digging any further into the building.

'Yep, I'm okay,' she called belatedly. 'Not much here though.'

She reached down to her thigh, which was no easy task in the cramped space, to pull forth the compact saw stowed there in a pocket sheath. With the saw free in hand she rolled carefully onto her back to get better access to the fingers of metal clawing down from above. The light revealed a couple of black cockroaches staring down, incredulous at her for disturbing their home. She brushed them away with her gloved hand, used to them by now. Roaches were perhaps the most prosperous of creatures still living in the Badlands.

'Just taking all the metal I can,' she called out to Coal, before setting to work with the small hacksaw. The serrated blade was sharp and cut fairly easily through the finger-thick pieces of metal, though it grated and squealed loudly in the process. Despite the keenness of the blade, it was vigorous work and after a few minutes Silver was breathing heavily and sweating inside of her overalls. Each time a piece of metal came away, she would tuck it into a hessian sack she carried with her. It was far from the most valuable material she had retrieved from the Badlands, but it would fetch a price nonetheless, and keep her place within the crew.

After a few minutes more she had cut away everything she was likely to get and carefully slipped the blade back into its pocket, making sure to secure the clasp.

'All right, pull me out Coal,' she called, rolling back onto her stomach in preparation for backing out. A rope fed through loops in her overall legs would enable Coal to pull and assist her as she carefully backed out of the rubble. It could also be used in an emergency, if something happened to her while inside the ruins.

'Coal?' she called again, after waiting a few moments for the rope to pull taut. A few breaths more and still nothing. 'Coal! Get back here!'

Her shout yielded nothing, the only sound her breathing within the cramped space. With no help forthcoming from the rope, she started to edge her way backwards the way she had come, but froze at what sounded like a gunshot from somewhere nearby.

'Fuck!' she cursed. Awkwardly, she reached for the small gun strapped into a holster over her shoulder. Before she could loosen the clasp, the rope around her ankles suddenly pulled tight and she was jerked violently a metre or so backwards. She gasped in pain and sparks erupted behind her eyes as her head struck an overhanging piece of concrete.

Fighting through the stars that clouded her vision, she found herself being dragged roughly towards the tunnel mouth. Frantically she reached out for something to grab onto, her fingers finding an edge of rubble. Her progress halted for a moment, but another violent tug ripped the piece out of her grip and continued to drag her inexorably toward the entrance of the tunnel.

Desperate now, she glanced back and could vaguely see a number of legs standing at the tunnel entrance. Though she couldn't make out much detail, she knew what they were: the mutated and sickly creatures that occupied the Badlands.

'No!' she screamed out as another tug dragged her closer towards them. Mutes hated those who dwelt within the protection of the Dome, and if they got their hands on her, she was dead—or their dinner.

Her right hand found another perch and grabbed it, while her left fumbled with the securing clasp that held the saw in place. Eventually her fingers cooperated and got the clasp open. Before she could pull the blade free, another violent tug caused her to lose her grasp, and she was dragged another metre closer to the mutes.

No longer clasped in place, the blade fell from its pouch with the next pull, tumbling to one side. She twisted to reach for it, her fingers teasingly close to the handle. The next pull jolted her further along, taking her out of reach of the saw.

She rolled over onto her back and tried pulling up with her legs, kicking and straining to loosen herself. Her efforts were futile, with the rope and her pants well made and unforgiving.

It was only then that Silver remembered the gift Coal had recently given her. She reached inside her overalls, down between her cleavage where she had fashioned a pocket to keep it concealed, and pulled forth a flick-knife. Clicking the release button, the sharp metal blade swooshed free of its beautiful engraved wooden casing. With the muscles in her legs straining against the continued pull of the rope, she reached down in the confined space and began feverishly sawing at the rope.

She was now only a couple of metres away from the entrance of the twisted tunnel, and could make out the legs of at least a dozen mutes crowded around. There was no sign of Coal or the rest of her crew. As she continued to saw, one of the mutes lunged into the hole towards her. Its skin was pale and sickly in colour, a pasty yellow white. Its body looked malnourished, eyes sunken within their sockets, greasy black hair hanging thin and limp.

Desperation lent her strength, and with a snarl, her blade cut through the last threads of rope and she was free. Silver scrabbled backwards away from the mute, but the creature darted forward and she felt its cold, bony fingers close on her ankle. She fought and kicked against the grip, but the cramped surroundings hampered her efforts, and the mute's grip proved surprisingly strong. Soon she found herself being pulled towards the tunnel entrance once more.

Reaching under her arm, she fumbled with the clasp that held her gun in place, eventually ripping it free. Twisting onto her back, she sighted the mute down the length of her body. The creature's eyes widened as it saw the gun pointed its way and it let out a pitiable moan, but its grip did not slacken. Closing her eyes, Silver squeezed the trigger, and the shot reverberated deafeningly in the confined space around her.

Blood spattered over her pants and boots, and the grip on her ankle loosened as the mute slumped, lifeless. Finally she was able to scramble back deeper into the tunnel. Only once she reached the spot where she had cut away the metal earlier did she pause for breath and to assess the situation. Her head hurt where she had banged it, and when she reached up to touch the spot, her hands came away wet with blood. A panicked sob escaped her lips as the gravity of the situation dawned on her. She was injured, separated from her crew and stuck inside a collapsed building deep in the Badlands with a bunch of hostile mutes waiting for her to emerge.

'Fuck you, Coal!' she screamed, throwing the full weight of her panic into the curse. 'How could you leave me?'

Her voice sounded hollow and tinny through the mask, the clear plastic fogging slightly from the outburst. Her heart thundered almost audibly in her chest, her lungs straining under the pressure of her quick, shallow breathing. Bracing herself against the wall of the tunnel and sitting up as best she could, Silver forced herself to concentrate on breathing, fighting for calm.

'Okay, get a grip, Silver,' she said to herself, talking out loud to help retain her calm. 'We never leave a man behind. Never leave a man behind.'

It was a mantra she had first heard her father say years earlier, and one she had heard repeated many times since by other crew members. Her crew would not leave her, so she needed to concentrate on getting to them. Sheathing her knife but keeping her gun to hand, she gingerly raised her hand to her head again. This time the wound felt wet, but gummy, indicating the bleeding was starting to slow. Looking herself over, she could see that her arms were covered in cuts and scrapes, but nothing that looked too serious. Her overalls were a mess, but the blood splattering them was not her own. Satisfied she had no serious injury concerns, she turned her attention to her equipment. Her cutting blade was gone, but everything else appeared to be in place. She considered starting back down the tunnel to retrieve the saw, when the sound of two distant gunshots caused her to freeze, head cocked to one side.

A few agonising seconds ticked by until a third gunshot confirmed that someone was nearby. The sound galvanised her into action and, slipping her gun into its holster, she pulled herself further along the passage, poking her head into spaces that at first glance appeared to lead nowhere. Her efforts were soon rewarded as she spotted a hitherto unseen space above her. The entrance was narrow and would be a tight fit, but looked promising beyond if she could squeeze through.

With a glance back the way she had come to ensure no mutes had decided to risk venturing in after her, she began manoeuvring herself up into the space above. Her muscles strained as she held her arms up to narrow her shoulder width and pressed upwards into the tight space. It was extremely claustrophobic, and at multiple stages she found herself jammed in place. But she had plenty of experience at climbing through tight spots, and she knew the trick was to stay calm and keep working to find the few millimetres that would allow her to squirm her way forwards.

After a couple of minutes of twisting and straining, she pulled herself clear of the tight squeeze. Above, there was a little more room, with a large concrete slab having fallen against another, leaving a triangular space under it. There appeared to be some room to her left, so she crawled along the space and found that a narrow way continued, leading inexorably up.

'Not ideal, but better than the alternative,' she muttered as she continued to squeeze her way along. Eventually, she detected some daylight filtering down from above and switched the light in her mask off. Making an effort to move a little more quietly now, she dragged herself towards the light and cautiously poked her head out of the entrance.

The light of day was a sickly yellow, weak from the dirty fog and haze, which was normal for the Badlands on a windless day. Silver was again thankful for her mask, the air quality outside no better than the mould and dust-filled air below. She had emerged just below the peak of the twisted ruin, and must have come out on the opposite side from where she had entered as there was no sign of mutes or other movement below. She eased herself out of the crawl space and, perched on top of a jagged piece of concrete, drew her gun. She was perhaps twenty metres above ground level, the rubble-strewn side of the ruin descending steeply down to the tarmac. She eyed the slope, concerned less about getting down and more about doing so quietly.

Poised to begin the descent, she instead changed direction and edged her way to the right. Keeping low to the concrete below her, she cautiously edged around, peering past a large piece of plastic piping so she could get a view of the mutes.

There were fourteen of them in all, mostly males, but some women and youths among them. All were clustered around the tunnel entrance, crouched around something on the ground. She bit back a horrified gasp and her hand flew to her mouth as she realised it was a body, and they were feasting on it like a pack of wild animals. As she watched, one of the mutes raised its head, a string of bloodied flesh hanging from its chin and her stomach rebelled, causing her to retch.

Some of the other mutes raised their heads at the sound and she pulled back behind the cover the pipe offered, panting heavily and squeezing her eyes shut against the image. 'Coal!' she whispered under her breath, her voice full of anguish. She knew there was nothing she could do for him now. All that was left for her was to try to get back to the rest of her crew and make sure they were okay. Together they could come back for his body.

Wiping her mouth, she backed away from her perch, keeping low initially. Once she was sure she would be out of sight, she stood and abandoned stealth, making her way down the opposite side of the pile as quickly as she could manage. She had not heard any more gunshots, which left her concerned that the other crew members were in trouble, or had retreated back to the trucks. Either way, she needed to hurry back. Rubble skittered and clattered down the pile, loosened from her passage.

Reaching the bottom of the ruined mess, she took off at a run along the bitumen remains of the road. Debris from the collapsed buildings had spilled out across it in places, along with fallen power poles. Time and nature had also taken its toll, with sickly yellow-brown coloured weeds and small bushes pushing up through cracks and holes in the road. As she ran for the truck at full pace, she vaulted over debris that had spilled onto the road, including large red block letters—'We'—all that remained of some retail outlet long gone.

The sound of engines starting caused her to break into a sprint. She took a left and ran another block as the sound of the trucks started to recede. She put on a last burst of speed to round the final corner, but was too late, glimpsing the tail end of one of the trucks disappearing into the fog over a hundred metres away.

'Hey!' she yelled, sprinting in the direction they had gone. 'I'm here, come back!'

But the trucks were swallowed by the fog, the sound of their engines gradually fading away. Silver pulled up, hands up behind her head, gasping for breath. She was alone on the desolate street, surrounded by the smog-enclosed ruins of what was once the central business district of Campbelltown.

She felt her chest suddenly tighten, her breath quickened into whimpering gasps. She felt like she was suffocating within the facemask and fought the urge to tear it off. She forced herself to breathe methodically, fighting down the panic that once again threatened to overcome her. Coal was dead, her crew had left, and she was a long way from the Dome. They had driven out a fair way; a necessity in order to find decent pickings among the ruins these days, with everything close having already been thoroughly worked over. With the day half gone, she doubted whether she could make it back by nightfall. The thought of spending a night alone in the Badlands did little to help her panic.

Nor did the skitter of a stone behind her. She looked over her shoulder and a jolt of adrenalin shocked her body as she saw a pack of mutes rounding the corner. Whoops and screams echoed down the street as the pack spotted their quarry and started towards her, causing icy fingers of terror to scratch down her neck and back. She didn't have enough bullets to take them all down, and didn't have much hope of outrunning a pack of fourteen. The image of them tearing at Coal's corpse like a pack of wild dogs flashed across her mind, and she imagined her in his place.

She pulled out her gun and, hand trembling ever so slightly, raised it at the mute leading the pack. The shot echoed weirdly across the fog-covered terrain, sounding like multiple shots fired from different locations. Her target stumbled and crashed to the ground and she immediately turned and ran, sprinting down the street away from them as fast as she could. She had heard that mutes were cannibals, and was hoping now that there was some truth to those stories. She kept her gun in hand just in case. If her ploy failed and they kept chasing her, she would save one bullet for herself.

# CHAPTER 2

The brakes emitted a brief high-pitched squeal as the truck pulled to a stop. As Lead killed the ignition and the rumble of the engine died away, the interior of the truck descended into silence. It had been a sombre trip home through the Badlands, knowing that they'd left one of their team members behind. Silver had been one of Lead's closest friends within the crew, and when Coal had returned on the run with news that the mutes had nabbed her, he had been devastated. He had wanted to take them on, regardless of their number, and go back and get her, but Coal had lamented that it was too late. He had seen her taken down while he fought in vain to get to her and he wouldn't risk further loss of life in a fight with nothing to gain. Lead had reluctantly given in, and they had retreated to the truck and started the long drive back to the Dome.

Now they were in one of the busy checkpoints that guarded the entrance in and out of the Dome, where salvage crews returned with their haul for the day and unloaded it for sale. Other work trucks lined the walls, though it was not as busy as usual, as many crews were yet to get back. The encounter with the mutes had forced Coal to cut their day short. Further within the cavernous warehouse was a market area where items salvaged from the Badlands could be laid out and put on sale for potential buyers. Nearby was a large weigh station, used for valuing the metal that was brought back. A huge set of heavy metal doors with interlocking panels opened every few minutes to admit rival crews as they returned from their time out in the ruins. Beyond them, another set could be glimpsed, forming the airlock that kept the noxious gases outside the Dome at bay.

The checkpoint itself was a hive of activity and sound; the clangs of scrap metal being loaded into the weigh crates, the idling of engines, the grating and dull boom of the airlock doors grinding open and shut, open and shut. Within the truck though, there was stony silence.

Coal was the first to break it, pulling off his respirator and jumping out of the front passenger seat. He hadn't spoken a word the whole ride home, and no one had been game to talk to him about what had happened. Silver had been more than a member of his team; she had been his girlfriend for more years than most could recall.

'What the fuck are you all waiting for?' he yelled, his deep voice booming threateningly. 'Get this pathetic load of scrap out of the truck and over to the weigh station. I want to get the fuck out of here.'

He slammed the door loudly behind him, the sound galvanising the crew into action. Coal stalked across the floor of the warehouse, heading for the latrines on the far side. He cut an impressive figure, standing just under two metres tall, and weighing in around a hundred and twenty kilograms. None of this was fat; he spent much of his time in the gym and his muscles bulged obscenely as he walked. Tattoos depicting women, skulls and guns started from his elbows and ran up his arms and across much of his back and chest, his grey-green sleeveless overalls obscuring many of them. Beyond his physique, he was also a reasonably good-looking man, with a strong jaw, dimpled chin, and tanned skin. A scar ran across his right cheek and his nose was slightly bent, both gained from some dust-up in the past. The imperfections only added to his look, lending him the appearance of a conquering warrior. A number of piercings lined both earlobes, while another one pierced his left brow.

Leaving the crew to carry out Coal's orders, Lead climbed from the driver's seat and hurried to catch up with his friend and boss. He dragged off his own breathing mask as he went, breathing in the tang of exhaust fumes and the stink of body odour. He was a big man himself, not quite matching Coal's height and build, but tall and well muscled nonetheless. That was where the similarity between the two men ended; Lead had dark-skin, having both Aboriginal and Islander blood in his veins. His teeth flashed pearly white, and his nose was broad. Where Coal had closely cropped hair, Lead's was tangled and black, forming a messy nest on top of his head, with stray strands sticking out like errant twigs. His skin was free of the tattoos that covered many of their crew, and he had an easy smile. The crew often joked that he and Coal should swap names, on account of his darker skin.

Lead caught up with Coal when he was almost at the latrines.

'Hey, boss! You all right?' he asked.

Coal glanced back at him, his eyes dark and emotionless. 'If you're offering to hold my cock for me while I take a slash, I'll pass.'

'No, about what happened out there today.'

Coal stopped outside the door to the bathrooms and turned to face him. 'What happened was Silver got nabbed by the mutes, and nothing we do or say now is going to change that.'

'But how did they sneak up on you? How did you and Sil get separated?'

Coal's eyes flashed dangerously and his voice lowered threateningly. 'What exactly are you suggesting?'

'Nothing, boss, I just thought talking about it might help.'

'It won't. She's gone. They came in hard and fast while she was roaching. I was forced away from her, and only dumb luck and stubbornness stopped me from going down under the weight of their numbers. By the time I recovered and got a few shots away, they had dragged her from the hole and there was nothing more I could do. Now, I need to take a piss, and then I've got to prepare for a meeting with Silmac, so I suggest you get over to the rest of the crew and help them unload the gear. And ensure they all conceal their guns properly this time. It doesn't help our cause with Silmac when he hears reports of one of his own crews being busted packing firepower inside the Dome.'

Coal turned and disappeared through the bathroom door, leaving Lead with the disturbing image of his friend being torn apart by mutes as he slowly made his way back towards the truck.

* * * * *

Her feet ached, her breathing came in ragged gasps, and her mask continually fogged up, but still Silver pushed on. The wind had picked up to drive the smog away, and she avoided looking behind her, knowing the sun was creeping ever lower in the sky. Her ploy with the mutes had worked, and they had given away their pursuit to feast on one of their own. But it would mean little if she could not make the Dome before nightfall. She had been running for a few hours now and the wind was a pleasant relief from the heat of the day. It also increased visibility, and she wanted to take advantage of the fog-free skies to check her progress and get her bearings. She laboured on up a steady rise, creeping closer to the top and the view it would afford.

Reaching the top, she saw the remnants of the inner-west of Sydney sprawled out before her. She was closer to the Dome now, a great, arching structure that climbed up out of the ruins and reached towards the sky before plateauing and beginning the long curve back to the ground. Made of a meshwork of metal and dark glass, it resembled the gigantic, many-faceted eye of a fly. Shadows of the sky-rise buildings under its umbrella could be glimpsed through the darkened glass. The most prominent building, Silmac Tower, was located at the very centre of the Dome and its top level and spire pierced the top, thrusting skyward.

The sun was getting low in the sky behind her, catching the glass panels and bathing the side of the Dome in a kaleidoscope of colours. The dazzling brilliance of the sight was a stark contrast to the surrounding landscape. The vibrant city and suburbs that once surrounded the city centre was the very image of destruction, as if a titanic bulldozer had methodically razed the buildings and homes that once covered the area. There were no intact structures left this close to the Dome, other than the once iconic Harbour Bridge. Being on the far side of the Dome, Silver could only glimpse the bridge's orange-splotched arch. Once the arch had been dark grey and seemingly indestructible, but even its majestic strength was succumbing to the volatile weather. On everything else, earthquakes, violent storms, tsunamis and time had taken their toll, leaving behind kilometres of broken and twisted ruins, black, brown and grey. Sickly weeds and small yellow shrubs were dotted here and there across the landscape, but there were no large trees left.

The wind whipped around her, cooling her body. But her relief was short-lived as she looked right and cursed. The wind brought with it great black clouds rolling in towards the city from the south-east. A storm was brewing, and Silver understood it meant death to be caught out in it. She looked back to the Dome and knew that reaching it before nightfall would be challenge enough, but there was no chance she would make it before the storm hit.

She scanned the surrounding area for anything that would offer her some protection against the storm and approaching night. Her only hope was to find some ruins with a tight squeeze, crawl in as far as she could and hope it gave her enough shelter, and that no mutes or other predators came across her during the night. Mutes were not the only thing that stalked the ruins; feral dog packs, vicious cats, large rats and other creatures haunted the wastes. Some even claimed they had seen monkeys and tigers prowling the Badlands, ancestors of a zoo population from times long past. Silver had never given much credence to such tales and hoped now she was right.

A set of crumbling but still partially intact buildings about a kilometre away was the only real promise of shelter Silver could find. She tightened her pack and took a few shuffling steps towards them when she heard what sounded like running footsteps from somewhere behind her. She immediately darted off the road, seeking cover behind a fallen power pole, one end of which was partially raised atop the rubble of a broken townhouse. It looked as though the pole had been the cause of the house's collapse in the first place. Burrowing in close to ensure she would not be spotted, Silver found a hole that afforded her a view of the road.

The footsteps grew louder, soon accompanied by a heavy wheezing sound. After a few more moments a mute came into view, running laboriously down the road in the direction she had come. He was stooped over to a greater degree than Silver deemed normal for mutes, and she realised that he was quite old. Wisps of a beard clung to his chin, long and white. He was incredibly thin, had sickly pale skin, and the few teeth that remained in his mouth were black and in poor condition.

As he half-ran, half-shuffled along, he looked over his shoulder and moments later three more mutes appeared in view, pursuing him and gaining quickly. They appeared much younger, probably late adolescent. Though still thin and sickly looking, they were far less stooped, had fuller hair and were less emancipated. Each held a crude club in hand. With a burst of speed, one of the pursuing mutes sprinted forward and swung its club in at the older mute's legs, causing him to fall heavily to the ground. The three whooped and jeered, circling the prone mute and jabbing at him with their clubs. The elder mute curled up into a ball, using one hand to swipe pathetically at the taunting clubs, and the other to try to protect his head and face.

Silver couldn't help but feel pity for the tormented mute as she watched the younger mutes grow more aggressive in their attacks. One launched a savage kick at the back of their victim, causing him to howl out in pain. Silver's hand unconsciously crept over to the handle of her gun and her eyes hardened as another kick was launched at the mute's midsection, sending him into a violent coughing fit.

It was too much for Silver, all too similar to scenes she had witnessed growing up, inside the Dome between humans. On those occasions she had been powerless to halt the beatings, but this time she was in a position to do something. As the mute wielding a metal club lined up for another kick, she rose from her hiding spot and levelled her gun at him.

The shot rang out, reverberating off the ruined piles of rubble around them, and the mute who had been about to strike instead fell to the ground in a howl of pain, clutching at his leg. The other two mutes twirled to face her, their grubby faces twisted in a mixture of shock and outrage. One of them started to advance towards her, but then gave pause as she redirected the gun towards him.

'Clear out!' she yelled at them.

They paused, glancing at each other and at their companion who continued to howl and clutch at his bloodied leg. It seemed to Silver that they were weighing up their chances of getting to her before ending up like their friend. She didn't give them the chance, aiming the pistol at the feet of one of them and taking another shot. The cracked bitumen before him exploded in a cloud of dust and debris and that was enough for the two of them to turn and flee the clearing. The wounded mute let out an angry moan at the back of his departing comrades, before struggling to his feet and hopping after them, throwing a last fearful glance at Silver.

Silver waited till they were well out of sight before turning her attention to the older mute, who by this time was in the process of slowly rising to his feet. His body shuddered under another wracking cough, and each breath was laboured. She took a step towards him to offer assistance, but hesitated. Having finally regained his feet, the mute turned towards her and their eyes locked. His grey-blue eyes seemed incredibly human to Silver and, while she could not read them, she didn't detect any malice or anger. Slowly she lowered her gun and re-holstered it.

'Gotta go,' she said, wondering if he'd even understand her. Either way, she did need to get going, as the approaching storm had gotten alarmingly closer in the last few minutes, looking darker and more ominous than ever. As if on cue, a jagged bolt of lightning rent the air to the south, lighting up the landscape momentarily. A threatening peal of thunder followed close on its heels and the ground seemed to tremble slightly at its power. The light had taken on the sickly yellow look it adopted right before a big storm as the sun continued to drift closer to the western horizon.

Silver gave the mute a wide berth as she made her way back onto the road while it watched her, unmoving. She was fifteen paces down the road and was about to break into a run when he called out, his voice hoarse and strained, sounding more akin to the bellow of a venerable seal than the call of a human. Silver paused and turned, her hand instinctively falling back towards her gun. He motioned at her: *come.*

Silver shook her head, and motioned over her shoulder in the direction she had been heading, walking backwards to keep moving. 'I'm going this way.'

He shook his head and took a few steps to his right, motioning to her again. *Come.*

Silver stopped moving now, but still had reservations on following the mute. What did he want with her? She shook her head again and pointed her thumb over her shoulder again.

The wizened mute took a few more steps until he was nearly off the road and would soon disappear into the surrounding piles of rubble. This time he pointed up in a different direction, and Silver followed his line until she was staring into the ever-approaching mass of clouds, a thick dark blanket that looked like it would smother all that lay under it. She blanched as another jagged line of lightning ripped across the sky, illuminating the landscape momentarily. Barely had the light gone when the boom of thunder struck, the ground trembling at its fury. Silver threw her hands up to her ears, deafened by the power and volume of the thunder.

When the mute motioned again, *come,* and disappeared off the road between the rubble and debris, Silver no longer resisted, but trotted after him, slowly at first, then hurrying to catch up. She could not imagine surviving a night out in this storm, but his existence showed it was possible to do so, that he must know of some shelter.

'Yeah, but will I be sharing it with a bunch of hungry mutes?' she muttered to herself. It was a real possibility and her hand instinctively found its way to the handle of her gun once more.

The pair wound their way through the piles of rubble, once comfortable homes and apartment blocks. The mute walked confidently through the debris littered terrain. Despite his limp and advanced aged he moved quickly, almost effortlessly. His bare feet, black with untold layers of dirt, had the uncanny knack of avoiding all obstacles in their way and made not a sound. Silver, who fancied her ability to move with stealth when needed, felt deafeningly loud by comparison, as if each footfall was that of a clumsy, lumbering giant.

It was not long before she had lost her way, her guide navigating his way through the ruins. She knew she would be hard pressed to make it back to the road, and she constantly looked over her shoulder, frowning at her inability to identify a landmark with which to determine her position. But a look at the approaching storm reminded her that she had little choice in the matter, for it continued to roll in with frightening speed and would be upon them any minute. Another jagged line of white light split the sky, forking into half a dozen claws that reached for the ground before fading from sight and leaving only their memory imprinted on her retinas. The boom that followed a few seconds later was much louder than the first, reverberating across the sky as if announcing the imminent arrival of the storm. A gust of cold wind whipped around them, stealing Silver's breath away momentarily. It had been a warm day out in the Badlands, but the air arriving with the storm was bitterly cold.

She hurried to close the gap between her and the mute. Like it or not, she was completely at his mercy now, and she hoped she had done the right thing following him. At least she wouldn't have to ride out the storm alone. She was generally not the type to give into her fear, but the thought of being alone, huddled in some hole while the storm raged above, was not a prospect she relished.

The wind continued to pick up, whipping dust and debris through the air, and making Silver all the more grateful she was wearing her respirator, which also protected her eyes. She could feel the bite of the cold, her sleeveless overalls and singlet offering little protection from the icy chill. Her sweat-dampened clothes gave it extra bite, causing her teeth to chatter and prickly goose bumps to rise all over her skin.

Hampered by the cold, Silver lost sight of the mute as he disappeared around a pile of shattered concrete. She hurried to catch up with him and was alarmed to find no sight of him when she rounded the bend. She looked frantically, left and right, but could not see where he had gone. Panic gripped her; had he left her to die, gotten her lost so that the storm would finish her off? There was no time to find adequate shelter now, a fact that was punctuated by another flash of lightning and a bone-shaking crack of thunder.

Something grabbed her ankle, and she nearly howled out in shock and fear. Looking down she saw the mute reaching out from a nearly invisible and incredibly tight hole amidst the rubble. He released her ankle and motioned for her to follow before disappearing from view once more. Silver looked dubiously at the tunnel, not particularly keen to join a mute inside such a tightly cramped space. But a gust of wind that nearly swept her from her feet made the decision for her; she would most certainly die if she stayed out in it much longer.

# CHAPTER 3

As the door to his office closed, Corbett Silmac rose from his desk and turned to the cabinet that ran along the wall behind him, grabbing first a glass, then a decanter filled with an amber coloured liquid. Silmac's office was simultaneously Spartan and opulent, the latter being as much a fact of the view laid out before him as the contents of the office itself. Situated on the top level of Silmac Tower, the office was palatial, a semi-circular shaped room with windows running the full length of its curved side. The windows offered a unique view as the only vantage within the city that afforded a view of the surrounding landscape, unobstructed by the panels and trusses of the Dome. The tower stood at the exact centre of the Dome and, being the tallest building in the city, its top level and spire actually poked through the protective structure. Instead of completely enveloping the tower as it did with the other skyscrapers, the curved edges of the Dome joined to the tower just below the top level, leaving the penthouse peeking out. From his chair, he had a one-hundred-and-eighty degree view of the west, looking out over the ruin that once was the city of Sydney. On a rare clear day he could see the Blue Mountains off in the distance. The other half of the level was his private premises, completing the three-hundred-and-sixty degree view.

Impressive as it was, the view was far from what it would have been in the past. On roughly four out of five days, smog, smoke or heavy rain prevented the occupants from seeing far beyond the edges of the Dome. On those rare clearer days, a brown and concrete wasteland was revealed, where once had stood a sprawling, green metropolis. The satellite cities once spread out north to south, the winding green avenues of the inner-west, the parks, stadiums and sports fields that were once dotted across the Sydney basin were all gone. The apartment blocks, the townhouses, the large brick and smaller fibro houses—all had been reduced to piles of rubble, or swept away altogether. The gums and other trees that had lined the streets and filled the parks had long since been cut down for lumber and firewood. Frequent tsunamis had deposited heavy loads of salt across much of the city and, combined with the intense cold of the big storms that periodically hit, had rendered nature's efforts to reclaim the land unsuccessful. The scene outside the windows was the only one Silmac had ever known, but he had seen faded photos of the city in its former glory.

The interior of the office was sparsely furnished, particularly given its size. The lift was in the very centre of the tower, though a wall screened it from view and ensured that Silmac's desk was not visible from the lift itself. Security tightly controlled access to the lift from the levels below, meaning Silmac was aware well in advance of the few people who were allowed up. To either side of it, backlit sky-blue cabinets ran along the internal wall in both directions all the way to the windows, giving the room the illusion of having windows on all sides. They brightened and darkened each day, in tune with the weather outside. The desk was large and empty, made of fine varnished wood. Its surface was only broken by two slits that allowed twin screens to rise from within the desk as needed. A keyboard and mouse were the only other two items adorning the desktop.

Silmac sat on a swivel chair made of unblemished black leather. Two matching armchairs faced him on the opposite side of the desk. The carpet was granite grey in colour, rich and thick, while in the south corner of the room a set of black leather lounges and armchairs faced each other for less formal meetings. The windows, backlit cabinetry and the grey carpet combined to give the office the feel of open space, as if standing on the summit of an urban mountain.

Silmac's fashion sense mirrored the décor of the office: expensive and high quality, but simple. His suit was black and looked plain at first glance, yet it was tailored perfectly to his build and made from high quality material. His pants and shoes were similar in appearance, plain but fitted to perfection, the shoes shined to a reflective sheen. The shirt he wore was sky blue in colour, well made, perfectly fitted, and left unburdened by a tie. His hands and face were free of jewellery or other accessories. There was little that was remarkable about the man himself. He was of average height and build, though on the slim side. His dark brown hair showed no signs of grey and was slicked back with gel. He kept a well groomed moustache and goatee and had a hooked nose, giving him a slightly hawkish appearance. His cheeks were marred and pitted from acne scarring from his younger days, his eyes his most defining feature: sharp and intense, calculating.

'Whisky?' Silmac asked, pulling the stopper from the decanter and pouring himself a quarter glass of the liquor. His voice had a slightly nasal quality to it.

'Please,' agreed the other person present in the room. Silmac's younger brother, Gavin, was seated in one of the chairs opposite his desk. As Silmac poured a second glass, Gavin rose and made his way around the desk to take it. Gavin did not much resemble his brother. At one-hundred-and-ninety centimetres, he was much taller than his brother, and carried far more weight, some of it muscle but much of it excess fat. He had big lips, a pudgy nose, close-set eyes and chubby cheeks, giving his face a squashed look. Like his brother, he wore a suit, but his was large and loose to accommodate his girth. The pinstriped style and looser fit did little to disguise his expanding waistline. His hair was the only real thing that resembled Corbett: dark brown and slicked back from his forehead, exposing a pronounced widow's peak.

'Looks like a storm,' Silmac said, gesturing to the southern edge of the office where a mountain of dark clouds, laced with flashes of lightning, was rolling in. Gavin only grunted a reply, his mind elsewhere.

'Why do you tolerate that Coal character?' Gavin asked. 'He is a simpleton and a fool and should not be trusted.'

They had just concluded a meeting with the Silmac Ops crew leader, who had delivered Silmac a report on the shape of the Badlands and news about decent salvage spots.

'Even simpletons and fools have their uses. And on the contrary, I think he is extremely trustworthy,' Silmac replied, making his way over to the lounges and taking a seat.

Behind him, Gavin narrowed his eyes, unsure if the first comment was targeted at him as much as Coal. He followed his brother over to the lounges and sat heavily in an armchair opposite.

'He may have his uses, but why him? There are dozens of men like him available to you who would be capable of running a far better operation than he does. I'm not sure that you can call someone who is stoned on drugs half the time and runs a crew made up of vagrants and addicts trustworthy?' The room was lit momentarily by a flash of lightning, the grumble of thunder that followed muffled by the thick glass of the office.

'But that's why he's trustworthy. While Coal is not the brightest, he is smart enough to know his own weaknesses, and understand that he has reached the position he has thanks to me and me alone. It's not that he can't be bought; rather there would be few who would buy him. He knows this and so is unlikely to do anything to jeopardise it, no matter what task I give him.'

'But you've got the police at your disposal as well as your own private forces; surely they are capable of carrying out your needs?'

'They are loyal to money, not to me. So in a way, they are less reliable than Coal, though in truth there is unlikely to be any who could afford to buy them out. Regardless, there are some tasks that are best left to look like they were a result of gang warfare and street squabbles. It is worth preserving *some* pretence of autonomy among the police force.'

Gavin snorted into his glass at the thought of the police force being anything other than a tool to carry out Silmac's commands, before taking a large swallow to finish off the drink. 'So have you found any more information on who it is seeking solar panels?'

Silmac's lips pursed disdainfully. 'Only rumours at this stage. But a rumour like that doesn't spring up of its own accord. Very few people are aware of the existence of such a technology. There is someone out there searching for the panels, and they've got access to resources. I mean to find them.'

'You need to relax. Grandfather took care of the problem four decades ago, hiring teams to scour the Badlands for any old panels out there and getting rid of them. He was thorough, also searching for and destroying any record of the panels. The knowledge of them is all but gone, and even if some still exist, no one can hope to reproduce them, and certainly not on a scale to threaten us.'

Silmac's eyes narrowed at his brother's words, and he rose from his seat, crossing over to the desk and pulling a thin cylindrical key from his pocket as he went. He inserted it into a small keyhole built into the desk and turned it. With a quiet whirring sound, the panels along the inside edge of the office slowly lifted, revealing a screen that featured a map of the city hidden beneath. The map was divided into buildings and sectors by a series of red lines, each with a label. Some sectors, most clustered in the centre of the map, were back-lit, indicating they had power. Most of the map was dark and lifeless.

One of Silmac's forebears had commissioned the map, wanting ultimate access and power over the grid at his fingertips. It ignited a feeling of strength and invulnerability within him each time he gazed upon it. He had the city at his mercy, with the ability to grant power or take it away as and when he pleased.

'Any talk of solar power is a threat to us and worth taking seriously. Look at the map. What does it show you?'

'It shows the grid and what areas have power switched on and which don't. So what?'

'The dark outweighs the light significantly, just as those with no access to power outweigh those with. Significantly. Just the thought of an alternate energy source among the Dome would be like throwing a flame to a barrel of oil. Once started, that is a fire you would be hard pressed to put out. I'd be surprised if solar power would ever have the capability of producing the energy needs of the Dome. But it is the idea of it that we need to be cautious of.'

Gavin sighed. 'So you think it must be one of the leading families?'

Silmac nodded, finishing off the last mouthful of whisky and heading over to his desk to grab the bottle. He brought it back to the lounges, topping up Gavin's glass and refilling his own.

'The common man within the Dome is too poor and uneducated to know of the existence of solar panels. The only plausible scenario is that someone with wealth and access to books and archives has uncovered some information about them. The culprit also needs to have access to money to fund a salvage crew. By focusing on panels, such a crew wouldn't be bringing in much money.'

Another flash of lightning lit the room and the boom that followed was powerful enough to rattle the reinforced windows of the office, causing Gavin to jump nervously.

'So we search and question every salvage crew in the Dome until we find them.'

'There are hundreds of crews operating within the Dome,' Corbett replied patiently. 'Doing so would be both impractical and highly detrimental to our cause. The fewer people that know about them, the better. We don't want to let every checkpoint guard in the city know what we are concerned about. Those guys are crooked as they get, and will sniff out any chance to sell information for a dollar or two.'

'Okay, so who of the ruling families could it be then? The Brownes?'

'The Brownes are motivated by one thing only: luxury. And they have ample means to continue to ensure it. I can't see them having the motive nor the energy to go stirring up trouble. What about the Nyugens?'

Gavin considered the suggestion. 'Could be, but they have the restaurant contracts stitched up, which gives them good prospects for continued prosperity. Besides, we've always had a good relationship with Ted, and he rules the family with an iron fist. What about the Adams? Or the Paxtons? Old Will is probably still smarting since his son got himself killed out on the streets, and he blames you for not having the police step in sooner.'

Corbett nodded thoughtfully. Either of the two families could be responsible. 'What do you think of Meldon? He's always bemoaned the gradual decline of the once powerful Meldon Corporation. Perhaps he is seeking a return to prominence?'

'No way.' Gavin rejected the idea. 'Ever since he married that young gold digger slut—what's her name? Tara? Sara? I'm not convinced he even knows about it. And she certainly doesn't have the opportunity to tell him, on account of her mouth being constantly occupied elsewhere. No, he's got other things on his mind and solar power is not one of them.'

Corbett's face remained expressionless, souring the smirk on Gavin's face from his comment. 'What about his son, Lance?'

Gavin shrugged, sullen. 'Don't know much about him. He seems to run the family affairs now that his father has taken a back seat. Keeps a pretty low profile. Let's face it, Corbett; we can speculate all night, but we need something solid to work off. Everyone has a motive: power. We've got it and they want it, so they start spreading a rumour of the existence of a lost technology to try to stir up some ill will towards us. Sitting here playing "guess who" doesn't achieve anything.'

Corbett pursed his lips at the comment, but did not respond, draining his glass instead. 'I will get Meek to look into it. If there is something to find, he will find it. Shall we head downstairs for some dinner? Italian?'

* * * * *

The tunnel sloped steadily downwards and was one of the tightest Silver had ever squeezed through. The light from her mask pierced the gloom but showed no sign of the mute. Apprehension caused her chest to tighten and breath to quicken. She felt like a mouse that had unwittingly descended into a snake hole while fleeing a cat. Behind her the storm continued to build in fury, wind whistling through cracks and holes in the ruins, creating a series of eerie screeches that did little to calm her nerves. Even down here in the tunnel she could feel the temperature dropping still further and she knew she had no option but to continue down.

After a few more minutes of progress, the tunnel opened up a little and overlooked a vent. Silver manoeuvred her body so that her legs dangled through the vent and she peered down. The thin beam of the torch illuminated a plain concrete stairwell leading downwards, with a landing directly below her. There was no sign of the mute.

With her body growing colder by the second, she turned around and began lowering herself down into the hole, her arms extending to full stretch before she was forced to drop the final half metre to the ground, landing in a crouch. With a better view now, she could see that to her right, the ascending stairs were completely blocked by rubble and debris, while to her left, the stairs descended into darkness. Her light, made for small cramped spaces, barely penetrated the darkness, but she could just make out a right turn at the bottom of the stairs.

Trying to prevent her body from shivering, she cast her eye back up the way she had come and noted there would be no quick exit if she was forced to flee. Other than an old crate sitting in the corner of the stairwell, there was nothing to aid with the climb back up.

She pulled her gun out again before making her way slowly down the stairway, watching and listening for any sign of movement below. She could faintly make out the sound of laboured breathing that indicated the mute was nearby. She imagined him hiding around a darkened corner, waiting to strike, and could no longer tell whether her body was shaking from the cold or trepidation. When she reached the bottom stair, she peeked apprehensively around the corner and found a short corridor leading to a closed door. Light emanated from under the door, a slight frown of confusion creasing her brow.

Still trembling, she edged over to the door and hesitantly turned the handle, gun held at the ready. Light and warmth spilled out from the room beyond and as Silver took in the scene, she lowered her gun absently to the floor and dropped her mouth open in wonder.

The room was a far cry from the dirty hovel she had expected. Some sort of basement, it had survived the destruction of the city and suburbs above remarkably well, particularly considering its size. A large central bench filled much of the floor space in the centre of the room, while an assortment of bookcases and shelves lined the walls. Every flat surface was filled with hundreds of relics from the past; but like none Silver had ever seen. There were model cars, toy planes hanging from the ceiling on string, beautiful blond-haired dolls and furry brown teddy bears staring out from shelves. Hundreds of books filled the bookcases; all arranged neatly, spines facing outward. There were toy figurines; soldiers, monsters, dragons and other fantastic creatures of all scales and sizes. A model train set dominated the table in the centre of the room, complete with toy houses, little plastic animals and electric locomotives. Silver had come across many of these types of things while salvaging, but they were always damaged, dirty and rotten. The toys and items before her were in great condition, as if fresh from the store.

The hunched mute was pottering around the table, working on a toy train with a set of tiny screwdrivers. A cold draft from the storm above gusted past Silver into the room, causing him to look over at her and hiss in agitation. He slammed down his tools and hurried around the table in her direction. Alarmed, Silver began to bring her gun back up to defend herself. But rather than being attacked, she found herself being ushered fully inside so the door could be shut behind her, chided like a belligerent child all the while. Once closed, the mute shuffled back over to the table and resumed tinkering with the train set as if she wasn't there.

Silver slowly lowered her gun, eventually tucking it back into its shoulder holster. While not warm, the room was much more comfortable than the air outside, and the sounds of the storm could still be heard but seemed now a muffled, distant thing. She slowly began to wander around the table, glancing repeatedly at the mute but otherwise allowing herself to take in the amazing relics on display.

Partway around the table, she recalled her confusion at the source of light in the room and raised her eyes to the ceiling. She was shocked to find a globe there, shining brightly. She glanced at the mute and back up at the ceiling, her frown at the sight deepening. Most of the buildings within the Dome didn't even have access to electricity, the occupants far too poor to pay the exorbitant price. It seemed impossible that a sunken basement in the middle of the suburbs could have access to power.

Silver returned her attention to the mute and studied him more closely. Before this day, mutes had seemed to her nothing more than savage and cannibalistic creatures, monsters to be feared. But the creature before her was seriously challenging that belief.

Now, under clearer light, the mute appeared much more human to Silver. It was not so much his physical appearance. His skin was too pale, with an unhealthy looking grey hue to it. His body was thin and malnourished, with stick thin arms and legs, a drawn face and sunken chest. As she had noticed earlier, he was bent over even more than what was normal for mutes. He had little hair on his head, just a few white wisps to match those on his chin. His skin was wrinkled and the teeth he still had were crooked, ranging from yellow to black in colour. But the way he fussed and worked at the bench had a decidedly human flavour to it. And his blue-grey eyes did not look so different from anyone she had met inside the Dome.

Silver was filled with a feeling of compassion towards the creature as she watched him apply the finishing touches to a toy locomotive against the backdrop of hundreds of toys, books and ornaments. It was amazing to her that he had survived this long.

As if in affirmation to her thought, the mute was suddenly wracked by a violent fit of coughing, doubling over so low that his head fell below the level of the table. The coughing grew in intensity. Overcoming her earlier uncertainty, she rounded the table and reached out to him, patting him firmly on the back. He was startled at first and made as though to draw away. But the coughing prevented him from evading her and she persisted until eventually the fit subsided.

When at last he stopped coughing and took his hand away from his mouth, Silver saw that it was wet with blood, and she felt immensely sad for him. They stood there for a few silent moments, looking at one another, he studying her, she him.

A muffled, but still powerful crack of thunder shook the room, breaking the moment and causing Silver and the mute to glance upwards. 'How long do you think the storm will blow for?' Silver asked, pointing upwards in emphasis.

'Mmmiimm numph urggh,' the creature gargled unintelligibly. Silver shook her head hopelessly, unable to make any sense of what he was saying. The mute pointed up, then made a large circular sweeping noise with both hands before closing his eyes and nodding his head to one side.

'The storm is a big one?' Silver hazarded a guess, repeating the motion he had made as she went. 'It will last through the night while we sleep? Maybe?'

The mute bobbed up and down, a toothy smile on his face, though Silver had no idea if what she had guessed was what he had been trying to convey. But the booms and high-pitched whistling of wind coming from above indicated the storm had settled in for some time.

Silver sighed and looked around the room, thinking of her bed back in the Dome, luxurious by comparison. It looked like it was going to be a sleepless night for her. While she had compassion for the mute, and by now had the feeling he wouldn't harm her, she still wasn't prepared to let her guard down and go to sleep in his presence.

As the mute returned to his tinkering, Silver found a clear spot on the ground on the opposite side of the table and sat down, groaning at the stiffness in her legs. As she settled down, her stomach growled and she realised she hadn't eaten anything since breakfast and was extremely hungry. She rifled through her pack, finding a solitary nutrient bar and a flask full of water. It wasn't much, but at least it might take the edge off. She opened the bar and was about to take a bite when she noticed the mute watching her.

The bar paused halfway to her mouth and, though her stomach grumbled again in protest, she broke the meagre portion in two and held out half to him. He trotted around the table and took the food, sniffing it, frowning slightly, before popping it whole into his mouth and chewing thoughtfully.

Silver undid the clasp on her mask to take a bite of her own and considered the flavour, or lack thereof. She knew the bars contained all the essential vitamins, carbohydrates, protein and fats the body needed, but little had been added to give the bar much taste. The texture was soft and slightly chewy, but the bar was extremely bland, something like the excess, starchy water left in a pot that had been used to boil rice. Feeling thoroughly unsatisfied by the meal, she popped the last mouthful in and re-secured her mask. The mute looked at her expectantly once more.

'No more,' she told him, holding out her empty hands and shrugging.

The mute turned around and walked over to a can sitting on the floor near the entrance of the room. Picking it up, he considered the contents for a moment, before reaching one hand in and emerging with a large cockroach pinned in between thumb and index finger. The creature squirmed in his grasp, its legs working wildly to try to get free. He held it out toward Silver, who shook her head vigorously, her stomach churning at the thought of eating the insect. Shrugging, the mute wasted no time popping the roach into his mouth. Silver looked away from him as he chewed it, the crunching sound alone causing her stomach to rebel and threaten to bring up the small amount of food she had just eaten.

Unconcerned, the mute continued to munch on the roaches. Seeking a distraction, Silver rose and began perusing the table and shelves again. She reached out for a brown teddy bear, pausing to glance at the mute to make sure he didn't react poorly to her touching his things. He paid no heed, so she took up the bear, finding it soft to touch. It had a patch of matted fur on its lower back but otherwise was in excellent condition, with a subtle smile on its sewn mouth and a twinkle in its black button eyes. She gently stroked the fur on its head a few times before reluctantly placing it back in its spot.

She spent a long time among the toys, looking and touching these relics from the past. A half-turtle, half-man plastic figure with an orange headband; a green and white truck built from tiny building blocks with a few pieces missing; a skinny, plastic doll with pretty blond hair and a tiny floral sun dress; and an assortment of balls—small and green furred, larger round panelled and laced, oval shaped.

Eventually, Silver moved over to the bookcases, running her hand gently across the spines of the books, reading the titles. The shelves contained more books than she had ever seen, hundreds more than she had ever read. Many were children's books. She recognised a couple as more intact versions of some books her mother had read her as a child. Those copies had been falling apart, the pages yellowed and spotted with mildew, but they had been magical nonetheless. *The Magical Faraway Tree*,

*The Cat in the Hat, The Hungry Caterpillar.* She smiled as she flipped through the pages, mouthing the words as she read through the familiar stories. Her eyes started to tear up as the books brought back a flood of memories from a time long before, spent with her parents. They had read books together as a family, and even though she had sometimes struggled to relate to the stories from a world so foreign to hers, it had been soothing lying with her head on her mum's lap, lulled to sleep by her dad's gentle voice. When she was a little older, her parents had taught her to read and with a limited selection of books available, the stories from the books she had practised on were etched permanently onto her brain.

She moved on and alighted on a section dedicated to architecture and design. There were books on houses, books on high-rise buildings, books on stadiums and entertainment venues. In among them, Silver's eyes were drawn to a beautiful, leather-bound book with no name on the spine. It was not a huge book; probably twenty centimetres tall and only two or three centimetres thick, including the bound covers. She pulled it forth from the shelf to find a slightly faded brown leather cover, complete with golden metal corners and gold metal clasp. She ran her hand over the cover. The texture of the leather felt good on her skin. The book did not have a title, so she flipped it over but found the back similarly unmarked, provoking her curiosity.

Glancing again at the mute, who had finished his meal by this time and returned to the bench top, Silver gently undid the clasp to the book and opened it to the cover page, reading the entry there:

*This diary belongs to Benjamin Adams*
*born 19<sup>th</sup> of July, 1981*

The words were handwritten in black pen and in a simple but neat script. The name danced at the very edge of Silver's memory, and though she couldn't place it, she felt certain she had heard or seen it once before. She flipped through the pages and could see lots of entries, though looking at the dates they were not particularly regular and had been entered over many years.

A big yawn forced its way from her mouth as she settled back down on the floor next to where she had left her pack. The air in the basement was starting to get a little chilled, but she figured it was a good thing as it would help her stay awake. Getting as comfortable as she could under the circumstances, and fighting off another yawn, Silver settled in to read.

# Chapter 4



*From the diary of Benjamin Adams*
*December 30th, 2001*

*Hi Ben! This is the Ben from the past. If you are reading this, it means that you have gotten old, become nostalgic and wanted to relive your glory years! And for my part (also you), it means I have persisted with this diary thing, which Nan gave us. Can't believe I'm trying this; I seriously need to get a girlfriend. Anyway, here goes ...*

*I sent off another three resumes today, but still no luck with finding a job at this stage. So much for a uni degree guaranteeing work—most of the people in my class are in the same boat. All the firms are seeking someone with two or three years' industry experience, but how do you get experience if you've never been given a chance to prove yourself? The casual job in the warehouse pays the bills in the meantime, so I guess I'll just keep plugging away.*

*I'm starting to get back into training for footy already, even though pre-season won't start until mid-January, and the season itself will not kick off until May. But, having missed out on first grade this year, I'm determined to make the team next season. Speaking of which, today's run took me along the Hume Highway, which was a big mistake. The amount of exhaust fumes I breathed in made me feel weak and had to change my route onto quieter roads. It can't be good breathing in that much crap! Anyway, my hand is cramping up and I'm tired, so I'll chat to you next time.*

* * * * *

Silver awoke with a start, scrambling upright and pulling the blanket draped over up to her neck. Wide eyed, she scanned the room, looking for danger. It was darker than it had been earlier, with the light above dimmed low, but there was no sign of danger. The only sound was the loud and irregular snoring of the mute, who Silver eventually located under the table, curled up among some dirty blankets.

Drawing in a deep breath and wincing as she rubbed her sore neck, Silver silently berated herself for falling asleep. The diary lay open on her lap, under the blanket and only a few pages in, though she couldn't remember falling asleep. She also had not had a blanket covering her before she fell asleep. While it was filthy and smelled musty, Silver was grateful for the extra warmth it provided given that the temperature in the room had dropped further while she slept.

She scratched at her facial filter, her skin irritated and red at having had the mask strapped on for so long. She wanted nothing more than to take it off and give her face a splash with cold water.

Instead, she rose to her feet and stretched, rubbing her lower back and shaking some of the stiffness out of her legs. She couldn't hear any rumbling above, which gave her some hope that the storm had passed and she might be able to get going, though she had no idea how long she had been asleep.

As she listened out for any sound above, she registered that the snoring had stopped and turned to find the mute staring up at her from his bed. She smiled uncertainly at him, still coming to grips with the thought of being face-to-face with a mute.

Slowly, painfully, the mute climbed out from under the table and rose. Barely had he gained his feet when a fit of coughing overtook him, lasting close to a minute and prompting Silver to once more thump his back in awkward assistance. When he had recovered sufficiently, he moved past Silver, opened the door to the basement, and disappeared out of the room.

Silver was left wondering where he had disappeared to for a few moments, but then shrugged and started packing away her gear. Once her pack was secure, she scooped up the diary and placed it back on the shelf, with a twinge of regret that she had not been able to finish reading it. Taking up her pack, she started for the doorway but pulled up short when the mute re-entered, a pair of large furry dead rats in hand, dangling by their tails.

The mute held the rats aloft, accompanied by a toothy grin, and mimed the act of eating with his spare hand. Silver smiled weakly back at him, eyeing the rats apprehensively. Her stomach felt like it had a hole in it, but the dead rat in front of her was not how she fancied filling it.

Oblivious, the mute turned a nob on the wall that caused the lighting to return to a brighter level, and set about skinning and gutting the small animals, dropping the offal into a stained bucket. Once done, he skewered them with practiced ease onto a couple of thin lengths of metal and moved over to an old oven in one corner of the room, which had been used as a fire pit. Using some yellowed, crumpled paper, he struck a piece of metal against a stone until he managed to generate some sparks and get the paper smouldering. Carefully adding some splinters of wood piled beside the stove, he blew on the paper until soon enough he had a small but bright fire burning, the rats held over it.

Silver watched on in amazement at the whole process, once again stunned at how a creature she had considered on par with an animal less than a day earlier could prove so industrious. And as the smell of cooking meat filled the room, her stomach rumbled hungrily and her mouth began watering despite herself. The aroma reminded her of wandering past the rich stretches of the city where a few restaurants operated, and those who could afford it paid large sums of money to dine on real food, rather than the processed food that the majority of people lived off. As a child she had spent as much time there as she dared, breathing in her fill of the delicious aromas and imagining the food was being prepared for her. It was never long before she was chased away by the security of the establishments, but the memory of the stolen smell and the fantasy of sitting at one of the fancy tables, about to tuck in to a delicious cut of steak and side of crisp, fresh vegetables went with her.

Soon enough, the mute finished cooking the rats and handed one over to Silver, blowing on his own to cool it enough to eat. Silver took the proffered stick, her hunger and the smell overcoming her reluctance. She loosened her mask with her spare hand, lifting it to take a bite. The meat was hot and the taste was not as bad as she expected, though there was precious little of it. In minutes, alternating eating and breathing, she had polished off the morsel and her stomach felt better.

The mute had finished his much quicker than her, and made his way to the other side of the room. When he returned, he was holding out the leather-bound diary for her to take. Silver accepted it uncertainly, but quickly offered it back to him. 'This is yours. I can't accept it.'

The mute shook his head vigorously and pushed the book back towards Silver.

'Thank you,' she said with a smile, conceding. She took the book and tucked it carefully into her pack. Once again, she felt herself growing emotional at the actions of the mute, touched by the gift and ashamed not to be able to offer him anything in return.

The mute pointed upwards and made the sign of walking using his fingers before heading out of the room. Silver followed him out, taking one last look around at the amazing relics collected in the basement. It was a sight few in the Dome would believe existed out here in the middle of the Badlands.

At the top of the stairs the mute struggled on the landing to climb back out of the hole, using the crate to assist. Eventually he made it up, and Silver followed, having to jump and grab the edge of the rim, then scrabble up with her feet against the wall. She wormed her way along the cramped tunnel after the mute and finally dragged herself completely out to the tail end of another coughing fit from the mute.

The storm had passed, and the day was still and calm. The Badlands were blanketed in a thick, soupy layer of fog that distorted sound and obscured vision beyond twenty metres. The air remained cold, and her breath puffed in clouds around her. Looking around she realised with some concern that she could not see the Dome and had no idea which direction it would be in. She struggled to remember where it had been in the day before, but each pile of rubble looked the same in the cloying mists, and she could not see far enough to identify any other landmarks. She looked helplessly at the mute, and he motioned for her to follow and began walking around the large pile that covered his secret home below.

Placing her trust in him yet again, Silver followed. The ground below was wet from the recent drenching it had taken, with large puddles formed here and there. She looked at the remains of the building from which they had emerged and guessed it may have once been a shop. There was no sign of tiles or other materials that indicated it was residential. Some shards of broken signage, faded beyond legibility, were strewn in among the debris. Halfway up the pile was a strip of black panelling, akin to things she had come across once or twice before but appearing more intact. They looked a little out of place, as if they had been placed there after the building had collapsed, rather than having fallen and come to rest there.

In danger of losing the mute in the swirling mists, Silver hurried to catch up, not wanting to get lost among the twists and turns of the rubble. She noticed his breathing was getting louder and more laboured from the exertion, broken by a regular, hacking cough. She felt real concern for him, wondering how much longer he could survive.

As they walked, the thick fog slowly began to thin and lift, until eventually the sun penetrated the water vapour more fully and Silver was able to get her bearings back. Studying the glare of the sun through the thinning mist, she was surprised and a little alarmed to see how high it was in the sky already. She must have slept longer than she realised. While she had come a fair way the previous day, there was still a long way to go before reaching the Dome, and haste would be needed to ensure she made it back before nightfall.

A couple of minutes later, they arrived back at the remnants of the main road she had been following before the storm forced her off-track. Vestiges of the fog still remained, but the air had cleared sufficiently that Silver could see the huge structure of the Dome, rising imposingly above the devastated landscape around it. The mute stopped and pointed towards it, wheezing loudly.

'I don't know how to thank you,' Silver said, her voice cracking slightly from emotion. She reached out a rested a hand on his shoulder, his skin rough like concrete. 'You saved me from the storm and kept me safe and warm overnight. You've shared a meal with me, given me a gift, and put me back on track. How can I possibly repay you?'

He lifted up his hand and gently touched hers, then extracted himself from her grasp and gave her a nudge in the direction of the Dome. 'Ooohhh,' he said, the gurgle of fluid evident in his voice.

Silver studied him for a while longer, her eyes rimmed in moisture. She wished she could give him proper thanks, or take him with her back into the Dome. It would never be possible of course; the checkpoint guards would shoot him on sight, and probably her as well for trying to bring him in. But the thought of him dying out here alone filled her was sadness.

Another gentle push from him prompted her to start down the road. 'Goodbye,' she whispered, wondering again if he understood any of what she said. She tightened her pack straps and started off at a jog in the direction of the Dome. After a few steps, she turned to look back, but the mute had disappeared.

The howling of a dog somewhere nearby prompted her to continue. She was not out of danger yet and had a long run ahead. Blinking to clear the excess moisture from her eyes and scanning the road for any sign of danger, she started towards the Dome.

# CHAPTER 5

*From the diary of Benjamin Adams*
*February 2<sup>nd</sup>, 2002*

*The holiday is over—I finally got a job today, at a firm called Raymond Architecture. Turns out the old saying 'it's not what you know but who you know' is spot on; Jess (from uni) got a job there two weeks ago, and they had another role going so she put my name forward. Not sure why she suggested me, but not complaining! I was pretty nervous in the interview but it obviously went okay.*

*It was great handing my notice in at the warehouse—I won't be missing that place! RA specialises in commercial buildings, so maybe I'll get to design a few warehouses. More than likely I'll have a whole lot of crap work to do before I get to design anything, but it's a start and Jess seems to like it so far. I'll have to buy her a drink to thank her. I start next week, so will have to party hard this weekend.*

* * * * *

The red orb of the sun was sinking below the horizon with alarming speed, and with every centimetre it dropped, Silver's anxiety grew. The Dome loomed huge before her, rising from the ground like the many-faceted eye of a colossal-sized insect. The dying rays of the sun caught the structure, reflecting on the panels in a dazzling rainbow of brilliance. While the sight was breathtaking, it also meant that the checkpoints in and out of the Dome would soon be closing and would not reopen until morning. Silver doubted her odds of surviving a second night in the Badlands, not liking her chances of meeting another mild-tempered and generous mute with a secret hideaway. Mutes were rare this close to the Dome anyway, but wild dogs were not, attracted to the rats that thrived close to the city.

Silver's run had been blessedly uneventful but frustratingly slow, with the hilly landscape and other natural barriers slowing her down. She had heard the sounds of returning crews passing nearby through the afternoon, but had stopped short of trying to flag one down. A rival crew would as soon run her down as pick her up.

With the light starting to fade fast and the howl of dogs becoming more frequent and drawing ever closer, at last Silver saw the large letter 'D' painted onto a set of large double doors in the wall of the Dome to indicate she had arrived at one of the checkpoints. The Silmac Ops crew typically used Checkpoint E, which meant she had come a little further north than intended. She hurried down across the last stretch of barren land towards the Dome, her legs aching and breathing laboured.

By the time she reached the small access door beside the larger gates, twilight was fully upon her. She pressed the intercom buzzer, hands dropping to her knees as she tried to suck in more air than the breathing filter would allow. She waited for a few seconds with no answer before she pressed the button again, looking around behind her to check for danger. Another howl sounded, this time not far away.

'What is it?' The sudden voice pulled her attention back to the intercom. The voice was male, and sounded irritated.

'The name's Silver, from the Silmac Ops crew,' Silver replied, finger on the intercom button. 'I got separated from the crew. Can you please let me in?'

'Checkpoint's closed for the night, come back in the morning.'

'The western horizon is still light, and we both know I won't live to see morning unless you let me in,' Silver objected.

'Tell it to someone who cares.'

'Fuck!' Silver screamed long and loud, her hand off the intercom button. The curse echoed off the surrounding ruins and barking broke out as if in reply, sounding alarmingly close.

She fought to compose herself before pressing the intercom button and trying again. 'I can trade,' she offered through gritted teeth. She looked back out into the night and fancied she could see multiple pairs of glowing eyes in the dark. The throaty growl that came out of the darkness towards her was unmistakable.

'Or I could just leave you and collect anything you've got of value in the morning,' the guard replied. 'I doubt you'll be able to negotiate by that point.'

'Yes, but you'll have to share it with the other guards,' Silver shot back, desperately grasping onto anything that might sway him.

There was silence for a moment, and Silver looked back out at the dark, seeing a number of dark shapes creeping nearer. She pulled out her gun and fired a shot off in their direction, causing them to scatter. It was a temporary respite, she knew, and she was running low on bullets.

'What have you got to offer?' the guard eventually replied.

'I'll give you my gun,' Silver replied. It was the only real item of value that she had on her.

'I was looking for something a little softer, something more pleasurable.'

'Well, that's not on offer, but the gun is. Take it or leave it.' Silver chanced another look over her shoulder and could see the glowing yellow eyes and dark shapes creeping forward once more.

'You're hardly in a position to argue.'

'And I'll never get into any position with you, so either you want the gun or you don't.' It was a gamble, but she was betting on the greed of the gatekeeper to win out. 'You can sell the gun if you want and go buy the type of service you're after, with plenty left over. Please!'

She looked out behind her again and the dogs were taking on more defined shapes as they drew closer to the light. While they varied in size and shape, they all shared the same lean, hungry look. The closest, a large one with a patchy black and yellow coat, snarled at her, its lips curled back revealing slavering jaws underneath. It was moving slowly, low to the ground and poised to strike. She raised her gun towards it, hoping that if she took down one or two, the others would back off.

Her finger was tightening on the trigger when she heard the click of the airlock door behind her. She immediately turned, grabbed the handle and hauled the sliding style door open and scrambled through. The dog sprang towards her, snarling. She reversed her grip on the door and dragged it closed just in time and the dog crashed into the metal. Silver stumbled backwards and half lowered herself, half fell to the ground. She ran her hands through her hair in relief, breathing heavily.

'Prepare for depressurisation, and disarm your gun.'

The voice of the guard echoed through the intercom. She complied with the request, releasing the clip from the gun, and then slowly climbing to her feet. The airlock she was in was fairly small: just two metres wide by three long. It was made of a strong but transparent Perspex, ensuring those within were fully visible. Next to her was the larger airlock, made for full vehicles. Beyond both was the large warehouse style space of the checkpoint.

A sudden rush of air caused her hair to whip around over her shoulder as the depressurisation commenced. Silver closed her eyes, finding the cool, clean air invigorating. As soon as the process was completed, Silver gratefully unclasped her facial filter and stepped through the interior door. It was liberating to be free of the mask after wearing it continuously for a day and a half. She stashed the filter and her gun clip into her pack before looking around.

The inner door of the airlock opened into an empty checkpoint. An assortment of salvage vehicles lined up neatly along both walls, ready for tomorrow's work. The middle of the floor was dominated by piles of material salvaged during the day, segmented by type. Most was metal, but there was wood, furniture, toys, books and a heap that appeared to comprise everything else. These would not fetch as high a price, but could be worth something to a rich buyer. Silver knew the buyers would arrive in the morning to bid on the raw material, with the profits going to the salvage team operator, and the crew only getting a small cut of that.

She shuffled wearily across the open space until she reached the door that led through to the office and eventually outside. As she approached, the door opened. A guard stood in the doorway, gun in hand and levelled at her.

The guard was not a good-looking man; middle aged, balding, and carrying excess weight around his gut. His nose was small, his eyes close set and his forehead looked large and square, exacerbated by the receding hairline. She knew he had been in this job some time, given she had seen him here on the handful of occasions the crew had used this checkpoint. She didn't like the way his eyes roved over her body.

'Place your pack, gun and belt on the ground and step to your right. Nothing tricky.'

Silver held her hands up and slowly cooperated with his request. It was difficult to part with her gun but after somehow surviving the last two days in the Badlands, she wasn't about to get shot now by a trigger-happy guard. She placed it along with her pack and utility belt on the polished concrete floor and took two steps over to her right.

'Good. Now hands up on the wall and spread 'em.'

The guard indicated the section of blank wall next to the door with his gun. Silver slowly carried out the instruction, turning her head to watch him as long as possible. Reaching the spot, she reluctantly placed her hands against it.

He followed her over, and she heard him holster his gun and felt his hands on her shoulders, running them down looking for any concealed weapons. He proceeded to search her thoroughly, his hands lingering uncomfortably in certain areas. Silver bit her tongue, wanting nothing more than to throw an elbow back into his face to teach him a lesson in manners. But an assault on a checkpoint guard would land her in a press gang heading north to the coal mines—no one came back from there.

He finally finished his search, failing to find her concealed flick knife. The guard then leaned against her, his lips touching her right earlobe. She could feel the bulge in his pants rubbing against her lower back and knew what he was thinking.

'What are you going to do without your gun, honey? You work in one of the crews, right? You know you'll be out on your arse without a gun, and no work means no money. I'll return it to you, if you do me a service.' His breath was hot and uncomfortable against her ear and had the stale smell of alcohol.

Despite herself, Silver did not answer immediately. She knew many women who would have happily done what he wanted, dropping to their knees and giving the guard a blow job, or bending over and allowing him to have his way. It would be a few minutes of discomfort, assuming he lasted that long, and she would be able to hang onto her gun, something she did not have the money to replace. But she just couldn't bring herself to fall that low, to let this sleazy fucker get his way. Besides, she should be able to claim an old gun of Coal's, or Lead would help her find a new one.

'Keep the gun. If you want a bitch, there's a whole pack of them outside.'

She started to turn, but suddenly found herself slammed hard against the wall, the guard pinning her in place with his hands and body.

'Such a tiny girl and such a big mouth. I was willing to trade, but I'm not feeling so generous no more.'

Silver strained against his grip, but he had a large weight advantage over her, and her struggling amounted to nothing. Meanwhile she could feel him shift his grip and start fumbling with his belt buckle below.

'I don't think Coal would be too impressed to hear his girlfriend had been forced to drop to her knees,' she gasped, clutching at anything she could think of and hoping he had not heard that Coal was dead. 'I think he might take a big exception to it.'

The guard paused for a moment, clearly familiar with Coal's name and reputation. 'If he cared that much for you, why'd he leave you in the Badlands? Way I hear it, crews never leave no one behind. My guess is he doesn't even know you're alive. Who says he's ever gonna find out?'

Silver knew she was in trouble now. The guard was right—no one would know she was here, other than him. There was nothing to stop him having his way and then killing her, disposing of her body back outside the airlock. The dogs would make short work of the evidence, even assuming someone investigated further. She slouched her shoulders and stopped struggling.

'All right, I'll do it.'

The guard's grip didn't relax, but he paused, leaning in close again. 'How can I trust you?'

'Well, last time I checked you were the one carrying the gun. And I'd prefer not to end up a corpse.'

There was silence for a moment while the guard apparently considered the pros and cons of continuing to use force against a more cooperative approach. 'All right, but try anything and yer dead.' He relaxed his grip and stepped back from her. 'Turn around.'

Silver complied, turning to find the gun levelled at her once again. The guard's belt was partially undone, but he had not yet managed to get his pants down, the bulge in his crotch possibly hampering his efforts. His finger twitched on the trigger, ready for her to try something. She longed to reach for the flick-knife concealed in her bra, but resisted, knowing there would be little chance of getting it out in time.

'On your knees.'

Again, Silver followed the order and the guard stepped forward, the bulge now centimetres from her face. 'You know what to do.'

Rather than reaching for his belt, Silver instead began slipping the straps of her overalls off her shoulders.

'What're you doing?' the guard snapped, and she felt the muzzle of the gun pressing in against her skull.

'If you're going to make me do this, I may as well do it right. Unless you'd prefer I left my shirt on?'

A lewd grin broke out across the guard's face and he nodded for her to continue. Silver wore a plain shirt under her overalls, so she reached over and used her left hand to slip her right arm out of its sleeve, discreetly grabbing the flick-knife from its sheath while her hand and arm were still under her shirt. She then slipped her left arm out of its sleeve and hesitated before she lifted the shirt completely over her head.

'You're going to have to move the gun for me to get this off.'

The guard, whose eyes were glued firmly to her cleavage, absently obliged, shifting the gun away to one side. Silver pulled her shirt all the way off and dropped it to one side and, as she hoped, he did not bring the gun back quite as close as it had been. She reached forward and took hold of his belt and zip with her left hand, as if to finish unclasping it. But with her right she suddenly jammed the knife, still sheathed, up between his legs, into his groin.

'Move and this will be the last time you see your cock attached to your body. What you can feel is the hilt of a flick-knife I have stashed for occasions just like this one. I keep it very sharp. Drop the gun.'

The threat had the desired effect, causing the guard to freeze in place. But he did not immediately drop the gun. 'A gun fires quicker than a flick-knife. You'll be dead before you can do any harm. You drop the knife.'

'Maybe, but I'd rather be dead than suck on your cock, so it's win-win for me at this stage. Shall we find out?' Silver pushed a little harder up into his groin.

'No!' the guard exclaimed, dropping the gun down next to the shirt Silver had just discarded.

Silver eyed the gun but was unable to easily grab it herself without letting go of the guard's belt or taking the knife away, neither of which she was willing to do. Still on her knees, she remained in a precarious position, with only the continued threat of having a knife put through his manhood stopping the guard from striking out at her. Without it, she would be at the mercy of his knees, feet and fists before she could regain her feet. Wanting to ensure the gun was far away from him, she manoeuvred one of her legs to kick it across the room.

She glanced up at the guard; his face was tense, nostrils flaring with every breath, brow furrowed in rage. He was only barely keeping himself in check, and the second she gave him an opening he would likely take it. There would be no second chances for her if he caught her again. She still thought she could take him in a fight, but he did have a definite size and weight advantage on her, and she would be starting from a position of weakness. Standing up or ordering him to turn around would force her to remove the blade momentarily, which would provide him the opportunity he was waiting for. Adding to her concerns, the overall straps currently off her shoulders would likely slip down the moment she stood up, and she didn't like the prospect of having them tangled around her legs if he did decide to make a move. But time was ticking away and she needed to do something.

'Okay, in a moment I'm going to pull the blade away and move back. When I do so, I want you to put your hands on the wall and do nothing until I leave. Do you understand?'

'Whatever you say, miss.' The words were spoken through gritted teeth, giving Silver little confidence in his cooperation. She shook her head and with a grimace, pressed the button on the flick-knife.

A muffled click preceded a howl of pain from the guard as the three-inch blade buried up in his groin. Silver wasted no time, pulling the blade free and simultaneously shoving him backwards. The guard stumbled back a few steps before falling onto his back, clutching his bloodied crotch all the while. Silver pulled the straps onto her shoulders and jumped to her feet before she realised that, whether by luck or design, he had fallen to his left, putting him right next to where she had initially been forced to drop her gear. Her gun was less than a metre from him, while his was lost somewhere across the room, tangled in her shirt.

She lunged forward and grabbed her pack, which was closer, then reached for her gun. But the guard saw her intention and snatched it first, brandishing it triumphantly with one of his bloodied hands. He brought it to bear on her and pulled the trigger. The ineffectual click caused his grin to turn into a scowl. His face contorted in pain and rage as he reached down to a pouch on his belt for a spare clip.

Silver briefly considered wrestling him for the gun, or rushing across the room to grab the other, but finally settled on the door as the closest and safest option. The wound in his groin would make pursuit impossible, but it wouldn't prevent him shooting her. She dashed towards the door, wrenching it open and ducking through.

'Come back here, bitch!' the guard yelled out after her, and a shot rang out, thudding into the closing door as she fled down the corridor beyond. 'You fucking whore, you'll pay for this!'

Taking a turn at the end of a corridor she pushed through an exit door and spilled out of the checkpoint onto the city streets. She had never been so happy to see the dirty, broken streets of the Dome in her life. The door closed behind her, blocking out the continued cursing and bellowing of the wounded guard. The streets were bare as few ventured out after dark, particularly on the fringes of the Dome. Even so, Silver forced herself to slow to a walk to avoid attracting unwanted attention as she left the checkpoint as quickly as she dared.

# Chapter 6

*From the diary of Benjamin Adams*
*January 29th, 2005*

*Well, Jess and I are now an item. In the five years I've known her, she's always had a boyfriend, so I'd never really considered her as more than a friend. But we caught up on Christmas Eve and she had just broken up with her most recent partner. Figured I'd have to move fairly quickly and after a couple of days' procrastination, finally plucked up the courage to ask her out. We'll take it a little slow and keep it under wraps for a while, given we work together and all. It's going to be tough, because I really like her.*

*The recovery efforts continue in Asia after the recent tsunami. I have not heard of anything like this before, and the images coming in are pretty horrific. They are saying the quake was one of the biggest on record, but the tsunami that followed was what caused the most devastation. Waves up to thirty metres high hit the coasts of surrounding countries; Indonesia, Sri Lanka, India and Thailand being the worst affected. We're getting most images from Thailand because of the number of Aussies who holiday there, and the pictures are simultaneously incredible and disturbing. Waves carrying away resorts, tall palm trees all but completely submerged, images of people in what would be their final moments on earth. The death toll is estimated at around 250,000 people, which is almost incomprehensible. Whole communities have yet to be reached, and it is feared that they no longer exist. I have donated a little money to the cause; it is not much but hopefully it will help a family somewhere. Feeling blessed that Sydney is a long way from any major fault lines.*

* * * * *

Silver gazed at her reflection in the cracked hard plastic mirror of one of the few public toilets still in working order within the Dome. She was pale and shaking, the adrenalin from the confrontation with the guard having long since faded, leaving her feeling weak and sick. She fought the urge to throw up. It was not the first time she had been attacked or threatened in that way, and probably wouldn't be the last. She had always managed to evade such attacks, through fight or flight, reasoning or bargaining. But this time it had been too close, and she knew she was only one attack away from her luck running out.

She looked down at her hands, bloodied and trembling badly. The flick-knife was still gripped tightly in her right hand and after staring at it absently for a few minutes, she turned the tap and began cleaning the blade. She had to take it slow, lest her shaking hands caused her to cut herself. Her attention then turned to her hands and she began scraping away at the blood with her nails, slowly at first but growing more and more frantic until she was scrubbing violently. Tears flowed down her face and she suddenly lashed out, kicking the one remaining cubicle door so that it bent in its frame. A tortured scream tore from her throat and she fell back against one of the walls, burying her face in her wet hands and sobbing uncontrollably.

It took a long time, but eventually she forced herself to calm down, and climbed unsteadily to her feet. Returning to the basin, she turned off the still-running tap and gazed into the mirror again. Two days in the Badlands had left her covered in grime and looking a mess. She still had red marks across her face, the result of wearing the breathing filter for too long. Her face was relatively free of grime but everything beyond the oval of the facemask was caked in layers of dust, dirt and blood. Her hair was a wild, tangled nest and, as well as being filthy, her overalls had a few tears that would require mending. The fact that she had also lost her shirt and was now wearing sleeveless overalls with just a bra underneath meant she cut a much more conspicuous figure than she would have liked.

Despite her appearance, she felt almost clean compared to the public bathroom in which she stood. The walls were buried under endless layers of graffiti, some of it in colour, but mostly grey or black tags and grotesque images. It was hard to tell that the walls were once tiled, but those that remained were cracked at best, or else lay shattered on the floor. The smell of mould was strong, and the once white enamel sink was grey-brown in colour, cracked and chipped so badly it was a miracle it still clung to the wall. The bathroom had two toilet stalls, but she tried to avoid looking at them, knowing they would be closer to brown than white, covered in filth. The smell wafting from them was bad enough, not helping with her lingering feeling of nausea.

For all its faults, the bathroom had access to running water, which was what she had come for. Water was the one resource in the city that was plentiful. The vast surface area of the Dome had been designed to catch rainfall and channel it into huge tanks built along its edges and underground. The wild weather also meant it was rare to go more than a week or two without rain. The storms brought it in great torrents, causing dangerous flash flooding outside and easily replenishing the Dome's tanks.

Silver turned the tap and splashed water onto her face and neck, washing as much of the grime away as she could. The water was cool and refreshing, and after washing herself as thoroughly as possible without soap, she used her hands to channel water into her mouth, drinking thirstily. She had finished her bottled water early that morning and was parched and slightly dizzy from dehydration.

After quenching her thirst, she pulled her greasy hair from its knot and retied it, doing her best to work out the worst of the tangles. Her bra and overalls did not combine for the greatest look, but without a shirt there was little she could do about it. She figured she resembled an out of work crew member who had resorted to prostitution to survive, a sight that was not uncommon within the Dome.

She wondered whether she had done the right thing with the guard. If he died from the injury, she would be in trouble. The police would be forced to investigate and it would not be too difficult to track her down with the video footage of the inside of the checkpoint. But assuming he lived, it was possible the incident would go unreported. The surveillance footage would be just as damning on him as her and would likely result with him being fired. Those without employment in the Dome didn't tend to survive long.

'At least the prick might think twice before trying to force himself upon anyone in the future,' she muttered to her reflection.

Taking some comfort in the thought, Silver left the building cautiously and once she was certain the road was clear, continued her journey across the city. She was still not far from the checkpoint on the south-west edge of the Dome and the Silmac Ops clubhouse was at the very northern edge. Despite feeling extremely fatigued, she set a brisk pace, keeping her head down, arms folded across her chest.

The city was gloomy at the best of times, with the frequent cloud cover above, the darkened glass of the Dome itself, and the skyscrapers all serving to block out much of the light, even during the day. At night it was extremely dark, the price of electricity so high that, outside of rare occasions, only the wealthy centre of the Dome was lit by street lamps. The buildings above looked down like giant sentinels, their windows lightless. The debris and cracked pavement made for a treacherous path. The sounds echoing out of dark doorways and darker alleys all combined to set her on edge. She saw dark, suspicious looking shapes at every corner and down every side street, though it was impossible to tell whether they were potential attackers or merely piles of rubbish, old dust bins or discarded pieces of junk.

Silver could only imagine what the city would have looked like in the past before electricity had become such a rare commodity. Hundreds of lampposts had once lit the city streets, though many of them had since been pulled down, leaving empty concrete pylons or star shaped drill holes in the pavement as evidence of their existence. Now broken neon signs and open-faced storefronts would have also contributed, lighting up the streets like day in a myriad of colours. She sometimes dreamt about it while she slept, imagining the coloured lights and the carefree citizens wandering the busy streets.

The city was a far cry from what it had once been. It was in decay, crumbling, cracked and vandalised. The frequent seismic activity and the lack of maintenance had left most buildings in poor condition. Windows were cracked or missing entirely, sometimes boarded up, but more often open to the Dome beyond. Graffiti covered virtually every reachable surface, regardless of height or accessibility. She had added her own fair share in her teen years, though not as prolifically as some. It had been something to do, an expectation of the crew culture.

The concrete exteriors of buildings were chipped and cracked, sometimes with great chunks missing. Many buildings had collapsed completely. Some of these sites had been claimed by Silmac, cleared, fenced off and then used for various reasons. Others remained as piles of rubble, with anything useful having been stripped long ago. Only concrete, twisted and broken furniture, and dust was left as a memorial to where they had once stood. The pavement and roads were in similar disrepair, cracked and pitted, and often obstructed partially or completely at spots where a building collapse spilled out onto the road.

Having squatted in plenty of them herself over the years, Silver knew that the interior of the buildings were often worse than their exteriors. What had once been well-fitted office blocks and luxury apartments had degenerated into the dens of the destitute. Most were over-crowded, with each collapse forcing the former occupants into neighbouring apartments. Graffiti covered the walls, the plasterboard was cracked and busted, furniture broken, and filth filled the corners. Dirty mattresses and blankets were strewn about for beds. Families doing their best to live a normal life shared spaces with prostitutes and drug addicts. It was chaotic and tribal, with alliances formed and broken daily, law dictated by those with the strength to enforce it.

With the streets dark and her vision limited, it was the sounds of the Dome that Silver became aware of as she made her way through the darkened streets. The deep laugh of a drunken man; the scolding of a mother to her child; the grunts of a man in the throes of orgasm, accompanied by the moans of his over-enthusiastic partner, a scream of pain or ecstasy or both; the clatter of rock being kicked along—all these sounds filtered down to her at various volumes and all with a strange echo that made it difficult to pinpoint their source.

Silver was relieved that most of the sounds she heard seemed to be coming from inside the buildings and there were blessed few people out and about to notice her passing. She did catch the eye of a street tough who made his presence known by making her a lewd offer. She pointedly ignored him and hurried on. But as she went, the fatigue of the last two days began to catch up with her and she found herself stumbling on broken edges of pavement or missing a turn she would have typically taken.

She passed a building where the words 'I will never leave a man behind' were scrawled in big letters across the wall. She had seen it before, but this time the graffiti caused her to stop and stare. They were the mantra of every salvage team, the vow that each salvager made upon being accepted into a crew.

The sound of footsteps somewhere nearby made her realise that she had stopped for too long, and with a glance over her shoulder, she pushed on. But the words remained burned in her vision, forcing her to consider the thing that had been bothering her since she had watched the trucks leaving without her: why had she been left? Coal had been taken down, which meant there would be a leadership challenge within the crew. Lead was the likely candidate to take Coal's place, and they had gotten on well. She considered him one of her true friends. Yet he had left her, along with Coal's body, out in the Badlands with not even a backwards look. The amount of time that it had taken her to get back to the trucks had not been excessive. It left little or no time for them to have mounted a search or at least an attempt to recover their bodies. She wasn't even certain she'd be welcome back into the crew when she arrived back. The thought caused a tightness in her chest and she developed a dull, throbbing headache, which seemed to increase in intensity with every step she took that brought her closer to the clubhouse.

The Silmac Ops clubhouse was located in an ancient building. Once a warehouse, it had been modernised at some stage and converted into office space. It had been many years since its last restoration though and, like the majority of buildings within the Dome, was now particularly run down. The brick façade was crumbling, the doors and windows boarded up, and every available surface covered in decades of graffiti—the most recent added by members of her crew. The Silmac logo, featured along the main wall, was a dark blue circle with a cross running through it. It represented the company's surveying history as they had made their fortune finding and tapping into increasingly scarce deposits of coal and gas. Silver had always thought it looked much more military, like the crosshairs of a sniper's telescopic sight. Either way, the logo gave the clubhouse credibility and warned off rival crews and gangs who would think twice before trying to muscle in and take over. The other images on the building were more typical of the gangs and crews that vied for space in the confines of the Dome; cartoon muscle men packing serious weaponry, skulls, chains, knives, blood and endless lewd imagery meant to intimidate anyone walking past.

Silver approached the single entrance maintained by the crew, a heavy sliding door that she knew was modified and reinforced on the inside for security. She raised a hand to knock, but hesitated, doubts still kicking around in her mind. Eventually she rapped out the code: three knocks, pause, another two knocks, pause, two knocks, pause, one knock.

She waited for a response, and the time ticked by, ten seconds, twenty seconds, thirty. She was about to raise her hand to knock again when finally she heard a muffled voice from inside.

'Who's there?'

'Is that you, Lead? It's me … Silver.'

A pause, then: 'Silver's dead. You think I'm dumb? Step away or I'll knock your arse down.' There was anger and hurt in the voice.

'No, Lead, it's me. I'm not dead. I got away from the mutes and made it back. Check.'

There was another pause before she heard the sounds indicating Lead was unlocking the peephole built into the door. While she couldn't see inside through the thick glass, she moved into a spot that would afford him a good view of her face, despite the darkness.

'Damn, girl. It is you! Hold on.'

A second later, she heard the bolts on the door being removed, and the heavy door was pulled to one side, allowing her entrance into the clubhouse. She made her way into the dimly-lit interior. Lead was waiting for her behind the door, his white teeth and the whites of his eyes seeming to glow in the darkness. He looked upon her for a moment, as if trying to ascertain if she was real, or a spirit from the Badlands come to haunt him.

'I'm real, Lead. Feel.' She held out her hand, and he clasped hers in greeting, hesitantly at first, but pulling her in for a hug when he felt she was indeed alive and real. The hug took Silver by surprise, and she didn't immediately return it. 'Why did you leave me, Lead?'

He released her and pulled back, looking her in the eyes. 'We thought you were dead, Silver. Coal told us the mutes had taken you.'

Silver's eyebrows furrowed in confusion. 'What do you mean Coal told you? Coal's dead.'

It was Lead's turn to look confused. 'No, Coal's alive. He's here, upstairs in his room. Your room.'

'What? I …' Silver felt the room start to spin and began swaying unsteadily on her feet. Lead reached out and grabbed her, directing her towards one of the lounges.

The clubhouse was cluttered with stuff. The crew sponsors had first rights at anything the crews brought back from the Badlands, but what they didn't want was left for the crew to take and use or sell. The clubhouse was full of such items—anything that had been unable to attract a buyer had been dumped in a corner and piled up with other unwanted things. Old chairs, twisted plastic toys, assorted crockery, pieces of plastic tubing, bricks, sheets of plasterboard, a plastic mannequin and a whole host of other things were scattered about. There was no metal among the piles—anything metallic was taken by the sponsors. Items of clothing and wood was also normally sought after, or else used by the crew. Most of the remaining stuff was junk, deemed too damaged to be worth much.

The clubhouse itself consisted of a large open floor space, broken by grey steel pillars that supported an upstairs section at the back half of the building, as well as the high ceilings above. A stairway ran up the right side wall leading to a balcony, off which a number of doors led to bedrooms, a kitchen and a large bathroom. At Silver's level, there was a clear open space in the middle of the warehouse used by the crew in their downtime, filled with old couches and stools, a section set aside for weights, and a bar that had been salvaged from somewhere. A table tennis table stood off to the right, propped up on bricks and its net long since torn away, replaced by an old strip of wood. A dart board hung on one pillar, and a couple of low tables housed worn decks of cards and an assortment of other old games to keep the crew members entertained. The area was dimly lit by a candle sitting in the centre of one of the low tables.

'Are you all right, Sil?'

'I … um … so Coal's not dead?' Her mind was swimming and she was having trouble processing the news. 'But if that's true, then …'

Before Lead could answer, another voice boomed down from above. 'Silver! Is that you? You're alive!'

Shirtless and sporting only a pair of jeans, which he was still in the process of buckling up, Coal stood on the balcony overlooking them. His classic V-shaped body cut an impressive figure, made even more intimidating with his full range of tattoos on display. He hastened along the balcony to the stairway and made his way down them two at a time, then hurried over to Silver. Others were following him down from above and soon a crowd had gathered around them. Coal had a huge grin on his face, and he took her up in a bear hug, spinning a half circle before placing her back on the ground. The strength of his embrace was comforting to her, but she pulled back quicker than normal and looked up at him in question. For a moment, his eyes flicked past her, up towards the balcony, before returning to look at her. To her right she noticed Lead was also looking up towards the balcony, the slightest of frowns on his face. Before she could turn to follow his gaze, Coal leaned in and kissed her, his lips familiar and gentle. When he finally pulled back, the grin was gone and his eyes were sombre, tear-filled.

'I can't believe you're alive, Sil. Those mutes came out of nowhere, took me by surprise. Before I knew it, I'd been struck in the head and could barely keep my feet. Then they were on top of me, forcing me away from you, catching me while I was still groggy. I tried to fight my way back through 'em, but then I heard you scream and thought they had you.

'When I heard the gunshot, I fought harder, took at least six of the buggers down with my bare hands. But then there was just silence and I thought you were gone. I wanted to get to you, at least to retrieve your body, but I had the others to consider. More mutes kept piling in and they would have threatened the truck, particularly if I hadn't made it back to warn everyone. So I made the decision to retreat. Had I thought there was any chance you were still alive I never would have left. Oh man, I'm so glad you made it back.' He leant in and wrapped her in another crushing hug.

Silver wanted to believe Coal's story. There was nothing in its delivery that she could detect other than sincerity. His embrace, his kiss, the look in his eyes … all seemed genuine. Her heart told her to accept the story and move on, but her mind continued to niggle at her, telling her it didn't quite add up. The lack of warning and the delayed gunshots didn't seem to quite fit. Why had it taken Coal so long to go for his gun? Dazed or not, she knew him well enough to know he was quick off the hip.

She opened her mouth to voice the question, but seeing the growing crowd around them, closed it again.

'How'd you escape, Silver? How'd you get away from them mutes?' The question came from Tip, a young member of the crew who had only been initiated into Silmac Ops a couple of months before. His wide-eyed face conveyed the wonder he felt at seeing her back there alive. It was reflected in most of the faces watching her. 'And what happened to your shirt?'

Coal released her and stepped back, and she felt suddenly nervous and vulnerable under the weight of eyes looking in at her. 'They tried to haul me out of the hole, but I cut the line and wasted the one that reached in to grab me. I managed to find another way out the back of the building. By the time I had circled around to the truck, you were gone, so I set off home on foot. The shirt got messed up with mute's brains so I took it off and lost it somewhere.' The lie about the shirt came to her lips unbidden. Silver had no desire to recount her ordeal at the checkpoint in front of everyone.

'It must have been the mute's body I saw them fighting over, not you!' Coal exclaimed. 'It was at the entrance to the tunnel, and there was a crowd of them around. I thought it was you, Silver.'

The same thought occurred to Silver; when she looked out and saw the mutes feasting on a body, she assumed it was Coal, but it must have been the mute she had shot.

'What about the storm last night? How did you survive a night in the Badlands?' This question came from Hawk, a grizzled veteran salvager, her body strong but her face weathered.

'I lucked out,' Silver said, not wanting to try to explain the bizarre encounter with the mute, nor thinking it would be wise to do so. She would be considered tainted or infected if the crew learnt she had spent the night in the company of a mute. 'I found a particularly large ruin and crawled inside, came across a half intact basement. It was empty, but shielded me from the storm.'

'But did you encounter any more mutes?' Tip piped up again. 'Or dogs? What about the giant rats and mutated 'roos?'

A few of the older members of the crew snickered at Tip's question, and one, a man named Schmidt, slapped him across the back of the head. A huge yawn forced its way past Silver's lips.

'All right, that's enough. Silver needs rest and we've got an early start in the morning,' Coal said, putting his arm across her shoulders and steering her through the crowd and towards the stairs. She was too exhausted to resist, so she allowed him to help her up. The crew followed them up the stairs, heading back to their rooms. Coal started to steer Silver towards the bedroom, but she pulled away.

'I'm tired, and in bad need of a shower.' She shoved her pack into his arms and headed down the hall to the door at the end that led to the shower rooms. It was empty and dark, so she struck a match, lit one of the candles at the door and wasted no time stripping out of her filthy overalls. Her skin underneath was dark, covered in dirt, mud and dust from the Badlands.

Venturing over to one of the five doorless cubicles, Silver turned on the tap and, closing her eyes, plunged her head and body under the cold water. It shocked her, but she forced herself to remain under the flow, scrubbing at her hair and body furiously to distract herself from the cold as much to get the dirt off. Hot water was a luxury afforded only by the wealthy, and while the weather was warm enough, the water was still uncomfortably cold. Despite the discomfort of the temperature, it was refreshing and invigorating, and she felt some of the exhaustion wash away along with the layers of dirt. She grabbed the bar of soap from the holder and methodically set about washing each part of her body.

After a few minutes, she turned the water off. Her body was covered in goose bumps and she shivered slightly from the cold, but her bare skin felt clean. Turning to reach for a towel, she started when she found Coal in the room, watching her. She had been so absorbed in the shower she had no idea when he had entered, or for how long he'd been watching.

Towel in hand, he stepped silently forward with the intention of drying her, but Silver snatched it from him, using it to dry her face. 'Never leave a man behind. I've heard you say it a thousand times, Coal. Why'd you leave me?'

'I could ask you the same question, Sil,' Coal cut back, a slight edge in his voice. 'You saw what you thought was me being eaten by the mutes and you did nothing.'

'But that was different,' Silver protested, clutching the towel to her chest. 'I was alone, the crew …'

'Hey, hey,' Coal interrupted, coming forward and holding her, his voice softer now. 'I don't blame you, Sil, but you can't blame me, neither. I thought you were dead and I had the rest of the crew to think about. I was devo, Silver, but now I'm just so relieved you're alive.'

His left hand nudged her chin upwards towards him so he could lean in and kiss her. Silver didn't kiss him back, but nor did she push him away this time. He gently extracted the towel from her grasp and started wiping the water from her skin, rubbing her shoulders and back dry, squatting down to towel off her legs. He was still shirtless and his muscles bulged, looking all the more impressive in the dim candlelight. His touch was firm and strong, comforting to her. She closed her eyes and lost herself in his touch as he moved around behind her, pulling the wet hair back from her face and using the towel to gently soak the water from it.

'You can't believe how happy I am that you are safe, Silver,' he whispered into her ear, leaning forward, his body against hers. She shivered under his touch, this time not from the cold. But she resisted, pulling away from him and taking the towel with her.

'Coal, I'm tired and still …'

'Shhh,' Coal cut in, stepping in again and kissing her, gently at first, then with more urgency. His strong arms enfolded her, and this time she didn't fight back but surrendered to the feeling of safety and warmth his embrace offered.

'I'm glad to be back too.'

He kissed her, passionately, hungrily, his hands roving from her thighs, over her stomach and up to her breasts. She tried to kiss him back but did not have the will or the energy. She could feel him rising against her as his hands found their way back to her thighs and buttocks and he started to lift her up. She grabbed his wrists and pulled away from his kisses, stopping him.

'What's wrong, baby?' he asked.

'Coal, I just can't, not now. I need rest.'

Their eyes locked for a moment but in the dim lighting of the room and with his back to the candles his face was bathed in shadow and she could not read his expression. After a moment, he stooped once more but this time swept her up sideways, one arm supporting her back, the other hooked under her knees. She snuggled in against his chest as he carried her from the bathroom and down the hall to their room.

'I love you, Silver,' he whispered gently into her ear as he lay her down on the bed and pulled the sheets up over her. She smiled contently, drifting off into an exhausted sleep.

# Chapter 7



*From the diary of Benjamin Adams*
*November 27<sup>th</sup>, 2007*

*So much has happened since my last entry! I've changed jobs, become a father, and Jess and I have gotten engaged. I can barely believe how fast the time has flown. Our little one, Jayden, is not a baby anymore—he's eighteen months old and big enough to walk the rings down the aisle at our wedding! It's only a month away now, which is exciting. Everything is just about done; all we can hope for now is some good weather on the day.*

*The federal election was decided last week and it was interesting. Climate change policy was one of the main battles on which the election was fought and won, which I think is a first, and a positive thing. It's probably thanks to the documentary An Inconvenient Truth, which has turned a lot of attention to the issues around pollution and the climate. Ever since having Jayden, I've been thinking more and more about this type of thing.*

*Look at me, talking about politics and social issues! I must be getting old ...*

* * * * *

It was black outside the curved window of Silmac's office, with the thick storm clouds from that afternoon having blocked out any light that the moon may have shed across the barren landscape. He stood, gazing out at the darkness. It was late; well past midnight and by this time all the lights in the Dome below had been switched off.

The silence was broken by the sound of the lifts operating, but Silmac didn't turn. Only Meek, his head of security, had access to his office at this time of night, and Silmac was expecting him.

'You know this light might be the only manmade light shining anywhere on Earth?' he mused. 'We could be the last civilisation left. Our international neighbours had it much worse than us; Europe, Africa, Asia and America were devastated by the wars, earthquakes and volcanoes. We got reports that there were other protective domes being built, underground bunkers, and even some space projects. But none of them were finished when comms went down. That would make me the ruler of the world.'

There was no answer from behind him, but Silmac hadn't expected one. He turned from the window and made his way over to his desk where Meek waited patiently. Meek was a small man, standing only one hundred and sixty-five centimetres tall and appearing slight as well. He had Asian blood in him, with a full head of jet-black hair, and a smooth, boyish face despite being in his mid-thirties. He dressed all in black, with a long-sleeved, buttoned and collared shirt, loose black slacks and black leather shoes.

Corbett knew that the man's size was deceptive, a strength rather than a weakness. People underestimated him, and he used that to his advantage. The first time Corbett had met Meek he had done the same, before witnessing him take down six armed and capable fighters, all of them bigger and stronger men. He fought using an unorthodox but highly effective combination of martial art styles and street fighting skills, and moved with a speed well beyond anything Corbett had seen before. He had been little more than a street urchin at the time, and had approached Silmac for a job in his security team. Finding the request amusing, Corbett had decided to interview the boy by setting his six-man security team onto him. Within little more than thirty seconds Meek had left two of them dead and the other four with severe injuries, and had won himself the job he was after. A few years later, Corbett had promoted him to head of security.

'What have you got to report tonight?'

'We've found three dead bodies in the last thirty-six hours, two males and one female. No one of note; all appear to be the victims of petty theft or drug related violence.' Meek's voice was neutral, devoid of emotion.

Corbett nodded. 'Next.'

'One of the tall buildings, the old Shangri-La hotel, is on the verge of collapse. The engineers fear it will not withstand the next quake.'

'What's the potential damage?'

'Minimal. You have no assets in or around that area. No one of note lives in the building itself, and only a few minor players live nearby. However, there are squatters and peasants currently occupying it.'

'How many?' Corbett enquired, his voice casual.

'I'd estimate approximately nine hundred, give or take.'

'They've been warned?'

'The building was officially cleared and locked down months ago, with notices posted on its structural weaknesses.'

'We could do with a few less mouths to feed. I want a team ready to strip the building of all valuable materials once it goes. They can also clean up bodies, to limit the smell.'

'Yes, sir. I've already got a team on standby,' Meek replied. 'They'll be on site before the last of the rubble has settled.'

'Good. Anything else?'

'Two things. I've heard rumours that the Homeless are becoming restless again.'

Silmac pursed his lips at mention of the Homeless, a group of outcasts who lived in the sewers and subways below the city.

'Are they a threat?'

'Not at this stage, but whispers say they have a new leader, someone who has united the separate groups together.'

'Find out what you can, and extract him if possible. If their restlessness grows, warn me at once. And the other item?'

'Yes.' Meek hesitated unusually in his normally military-style debrief. 'This report has only just come to me so I haven't had a chance to investigate it, but it sounded interesting. One of the overnight guards at Checkpoint D got himself stabbed in the groin earlier tonight.'

'Dead?'

Meek shook his head. 'No, and he didn't report it either. Called in one of the other guards to cover for him.'

Silmac raised an eyebrow. 'Odd, but I've heard stranger. Who stabbed him?'

'A woman. Appears to be a member of a salvage crew who was left out in the Badlands and talked her way in after hours.'

'So the guard broke protocol and let her in, then tried to get lucky with her and got himself stabbed. Since he had broken the rules, he decided to cover it up rather than report it. Doesn't sound overly odd to me.'

'I agree; the guard's actions were predictable. This particular guard is known to be a frequent visitor of some of the more eccentric and depraved brothels operating in the Dome. The odd part is that no crews reported anyone missing today, and counts suggest that the same number that went out came back in.'

'So who's the girl?'

'I can only assume that it is a member of one of your crews, reported lost and dead in the Badlands two days ago.'

'She survived a night out in the Badlands?' Meek's nod caused Silmac to raise an eyebrow. 'There was a significant storm last night.'

Meek nodded again. 'If it is the same woman, then she would have survived a night and full day out in the Badlands by herself, before taking down the guard and escaping into the Dome. Plus, she was reportedly lost in the old Campbelltown region.'

'Campbelltown? That's forty or fifty kilometres out from the Dome, isn't it?' At Meek's nod, Silmac whistled and leant forward in his chair. 'Find out who she is. I'm not sure I'm comfortable with stories of survival like that spreading through the Dome. Which crew is she with?'

'Silmac Ops.'

'Coal's crew. Drop by there in the morning and bring her to me.'

'I'll get onto it.'

'Oh, and have you got footage of her encounter with the guard?'

'The security cameras caught most of it on tape, yes.'

'Send it up. I want to see it.'

'Very well, sir. You'll have it within the hour.'

* * * * *

Silver awoke slowly. She looked around in a daze, taking a few moments to realise that she was in her bed, back with her crew. She dimly remembered Coal carrying her back to their room and tucking her into bed before climbing in himself. A towel covered her pillow, protecting it from her still damp hair. The pillow beside her was unoccupied, with Coal nowhere to be seen. Blearily she looked around and figured it was still night time judging from the lack of light coming in from the circular window high above the bed.

Her mouth was dry and rough as sandpaper. Slowly, she dragged herself out of bed, pulled on a long shirt of Coal's to cover her nakedness and made her way out of the room, heading for the kitchen. As she passed the bathroom door, she registered the sound of whispered voices coming from within and only then noticed a dim light emanating from under the door.

Curious, Silver slowed down and quietly approached the entrance to the bathroom, straining to determine who was in there and what they were whispering about. She could make out a male and female voice.

'… finally get you all to myself, and then she turns up and you're with her again!'

'It was as big a shock to me as it was to you, believe me. It seemed impossible that anyone could make it back from that far out.'

'It didn't look like shock from here. It looked like you were ecstatic to have her back. I heard you two in the shower.'

'How was I meant to react? It was all a show for her until we can work out what to do.'

Silver's heart grew cold as she listened to the whispered argument. There was no doubting the male voice was Coal's, and it was obvious whom they were talking about. She wasn't certain, but she thought the female voice was Arlia's, a long-legged blonde crew member whom Silver suspected had had her eyes on Coal for some time.

'What are we going to do? I've waited for this for so long and you promised me she was gone for good. I can't go back to how things were, having to watch you with her all day and creep around like this. Do you know how embarrassing it was for me to sneak out of your room last night, with the rest of the crew snickering away?'

'You're going to have to be patient while I work something out.'

'I'll walk.'

'No you won't. You'll stay with me and we'll be together. I just need some time.'

There was silence from within until Coal whispered again. 'You know what else I need?'

'What, are you serious? You were trying to fuck her less than an hour ago!'

'Yeah, but she interrupted us tonight, Arli, and what you were doing to me earlier reminds me why I want to be with you.'

It seemed pathetic to Silver, but Arlia clearly fell for it, because a moment later she heard satisfied moans from Coal and could well imagine what was going on. Pathetic, maybe, but no less than she, pushing aside her doubts and allowing herself to be manipulated by him. For how long had he cheated on her? Weeks? Months? Years even? And with how many women? Was it just Arlia, or were there more?

The sounds of pleasure coming from Coal increased and Silver had heard enough. Her thirst forgotten, she hurried back to her room and climbed back into bed, only belatedly remembering to pull off the shirt she had put on. It took a few minutes but eventually she heard Coal enter the room and slip into bed beside her. She lay still and kept her breathing even, feigning sleep. She needn't have worried; within minutes he was asleep, breathing heavily.

Silver waited until she heard the familiar sounds of snoring come from Coal before she peeled back the covers and cautiously crept out of bed. Standing there naked, she gazed down at the man who had been her one and only lover for over a decade. He had provided her protection and security during that time, but his actions earlier in the evening had shown how easily she could be replaced.

She pulled on her clothes and came across the flick-knife he had given her two years before. It was priceless to her, made of metal and engraved with 'Silver' on the handle. It had been akin to a proposal, like the rings that had been traditional in the past. She pressed the trigger and the blade sprang instantly free. Dried blood was visible at the base of the blade as she had not cleaned it properly after her encounter with the guard at Checkpoint D.

With blade still bared, she turned back to Coal's sleeping figure. She felt the urge to return it to him—blade first—to pay him back for his betrayal. Her knuckles whitened as she gripped the handle tightly and toyed with the idea of making him hurt the way she did inside. Eventually she pressed the button again to retract the blade. Stabbing him would ultimately not change the way she felt, or the wrong she had suffered.

She grabbed her pack and gathered together the few meagre possessions she owned. There was pitifully little: a few changes of clothes and a handful of books she had salvaged from the Badlands. She was almost surprised they were still there, that Coal hadn't gotten rid of them the second he thought her gone. She had no gun, which would be a problem trying to find work with another crew. If she couldn't scavenge, the only likely work she would find was with one of the many brothels scattered around town, and while that worked for some, it was not an option for her.

She tiptoed around the bed to where Coal had discarded his clothes, hanging his belt over the bedhead as was custom. Holding her breath, she reached out slowly for the belt, half expecting his arm to shoot and grab her before she could secure the weapon. But he continued to snore noisily, oblivious to her actions, and she quietly lifted the belt, pulling the pistol from its holster. It was bigger than she was used to, and heavier, but it was a gun and would do.

She tucked the weapon into her pants and pulled the shirt over to conceal it. Despite being ready to go, she hesitated, before reaching into her pack again. She took out one of the books within and slowly tore a blank page from it, grabbed a pen that was sitting on a side table and scrawled a message.

Reading back over it, she knew it was petty, but it gave her some satisfaction all the same. She retrieved the flick-knife he had given her and used it to pin the page to the back of the door where he would clearly see it when he awoke in the morning. It was shame to leave the knife, but what had once been priceless to her had suddenly diminished in value.

She stepped out of the room and pulled the door gently closed. Creeping along the balcony, Silver made her way quietly downstairs, scanning the darkened space below for whoever was on watch. But it was dark, and she could see no sign of movement below. It was possible they had headed to the bathroom, or gone to get a drink.

Reaching the bottom of the stairs, she crept over towards the door that would take her outside.

'You're leaving.'

It was a statement rather than a question, and came from behind her. She answered without turning. 'There is nothing here for me, Lead. I have to go.'

Lead emerged from the shadows to her right where he had been concealed in the darkness. He gazed at her, his eyes sad. 'I tried to make him wait, out in the Badlands. He ordered us to drive. Said he had seen you taken by the mutes. Said you were already dead.'

'Were you in on it, Lead? Did he tell you what he was planning?'

'Planning? What are you saying? He *meant* to leave you out there?' The horror splashed across his face seemed genuine.

'If the conversation I just overheard him have with Arlia is anything to go off.'

Leads eyes flicked away momentarily at mention of Arlia, but Silver spotted the look. 'You knew about Arlia, didn't you?'

Lead nodded reluctantly, his brow creasing in consternation. 'I knew, but I didn't know you were in danger, Silver, you have to believe me!' He reached forward to touch her arm but she stepped back from him.

'I don't know what or who to believe, Lead. How long?'

'Coal and Arlia? Long.'

'Were there others?'

Lead hesitated before nodding. 'Yeah, there were others.'

'Why didn't you tell me, Lead? I thought we were friends.'

'Honestly? I wanted to, but I didn't think you wanted to know. There are others who would have been comfortable with the arrangement. It seemed to me you would have found out if you really wanted to.'

The slap caught him squarely across the cheek, but Lead didn't flinch away. A red handprint appeared faintly on his face, but Silver's cheeks burned brighter still, incensed at his comment. 'You think I'd happily sit by and let him get away with it? Turn a blind eye? Fuck you, Lead.'

She turned back to the door, and furiously began working on the bolts that kept it locked. Lead remained still behind her. 'Are you angry at me and Coal, or yourself, Sil?'

'I just need to get out of here, now.'

'Where will you go?'

'I don't know. I'll find another crew.' The door was open now, the night yawning beyond. She started to step out, but Lead stepped forward and grabbed her arm, stopping her.

'Let me come with you. It's dangerous out there alone, and I know you don't want to return to that. Together we have a better chance to make it.'

'I'm too pissed at you right now, Lead. I need time and space from everyone here.' She shrugged her arm free of his grip and stepped out into the night.

* * * * *

Silver made her way east, with no particular destination or plan in mind—just a need to put some distance between Coal, Lead and herself. The night was dark and the streets darker, but she had Coal's gun and was dressed more appropriately than she had been earlier, so she felt safer. *Mercy to the fool that tries to mess with me now,* she thought.

It was much quieter on the streets, with the majority of the Dome's occupants in bed and sleeping by this late hour. Those few who were out must have sensed her mood, because though she spotted a few guys who looked like potential trouble, no one approached her. After about fifteen minutes of hard walking, the anger that had fuelled her began to ease and her fatigue returned. Her body ached and she needed to get off the street. Sooner or later trouble would find her, and while a part of her recklessly craved a fight, she knew it would not be a wise choice.

*It's dangerous out there alone, and I know you don't want to return to that.* Lead's words echoed in her thoughts. It had been many years since she'd been alone, on the streets. It was after her parents had died, around the age of nine or ten, before she'd fallen in with Coal. It had been the loneliest time of her life, and was also the most vulnerable she'd ever felt. She could feel her anxiety rising at the thought of it, her pulse quickening and chest tightening.

At that time, she'd resorted to climbing multi-storey buildings and finding a concealed spot on a ledge to sleep. She had quickly worked out that decent spots inside the skyscrapers were either already taken or else offered little protection from those who would seek to take advantage of a young girl on her own. The outside of the buildings offered concealment of a sort and, more importantly, distance from would-be attackers.

Having a course of action helped to ease her panic, so she focused on it, scanning the surrounding buildings as she looked for a suitable spot. Eventually she found one she had used before. The building in question had an external pillar about six storeys up. The ledge behind it would provide a good spot to sleep, while the pillar itself would provide some extra cover from prying eyes. Tightening the straps on her pack and ensuring everything was secure, she moved over to the base of the building. Her hands felt the cold, rough surface, searching for the lines and cracks that would offer her decent hand and footholds.

It was slow going at first as it had been a long time between climbs of this nature, and it was harder work than she remembered. Before long she was breathing heavily and sweating from the exertion. But as she got higher, her confidence grew and she found herself grinning. She had forgotten how much she loved the challenge of the climb, the rush of adrenalin and the feeling of freedom that came with it. Her pace quickened, and while her muscles burned from the strain, her smile broadened. Soon enough she reached the pillar, and with one final effort, she pulled herself up and swung a leg over, rolling onto the flat ledge. She lay there for a moment, breathing heavily, one leg still dangling over the edge.

The skyscraper continued upwards, pointing at the Dome arching above it. This building, even at its peak, came nowhere near reaching the ceiling of the Dome. Only one building did that. She scanned around and spotted it in a gap between a few other skyscrapers: Silmac Tower. Silver thought that the building resembled a giant arrow, pointing skywards, with a long cylindrical body supported by metal cable fletching. At its top it mushroomed out, with an almost conical shaped head balanced on top of the narrow body, tapering to a point. From the Badlands, the Dome resembled a giant bow, pulled taut and ready to fire up at the clouds.

Silver gazed at it, wondering what it would feel like to be so high up. Coal had been up there a couple of times when meeting with Silmac, and had spoken of the view of the surrounding landscape. Silver could only imagine what it would be like to live in the tower, to have access to the kind of money and power that Silmac enjoyed.

She turned her gaze towards the rest of the city, buildings rising from the darkness below and reaching into formless black masses above, with the Dome a huge dark blanket thrown over them all. Even the lights of the wealthier buildings were out at this late hour. It was hard to picture what the city would have looked like in a time when electricity was cheap. She imagined lights, colours, sounds and activity, in contrast to the dark and sinister maze of crumbling buildings it was now.

Pulling her leg up over the edge and rolling over to try to block it out, she found a familiar image scratched into the concrete wall behind her. It was a simple flower, and she knew it because she had put it there, years before. She must have slept in this very spot in the past. It brought back a flood of memories; her parents, being alone on the streets, meeting a young Coal who offered her protection and an escape from loneliness.

Silver felt tears brimming and rolled away from the image angrily, using her backpack as a pillow and trying to get comfortable on the hard concrete ledge. She had learnt long ago that crying got her nowhere, and led to a path of self-pity and despair. What she needed was rest, and once rested she'd set out and find a new crew. She closed her eyes and tried to sleep, but still the tears came.

# CHAPTER 8



*From the diary of Benjamin Adams*
*September 4th, 2010*

*I'm clearly fighting a losing battle with time! With two kids now, sleep is at a premium and Jess and I are forever busy. It's Alex's second birthday this weekend and we have a party with the family planned, which should be fun. The boys are both growing so fast. Another year and we'll put Alex in pre-school a couple of days a week for the social interaction, and Jayden will start kindergarten! It will be good for Jess—being a mum is challenging and isolating and it has been a tough four years for her. She's been amazing, giving the boys such a strong, loving start to their lives.*

*Work is tracking along well; I'm working on interesting projects with good variety. The firm is happy with my performance and my salary is steadily rising, which helps with the increasing costs at home, as well as the solar panels we just had installed. With our own family, Jess and I are more conscious than ever of trying to do our part for the environment. The panels will help reduce our energy costs longer term, which is a bonus.*

*Speaking of which, the latest federal election results are in—and what a contrast to the last election! Action on climate change was such a key factor in the last election, but three years on it has contributed to the fall of the incumbent government. A mining-funded propaganda campaign led to a huge slide in opinion and saw them oust their leader only months before the poles. While they have clung to power by the narrowest of margins, they are going to be challenged getting any laws through the senate, and this doesn't bode well for environmental interests.*

* * * * *

'Coal, you'd better wake up. Silmac's man is here and wants to talk to you.'

'What? Who?' Coal raised his head off his pillow and looked around. He was bleary-eyed and took a moment to gather his senses. Lead leant in through the door.

'It's Meek. He's outside and wants to see you.'

'What the fuck does he want?' Coal said, scowling.

'Don't know, wouldn't say.'

'All right. Piss off for a sec while I get dressed.'

Coal pulled himself out of bed as Lead closed the door. He dug around in his drawer and pulled out a small bag of white powder. He tipped a portion of it out onto the dresser next to him and used a piece of card to straighten it into a couple of lines before snorting it through a rolled-up piece of paper. Wiping his nose and stashing the remaining powder back in his draw, he stood and grabbed his pants from the floor and pulled them on. Grabbing for his belt, he felt that it was far too light and immediately realised the gun was missing from the holster. He looked around the room and only then noticed that Silver was not lying next to him as she had been when he went to sleep. He scanned the room in confusion, noting that her clothes and pack were also gone. Finally, his eyes alighted on the note, visible now that the door was shut. It was held in place to the back of his door with the flick-knife he had given her.

He strode over and snatched the note, scanning it. The words meant nothing to him as he had never bothered to learn to read. But he didn't need to read it to understand what had happened. His face darkened, and he wrenched open the door. He thrust the piece of paper at Lead, who was waiting there.

'What does it say?'

Lead took the note and read. *I've left and I've taken your gun. You can find a replacement for both at Checkpoint D. The night guard there took my gun, and would be well suited as your bitch. I hope you enjoy that slut Arlia and the ugly rash she is always scratching at whenever she showers. You've earned it.*

'I'll kill that bitch!' Coal screamed, returning to his room and kicking at the wooden crate that sat at the end of his bed, serving as a chest. The crate shattered under the impact, reduced to a pile of kindling. 'She'd dare leave *me*? Find her and bring her to me!'

'Why don't you let her go, Coal? You earned this.'

'What the fuck did you say?' Coal asked dangerously.

'I said, you earned this,' Lead clarified, holding up the note. 'Think about that while you go and chat with Meek.'

Coal's eyes simmered, and he pushed past Lead roughly, descending the stairs and strapping on his belt as he went.

The rest of the crew, awoken by the shouts, were cautiously looking out through their bedroom doorways. Used to Coal's raging, they hoped to find out the cause without becoming the focus of his ire.

Coal arrived at the front door and wrenched it open. Meek stood outside, unaccompanied. It was still dark beyond him, before dawn.

'What do you want?' Coal asked threateningly, moving towards the man until he towered above him. Meek held his position unflinchingly, infuriating Coal all the more.

'Nothing. But Mr Silmac wants something, or rather, someone. The girl who spent the night out in the Badlands. He wants to speak with her.'

The request took some of the wind out of Coal's sails. What could Silmac want with Silver? How did he even know of her? She had been part of the crew for years and he hadn't shown the least amount of interest in her. And now, when she had up and left, suddenly he needed to see her?

'Well?' Meek prompted, causing Coal to realise he had been standing there mutely.

'She's gone.'

'Gone?'

'That's right, she's not fucking here.'

'Where is she?'

'Fucked if I know.'

Meek pursed his lips slightly, the closest thing to an expression Coal had ever seen him make.

'You gave her leave to go?'

Coal suddenly realised he was treading on dangerous ground. Silmac would hear about this conversation and he didn't want to come off sounding incompetent.

'No. She got back last night and was gone this morning. It won't take long for me to find her though, and when I do, I'll bring her to Silmac.'

'I see. Bring her to me, not Silmac, as soon as you find her.'

'Of course.' *Like hell I will, you fucking son-of-a-whore. I won't have you taking fucking credit for it.*

Meek turned to leave, but paused after a few steps and turned. 'Your quota of salvage is down this week. Be sure that it picks up, or Silmac might choose to withdraw his backing.' With the threat left hanging in the air, Meek melted away in the darkness. Coal slammed the door shut. Turning, he found Lead and Arlia waiting for him. Arlia sidled up to him, a smug look of satisfaction on her face.

'Don't worry, baby. It's a good thing that she's gone. I'll soothe your worries.' One of her hands slid down to his crotch, rubbing at his manhood through his pants.

'Get away from me, slut,' Coal said, snatching her hand and shoving her roughly. 'It's your fault she's gone and we're in this mess. We've got work to do.'

Arlia looked hurt for a moment before the expression was replaced with one of anger. She spun around, storming off up the stairs. Coal ignored her.

'Lead, assemble the team. We've got a long day in the Badlands ahead of us, and we're going via Checkpoint D. When we get back we'll find that bitch Silver and drag her back here kicking and screaming. No one leaves this crew without my say-so.' He moved up into Lead's face, white nose almost touching black. 'And then we'll continue our discussion about what I've earned.'

* * * * *

Silver awoke to violent shaking. She sat up with a start, disoriented for a moment before remembering that she was on the ledge she had climbed to the night before. The shaking intensified, and she realised the building and whole city around her were shaking along, accompanied by a grumbling that was growing in volume. The sound was deceptively loud; not the piercing volume of a gunshot or the high-pitched scream of a child, but a low and constant sound that filled her senses completely, like radio static turned up loud.

Quakes occasionally brought buildings down and this one felt unstable enough to cause some damage. But the more immediate risk, and one just as lethal, was the very real possibility of being shaken right off the ledge and falling six storeys to the road below. Silver braced herself against the pillar in front of her and the wall behind her and placed her hands flat on the ground either side for extra stability.

Once secure, she closed her eyes and gritted her teeth against the intensity of the shaking. She was used to quakes, but still found them scary. The tremors continued for another thirty or forty seconds before gradually subsiding. The roar that had filled her ears eased, leaving them ringing slightly. Silver relaxed her muscles and allowed the breath she didn't realise she had been holding to escape. Judging from the intensity of the quake, Silver reasoned there was a fair chance it would trigger a tsunami.

Rubbing cramps out of her legs, she looked up and could see light beyond the panels of the Dome, indicating it was some time in the early morning. Looking down, she could already see people migrating towards the north-east edge of the Dome where the water would hit. The threat of a wave required all the checkpoint gates to be secured, locking all those crews that had not already departed for the Badlands inside. The day became a public holiday of sorts, with people gathering to watch the often spectacular show of the wave hitting the Dome.

Silver yawned and rubbed her red-rimmed eyes. Though she felt like nothing more than curling up and going back to sleep, she resisted the urge to lie back down. With the gates closed, and all the crews who hadn't already made it out stuck inside for the day, it was a great opportunity to try to find a crew with a vacancy. She could be fairly sure that she would not run into Coal; he generally got his crew out before sun up so they would already be outside the gates heading west.

Turning so her legs dangled over the edge, Silver rolled her shoulders to get the blood moving. After a few seconds she turned around and gingerly lowered herself down, working her feet against the wall until she found a foothold. There was a heart-stopping moment where she couldn't find anything and the strain on her arms intensified. But then her toes found a crack, and her other foot searched for the next, a pattern continuing down towards the pavement below. She dropped the last couple of metres to the ground, wincing as she failed to absorb the full impact with her knees and felt a jolt of pain run up through her heels. Rising to her feet, she joined the stream of people heading towards the Dome edge, limping slightly.

The crowds got thicker as she walked through the old Circular Quay district, with more people joining the commute. Kids as young as nine or ten marched up and down the street, and Silver kept her hand close to her pockets to discourage any unwanted attention. They headed along Alfred Street and then climbed up Albert and headed up towards the old Government House building, now little more than ruins. The Dome edge ran along the headline just beyond, and it was here that a healthy crowd had already started to gather.

The siren sounded just as Silver was approaching the building, and a cheer went up from the crowd, followed by a surge from those still making their way in, jostling to get a good spot. The warning wail signalled to the crowd they would get what they came for—a wave was on the way.

Silver pulled out of the surging crowd heading for the very edge of the Dome; instead hopping up once, twice, three times to a ruined wall edge of the Parliament building. A few others had taken similar perches, and she knew the remaining spots would fill up quickly. The vantage point afforded her a fair view of the Dome wall and allowed her to see over the crowd.

She couldn't see the approaching wave yet, for the headlands outside of the Dome blocked the view of the open sea. However, she had a good view of the harbour beyond the Dome. Directly below the point the crowd were gathered, outside the protection of the Dome, was the spot where the iconic Opera House once stood, its white peaks curving like the sails of a great ship. Now there was only open water. Rising sea levels had left the strip of land on which the Opera House had been built under water, and the building itself had been destroyed over a number of years by the waves that buffeted it.

To her left the Harbour Bridge loomed; still intact, but time and the weather had taken its toll. The sandstone pylons at either end had long since crumbled and fallen away, now only stumps sticking out of the encroaching water. The metal of the bridge was pitted by rust and erosion, its once dark grey colour now patched with the red-orange of rust. Some of the arms had already rusted through and fallen away, and the whole bridge sagged slightly. It seemed to Silver only a matter of time before the structure collapsed into the harbour.

Most of the assembled crowd was facing north-east though, looking to Silver's right. The old Mrs Macquarie's Chair headland poked out from the Dome, looking forlorn. The once lush, gardened strip of land was mostly rock, with a few stunted bushes clinging to life among the windswept rocks. Like those that had struggled to life before them, the bushes cowered in the breeze, as if aware of the approaching wave that would likely drown them.

'Want to put a wager on the bridge, missus? It's looking mighty shaky. I'll pay three-and-a-half for the dollar, best odds you'll find here.' The speaker was a portly, middle-aged man, balding on top, with ruddy cheeks. He was flanked by a much larger, imposing man, arms folded across his chest and his battered face expressionless.

'Not this time, thanks. I reckon it's got a bit more life in it yet.'

The bookie frowned and moved on, his bodyguard faithfully on his tail. Silver could see other bookies working the crowd, no doubt offering similar wagers. Many were surrounded by groups of punters willing to put their money down in the hope of making some cash. Elsewhere, circles had gathered, with a traditional coin game known as Two-up offering more entertainment.

Excited chatter from the crowd drew Silver's attention back to beyond the Dome. They were pointing to the water at the edge of the Dome, which was rapidly retracting, sucked out into the oncoming wave. Looking out towards the headlands Silver saw it: a dark line cresting the cliff top. The crowd fell silent, all eyes turned in that direction. The line seemed to remain static, unmoving for a minute, then two. Then, rapidly, it grew in size and struck the headland, sending plumes of water shooting dozens of metres into the air. The wave itself kept going, spilling over the top of the rock and plunged back down into the harbour below. More water surged through the gap in the headland, its momentum unhindered by the rocky wall.

The crowd gave a collective gasp and Silver's pulse quickened as the size of the wave became apparent. The wave surged across the harbour towards them, a black churning wall bearing down on the Dome. Silver estimated the wave face to be around twenty metres high, more than enough to reduce the city to rubble if the Dome wall gave out.

Screams of excitement erupted from the crowd as the wall of water covered the last dozen metres and struck the Dome. The wall shuddered under the impact but held strong, the crash of the wave deafening despite being muffled by the protective layers of reinforced glass and steel between them. The crowd at the wall edge flinched backwards involuntarily, causing many to fall over. Water surged up the curved Dome wall, driven upwards by the millions of litres pushing behind the initial wave. The rest of the wave drove around the Dome edge, rolling over where the Opera House had once stood and pushing onwards towards the bridge.

The eyes of the crowd followed the wave's progress, with another gasp of anticipation as it hit the base of the bridge. The structure shuddered much more visibly than the Dome had, trembling under the weight of the water. But it held; the wave continued on under it and the crowd let out an almost disappointed sigh, many having clearly taken up the wager that Silver had avoided.

Silver found herself holding her breath and let it out quietly. Her heart rate began to slow as the rush of adrenalin subsided. Her eyes lingered on the bridge, and she was buoyed by the fact that it still stood. For her it was a symbol of hope. The day it fell would be a triumph of nature over man, and would signal the inevitability of the Dome one day enduring the same fate.

The rest of the gathered crowd was oblivious to Silver's thoughts of hope and survival. A chaotic scene was spread out before her, with those who had fallen trying to pick themselves up, punters who had come out on top chasing bookies for their payout or celebrating their win. Adolescents weaved through the crowd, playing tag or fleeing with a wallet or bottle of rum they'd snatched. Many in the crowd were dispersing, while other latecomers were still flooding into the area. Many more were milling around, pulling bottles of alcohol from pockets and packs, resuming games of Two-up, or taking up instruments for entertainment. Fights had broken out throughout the crowd: some organised sport, others clashes between individuals or groups.

She couldn't help but smile from the irony of Coal's absence. It was now his turn to spend a night out in the Badlands, as the checkpoint gates would not be opened for at least twelve hours while the waters subsided.

Her mood sufficiently lightened from that thought, Silver climbed down from her perch and began weaving through the crowd. The atmosphere was jovial and light, like a carnival. Music from pipes, guitars and drums accompanied the laughter and boisterous discussions taking place. Here and there groups of people danced to the music. Later it would likely turn violent and dangerous, fuelled by alcohol, macho egos and deadly vendettas. But for a few hours at least, most were relaxed and having fun.

Unfortunately, that wasn't a luxury Silver could afford, as she needed to take the opportunity to try to line up some work. Anything would do, but salvaging was what she was good at, and what she enjoyed. For all its dangers, it got her out of the sometimes stifling confines of the city, challenged her and added an element of danger that she thrived on. It also offered board and companionship as crews typically had a clubhouse where the majority of members lived and socialised. Though she felt weary beyond belief, and her body still ached from the ordeal in the Badlands and last night's less than restful sleep, she continued through the crowd looking for familiar faces.

After a few minutes, Silver spotted a face she recognised, but it was not one she was pleased about seeing. Known as Slip, the young man had sought a position within the Silmac Ops crew, and Coal had set him a number of tasks with which to prove himself. Slip had taken to the tasks eagerly and was nearing completion. Silver knew that the last item on the list was to take down a member of a rival crew.

Slip had not seen her, but he was alone and seemed to be moving through the celebrations with some purpose. Cautiously, Silver set out after him, following some way behind so as not to arouse suspicion. Eventually, his pace slowed as he entered a particularly dense section of the crowd. His attention seemed locked on a woman ahead and to his right, her back to him. She was remarkable looking, even from behind, with a slim figure and beautiful chocolate coloured skin. Her hair was an explosion of colour, thick and tightly braided into hundreds of thin strands, each dyed brightly in yellows, oranges, reds and purples. While most of the strands had been tied back into a single, thick knot, one slightly thicker purple hued braid had been left free, hanging from her right temple and hooked back over her right ear, like a draped poisonous viper.

Her hair wasn't the only source of colour on the woman though. She wore a plain, figure hugging white singlet top, leaving her arms and shoulders free to display the python tattoo she sported. It was unlike anything

Silver had ever seen; the python's tail began at her left wrist and wound its way up around her arm and across her shoulders, disappearing briefly under the singlet before it continued its winding path down her right arm, its diamond shaped head ending on the underside of her wrist. The snake was of exquisite detail, with each scale coloured in the same hues as her hair, creating a glistening spiral running from wrist to wrist.

The woman was with a small group, listening to a man belt out a tune on a banjo. Drink in hand, she appeared absorbed in the music and oblivious to the boy creeping up behind her. As Silver watched, Slip pulled a wicked-looking knife out from under his jacket, holding it low and inconspicuously down by his side. Alarmed, Silver tried to close the distance between them, fighting through the crowds to reach them before Slip could do anything to harm her. As she went, she reached into her pack, pulling out the gun she had taken from Coal.

Slip positioned himself directly behind the tattooed woman, his arm pulled back to deliver a stab to her back as he passed. But Silver got there first, ramming the nozzle of the gun into his back, and grabbing his shoulder with her left hand to hold him still.

'This ain't a toy, Slip, and if you don't drop that knife quick smart, it'll be making mincemeat of your innards.'

The man froze in place, knife dropping from his hand and clattering to the asphalt. The noise alerted the tattooed woman, and she spun around, hand darting to a knife that was sheathed in a pouch at her side. From the front, she was even more beautiful than she had appeared from behind. Her skin was smooth and flawless; she was tall, standing on par with many of the men around her. She had an athlete's figure, with small breasts, a slim waist, and shapely arms and legs. She wore tight fitting faded denim shorts, torn in intervals down her thighs, front and back. On her feet she wore a simple pair of brown leather thongs, and on her left ankle was a beaded wooden bracelet. She had large, beautiful chestnut brown eyes, and they flashed dangerously as they took in Slip, Silver, and the discarded knife. Two men standing nearby moved over to flank her threateningly.

'What's going on here?' the woman asked, her voice low and dangerous.

'Slip here was just leaving,' Silver answered, shoving the man forcefully to her left. He stumbled but recovered quickly, putting a couple of steps between himself and his assailant, before half turning to look back at her. His eyes widened momentarily in recognition before narrowing dangerously, spitefully. Then he was gone, disappearing into the crowd.

Silver turned and found the trio now facing her, arms folded and stern expressions on their faces.

'Friend of yours?' the tattooed woman asked.

'Hardly.' Silver lowered her gun and tucked it into the back of her jeans, casting her eyes around for any police officers working the crowd.

'I know enough about him to know he's generally up to no good. He seemed to be showing some interest in you,' she stooped to pick up the knife, flipping it over and holding it handle first towards the woman, 'and I also know that when Slip takes an interest in a woman, he's not planning to buy her a drink.'

'He was going to use that on me?' she asked, gesturing to the knife.

'Looked like.'

The tattooed woman reached out and took the blade.

'Why did you step in?'

Silver hadn't expected the question and stood there stupidly for a moment.

'Don't know.' It was the truth. She didn't know the woman and had little motive in risking her own life to assist her. 'I guess I'd hate to see those amazing tattoos damaged,' she said at last, gesturing to the snake.

'Well, I guess I owe you thanks then?'

'You don't owe me anything.' Silver turned and started to make her way off through the crowd.

'Wait!'

Hesitating, she turned and looked back at the tattooed woman.

'You salvage? You've got the look about you.'

Silver nodded. Yes.

The woman motioned to the heavy pack over Silver's shoulder.

'You're travelling heavy and packing heat. Risky here with the cops about. You got a crew?'

This time Silver shook her head. No.

'We could use an extra gun. Hold on a sec.'

The lady said a few quiet words to her male companions who shrugged and turned around once more to continue to enjoy the show. She then approached Silver, this time wearing a genuine smile and offering her hand. 'I'm Asp.'

Silver clasped the offered hand but did not quite return the smile. 'Silver. You run a crew then?'

'I don't run the crew, but from what I've seen of you so far I think Grave will be glad to have you on board. Grave runs the crew. We're known as the Ash Walkers. You look dead on your feet—wanna get something to eat?'

Silver nodded, and Asp motioned for her to follow, pushing a path through the still celebrating crowd. Following hesitantly behind, Silver hadn't heard of the Ash Walkers, but there were plenty of crews around the city, so that meant little. While she wasn't certain she could trust Asp, she gave off a good vibe, and seemed genuine. She could have taken Silver down easily enough with the help of her two male companions but she hadn't. Besides, this was the reason Silver had joined the crowd in the first place, though she had not expected to be successful quite so quickly. Assuming this Grave character agreed to take her on, she might have to send Slip her thanks.

Before they had gotten far, however, an after-shock from the initial earthquake set the Dome trembling again. It was not unusual to experience tremors hours or even days after a big quake and this one lasted only a few moments. But a shrill scream alerted Silver to danger, and she turned to see a building coming down, to the west of their position, a few streets away. It was a tall, old building, a hotel in its former life. She watched as the top of the skyscraper disappeared from sight behind intervening buildings, leaning slightly as it went, leaving only a series of booming concussions to show that it continued its descent.

'What're you doing?' Asp asked as Silver began to race towards the building, digging in her pack for a respirator as she went.

'I know that building, and it was full of people!'

Asp's expression betrayed her surprise, but she nodded and hurried to catch up. 'You got another filter?'

Silver handed Asp her mask and then pulled out a spare shirt and tied it around her nose and mouth. It would not be as good as the filter, but it would stop the worst of the dust.

Rounding a corner, they were hit by a second tsunami, this one made of dust and grit. The grey wave rolled over them, reducing visibility to a couple of metres. The tremors and concussions had subsided by this stage as the building had finished its collapse. The sound was replaced by human cries and screams, though pinpointing where exactly they were coming from within the dust cloud was almost impossible.

Silver pushed on, following the road to where she knew the building had once stood. Asp was gone, though she could have been two steps away and Silver wouldn't have seen her. Only the cries and coughs of the wounded and dying remained, and the inescapable grey.

The sound of a woman wailing guided her through the cloud and at last she came to the owner of the cries, lying at the very edge of the rubble. Silver nearly missed her at first, painted in the same grey colour as everything else within the cloud. The woman was lying on her back, legs pinned under a giant slab of concrete. Her face and arms were covered in lesser scratches and cuts. She reached out a hand for aid when she saw Silver.

Before Silver could go to her, she was grabbed roughly from behind and spun around. She found herself face to face with a policeman, his face obscured behind a breathing filter, a gun held threateningly in his other hand. More policemen flanked him, similarly attired.

'This area is off limits. You must return to the street and remain behind the barricade.'

'Please, help me pull this woman free. She needs help.'

One of the other men stepped up and grabbed her by the other arm and began physically moving her back off the rubble, away from the pinned lady. Silver struggled to break free, kicking and screaming, but it was no use; the men lifted her off the ground and she felt her energy slipping away. Looking back, Silver caught a glimpse of the lady slumped back on the rubble behind her, resigned to death or possibly dead already. And then she was gone, melted into nothingness in a sea of grey.

Silver had not ventured far into the rubble, so it was only a moment before the police had cleared the edge and thrust her beyond a hastily erected barrier around the perimeter of the fallen building, manned by more armed police. A small crowd had gathered beyond the picket, but there were pitiful few of them. Asp was among them and she hurried over when Silver was thrust out.

'The police threw you out too?'

Silver nodded dumbly, her body feeling numb. The previously colourful Asp was reduced to uniform grey now, her hair and tattoos blanketed under a thick layer of dust.

'The bastards must have known it was going to collapse, getting here so quick,' Asp said, speaking loudly enough so that the police standing guard could hear.

'I found a woman still alive, trapped. They wouldn't let me help her,' Silver replied, her voice cracking from emotion. 'I tried, but they threw me out.'

'Hey now,' Asp soothed, pulling her into a hug as the tears threatened to spill. 'Come on, let's get out of here.'

With Asp's arm still around her, Silver allowed herself to be led away from the barrier and eventually out of the dust cloud. Her legs wobbled, and she was thankful for the support. When they had made it out of the cloud, Asp unclasped the breathing filter and gently pulled the shirt down from Silver's face.

'Come, let's get you back to the clubhouse and cleaned up,' she said gently. 'You tried to help, but Silmac controls the site now and there's nothing to be gained in staying.'

The trip was a blur to Silver. She vaguely remembered Asp supporting her and encouraging her along, but she was in a daze, physically and emotionally drained from the events of the last few days.

The clubhouse was located in an old run-down shop on Smith Street in Surry Hills, with four levels above. Fortunately, most members of the crew including Grave were out, and Asp hurried Silver inside, only briefly pausing to introduce her to an immense man she called Blocka. Silver allowed herself to be led upstairs to a bathroom, where Asp helped her strip out of her clothes and wash up. She was dimly surprised when she realised the water was pleasant and warm, but not in much of a state to question the luxury.

Once Asp had helped her to dry and handed her a faded, over-sized T-shirt to put on in lieu of her filthy clothes, she was led up another flight of stairs and into a comfortable looking bedroom with two single beds inside.

'Someone has to do something, Asp,' Silver whispered, her voice hoarse.

'About what, Silver?

'About life. About Silmac. We can't go on like this.'

Asp gently eased Silver down onto the nearest bed and tucked her in. 'I'm not a fan of Silmac either, but no good will come from taking him on. He holds all the cards. You need to rest—there will be food when you wake.'

Asp moved out of the room and closed the door quietly, leaving her alone. Silver curled up into a ball, cozy in the bed. But the screams of the trapped woman echoed in her mind as she fell into an exhausted sleep.

# CHAPTER 9

*From the diary of Benjamin Adams*
*March 19th, 2011*

*It's been over three months of natural disasters! Floods in Brisbane and Queensland in December killing about 35 people and doing damage estimated at $2.4bn. New Zealand is still recovering from the Christchurch earthquakes in February that claimed one hundred and eighty-five lives. And now another quake and tsunami, this time off the coast of Japan. Waves up to forty metres high and water swept inland as far as ten kilometres! Thousands dead and hundreds of thousands dispossessed, in the middle of winter. And to cap it off, one of their nuclear reactors was damaged and is seriously unstable and leaking radiation. Days have passed and authorities are still not confident that it will be brought under control.*

*Is it just me, or is the world becoming less and less stable? And are they really 'natural' disasters or are we playing some part in them? Either way my heart goes out to the Japanese.*

* * * * *

'I see the Shangri-La has gone.' Silmac sat in his office, on the comfortable couches that faced the long curved windows. It was windy outside the Dome, with the shadows of the patchy cloud cover racing each other across the barren landscape below. The wind kept the smog haze down, providing a relatively clear view from Silmac's windows. Muddy water covered much of the land directly around the Dome, and it would take some time for the waters from the morning's tsunami to fully recede.

Silmac sat with Gavin who, but for the view and the occasional and heavily muffled wail of wind, would be completely oblivious to the wild weather conditions at play outside. They had been discussing business when Meek had arrived to report.

'Yes, sir, it fell in the aftershocks of this morning's quake.'

'How many dead?'

'Two hundred and thirty-nine bodies have been retrieved, sir. There are many more as yet buried among the ruins.'

'They shouldn't have been living there,' Gavin commented, leaning forward to grab his scotch and rocks from the table and take a sip. 'There was ample warning that the building was unstable.'

'Have you secured the site?' Silmac asked, ignoring his brother's comment.

'Yes, sir, and we've already stripped a considerable amount of metal from the building.'

'Crews are already mobilising to begin hauling the remaining rubble from the Dome,' Gavin added. 'It should be cleared within three weeks. I would like to propose a new headquarters for my team be built at the site.' As head of constructions within the Dome, his team actually did more work removing and clearing collapse sites than they did building new ones. Gavin had been trying to get a new office approved for some time.

'Meek has indicated a need to turn the site into a new greenhouse?'

'While we are well stocked with fish in Darling Harbour, the livestock at the Domain need more room to pasture to keep up with required output. You could open up parts of the old gardens to them, but you'd need a fresh piece of land to accommodate the resulting loss of vegetable production. Our current production levels are only just keeping up.'

'I have noticed a shortage of fresh ingredients in some of the restaurants of late. Gavin, I'm going to give the land to Meek. I want it up and running in four weeks, with an electrified fence put in place to deter thieves.'

'I have already sourced uncontaminated soil,' Gavin replied, a sullen note to his voice. 'I'll have it brought in at once to fill the site once cleared. We've got materials for the fence already set aside so that shouldn't be an issue.'

'Good. What about the air quality within the Dome, Meek?'

'It remains poor, sir, loaded with dust from the collapse. The vents have been turned up to full capacity to help clear the air, but the

Shangri-La was a big building. I anticipate it will take two days for air quality to return to safe levels.'

'Have all my meetings and dinners relocated to here. Anything else to report?'

'There have been more attacks on various food production facilities. Two on the Darling Harbour fisheries, one on the fruit orchards at the south end of the gardens, and one on live stock. None were successful and three of the four perpetrators have been taken into custody and await shipping up to the mines. I have increased security as a precaution against further attacks.'

'Good. Anything else?'

'Just an update on the girl you were interested in. When I spoke with Coal, he claimed he had no knowledge of her whereabouts.'

'And you believed him?'

'Not entirely. After I left, I had him and his crew watched. He was clearly agitated, and the crew departed, equipped for a day in the Badlands. However, they first paid a visit to World Square, where the guard who let her in lives. They spent some time in conversation with him before making for Checkpoint E and exiting the Dome. There was no sign of the girl.'

'And on the streets?'

'I have my men keeping an eye out for her. So far, nothing.'

'Keep looking, and bring Coal to me the minute he returns from the Badlands.'

'Yes, sir, though it may not be today as water currently blocks all the gates into the Dome. The crews who made it out this morning will most likely be forced to spend the night outside.'

Silmac nodded, and Meek gave a formal bow, before backing out of the study and disappearing into the lifts.

'So who's this girl you are interested in?'

Silmac stared at Gavin, his eyes devoid of emotion. 'She survived a stormy night out in the Badlands. I want to quiz her on how she managed it. The last thing we need is someone prancing around spreading rumours on how one might survive outside the Dome. Now, back to business.'

* * * * *

Silver awoke to the sound of shouting somewhere nearby. The room she was in was dark, with only faint light filtering in through the boarded-up windows. Listening to the shouting, her heart sank as she recognised Coal's voice. He had made it back inside the Dome and found her already. She guessed she had Slip to thank for that.

She climbed out of bed and checked for her things. Her possessions were by the side of the bed, including the gun she had taken from Coal. The pack was where she had left it on the floor by the bed and seemed to have been left untouched. She reached out and touched her clothes, clean and folded neatly next to her pack. All the dust from the previous day was gone.

Shrugging, Silver quickly got dressed, then grabbed her stuff and headed over to the door, cracking it open onto an empty corridor. Seeing a stairway, she made her way over and descended quickly and quietly.

She hadn't taken in much of her surroundings when Asp brought her in that morning. She remembered thinking the clubhouse looked pretty run-down from the outside, but it was quite comfortable inside. While it was a smaller space than they had at Silmac Ops, it was much less cluttered and looked well furnished. The bottom level was an open plan, and when she descended the stairs, she found the Ash Walkers crew gathered around the front of the shop, peering out through cracks in the windows.

'If you know what's good for you, you'll send that slut Silver out now. She's my property and I'm prepared to come in and get her.'

Coal was shouting at the top of his lungs, his voice bristling with anger and aggression. The Ash Walkers still hadn't seen Silver and were whispering heatedly among themselves. Silver's cheeks flushed red and her face hardened. She hurried over to the door, reaching for the bolts that secured it.

'What do you think you're doing, Silver?'

'It will be best for you if I just go, Asp,' Silver replied, pausing by the door. 'I've been here less than a day and already I've brought trouble down on you.'

Asp moved over to her and gently pulled her hand away from the door latch. 'You've been here more than a day—you slept through the night and another full day you were so exhausted. And you'll do no such thing. Grave will be down shortly and we'll follow his lead.'

She was thrown for a minute with news that she had slept so long. She couldn't remember ever sleeping for thirty hours. Trying to refocus on the business at hand, she shook her head. 'You don't know what Coal is like, he won't back down.'

'On the contrary, I think I know exactly what he is like.'

With the string of profanities and abuse continuing to filter in from the road out front, Silver had failed to notice the newcomer until he was right behind her. Before she could respond to him, he was past her, opening the front door.

'Blocka, Sarge, with me. The rest of you, stay put. Guns ready.'

The two men he had indicated fell into step behind. One of them, the mountain of a man Asp had briefly introduced her to when they had arrived at the clubhouse, walked with a limp. Grave, Silver presumed, opened the door, and the three filed out.

Asp led Silver over to a window where they could watch the encounter. Coal and his crew were arrayed outside, all of them carrying guns. She scanned the line and noted that Lead was absent, but Slip was with them, lurking to Coal's right.

Grave marched up to Coal, stopping a couple of paces away. Next to her former partner, Grave appeared small and vulnerable. He stood almost a full head shorter than Coal and was further dwarfed by Coal's broad shoulders and barrel chest.

Grave's hair was dusty blond in colour and shaggy on top. Light coloured stubble lent further to his casual, comfortable look. His skin was pale, made to look more so by the long black coat he wore, hanging to mid-calf. Underneath, the black theme continued, with a thin, well-fitted long-sleeved shirt, black jeans, belt, and boots. A gun was holstered on his right hip, and a large knife was sheathed on his left. Silver couldn't take her eyes off the two men, horrified at what Coal might do to Grave. She took some confidence in the larger form of Blocka standing behind Grave, out-sizing even Coal in height and girth.

Despite the fact that Coal dwarfed him, Grave was deadly calm and commanded a quiet power of his own, at complete odds with Coal's loud, physical presence. His blue eyes met Coal's and held them, forcing him to quit his ranting and move over face-to-face. He stepped forward quickly, threateningly, but Grave held his position and did not flinch, simply crossing his arms in front of him. Concerned with what Coal would do, Silver made a move to head outside to join the two men, but Asp's hand shot out and restrained her.

'Stay. He has come for you and your presence will only enrage him further. Grave will handle it.'

Silver was doubtful of the claim, but didn't try to push past.

'What is the meaning of all this?'

Silver had to strain to hear Grave's words, as his voice was calm and level, in control.

'You've got something of mine in there and I want it back.' Coal's voice was louder, but had lost some of the aggression that his earlier shouting had displayed.

'Who? This "Silver" you've been blustering about? Last time I checked people don't belong to other people, but are free to come and go as they choose. If your girlfriend has had enough of you and wanted to get away, personally I wouldn't blame her. Besides, I've never met anyone called Silver. Now if that is all, I suggest you clear off my patch.'

Silver flinched at Grave's words, waiting for Coal to lash out in rage. Miraculously he didn't, actually seeming a little lost for words. 'One of my men saw her with one of yours and followed her back here. She's also got my gun; she stole it and I want it back.'

'I saw 'er come in 'ere,' Slip echoed, stepping out briefly from behind Coal's girth.

'How long have you two been together, before tonight?' Grave asked, ignoring Slip.

'What?'

'I asked how long you and this Silver have been together, before she left you?'

'Five years? Ten? What the fuck does that matter?'

'According to Australian law, a relationship of that length effectively means that she is entitled to half of what you own. You own the clubhouse on the north side, right? When is it up for sale?'

'What!?'

'Well, I assume you will be selling the clubhouse, and splitting the profits with her?'

'The fucking clubhouse is mine. That slut will have to beg for mercy before she steps foot in it again.'

'Well then, I think the matter is settled. You get the house, and her only claim in recompense is the gun. I think you'll agree you've won out?'

While Grave had his back to them, Silver had a clear view of Coal's face throughout the encounter. The big man's mind struggled to catch up with Grave's negotiating. It was almost laughable, except that Silver knew he was liable to snap at any time. He leaned in threateningly now, trying to intimidate Grave with his size.

'No more talk. The only law in the Dome is force. You'd better bring out the girl and my gun in the next ten seconds or ...'

'Or what?' Grave cut in. 'Like I said, I haven't met anyone called Silver. Besides, it sounds like the girl clearly doesn't want to go with you, and even if she were here I wouldn't be inclined to make her. You're on my turf, and every member of my crew currently has a gun trained on you and your men. They don't like being kept waiting, so I suggest you back up your threats with some action, or else clear off and stop wasting everyone's time. Oh, and I forgot to mention I'm carrying this, and I seem to have lost its pin.'

He held out his hand and though Silver could not see the contents, she saw Coal's eyes widen.

'You wouldn't. It would take out all of us.'

'Yes,' Grave said simply.

The two men stared at each other. Coal's nostrils flared and his face twitched, and Silver braced for action, finding her hand on the hilt of her own gun. She contemplated Grave's bluff, trying to decide whether Coal would be arrogant enough to call it. While the Silmac Ops crew outnumbered the Ash Walkers and could probably take them down, they were mostly out in the open and would not walk away from the encounter casualty free. A gunfight within the Dome would also bring the ire of Silmac down on all who took part in it.

'Enjoy the slut, you can fucking have her,' Coal said eventually, breaking the deadlock. 'But I guarantee you'll come to regret tonight.'

He turned and strode away, the rest of the crew following, glaring threateningly at Grave, Blocka and Sarge as they departed. The trio remained where they were until the rival crew was out of sight.

'Told you!' Asp nudged Silver with her elbow, her face lit with a grin. Silver was left shaking her head silently as she watched her old crew depart and three who had faced them return inside.

'Thank you for not handing me over,' she began as Grave re-entered. 'I never intended to bring trouble to your crew. If I can …'

The thanks died in her throat as Grave strode right past her with barely a glance.

'I want a double watch tonight, in case they come back,' he instructed over his shoulder. 'We roll out early tomorrow.'

He threw what he had been holding to the smallest member, who caught it gingerly and muttered, 'Hey, careful with that.' But Grave was gone, disappeared up the stairs.

Silver's face turned a deep shade of red, partly from humiliation, partly from anger. The jerk had completely ignored her and then made it clear to the crew that they would be doing a double watch on account of her. She could imagine the dagger-like looks that were being thrown her way at the moment.

She slowly turned to face the rest of the crew, and while most eyes were on her, she was surprised to find no obvious signs of anger at the increased workload.

'I don't think he likes me,' she said meekly, needing something to break the silence.

Asp waved her comment away and walked over to her. 'That's just Grave's way, you'll get used to it. I think it's where he got the name Grave from; his social skills are about on par with that of a zombie.'

A few of the gathered crew members chuckled, and Silver felt the heat in her cheeks easing.

'I think a few introductions are in order. Everyone, this is Silver, our newest crew member. She'll be joining us as a roach, and if the last ten minutes are any indication, her presence should keep things from getting boring around here.' The comment won a few more chuckles, before Asp continued. She gestured to the man Silver had briefly met the day before, who stood closest to them on Silver's left side. 'Blocka you've met. He's our deterrent, making rival crews think twice about attacking us. He's quiet as a mouse, but the best to have on your side in a scrap. And he's spoken for, so don't even think about it.'

'You know I only have eyes for you, baby,' Blocka replied, before extending a hand to Silver. 'Welcome to the crew, Silver.'

Silver took his offered hand, which completely enfolded her own in its immense grip. She could well imagine him acting as a deterrent; standing close to two metres tall, and weighing at least one-hundred-and-thirty kilograms, if not more. His chest was like a large barrel, his arms and legs like tree-trunks. He wore a simple black T-shirt and pair of grey-green overalls over the top, with a large pair of black boots covering his huge feet. His head was a smooth, round dome, clean-shaven and shining in the lamplight. His skin was pale white, and Silver could see no evidence of tattooing, which was unusual. His face was not a handsome one, with close-set eyes and a somewhat small, squashed nose, but his expression was kind and, despite his immense bulk, she felt at ease with him.

'This is Sarge,' Asp continued, indicating to the next man in line. 'Sarge is ex-military, and self-appointed security of the crew. He is also a stickler for time and keeps us organised and on schedule when out in the Badlands.'

'Damn straight, and don't you forget it,' Sarge barked. 'Staying to schedule could save your life outside the Dome.'

Silver could tell Asp wasn't joking about him being ex-military. He was an older man in his late forties and had close cut, silver-grey hair. Despite a face creased with care lines and a perfectly manicured moustache, he was still good looking. He was slightly taller than Asp and had retained a well-toned figure.

His dress was military through and through: a tight fitting grey shirt; camo black, grey and white pants covered in pockets and pouches; a black utility belt also sporting a number of sheaths and pouches; and a pair of black boots, shined to a glistening sheen.

He had been standing at ease when Asp introduced him, legs spread, arms behind his back. It wasn't until he extended his left hand to shake Silver's that she realised he was missing his right arm, from just above the elbow. She had been so absorbed in the encounter with Coal that she hadn't noticed it earlier.

'An old war wound,' he explained, as she shook his hand, noticing her gaze move to the rounded stump where his arm should have been. 'Arm got gnawed on by a couple of mutes while protecting a convoy from the mines. Had to wait to get it seen to, and by that point it had become infected from their filth and had to come off.'

Though he told the tale in a matter-of-fact manner, Silver could detect a note of bitterness in his voice. She wasn't sure how to respond, but luckily Asp cut in to continue the introductions.

'You met Muzzle and the Rat yesterday, at the wave.'

Though she had not paid much attention to them at the gathering by the Dome edge to watch as the tsunami hit, Silver recognised them as the two who had been standing with Asp when she was approached by Slip.

Muzzle was a young man, probably just twenty or so. Silver guessed he had probably not yet finished growing, but already he was developing a well-muscled body. He was tall, though not quite as tall as Blocka, who dwarfed anyone near him. He'd spiked his hair up into a mohawk, which gave him the appearance of being taller again, and it was dyed a bright blue in colour, matching his faded denim jacket, white shirt and blue jeans. His face was full of youthful energy and he flashed Silver a confident smile as they were introduced, his eyes giving away the fact that he liked what he saw. Silver smiled back at him. He was handsome enough, though a little on the young and inexperienced side.

Next to Muzzle stood a small, mousy man, the one Asp had referred to as Rat. He was slight of build and short for a guy, standing eye to eye with Silver. His hair was long and greasy, tied back in a knot. A long but thin and wispy beard and moustache obscured much of his face. His arms and legs were visible, covered in dark hair—a contrast to his otherwise pale skin. He wore a dirty grey cap backwards on his head and a short-sleeved grey, baggy T-shirt over a black long-sleeved shirt, with the sleeves pushed up to the elbows. He had a tattered pair of sneakers on his feet, poking out from below his baggy, unbelted pants. He nodded at her nervously as he was introduced, and his nose twitched involuntarily. Between his look and the twitch, Silver could well understand how he had ended up with his nickname. He was still holding the object Grave had thrown him.

'Rat is a roach, and has an interest in the construction of explosives, which often comes in handy out in the Badlands. And sometimes inside the Dome too, as you've just seen. Muzzle is our youngest team member, still learning the ropes but with plenty of promise.'

Silver nodded to both of them. 'Where's the rest of the crew?'

'That's it, hun. We're a small but effective unit.'

Silver was taken aback but tried to hide her surprise. The smallest crew she had come across before had nine members, and she had wondered at the time how they protected themselves, both in and outside the Dome. It appeared this crew was doing it with six people, with her addition making it seven. She started to have some doubts about joining them, wondering how they would handle an attack by a large group of mutes. Still, apart from perhaps the leader, Grave, they seemed nice enough, and the clubhouse was well stocked and comfortable. She didn't have anywhere else to go at this stage, so looked like she'd have to stick it out and see how they operated. Her stomach grumbled loudly and Asp looked at her and laughed.

'Your stomach clearly doesn't want to be left out. Let's go introduce it to some food. Come on, the kitchen's this way.' Asp led her around to the back of the shop where a small kitchen was tucked away under the stairs. 'We don't have much choice to offer, but we are never short of food so have as much as you like.'

The pantry was well stocked with nutrition bars, packets of porridge-like gruel and a few other fairly unappealing foodstuffs. It was normal fare for most within the Dome, the only difference being that this crew seemed to have a lot of stock.

'All you need for a healthy balanced diet,' Asp joked as Silver took down one of the packets, poured the contents into a bowl and added water. 'So what was the go with you and that Coal guy? He seems like a jerk-off.'

'It was more a relationship of convenience I guess,' Silver replied, admitting it to herself at the same time. 'I met him very young, when I was on the streets alone. He was strong, confident and capable, and offered me an escape from solitude. I guess I knew lots of the things he did were wrong, but I turned a blind eye to it because I couldn't handle the thought of being left by myself again. After a few years he got a gig in a crew and got me in as well. We made a pretty good team and rose up through the ranks until he was running the crew. Eventually word got out, and he got poached by Silmac Ops to run their top crew, and we both came across.'

While she spoke, Silver had been mixing up the powdery porridge until it had become a thick, pasty consistency. She paused to take a mouthful.

'So what made you leave?'

'He left me out in the Badlands, doing the runner when a group of mutes came across us while I was roaching. Didn't even give me a warning, just hot-footed it, leaving the mutes to reel me in like a fish on a line.'

Asp shook her head in disbelief at Coal's actions, breaking one of the unspoken but firmly entrenched rules of salvaging: never leave a crew mate behind. 'So how did you get away and get back? Another crew pick you up?'

Silver swallowed another mouthful of the porridge before relating the rest of the story. Asp was a good listener, different to the other women Silver had met who, like herself, tended to put up a front of bravado in order to compete and fit in to the male-dominated world of the salvage crews. Asp was relaxed and had a manner that invited openness and honesty. Silver even told her about the strange encounter with the elderly mute, letting it slip before she registered what she was saying.

'So you actually spent a night out in the Badlands in the same place as a *mute*?'

'I didn't touch him and he didn't touch me!' Silver objected. 'I'm not tainted or anything.'

'Whoa, girl! Easy. I'm not accusing anything, just surprised is all.'

Silver eyed Asp for a moment, hesitantly continuing with her tale. 'It was weird, I know, but this one was different. He had found a way to survive that didn't involve savagery and cannibalism and so I felt safe in his presence. He was very human.'

'That's incredible. I never would have thought it possible,' Asp admitted. 'So what happened when you got back? Is that really Coal's gun?'

'I had to trade my gun to get in through the checkpoint or spend another night out in the Badlands. When I made it back to the Silmac Ops clubhouse I found out that Coal had already started something with another member of the team. Turns out it hadn't just started, but it was the reason I was left out there. I guess I often suspected it, but thought I was happier not knowing, you know?'

Asp nodded, and Silver continued.

'So I waited till he was asleep, grabbed my stuff and his gun and left. I spent last night on the streets and then bumped into Slip and yourself in the morning and now I'm here.'

'I never properly thanked you for that,' Asp said, referring to the incident with Slip. 'I can't believe I let my guard down and nearly got stuck for it.'

'You've thanked me by offering me a place in the crew and then gone well beyond when you didn't hand me back to Coal. But what was Grave's problem? I guess he was pretty pissed at me bringing heat down on the crew, but he just brushed me off. No offence, but he comes across as a bit of a tool.'

'Grave's an odd one, there's no doubt about that, but he's the best boss I've had. He's just not much of a talker and can take a bit of getting used to. It wasn't anything personal; he didn't hand you over after all.'

Silver nodded, conceding the point, but still not completely convinced. She finished off her bowl of porridge and looked longingly at the other food in the cupboard. Asp laughed and proceeded to grab two of the nutrition bars and pass them to her.

'Go on, they don't taste like much but they should fill you up at least. Then I have to see about organising the watch.'

'About that, I'll watch the full night. I've just had a good sleep, and it's on account of me that we're having to double the watch, so it's only fair.'

'Absolutely not. We'll be heading out into the Badlands early tomorrow and you need to be fresh. You can pull a double though, take the watch first up with me, then I'll put you on with Muzzle. Sarge and the Rat can go next, then Blocka and Grave. Sound okay?

Silver nodded, happy with the compromise. She just hoped that if Coal chose to return, he did it on one of her watches. Her hand fell to her gun, comfortingly.

# CHAPTER 10


*From the diary of Benjamin Adams*
*May 3$^{rd}$, 2011*

*City Design has completed its buy-out of another company, Urban Architecture, and I've taken on a new role within the greater company, which is exciting. I'll be overseeing a relatively large team of people at Urban, and have the opportunity to work on large-scale projects. It's a little daunting as the two companies have fairly different cultures, which will take some getting used to. But it is a big step up in career, and I'm looking forward to the challenge.*

*Jess and the boys are going well. Jayden and Alex continue to grow at a rate of knots, with Jayden about to turn five. He'll start school next year, which seems ludicrous. Time seems in a perpetual state of acceleration!*

* * * * *

The morning became a surreal experience for Silver, a strange mix of familiar and foreign. Despite sleeping the best part of a day and night, she was tired after her double watch and climbed gratefully into bed. This time it took a while to fall asleep; the sounds of the clubhouse were different, unfamiliar.

She couldn't remember falling asleep, but next thing she was being awoken by Sarge, shouting at everyone to get up and ready to leave, lamenting the fact that they were already behind schedule. The grey outside indicated it was early. She helped get the gear ready for the day's work as usual, while struggling to remember everyone's name, and being slightly out of kilter with their habits and practices.

When they arrived at the checkpoint, she found that their truck was not like the big machine she had been used to with the Silmac Ops crew, but little more than an old four-wheel-drive with a trailer on back. It was cozy with six of them squeezed into the car as it bumped and ground its way out into the Badlands, Sarge at the wheel. Silver found herself in the back of the car, sandwiched between Asp and Rat, with the latter focusing his attention out the window and muttering constantly. Grave was absent.

Once they were out, Asp began doling out small bowls of gruel from a larger jug she had prepared back at the clubhouse. Silver took hers and ate hungrily, knowing she would need her energy for the work ahead. She was nervous and excited about the day, keen to prove to her new crew that she was as good a roach as any.

It wasn't until she had finished her breakfast that she realised they were heading north and west, winding their way through what was once the inner west.

'Where are we going?' she whispered to Asp, who was still finishing off her breakfast.

'To salvage of course. Why?'

'We're going the wrong way. All the untouched salvaging spots are in the far south-west, and it's much better to take the old main roads out that way. These areas have been picked clean of any precious metals long ago.'

'We're not out here for precious metals.'

'Right.' Silver's reply belied her confusion. 'What are we meant to be looking for then?'

'Other precious things, books, toys—relics from the past.'

Silver's mind shot straight to the mute's place where she had stayed three nights earlier, but she kept her peace.

'Oh, and keep an eye out for black glass, kinds like this.' Asp produced a shard of blackened glass panelling. Silver had seen its like once or twice before among the ruins, but had been told by Coal it had no value.

'What does it do?'

'Not sure to be honest, but Grave, or one of his buyers, has an interest in it.'

'And you make money off all this stuff?'

Asp nodded. 'Modest money, but enough to get by.'

'What about the mutes?'

'Yep, it is true what they say about a higher concentration of mutes in this part of the city. There weren't many a few years ago, but since the crews moved on from the area, they have steadily crept back in. Keep your gun close and your wits about you.'

Silver nodded and fell silent. She was perplexed as to how they could make enough money to survive, let alone fund the well-equipped clubhouse they kept, by searching exclusively for black glass and relics from the past. Coal had occasionally brought home things other than metal, but was extremely selective, limiting it to things they could use in their house or things he already had buyers lined up for. Their bread and butter was in the metal. Grave must have some fairly wealthy collectors lined up who funded the team.

'Where is Grave anyway?'

'He has a meeting lined up with a prospective buyer. He doesn't always accompany us out into the Badlands.'

*Typical*, Silver thought. What sort of leader left the crew to face the danger and do all the dirty work, in order to attend meetings with prospective buyers? She didn't know how he had fooled Asp into thinking he was the best boss she'd had, but he wasn't shaping up to be anything special in Silver's eyes. Maybe they had history?

Her line of thinking was interrupted as they came to an abrupt halt from their bumpy journey, the brakes squealing loudly in protest. The crew began pulling on their air filtration masks, so Silver followed suit, taken by surprise at the speed of the journey. As they piled out of the car, she looked around and saw the Dome looming near and large.

The area itself was a hilly district, once residential. The houses facing north-west were a little more intact than many Silver had seen, having been afforded protection from storms rolling in from the sea, and located high enough to avoid flooding and tsunami damage. They were still in very poor condition, but only semi collapsed.

There was also much more foliage in this region than usual. The trees and bushes were short and stunted, but they were growing. In many regions the land was barren and desert-like, but in this area nature was struggling onwards.

Having killed the engine and locked up the truck, Sarge circled round to where the others had gathered.

'All right, same pairing as usual; Asp and Blocka, myself and the Rat.

Muzzle, you are off watch duty today and can anchor for Silver. There will be mutes about, so keep your eyes open and your guns handy. Two rapid shots in the air if you need help. Do not stray too far from the truck. Let's go.'

Once he had finishing issuing the orders, he turned and headed towards some of the dilapidated buildings nearby, Rat in tow. Asp gave Silver a quick wave before heading off with Blocka in a different direction. Silver turned to find Muzzle grinning at her.

'Don't worry, you're in good hands.'

Silver wasn't so sure. Her palms were sweaty, and she found herself startled at every sound, her eyes raking over the surrounding ruins in search of danger. 'I'll lead, you just keep an eye out for danger and give me plenty of line. One pull means you need to give me some slack, two pulls you need to take it up.'

'Yes, ma'am! I like it when a woman takes control.'

'Come on.' Silver motioned, turning to mask the smile that crept to her face. She was secretly grateful for his youthful confidence as it eased her anxiety from her venture into the Badlands. And despite herself, she was flattered by Muzzle's evident interest in her. His confidence and exuberance was contagious.

Picking a direction away from where the others had gone, the two got to work.

* * * * *

Silver was impressed with what she saw of the Ash Walkers. The day was humid and bright, which made for uncomfortable working conditions. There had been rain overnight, and coupled with the water left in the city from the tsunami the day prior, the air was wet and thick with insects. The sky was a mixture of blue and white, but the combination of sun and cloud made for an eye-wateringly glaring day.

Despite the uncomfortable conditions, everyone worked hard. Muzzle was young and, while a little inexperienced and in need of some direction as an anchor, he was eager and strong. Working up until lunch time, they had found a whole manner of bits and pieces that would be saleable, including a tattered but intact and readable book titled *The Two Towers*, a shell necklace, a coffee mug, slightly chipped but otherwise intact and an orange action figurine that looked like a cross between a dog and a man, with the faded words Ben Ten on the back. Silver took a little while to get accustomed to looking for items other than metal, and as she had suspected there was precious little of it about. But once she got the hang of it, she found herself enjoying the search for other items. It proved far more interesting than simply stripping the ruins clear of metal.

When they met back at the truck for lunch, each of the teams brought with them a pile of small treasures, which they placed in the trailer. Toys, ornaments, pieces of furniture. Much of it looked in pretty poor condition, but Asp assured Silver most of it would look great once cleaned up. The rest would be used for parts to complete other broken items salvaged from the Badlands.

The crew ate together in the car so they could take their masks off. The nutrition bars were bland as ever, but the morning had been kind and they were in a jovial mood.

They returned to work after lunch, and it wasn't until mid-afternoon that they ran into trouble. Silver had ventured inside a once large double-level house and had already found a few items of use when she heard a call from Muzzle.

'Silver! Mutes! I'm pulling you out.'

His words sent an icy shiver running up and down Silver's spine, as memories of her recent ordeal immediately surfaced. She heard two rapid gunshots, and then she felt the rope tighten. For a moment she resisted, frozen and unsure whether it was Muzzle trying to pull her out or the mutes.

The pressure on the rope was far more even than previously, and Silver forced herself to breathe before allowing herself to be pulled, using her hands and knees to take her weight and keep her body clear of anything harmful.

As she cleared the entrance, she was faced with Muzzle's straining form, beyond which were a trio of mutes rapidly bearing down on him. They looked wild and aggressive, their faces twisted in hatred and hunger, their bodies lean and sinewy, hunter-like. Still lying in the entrance of the space she had crawled in to, she reached for her holstered gun and pulled it free.

'Get down!'

Muzzle immediately dropped to the ground at her order, and she pulled the trigger on the closest of the three mutes, just footsteps away from him. The shot rang out like a thunderbolt, and the gun recoiled violently in her hands, Coal's pistol being much larger and more powerful than the ones she was used to firing. But her aim had been good, and the mute was hurled backwards from the force of the impact, striking one of the mutes behind it and taking them both to the ground.

However, before she could redirect the gun, the third mute bound forward and launched itself at Muzzle's vulnerable back, teeth and claw-like hands bared ferociously.

Another shot rang out, and the mute lurched suddenly sideways in mid-air, crashing head first into the dirt and rubble next to Silver. She looked in the direction of the shot and found Asp and Blocka running in towards them, Asp carrying her gun in hand.

Silver scrambled fully out of the hole and moved over to help Muzzle, but Blocka arrived first. The big man grabbed the back of Muzzle's overalls and hauled him bodily to his feet. Another shot rang out causing the three to duck and turn reflexively. The second mute, who had been knocked down by the first, had risen to his feet and been poised to leap at them but Asp's sure aim had taken him down.

'Thanks,' Silver said to Asp and Blocka.

'We're not out of trouble yet. Look!'

Asp pointed beyond them in the direction that the three mutes had arrived from and saw another half a dozen running their way.

'Back to the truck!' Blocka yelled, but when they turned in that direction, they saw a second and then third group of mutes swarming between the gaps in the rubble and blocking their exits.

'Fuck, we're boxed in!' yelled Muzzle, reaching for his gun with a slightly trembling hand.

'Quick! Up on top of the rubble,' Silver ordered. 'If we stay on the ground, we're gone.'

Silver started scrambling up over the loose debris, working her way up towards the peak some fifteen metres away. She moved quickly and surely despite the treacherous and shifting ground underfoot.

At the top of the pile was a relatively flat and stable position. Turning, she found Asp close behind her, with Muzzle and Blocka beyond. The men were moving much more slowly up the pile than she and Asp had, and what seemed like dozens of mutes were swarming in on them fast.

Silver aimed the pistol out at them, steadying herself this time and preparing for the considerable kick back of the weapon. Her first shot rang out, and a mute fell, then another with her second shot, and a third.

By this time Asp had reached her side and brought her gun to bear as well, a mute falling with each shot. But even so, the mutes were gaining on the men and there were more of them than Silver had bullets.

Silver fired off two more rounds, and the two mutes closest to Blocka fell. When she tried for a third, the trigger kicked with no recoil and she realised she was out of ammo. Bullets were expensive, and though she normally carried a spare clip, she was carrying Coal's gun and hadn't had a chance to acquire spare bullets that fit.

'Muzzle, gun!'

Muzzle, who was almost at the top of the pile hesitated for a second, and then passed his gun out to Silver's outstretched hand.

'I'm out!' Asp holstered her now useless gun and stuck out a hand to help pull Muzzle up to their position.

Silver aimed Muzzle's gun at the mutes that were now scurrying up the pile, trying to buy Blocka enough time to reach their position. What they'd do then, she didn't know, but they had a better chance of fighting the mob off on the higher ground.

A mute caught hold of Blocka's leg, digging its dirty nails in and causing the big man to slip and lose grip on his gun, which fell down in between a gap in the rubble. A shot from Silver sent the creature flying backwards off the pile, with a second shot catching another one nearby. But as Blocka came back up to his feet, she lost her shot on a third, which launched itself up onto his back. He grunted as the thing bit into him and Asp cried out in dismay. Reaching over his head he grabbed the mute by the neck and tore it away, throwing it with a grunt of brute strength in the path of another one creeping up on him and sending them both crashing down to the ground.

Silver took another three rapid shots, felling two of the mutes nearby, while Muzzle leant forward and offered Blocka his hand to help him up the final few metres to the top of the pile. Blood streamed from the wound on the back of his neck. Silver got off another three shots, felling three of the mutes before the gun clicked empty and she was again out of bullets.

Despite the number of mute bodies surrounding the pile of rubble on which they stood, there were about that many again still standing. Some had taken cover to wait out the gun fire and now, hearing the shooting stop, emerged from hiding and began making their way towards the edge of the pile.

Silver reached to the side and took up a piece of wood from the debris, hefting it to use as a club. Muzzle followed suit, while Asp pulled out a long knife from a sheath at her back and Blocka rolled his shoulders, displaying no sign of pain from the wound on his neck.

'Well, it's been nice almost knowing you,' Silver said, as the mutes regrouped and began making their way up the pile.

Before anyone could answer, they heard a whoop and something dropped in near the base of the pile, where the mutes had amassed.

'Get down!' Asp yelled, pulling Blocka with her.

Silver was slower to drop, but Muzzle dived at her, bearing her to the ground underneath him just as the object exploded in a fiery ball of flame.

The two mutes standing next to the ball were completely engulfed in the flames, while those nearby also fell, knocked down by the force of the explosion, and the debris that flew out from it. Pieces of shrapnel flew above the companions, one of them opening up a bloody wound on Muzzle's thigh.

As the sound from the explosion died away, gun fire replaced it, and Asp peeked over the top of the pile to see Sarge coming around one of the piles nearby, opening fire on the mutes that remained standing, Rat just behind him.

It was too much for the surviving mutes, who turned tail and fled, leaving behind over a score of their comrades either dead or dying.

'You took long enough!' Asp called down to the pair, her voice belying her gratitude at their arrival.

'Looks to me like we got here at just the right time,' Rat called out. 'My device worked perfectly!'

'A little more warning would have helped,' Asp shot back.

'Anyone injured?' Sarge called out.

'Yep. Blocka took a bite to the neck and looks like Muzzle took some shrapnel to the leg. Both are okay though.'

'Get down here now! We've got to get him back to the Dome and get that seen to. Besides, we better not linger here. Won't be long before the dogs or more mutes come looking for all this meat.' Sarge indicated to all the dead bodies around the base of the pile.

While Asp and Sarge had been talking, Muzzle remained where he was on top of Silver, gazing into her eyes with an intense look on his face.

'Well, that was pretty full on, though at least it ended pleasantly.'

A little uncomfortable at the look he was giving her, Silver gently extracted herself from underneath him, causing Muzzle to wince in pain as he shifted.

'Thanks for pulling me down. You okay?'

'Yeah, just a scratch on the leg.'

Silver leant over to look at the wound and realised it was more than a scratch, and quite a deep gouge. She tore away the leg of his overalls and used the material to bind the wound as tightly as she could, eliciting further groans of pain from the young man. As she finished with the leg, she noticed that she was kneeling on black panelling.

Looking around, she quickly realised that the section where they had made their stand was a series of black panels, twelve in all. They were rectangular, each roughly half a metre wide by a metre tall. All were cracked and broken, and probably trampled and crushed further by the four of them. Silver reached down and pulled away a broken shard of the glass. Muzzle's eyes widened as he realised what she was looking at and seeing how much of it there was around them.

He whistled. 'Ah, Asp. I think we struck gold.'

Asp was doing her best to staunch the blood flowing from Blocka's neck and looked distractedly over at Muzzle to see what he was talking about. She raised her eyebrow in understanding before turning back to Blocka. 'You all right, babe?'

'I'll be fine,' he confirmed.

'Come on! Let's get moving!' Still waiting below, Sarge was clearly impatient to get on the road.

'Sarge, go get the truck and bring it here. We're coming down, but we're bringing a stack of the black glass with us!' Asp yelled in reply.

'No time, we've got to get back!'

'We'll make time, Sarge. This is the biggest haul of the stuff I've seen, and Grave will want to see it.'

Sarge grumbled something Silver failed to catch, but turned and ran off towards the truck, Rat on his heels. Asp and Silver helped the men to their feet and while they assisted each other down the rubble, the women started gathering what they could of the panels. Soon enough the truck returned at speed, tyres sliding a little as Sarge pulled it up as close to the pile as possible. Silver and Asp started making their way down the rubble, arms laden with as much of the panelling as they could manage.

Rat whistled softly when he saw what they were carrying and how much of it there was. Asp indicated to the top of the rubble pile they had just climbed down.

'There's another load up there.'

Sarge and Rat climbed up, and Silver made another trip to bring down all the panels and load them in the back of the truck. Asp meanwhile retrieved Blocka's gun, her slim arm sliding into the crevasse his could not. Once she had it, she and Blocka stood guard, watching for any sign of returning mutes, roving dog packs or other dangers. When all the panels had been loaded into the trailer, they piled into the truck and it roared to life as Sarge hit the accelerator. With the back tyres kicking up dirt and debris, Sarge spun the truck in a U-turn and they were soon bumping down the track, heading back towards the Dome.

Silver found herself sitting next to Muzzle, who winced every time they went over a particularly nasty bump.

'How's the leg?'

'It's not too bad, though walking hurts. I might be out of action for a few days.'

'Thanks for pulling me out of the hole.'

'Of course, that's the job of an anchor.'

'Yeah, well not all of them stick to their job description, so I appreciate what you did.'

Another grimace flashed across Muzzle's face as the truck jolted into a particularly deep rut in the road. 'I owe you thanks as well, for keeping them mutes off my back. I thought I was toast, but you're a crack shot.'

'Pays to be,' Silver replied. She noticed that with the last jolt, Muzzle had edged closer to her in the seat, and he was now leaning lightly against her. She wasn't sure if it had been intentional, or merely a by-product of the bumpy ride. 'I spent a bit of time on the range in my old gig and have been in my share of scrapes over the years. Not worth letting yourself get rusty in a skill like that.'

'I'll drink to that, and happy to have you watch my back anytime. We make a good team.' Muzzle's hand edged over so that his fingers brushed gently against Silver's thigh. This time there was no doubt about the movement.

She realised the car had fallen silent and was starting to feel a little awkward, so she changed the subject. 'Have any of you seen such a high concentration of mutes like that before?'

Most of the car shook their heads but Sarge, behind the wheel, nodded.

'Just once before; when I lost my arm, nearly seven years ago. Something had 'em stirred up that day, that's for certain. Corbett had decided to take a tour of his mine and power station up north and I was a member of the squad selected to guard his convoy. Not long outside of the Dome, we were ambushed by a group of mutes at least three times the size of what we faced here today. It was like they knew Corbett was in the convoy and they were attempting to get at him. Don't blame 'em really.'

Silver shuddered at the thought of such a large pack of mutes. 'How many of you were there?'

'We had a squad of twenty or so, but the mutes had picked their spot well and we didn't get a good chance to open fire at 'em. In moments they had made it into hand to hand. We were well equipped, but I took a nasty bite on the arm, like the one on Blocka's neck. Nothing too serious at the time—barely felt it in the heat of battle. Eventually we fought them off, leaving many of the dead on the road. I wasn't the only one injured—three soldiers had been killed by the mutes and another five had injuries like me. Rather than turn back and venture out the following day with a fresh squad, Corbett ordered the convoy onwards, leaving the dead on the roadside and forcing us to tend to our own wounds as best we could. We were hit by some bad weather heading north, and by the time we reached the mines four days had passed.

'Needless to say, the wounds we had sustained didn't look pretty by this stage. By the time a doctor could see us, it was too late. I lost my arm, another soldier lost his leg and the three others eventually lost their lives. When we made it back to the Dome, I was handed my marching orders, told I was unfit for service. No pension offered, no thanks, no nothing.'

Sarge lapsed into silence, but Silver noticed Asp's grip on Blocka tighten, her face betraying the worry that his wound might become infected. Silver reached out a hand to squeeze Asp's leg, briefly sharing a quick smile with the woman.

Silver was surprised at how much she shared Asp's concern. In contrast to Sarge's story of the type of loyalty Silmac offered, the Ash Walkers had demonstrated a fierce loyalty to each other, even extending that to her. She admired them, felt more valued in her two days here than she had been after years of working with Coal. As the Dome loomed ever nearer, a private smile crept across her face. She could see herself making a home and life here as an Ash Walker.

# Chapter 11



*From the diary of Benjamin Adams*
*September 9th, 2011*

*Work has been tough. Managing a larger team has been a pretty big learning curve, and I've still got some work to do there. It's been challenging dealing with some of the egos and politics of a much larger office.*

*Speaking of politics, we are creeping towards an election again and the tide has turned firmly away from climate change and environmental issues, to the point where the parties are promising to abolish most of the progress that has been made in the last five years. Propaganda campaigns backed by big business continue to play a part in this.*

*Politics at work, politics on the news; thank god for some sanity at home. Jess is a pillar of love and support for me, and I adore her and the boys. Alex is turning three in a few days and growing into a lovely young lad. The family will be coming over for a party, which will be nice. Jess has a cake planned as always—it will no doubt be a mission getting it done the night before, but it is always worth the stress when the boys see the creation she has made.*

* * * * *

It had been a long wait getting back inside the city, and Asp had started to get agitated, wanting to get treatment for Blocka's injury as soon as possible. Silver had also wondered what the hold up was about, but soon realised the delay was normal for most crews; it was her old crew's status as a Silmac Ops crew that gave them preferential treatment, allowing them to jump the queue.

Eventually they got to the checkpoint, and the guards did their usual inspection of the goods.

'You've bought back rubbish!' one of them complained, agitated that there had been nothing there they could confiscate for a bit of extra cash for themselves. He added the items to his inventory list with little enthusiasm.

Given the state Muzzle and Blocka were in, the crew had opted to leave the bulk of what they had found in the truck and return for it later, taking just one panel with them, carried by Sarge and Rat. Silver supported Muzzle on the walk back to the crew quarters, while Asp walked with Blocka.

The place was empty when they arrived, and Asp went straight upstairs and returned carrying a large medical kit. Silver was impressed; the kit would not have been cheap and again she was a little perplexed at how well stocked and resourced the small crew was, particularly given what they had salvaged. With the antiseptic ointment and bandages in the kit she felt reasonably confident that neither Blocka nor Muzzle would suffer any long-term effects from their injuries. She was surprised at the relief she felt from this.

It was still relatively early in the evening, so after getting cleaned up, most of the crew gathered downstairs for some food and drinks. Sarge and Rat played a game of pool, while Silver sat with Muzzle and Asp sat with Blocka. Not long after, Grave arrived, looking identical to the previous day. Silver watched as he entered and felt her disdain growing when he didn't spare her a second glance. He did seem genuinely concerned when he saw Muzzle's and Blocka's injuries, and demanded to know what had happened.

'You would know if you had been there,' Silver muttered quietly to herself.

Asp recounted the story, retelling what had happened and mentioning the role Silver had played in fighting off the mutes. Silver blushed with modesty, then bristled as Grave continued to avoid eye contact.

'Just when we thought we were done, Sarge and Rat turned up, and one of Rat's homemade grenades was enough to shake the resolve of the rest of the mutes.'

Rat beamed with pride and Grave smiled at him.

'And you've dressed the injuries?'

'Yes. We found something else you might be interested in too.'

'That can wait a moment. I'd like to take another look at them, just to be sure. It's not worth running any risk when it comes to wounds inflicted by mutes. Rat, can you grab the medical kit again please?'

While Rat trudged upstairs to retrieve the kit, Grave got Blocka to turn around and gently unwound the bandage around his neck, wincing when he saw the injury underneath.

'It is a nasty bite. You've done well in cleaning it, but I might give it another go over, just to be on the safe side. Asp, get some drink, and make it the hard stuff.'

Rat returned with the kit and Asp returned with a bottle of brown rum, handing it to Blocka, who took a large swig. Grave pulled on a pair of latex gloves from within, along with an assortment of tools. He set to work on Blocka's neck, his hands moving methodically.

'Pass the bottle to Muzzle—he's next.'

Muzzle took the bottle of rum and took a few swigs of his own while Grave finished up with Blocka, re-bandaging the wound skilfully. He took off the gloves and pulled another pair from the kit as he moved over to Muzzle and squatted down in front of him. When Muzzle pulled up his trouser leg revealing a bloodied bandage underneath, Grave shook his head and started unwinding the bandage.

'Looks like it will need stitches. This is going to hurt.'

Muzzle gritted his teeth and took another long swig of the rum while Grave dug needle and thread out of the kit. Silver watched on in fascination as Grave began his work, using one hand to pull the edges of flesh together and the other to thread the needle through. Muzzle let out a few gasps of pain but the rum, and perhaps the presence of crew watching on, gave him the strength to endure through it.

Once done, Grave packed away the medical equipment, discarding the latex gloves, leaving the instruments he had used aside and packing everything else back into the kit.

'Now Asp, what was it you were going to tell me about?'

The black panel they had retrieved from the truck had been left resting against the wall at the back of the room, a towel thrown over it for a little added protection. Asp and Blocka moved over and lifted it together, bringing it over to the pool table, setting it down and pulling the towel back in a dramatic reveal. The panel was covered in a spider web of cracks, but otherwise intact, set in a slightly bent aluminium frame.

Grave raised his eyebrow in interest, running his hand gently over the surface.

'Silver found it by accident when we were looking for a position to defend against the mutes. I'm afraid we may have broken it ourselves, standing on top of it before we properly realised what it was.' Asp looked somewhat guilty as she explained how they had come across the panel.

'Your lives are more important than the panel. Even with the damage it will attract a good fee from my buyer. Well done.'

'There's more,' Asp added. 'There are other panels in the truck, a couple in better shape than this one. With Blocka and Muzzle unable to assist with carrying, we decided to leave them there and come back for them.'

'More?' Grave asked, his interest growing. 'How many?'

'Another eleven panels I think. That right, Silver?'

Grave finally looked at Silver, and she nodded. 'That's what I counted. Twelve in all.'

'We need to go and pick them up. Blocka and Muzzle, hold down the fort. Everyone else can come with me. Sarge, grab the trolley. We leave in two minutes.'

'The place will be locked up by now anyway,' Silver objected. 'Is it worth the risk or expense of breaking or bribing our way in? It's not like they are going to be stolen or anything—no one else is interested in the panels.'

Already over to the foot of the stairs, Grave paused and glared at her. 'I'll decide what risk is or isn't worth taking, or what expense is or isn't worth incurring, thank you. We leave in two minutes.'

Silver opened her mouth, but saw a warning look from Asp and shut it again. Grave disappeared up the stairs while Sarge fetched the trolley; really just a wooden panel with some old shopping trolley wheels bolted to the bottom. Silver busied herself with grabbing her air filter and gun. She released the clip and remembered that she had used all her ammo in the gunfight with the mutes.

Before she could raise her dilemma, Grave was back downstairs, carrying a pack with him. He pulled out a couple of ammunition clips and passed them around the crew members waiting to go, including a box of bullets to fit Silver's over-sized handgun, which he shoved in her direction without making eye contact. Once the team had loaded their weapons, he headed out the door, setting a brisk pace towards the checkpoint.

By this time it was well after dark and the streets were fairly bare, becoming even emptier as they got nearer to the Dome edge. Grave called a halt when they neared the checkpoint.

'We get in quick and fast, take down the guard without killing him. Get to the truck, load the panels, and get out. Rat, hold here and signal if anyone approaches. If that happens, don't wait for us. Get back to the clubhouse, but make sure you're not followed.'

He reached into his pack and pulled out two spray cans, passing one each to Silver and Asp. 'Use these on the cameras. Ready?'

Without waiting for a reply, Grave ducked from cover and scurried over to the door, Asp and Silver following suit. With practiced ease, he inserted a tool from his pack into the lock of the door and wriggled it for a couple of seconds until his efforts were rewarded with a faint click. He pocketed the tool and stood, easing the door carefully open and peering inside.

'Clear', he whispered, before disappearing into the hall beyond. Silver signalled for Asp to follow before pushing the trolley in through the door behind her and slipping inside. She eased the door closed, making sure to avoid it banging.

Every checkpoint Silver had been in were identical, and the hallway she found herself in was familiar, with a number of doors leading into offices and storage rooms. It ended at a door to the warehouse where the trucks were parked and goods unloaded. Asp was in the process of spraying a security camera in one corner with black paint, while Grave made his way down the hall, ignoring the doors on his left and right. The passage turned right, and he disappeared around the corner. Silver pulled her gun out and she and Asp made their way down the hall, trolley in tow.

Hearing the briefest of bumps, Silver and Asp rounded the bend to find Grave easing a checkpoint guard to the ground, unconscious. Despite herself, Silver was impressed at the skill with which he had taken the guard down. Grave then took the guard's keys from his belt and hurried over to the door that would take them to the main warehouse.

Another faint click and the door to the warehouse opened, giving a slight squeal of protest. Silver checked over her shoulder, but the checkpoint was quiet except for them. She pushed the trolley through into the warehouse while Grave and Asp held the door open for her.

The large space beyond was dimly lit by an orange light high above, casting a reddish-orange glow over everything. It looked normal to Silver; trucks lined up in their correct spots, the airlock doors closed and secure, items salvaged during the day already taken away by the buyers. The Ash Walkers truck stood silently where they had left it, halfway along the row of parked cars and trucks.

Silver and Asp spread out, using their spray cans on the security cameras scattered around the cavernous room. Meanwhile, Grave took the trolley and strode towards the truck. By the time Silver and Asp joined him, he had pulled back the faded black cover for the trailer, revealing the panels underneath. The three of them worked together lifting the panels quickly and quietly over to the trolley. Each bump caused Silver's eyes to dart over to the door in, but no guard emerged.

After a few minutes, Grave and Silver lowered the last of the panels onto the now full trolley, and Asp pulled the cover back over the top of the trailer, securing it in place.

'Let's get moving,' Grave whispered, getting behind the trolley and carefully backing it out of the space between their truck and the next one. They had only just started back out across the floor when a thud on the big roller doors leading back into the door caused them all to freeze. A second thud sounded a moment later.

'Rat?' Asp whispered.

'Trouble,' Grave agreed.

'What do we do?' Asp asked.

Silver waited a moment for a response, but Grave stood there frozen in place, his knuckles white on the handles of the trolley.

'We find another way out of here, that's what we do,' Silver hissed. She ran over to the door they had entered through, grabbing a chair by the wall on the way and propping it up under the handle. She could hear the thud of multiple feet reverberating down the hall beyond. She ran back over to where Grave and Asp stood, Grave still grasping the bar of the trolley. 'Well, don't just stand there, come on.'

'There's only four ways out of this place,' Grave objected. 'The way we came in, the roller doors, and the two airlocks that'd take us out into the Badlands.'

'Only three conventional ways,' Silver countered, scanning the ground of the warehouse.

'Not the sewers!' Asp objected, a horrified expression on her face.

'Bingo!' Silver replied. She pulled the trolley from Grave's grasp and gave it a push, sending it careening down the row of trucks until it clattered into the side of another truck and came to a rest. An annoyed look on his face, Grave took a step towards it, but then thought better and followed Silver and Asp as they jogged along the row of cars. Silver's eyes roved the ground, straining in the dark to find a manhole that would take them down.

'THIS IS THE POLICE. WE HAVE THE BUILDING SURROUNDED. COME OUT WITH YOUR HANDS UP.'

The amplified voice filtered in from beyond the big roller doors that led back out into the Dome. It was followed closely by a shudder at the inner door as someone there tried to enter and found their way barred by the chair.

'Even if we can find a way down, any sane person knows it's not a good idea venturing into the sewers,' Asp hissed at Silver.

'If you hadn't noticed, it looks like we're about to be nabbed by the police. Now, correct me if I'm wrong, but breaking into a checkpoint, and stealing property will see us shipped to the mines at best.'

'But it's *our* property that we're stealing,' Asp objected.

'Whatever the case, this is not going to end well for us. I'll take my chances with the sewers.'

'Silver's right. We've got to find a way out,' Grave finally conceded. The three spread out across the warehouse, running down looking for signs of a grill or grate.

'THIS IS YOUR LAST CHANCE. COME OUT WITH YOUR HANDS UP.'

Within seconds, the sound of the roller doors cranking to life reverberated through the warehouse. As Silver and Grave continued to scurry down the isles looking for an exit, Asp pulled up, whipped out her gun and let off two shots at the auto mechanism just inside the roller doors. It exploded in a rain of sparks and the door ground to a halt, barely half a metre off the ground. However, the silence was soon broken again by the thump of bodies on the interior door, attempting to bust into the room by the same way the three had come.

'There!' hissed Silver, spying a hard plastic grate, sticking out from underneath a large salvage truck. It had probably been metal once, but as with many things in the city, had been replaced with other materials so the valuable metal could be used elsewhere.

Asp and Grave turned and started to hurry towards her, just as the internal door burst open and a squad of armed and armoured police began pouring into the warehouse. As they levelled their assault rifles at the fleeing pair, Silver raised her gun and fired three quick shots, taking out the two dim lamps on the ceiling and plunging the warehouse into darkness. Asp and Grave dived in to join Silver behind the truck as the police returned fire, spraying the truck and ground around it with bullets.

'Help me with this lid.'

Grave scrambled over to Silver's side and together they attempted to pull the grate free. Meanwhile, Asp fell to her stomach and aimed out underneath the truck. As the police started to advance towards them, backlit by the light spilling from underneath the partially open roller doors, she let off a few shots, sending them diving into cover.

The grate wouldn't budge, so Silver took up her gun again and rose.

'It's bolted in place. Stand back.'

She fired off four shots at the edge of the grate where she had felt the bolts. Grave leant in again, and this time when they tugged at it, the grate came free, banging loudly against the edge of the truck above.

'You go.'

'Such a gentleman', Silver replied sarcastically, but wasted no time in lowering her legs into the darkness of the hole, finding rather than seeing the ladder bolted to one side of the tunnel wall. She began climbing down, plunging into darkness.

'Asp, your turn.'

Above her, she heard two more shots and then felt the ladder shuddering under the weight of a second body. Silver reached the ground a moment later, feeling the hard concrete below but blind to anything else around her. Above, she could just make out Asp halfway down the ladder, and beyond her Grave's silhouette as he climbed into the manhole. Suddenly, the dim circle of light from the checkpoint above closed over and disappeared with a scraping sound, as Grave slid the manhole cover back into place and they were plunged into an even deeper darkness.

# Chapter 12

*From the diary of Benjamin Adams*
*November 6ᵗʰ, 2011*

*The lead up to Christmas is proving hectic as usual. We are having it at our place this year, which is nice, but it means I'm going to have to pick up the pace on the renovations in the front room. I've also got Jess's 30ᵗʰ birthday to think about. I want to make sure it's a good one.*

*Work is still a challenge. I seem to be making some progress, but it's always three steps forward, two steps back. I've just got to try to focus on the things I can control and let go of the rest.*

* * * * *

It was pitch black below, and the ground was wet and slimy. The smell of mildew was strong, accompanied by the sour tang of human waste. The grate above was almost invisible now that Grave had put the lid back over it; just a slightly less-black patch of darkness. More gunfire echoed down to them from above, those responsible yet to realise their targets had slipped away. A rhythmic swooshing sound echoed from the tunnel that headed out towards the Badlands, and a steady draught of air flowed in the same direction.

Silver heard Grave reach the ground, a squelching sound indicating he had alighted from the ladder.

'Asp? Silver? Are you here?'

'Yes, I'm here,' Asp replied. 'We need some light.'

'Not yet we don't,' Silver whispered. 'Light isn't an option until we put some distance between us and the grate above. Those cops meant business, and a light down here would make us stand out like dogs balls. Here, grab my hand.'

Silver found Grave's arm, quickly working her way down until she found his hand and clasped it tightly. Though she was putting on a brave face, the thought of venturing into the sewers without a light scared her, and she hoped he didn't notice the slight tremble in her touch.

'Now you take Asp's hand,' she instructed.

'Got it.'

Silver began edging cautiously along the tunnel, leading Grave and Asp along. She held Grave's hand in her left and kept her right hand on the wall. The brick was cold and slimy under her touch, but she knew it was the only way to navigate in the darkness. Though she could see nothing, she headed against the direction of airflow, leading them towards the centre of the Dome. As they moved along, she also fancied there was a slight curve in the path they were following, though it was hard to tell for certain.

Imaging all manner of creatures lurking ahead, Silver kept an ear out for what might be coming behind them. Some muffled shouting filtered down from the grate but faded as they moved further along. As far as she could tell, they had either not worked out where the three had gone, or else had decided against following them into the sewers. Probably the latter.

'It's not quite as bad a smell as I would have thought,' Grave whispered. 'Not pleasant, but not too overpowering either.'

No one responded, and they shuffled along in silence for a few more moments until Asp spoke up. 'You do have a light source, don't you?'

Silver detected a slight tremor in her voice. It was the question she was avoiding, because she knew they wouldn't like the answer, and in truth, she had not thought the sewers would be *this* dark.

'I do.'

Grave's answer caught her by surprise, and she let out a silent breath of relief. She felt his grip on her hand tighten, forcing her to come to a stop before letting go of her hand. The loss of contact caused her to feel immediately panicked and isolated, and she had to resist the urge to reach out and grab hold of him again to make certain she wasn't alone.

She heard some fumbling, and then a thin beam of light appeared, forcing her to momentarily shield her eyes from the glare.

The torch Grave held was a focused and bright beam, creating a circle of light on the ceiling above, and casting enough of a glow to dimly illuminate their surroundings. It was a compact silver torch, only about ten centimetres long. She knew that torches were not cheap, mainly due to batteries being so hard to come by and extremely expensive. She was relieved that he had it though.

They were in a concrete passageway, roughly two metres wide, with an arched ceiling a little over two and a half metres high at the apex. The ground sloped slightly towards the middle, creating a channel for water to flow. The ceiling and walls were lined with cracks from which moisture dripped down to the floor. The channel in the centre of the passageway had a thick brown green sludge filling it, probably ten to twenty centimetres deep at the centre, but not much more than a thin film closer to the wall where they walked. Looking back the way they had come, the passage indeed curved away. Ahead it appeared to straighten out, though the torchlight did not penetrate far into the darkness.

'What now?' Asp asked. Her eyes were wide, and the smile that Silver had grown accustomed to was conspicuous in its absence.

'We keep heading this way, until we find another grate leading up. With a bit of luck, there will be one not too far along'.

'What about the Homeless?' There was a tremor in her voice at mention of the group.

'It's unconfirmed whether they exist or not,' Grave responded. 'Either way, we don't intend to stay down here long so there is a fair chance we'll remain undetected.'

'We best keep moving.' Silver held her hand out for the torch. Rather than handing it to her, Grave moved past her and took the lead. Her brow furrowed for a moment, but then she shrugged, realising she was happy not to be up front if the Homeless turned out to be more than a myth.

'What do you know about the Homeless?' Silver asked softly as they resumed walking. 'My parents told me a little about them when I was a kid, but I'm not sure how much of that was fact or fiction.'

'Long before the problems that led to the building of the Dome, a growing number of poor and homeless people lived in the city,' Grave answered. 'Many lived on the streets above, but a few made their homes in the tunnels below, mostly in the underground train tunnels. Many were drunks or junkies, but some were just down on luck, unable to find work, and estranged from family and friends.

'As the price of electricity grew, the gap between rich and poor widened, causing more and more people to lose their homes and take up residence on the streets, or in the tunnels. The authorities of the time tried to uproot them, but offered no alternate solution and so any upheaval always proved temporary.

'When the Dome was built, a new effort was made to turf them out of the city entirely, along with a number of people from the poorer areas of the city. Some were caught and expelled, but most fled and hid, delving ever deeper into the sewers below. With bigger problems on their hands, the authorities gave up on their efforts, deciding instead to board up the sewers and starve them out. They did so for three weeks, but no one emerged. It was assumed the tactic had worked, and perhaps it did. It is said that since that time any who ventured down into the sewers fail to return. Allegedly, that's what happened to the police who ventured below following the starve-out attempt, fuelling the stories that the Homeless still live here.'

Grave lapsed into silence, and Silver stopped herself from asking any further questions given the paled colour of Asp's face. They kept walking down the tunnel, passing a number of pipes and side passages—gaping black holes in the wall, some of which dripped water into the tunnel. It had only been a few minutes when Grave spotted another grate above. He looked back at Silver and Asp, pointing up at it excitedly, before picking up his step to hurry towards the rusted metal ladder that hung down from the opening above. But as Silver watched, she heard voices above and saw a flash of light come down the grate. She threw herself forward, grabbed Grave's hand and wrenched the torch from it, covering it with her hand and plunging them into darkness once more.

'What the hell are you doing?' Grave hissed, before a beam of light pierced the darkness from above and voices filtered down.

'Do you see anything?'

'No, and I don't expect to. They'd be well and truly lost down there by now, and at the mercy of the Homeless.'

'You'll never see anything with that torch anyway, switch it off.'

The light turned off abruptly, and tunnel was plunged into darkness once more.

'So what do we do?' the voice above continued.

'What do you think? We wait until we're told we can go.'

'How long do think that'll be?' The guard's voice was whiny, clearly irritated at the prospect of sitting and watching the hole.

'Who knows? But I'm not about to go against orders, so we wait.'

Silver felt for the torch switch and turned it off before groping around until she found Grave's and Asp's hands. She quietly led them past the grate, moving close to the wall to avoid being seen. She didn't pause until she was sure they would not be heard by the cops.

'What do we do now?' Asp asked quietly, her voice still shaky.

Silver switched on the light, though kept the beam partially covered with her hand, bathing the tunnel in a soft glow once more.

'We keep going till we find an exit that isn't being guarded. They can't have possibly covered all the exits; probably just the ones near the checkpoint. What I want to know is why they are after us so badly? Is there something more to those black panels than you are letting on, Grave?' Silver folded her arms and waited for a response. Asp stood next to her, looking curiously at Grave.

'I don't have time to explain it right now ...'

'What do you mean? We have plenty of time while we're stuck down here waiting for the cops to give up on us.'

'No, I mean I really don't have time to explain it right now. We've got company.'

He pointed over Silver's shoulder and she turned, aiming the torch down the tunnel. There, a crowd of dark, shadowy figures stood at the edge of the light, their eyes seeming to glow in the dark. Silver's heart quickened, while Asp only half suppressed a scream, the sound coming out as more of a yelp. Silver flashed the torch back up the tunnel and found that more figures were edging up the passage behind them, blocking their escape.

'Well, at least we know they're not a myth,' Grave said, though his voice sounded strained.

For a few moments, the two groups stood there quietly, studying each other. Silver's hand had strayed to her gun, as had Asp's, but she had noticed the figures were armed with an assortment of clubs and rocks, and there were enough of them that she didn't fancy their chances in a shoot-out. It was Grave who broke the silence.

'What do you want? We mean you no harm.'

One of the figures stepped forward from the group, coming more fully into the light. He was short, appearing more so due to the fact that he was stooped over. His skin was pale white, untouched by the sun. His hair was long, dark and greasy, hanging in thick strands across his face. He had a long, wispy beard. His clothes were tattered and filthy, his skin covered in dirty marks. Despite appearing short, he looked muscular and strong. His eyes squinted in the light from the torch.

'This is our domain and you are trespassing.'

His voice was low, threatening. For a fleeting moment Silver was surprised that he spoke English, sounding just like anyone above. The look of the man was so foreign that she had absurdly expected him to speak with an accent.

'We have only ventured into these tunnels to escape wrongful persecution at the hands of the police,' Grave replied, stepping past Silver to address the man. 'I am Grave, and this is Silver and Asp. We have no wish to impose upon you, and will not linger if you will lead us to an exit that will not place us directly into police custody.'

The Homeless man studied Grave for a long time in which neither moved. Complete silence descended on the tunnel. With much of his face covered by hair and beard, and the poor light casting a shadow over the rest, Silver could not read him. She looked at Grave, and she noted that he stood straight and proud, showing no sign of weakness under the extended scrutiny. Nor did he attempt to fill the silence as many would have in a similar circumstance. Eventually, the spokesperson of the Homeless broke the silence.

'Fleeing the police, eh? Now you know how we feel. Why should I not just have you killed? We would get meat, and the items you carry, and the police would be rid of you. It would be win-win for us and the police; not so good for you.'

Silver shuddered at the thought of being eaten by the Homeless. It seemed she couldn't go anywhere these days without being considered a meal.

'There's little we can do to stop you taking that course of action,' Grave admitted. 'However, I think you have little love for the police, so on that count I guess you would not be overly keen to do them any favours. As for us, if you kill us, then you get short-term gain, but little long-term benefit. If you let us go, I can perhaps assist with your needs over a longer term? And, if it helps, I don't think we would make particularly good meals, given there is not much meat between the three of us.'

Silver looked at Grave incredulously. Surely now was not the best time for humour? However, the expression on his face was serious as he patiently awaited the Homeless man's response. Asp quivered slightly, her fear of the Homeless turning to near terror in their presence. Silver took her hand and squeezed it gently, trying to offer some comfort.

'You are right on two counts at least, though I am sceptical as to what you can offer us long term. I will take you to meet the Shepherd, and she shall decide. You will hand over your weapons. Do not resist.'

The Homeless spokesman turned and glided silently back through the crowd behind him, disappearing from view while a group of five Homeless approached, beckoning at them to pass over their guns. Silver and Asp were reluctant to do so, but Grave handed over his and nodded at them, urging them to do the same.

*The Shepherd?* Silver mouthed at Grave, who gave a slight shrug of his shoulders in response before allowing himself to be herded forward.

The trio were led through the tunnels, following the group ahead and forced ever onwards by the group behind them. It was not long before they were hopelessly lost, having passed through numerous turns and forks, and descended ladders at a couple of points. Some tunnels smelled so bad they made Silver's eyes water and her stomach try to rebel, whereas others appeared to have relatively clean, fresh water running through them. It seemed that they could have crossed the diameter of the Dome and back again in the time they walked, so Silver got the impression they were being led around in circles.

Silver kept the torch in hand and switched on so that they could at least see where they were stepping, but she couldn't tell how the Homeless, most of who travelled outside of the sphere of light it cast, found their way through the tunnels.

At last the tunnel opened out into a large chamber, with a ceiling forming a great arc over six metres above them. It appeared to have once been covered in a mosaic of pale yellow coloured tiles, but most had since dropped away, leaving the ceiling a dirty grey in colour. A few of the small tiles still clung here and there, catching the light of the torch and reminding Silver of twinkling stars.

The hall was roughly ten metres wide, but appeared to be far longer, stretching out beyond the limit of their sight. A central channel ran down the length of the hall, with platforms on both sides. Silver realised that this was once a train station, though the tracks had long since been removed, probably salvaged for metal many years before. The platforms were covered in an assortment of ramshackle buildings, some made of brick, others cobbled together from wood and rubbish. Few of them had roofs, and being underground and out of danger of the elements, she supposed a ceiling was unnecessary.

As the three were led down the central channel, more Homeless emerged from their huts to stare at them, most squinting or shielding their eyes against the light of the torch, though Silver covered it once more to minimise the light it cast. Many of the Homeless who had escorted them began to filter off, climbing out of the channel and disappearing inside the buildings, or joining others who watched from above.

In what she guessed was the centre of the old station, Silver saw that a bridge had been built across the channel, joining the two platforms. It was a wide bridge, and in the centre a large structure had been built: a mini hall of sorts running across rather than along the length. A ramp had been built into the side of the channel and they were urged upwards, bringing them onto the platform at the point where the bridge began. At this point the Homeless ahead of them parted, allowing them to pass through a curtained door leading inside the hall.

Within, the room was long and narrow, and devoid of any furniture. At the far end, sitting in a worn but beautifully carved antique armchair, was an elderly woman. She had grey hair, but sat tall and alert. Silver guessed she was probably in her sixties. She wore a brightly coloured and quite beautiful dress, adding a refreshing splash of reds, oranges and yellows among the otherwise monotonous grey of the tunnels. On her head she wore an elegant tiara with stones that sparkled in the torchlight. A sceptre, of sorts, rested in her lap: an ancient looking umbrella, black with a pointed metal end and a hooked handle. Silver had seen umbrellas in books her mother had read her as a child, but had never seen a real, intact one.

The look was simultaneously regal and ridiculous. The hall they stood in was more like a parody of a throne room and, while beautiful, the dress the Shepherd wore was not befitting a queen. Yet there was something royal about the way the Shepherd held herself, her bearing giving Silver the feeling that they were indeed facing a monarch. The Homeless man who had addressed them in the tunnels stood before her.

'Shepherd, we found these three Dome Dwellers trespassing on our territory. They claim to be fleeing the police. They seek to bargain their freedom, so I have brought them to you for your guidance and judgment.'

The Shepherd nodded almost imperceptibly before turning her steady gaze onto the three. She looked over each of them in turn. Asp shifted uncomfortably under the scrutiny, averting her eyes. Grave stood erect and proud, meeting her eye as he had with the Homeless man earlier. When it came to Silver's turn, she tried to do the same but found it challenging, as if the Shepherd were staring through her into her thoughts and soul.

'Come forward,' she eventually commanded them, her voice stately, carrying authority.

The three of them moved up the hall to stand closer to her, Grave moving to the front. The Shepherd focused her attention on him.

'Tell me, what brings you to my realm?'

'We did not lie before and neither will we now. We were cornered by the police while trying to retrieve salvage we had rightfully brought in from the Badlands. The tunnels below were our only chance of avoiding arrest and likely exile.'

'I am familiar with this tale, for it is the same one suffered by the Homeless many years ago. Yet we were given no help at the time, no assistance. I don't see why we should aid you now.'

'You should aid us because we should learn from past mistakes, not repeat them!' Grave snapped, his voice sharp. 'Lack of compassion left your people down here. Lack of compassion left those above living in the abject state they do. The Dome is surrounded by evidence of what a selfish approach does to the world, and we will never heal it until we start looking out for others. If we don't, we will soon be extinct.'

Silver stared at Grave, taken aback by the outburst.

'Dare you lecture me on how humans should behave?' The Shepherd's eyes flashed with anger, her ire clearly raised. 'According to the Dome Dwellers above, we were not deemed human, condemned to be expelled into the Badlands like animals. We no longer abide by human rules since that status was stripped from us. We have no obligation to extend compassion to those who expelled us.'

'Then that is your decision? You will not help us?'

'Fear of the tunnels is our security. If we allowed those who ventured into them the opportunity to escape, then it would not be long before we would again face expulsion, and this time we would have nowhere left to run. We cannot allow you to leave.'

'If that is your decision, I am disappointed.'

'I care not. John, take them away.'

The Homeless man who had stood by silently for the entire encounter stepped forward to usher them from the hall. Asp had started to whimper quietly, while Silver had become defiant, ready to speak out. As Grave turned, however, he saw her intention and grabbed her arm roughly, turning her towards the door.

'Don't say anything we'll regret,' he whispered, low and threateningly. 'Further words at this time won't help.'

Silver wrenched her arm from his grip. 'You're right,' she hissed as they were marched from the hall. 'You've said enough for all three of us. No emotion for three days and you choose now to lose it? Nicely done.'

She moved ahead of him, fuming as John led them through the ramshackle village until they arrived at an empty stall. John ushered them in.

'What will happen to us?' Silver asked him.

'It is not for me to say. For now you will be given some food and the chance to rest. Do not try to escape or do anything rash. You will not succeed.'

With no further ceremony, John turned and limped off through the shantytown, leaving the three to their devices. Asp immediately moved into the stall and sat down in the corner. She was trembling ever so slightly, as she had been since they ventured into the sewers, and she closed her eyes and rested her head back against the wall. In contrast, Grave stood calmly at the entrance to the stall, arms folded. Silver moved up level with him, scanning left and right for any signs that they were being watched. In the darkness, she could see no one.

'What are you doing?' Grave asked.

'I'm looking for a way to get us out of here,' Silver hissed at him. 'At least one of us should be trying to find a way out, especially after your performance.'

Grave turned to face Silver, drawing himself up to his full height. While not as tall as Coal, he was still much taller than she.

'Do not make an attempt to escape. They know these tunnels far better than us. It would be a pointless exercise.'

'What are we meant to do then? Wait for them to come and hang us, or roast us over their cook-fires? Or prepare to join them and live out the rest of our days among the cursed tunnels? Neither option looks particularly appealing to me!'

Grave moved a little closer and lowered his voice. 'I have a plan to get us out of here, but it needs some time. I would be grateful if you can sit with Asp. She doesn't handle enclosed spaces too well.'

Silver looked over at Asp; her shaking hadn't subsided and she was muttering something under her breath. Silver started to object, but Grave had already stepped back and turned away from her, facing the mouth of the stall. She stared at his back disdainfully for a few seconds, her dislike for the man ever growing.

Her glare was interrupted by the arrival of a shambling Homeless man bearing a bowl of food with two wooden spoons. Without preamble, he thrust the bowl at Silver before departing. Silver looked at the food, some sort of stew with white pieces of flesh floating in it. She sniffed at it doubtfully, but the aroma was not bad and her stomach rumbled hungrily.

She moved over and sat down on Asp's left, offering her a spoon. The offer roused the woman from her reverie, but she studied the bowl's contents fearfully. 'It's not human is it?'

'Surely not.' Silver frowned, using the spoon to scoop up a piece of white meat. She examined it critically, sniffed it and then tentatively bit off a tiny morsel. 'It's good. Fish, I think.'

Asp took up the other spoon and began to eat. Silver took a bigger bite and found the meat soft and tasty; far better than the nutrient bars she was used to. 'Who'd have thought the Homeless would eat better than us!' she whispered.

Together, the women polished off the stew and Silver set the bowl gently to one side. When she turned back, Asp had her eyes closed again and was rocking back and forth ever so slightly. Silver looked at her for a moment, unsure how to go about comforting someone. Her mind flashed back to memories of her mother, cuddling her when she was scared or cold, holding her tight.

She hesitantly reached out and took hold of Asp's hand, holding it in both of hers. Her hand was cool to touch, and Silver instinctively rubbed it to warm it up. It was then that she noticed Asp was missing her little finger at the first knuckle. Struggling to take on the caring role, she instead opted for providing a distraction.

'What happened to your hand?'

The tactic seemed to work. Asp paused in her rocking and opened her eyes to regard Silver.

'It happened a long time ago in my parent's shop, when I was still a teenager.'

'Your parents owned a shop?'

Asp nodded. 'Yes, still do. The clothing shop over on York Street.'

'You mean Smart Design? I bought my overalls from there! They're good quality.'

Asp smiled. 'Yeah, that's the one. I worked there when I was younger.'

As she had hoped, the conversation had distracted Asp from her fear, and Silver wanted to keep her going.

'So how did you lose the finger?'

'Had a gang of five crims come into the shop one day, trying to get a refund for some overalls they claim to have bought there the day before. Only the overalls had a bullet hole in the gut with bloodstains around it. Dad remembered the guy who had bought them; poor bastard had probably been shot and killed by the crims. Anyway, he refused to refund them and they started to get angry. I made the mistake of entering the shop after dropping off a parcel to one of our wealthier clients. One of them grabbed me and threatened to stick me unless Dad handed over his cash. Dad gave them everything in the till, which wasn't much. But the crim thought Dad was holding out on them, so he sliced off my finger and threatened to keep going till he got more cash.'

Silver shook her head, not in surprise, but more from consternation. 'How'd you get out of there?'

'Well, up until that point there had been another customer in the store who'd been keeping a low profile. It was Blocka, but I didn't know him then. When they cut off my finger, I screamed from the pain, and he snapped. He walked straight up and knocked two of them flying before punching the one who had cut me so hard he was dead before he hit the ground. Broke his nose and sent the bone up into his brain. The leader of the group pulled his gun and got off two shots before Blocka reached him. Next thing he was on the floor in a screaming heap with a snapped arm and a dislocated knee. That was enough for the rest, who cut their losses and fled the store.'

Silver was dumbstruck by the story. She had seen that Blocka was big and strong, but to overcome five armed opponents with his bare hands was fearsome.

'Blocka walks with a limp—was that from the fight?'

Asp nodded. 'One of the bullets hit him in the leg and is still lodged in there. The other went through his shoulder, but didn't go so deep that it couldn't be fished out. Funny thing was, we didn't even realise he was hurt until a few minutes later. First thing he did when the danger had passed was come over to see if I was all right. Only when we saw the blood did Mum insist he sit and let her tend to him. We've been together ever since.'

'He would have been young as well, right?' Silver asked.

'Yep, he's only a couple of years older than me. And the guys he took would have been late twenties, early thirties, with years of dust ups and fights under their belts.'

Silver whistled at the story, impressed.

'Coal was a big man, and strong, but even he couldn't have handled five armed men. Two, maybe three at most!'

'Why were you with him for so long?' Asp asked. 'Coal, I mean. From what I've seen, you two were complete opposites.'

'Coal wasn't that bad.'

Grave snorted from where he had been standing quietly up until that point. Silver looked sharply over at him, incensed. He shook his head and walked from the stall.

'Man, what's that guy's problem?'

'Well, you have to admit that Coal was bad.'

'Okay, so he was a dickhead, always has been,' Silver conceded, her gaze lingering on the vacant space left by Grave. 'I thought I was in love with him. Maybe I was. He came along when I was completely alone, and offered me security, a home and an opportunity to learn a way to make a living. He offered me a love, of sorts. Those things helped me to survive when I otherwise wouldn't have. Why I stayed with him for so long is probably the better question, and one that I can't say.'

'I get it,' Asp replied, smiling and squeezing her hand. She leant in and rested her head on Silver's shoulder. 'Sometimes we're blind to things that are obvious to others and it takes something extreme to see them. You being left out in the Badlands for a night was probably a blessing in drag.'

The pair fell quiet, and over the next few minutes Silver felt Asp's breathing gradually slow and fall into a steady rhythm as she drifted off to sleep. Her presence felt warm and comforting to Silver, and sleep started to overcome her too.

She glanced over to the stall door and saw Grave silently re-enter. 'Sleep, I'll watch,' he said simply, before turning and facing the mouth of the booth once again.

In some corner of Silver's mind she knew she should reject the offer, stand up and take watch herself. But sleep beckoned, and she felt strangely safe with him standing over them. She rested her head against Asp's and the wall behind her and allowed sleep to take hold.

# CHAPTER 13

*From the diary of Benjamin Adams*
*February 15th, 2012*

*It feels like summer didn't come this year. I can count the number of days the temperature has approached forty on one hand, with fingers left over. It's been cold on other days. The constant rain has been great for the plants but has started to wear a little thin.*

*Jayden began school two weeks ago. We took the traditional photo of him in school uniform at the front of the house. He looks so grown up and mature and he loves school, which is great. Alex took it all in stride— didn't get too upset or jealous.*

*Work is going well. I'm working on a major project that is keeping me busy. It's the biggest building I've worked on, and being a stadium with an enclosed top, it's got some interesting challenges that you don't encounter within a normal high-rise. The shape is one I like dealing with, and I think I can make some significant improvements and efficiencies on the standard designs I've studied, while actually making a stronger structure.*

* * * * *

'Wake up. It's time to go.'

Silver started awake at the voice, her movement shaking Asp from her sleep as well. She looked around, the tattered threads of her dream causing her to check for a Homeless lynch mob waiting outside the stall to string them up. Everything was dark and peaceful, however, and it was only Grave who had given Silver a gentle shake to rouse her.

'We're sneaking out?' she whispered.

'No, they are letting us go. John will escort us to a point where we can get back up onto the streets.'

'But how? What about the Shepherd?'

'She came around. There will be time for questions later, but we have to go now.'

Grave offered Silver a hand, but she ignored it and rose to her feet on her own. Shrugging, he offered the still outstretched hand to Asp, and she took it, allowing him to pull her to her feet. Without a word, he walked out the stall and out of view to the right.

Silver and Asp shared a confused look but then hurried to catch up. The words of the Shepherd had sounded final when she had declared they would not be allowed to leave. Something had happened while she and Asp had slept and Grave was acting cagey about it. She cursed herself silently for having allowed herself to drift off. She would hold him to his promise that there would be time for questions later.

Grave had made his way back down into the channel that led between the two platforms and was heading to the far end of the hall where Silver could just make out a dark figure waiting for them. Silver and Asp followed him down, and caught up just as they reached John, waiting for them at the dark mouth of the tunnel.

He didn't say anything, merely turned and started walking down the tunnel with his steady limping gait. Silver took one last look at the shadowy shantytown as it faded into the darkness behind them. It had sat there below them for a long time, and most in the Dome above had no idea of its existence, other than a seemingly mythical bedtime story to keep children from venturing into the sewers. She wondered if this was the only Homeless community, or if there were others scattered about beneath the city.

They proceeded in silence, broken only by the incessant dripping and the occasional sound of a rat or cockroach scrabbling away at their approach. Silver had expected a long journey through the tunnels, but was surprised when after only fifteen minutes, and a handful of twists and turns, John pulled up and turned to Grave, pointing at the dim light filtering down from a vent above.

'There's your way out. Should bring you up close to where you need to go.'

'Thank you.'

'Just remember your promise.'

'And you,' Grave replied.

'If you use the signal, we'll be there. Nothing happens in these tunnels without us knowing of it.' Without further comment, John turned and shambled off into the darkness, fading from view in a matter of seconds.

Silver turned to ask Grave about the promise, but he had already started climbing the ladder. She motioned for Asp to follow, and once Grave had removed the vent lid and disappeared above, she started her own ascent.

As she emerged from the manhole, Asp gave her a hand, pulling her up to her feet, while Grave waited with the cover, ready to put it back in place. It took her a few seconds to get her bearings, but soon realised they were just around the corner from the Ash Walker's clubhouse. There was a hint of pre-dawn turning the black above to grey. Asp's familiar smile had returned to her face, absent the whole time they had been below ground. Grave's face was its usual neutral, unreadable set.

'We cannot speak a word of this to the others when we get back, all right? Our story is we escaped the checkpoint into the sewers and made our way back out onto the street a hundred metres down the road. However, the police were out looking for us and we were forced to lie low for the night until they had given up. Promise?'

'No problems, boss,' Asp replied, before starting off down the road towards the clubhouse, eager to get home to Blocka.

Grave and Silver fell in behind her, moving a little slower. The city streets were dark but quiet, with few people out and about in the couple of hours before dawn.

'Silver, I'd like to thank you for …'

'Why did they let us go?' Silver blurted, cutting Grave off. 'What did you promise them?'

'Nothing,' Grave said, annoyed at being interrupted.

'I don't accept that. And until you tell me, I won't promise that I'll keep quiet about what really happened tonight.'

A look of weariness crept over Grave's face and for a moment Silver felt sorry for him, remorseful for pressing the point. But she was certain he was hiding something; not only from that night, but something bigger, and she intended to find out what it was.

'Not now, Silver. I am hungry and exhausted, and need to sleep. We can discuss this another time. Just promise you won't say anything about the Homeless; it's a condition of our freedom.'

Silver held his gaze for a while without responding. She could detect no sign of exaggeration in his show of weariness.

'I promise not to say anything for the next two days,' she conceded eventually. 'But unless you answer my questions, my promise won't extend beyond that.'

A look of exasperation flashed briefly across Grave's eyes. 'Fine.'

They walked on in silence around a corner in the road. The club-house was up ahead, with Asp almost at the door.

'What were you going to thank me for?' Silver asked, recalling what Grave had started to say before she had cut him off.

'For being a pain in my arse ever since arriving unannounced and unwelcome.'

Before Silver could respond, Grave strode pointedly away from her, meeting the rest of the crew as they burst out of the clubhouse. Blocka was out first, running over to Asp and sweeping her effortlessly up in his arms and wrapping her in a bear hug. The rest of the crew flooded from the house behind him.

Silver was still watching Grave, fuming from his parting comment when Muzzle limped over to her, a big smile plastered across her face. 'You had us worried there, Sil. When Rat came home, we thought the coppers had you nicked. I'm glad to see you're okay.'

Silver's gaze flicked over to Grave once more, and she noticed him looking at her while Rat spoke of how he had evaded the guards but had been helpless to aid the three of them inside. An impulse overtook her, and she turned her attention back to Muzzle, leaning in and kissing him on the mouth. Muzzle was shocked at first, but quickly returned this kiss.

'I'm glad to see you too,' Silver said as they came apart, and the grin on Muzzle's face widened further. Silver glanced over to Grave again, catching his eyes on her for a split second before they moved away. A moment later he excused himself from Rat and headed inside the club-house. The others began to follow, and Muzzle reached for Silver's hand, taking it in his as they also made their way in.

'So you ended up in the sewers? How was that?'

As they walked inside, the talk turned to the events of the night, and Asp took up the story on how they had fled into the sewers and found another way out but had been forced to lie low while the police roamed about outside. She improvised well, and the mood in the clubhouse was jovial, particularly when Grave ducked upstairs and returned with a couple of bottles of rum to celebrate.

Muzzle stayed by Silver's side, his arm planted around her waist as he drank and chatted. Silver liked the attention, but found her eyes constantly drawn to Grave. She thought she saw his eyes dart away from her once or twice, but wasn't certain.

'What do you know about him?' she asked Muzzle abruptly, gesturing with her cup over to Grave.

'Who? Grave? Not much really. Just that he gave me a chance in his crew when I was struggling to find another crew to take me. He spends a lot of time away, off-site.'

'Really? What does he do when he's out?'

Muzzle shrugged. 'Dunno. Business? Pleasure? He pays the bills so I don't ask.'

'But how does he afford it? With the stuff we pull from the Badlands, he'd struggle to cover food for the crew, let alone paying us and hot water.'

Muzzle shrugged again. 'Like I said, he pays the bills so I don't ask. Back in a minute.' He put his drink down and hobbled off to relieve himself.

Silver saw Rat go off to raid the kitchen for something to eat. Blocka sat in the corner on the old, worn couch, with Asp on his lap, the two snuggling into each other, while Sarge, whom Silver had not seen drink all night, appeared to have retired. Grave stood alone, looking haggard and worn; a night with no rest starting to catch up to him.

Silver started to feel a little guilty again for pushing him. He had somehow won their freedom from the Homeless and otherwise handled himself well down in the tunnels. But his interest in the black panels had her stumped, and now she had a feeling he was not the only one interested in them either.

She took another sip of rum, and started over towards him, thinking she should apologise for the hassling him earlier. But as soon as she started moving in his direction, he threw back the remains of his almost full cup and put it down on the bench top beside him. Then, without making eye contact, he headed over to the door of the clubhouse, leading out onto the street, and made his way out, pulling it shut behind him.

Silver stood there gaping at his rapid departure, heat rising to her cheeks in anger at his snub. He was so fucking rude, it grated upon her. Left standing awkwardly by herself, she moved over to the table where the bottles of rum sat. One had been completely polished off and had been tipped over onto its side, but the other was still half full of the amber coloured liquor. She downed the rest of her glass, feeling the fire spread through her throat and chest, then poured herself another.

Rat returned to the room bearing a bowl of gruel. 'Grave gone?' he asked Silver, with a mouthful of food.

She nodded in reply, indicating the door he had left by. 'Where does he go anyway? Doesn't he sleep here at the clubhouse?'

Rat shrugged. 'Sometimes. Probably stays with a lover or something the rest of the time.'

Silver took another large gulp of her drink, shaking her head as the rum burned down her throat. Rat didn't linger, wandering upstairs while still shovelling gruel from the bowl into his mouth. When Muzzle returned from the toilet, she had polished off three quarters of her glass.

'Wow, someone's going hard this morning!'

Silver threw back the remainder of her glass and put it down heavily on the table, then leant in and kissed him again, hard, urgently, pulling his head down to meet hers.

'Let's get out of here,' she whispered in his ear, and without giving him a chance to respond, she took him by the hand and led him to the stairs.

* * * * *

Silver couldn't sleep. Next to her Muzzle snored gently, lying on his stomach with a content look on his face. When they had gotten upstairs, she had ripped his clothes off and then helped him strip off hers, before jumping onto the bed. The sex had been okay; he had lasted long enough for her to climax, but he was young and fairly inexperienced. Soon after, he drifted off. She didn't normally have trouble getting to sleep, but she found herself tossing and turning restlessly. She rolled over for perhaps the thirtieth time and found daylight filtering in from between the thin curtains, landing on her face.

With a sigh, she sat up and rubbed her hands wearily over her face.

Climbing laboriously to her feet, she walked over to the curtains, dragging at them in an effort to minimise the light spilling into the room. As she headed back over to her bed, she spotted her open backpack lying against the wall, and caught sight of the book the mute had given to her sticking out of it. In the excitement of the last couple of days she had all but forgotten about the book.

She pulled it out and climbed back into bed, sitting it in her lap and studying the faded brown leather of its cover. It was a beautiful book, though it had seen better days. She opened it to the front cover and read the words there once again.

*This diary belongs to Benjamin Adams*
*born 19<sup>th</sup> of July, 1981*

She had not read much of his story in the mute's basement, falling asleep just a few pages in. It was penned by a man who had lived sometime before, when the world was a better place, and had seemed pretty mundane to her so far. The name still niggled at the edge of her memory, familiar but elusive. She flipped through till she had found the last entry she had read and began reading.

# Chapter 14



*From the diary of Benjamin Adams*
*May 11ᵗʰ, 2012*

*It's Jayden's sixth birthday in a few days, and he's getting so big! He's still enjoying school, which is great. Jess is working part-time from home but finding it difficult to balance the work with the kids, especially given Alex is still home five days a week.*

*I heard on the news today that another mining mogul will be challenging the seat of the current treasurer in parliament. That's the second I've heard of in the last twelve months; they'll be running for prime minister next! Mining commercials are a constant fixture on TV, and miners are cropping up on the boards of media companies. The solar industry seems to have peaked and started declining, which is disappointing. I don't want my boys to inherit a toxic world, especially when there are clean and viable energy options available.*

* * * * *

When Silver awoke her head was pounding painfully. It was dark outside, but she couldn't tell how long she had slept. Muzzle remained asleep on the bed beside her, and the diary she had been reading lay on the other side. The last vestiges of a fast fading dream hovered at the edge of her mind. She was sure Grave had featured in it, but the details of the dream proved elusive.

She pushed herself up onto her elbows and quickly wished she hadn't as the throbbing in her temple intensified. Gingerly, she climbed out of bed and staggered to the door. Why had she drunk so much rum? She was generally a pretty light drinker, happy to let the men make fools of themselves before passing out. But Grave had caused her to do the same last night. His behaviour grated on her.

She stumbled out the door and down the hallway to the bathroom. She could feel her stomach muscles tightening, and she could tell she needed to throw up. She rushed into the room and just made it to the toilet, sending a torrent of red-brown liquid into the bowl. Sensing more to come, she stayed crouching next to the toilet and heaved four more times, though the last one was a dry gag, as if her stomach was berating her.

Finally, the muscles in her abdomen relaxed, and she felt a little better, though her head still pounded. She grabbed some toilet paper and wiped at her face and mouth before standing up and flushing the contents of the bowl away.

She nearly jumped out of her skin when she turned around to find Grave at the door, leaning against the frame watching her. She fancied he had the slightest of smirks on his face.

'What are you looking at?'

'I see you enjoyed the rum last night.'

'I'm clearly used to much better quality rum than the swill you fed us.'

'Right, I'll try to cater a little better to your needs next time.'

'Don't bother. I wouldn't want to jeopardise you taking care of your own needs.'

Silver moved over to the washbasin and began scrubbing at her hands. After a moment's silence he asked, 'Have you seen Muzzle?'

'He's in my room.'

Silver looked at Grave once more as she grabbed a towel to wipe her hands. Any trace of a smirk was gone, and his face looked serious, business-like.

'We roll out in twenty minutes. Better clean yourself up and be ready to go.'

Before she could protest, Grave was gone. Silver groaned inwardly, not feeling up for heading out into the Badlands. She returned to the tap, turned on the water and lowered her head, using her hand to channel some into her mouth, and then splashing the rest over her face and neck. Her stomach turned slightly at the fluid she drank, nervous it contained more alcohol, but the water was cool and refreshing and helped her headache a little. She towelled off her face and sighed. She had a feeling it was going to be a long day.

＊ ＊ ＊ ＊ ＊

The trip out into the Badlands had been a quiet one. The crew was missing Muzzle and Blocka after Grave insisted they remain behind and rest, not wanting to risk infection or further injury out in the field. Of those present, Sarge was his usual self, driving the truck and shouting out an occasional warning about a dip in the road or bump, but otherwise not contributing to any conversation. Grave had joined them this time, sitting up front next to Sarge, eyes alert and on the surrounds.

In the back sat Asp, Rat and Silver. Asp had been in good spirits on their way to the truck, but had yawned the whole time and now dozed in her seat despite the bumps and jolts. Rat was not a talker at the best of times, but seemed particularly quiet and sullen that morning. Silver slouched in the back of the truck, sipping on a bottle of water. Her stomach was feeling better after having thrown up, but her head was still not in the best shape. She gazed out the window at the ruins rolling by, some covered in tangles of sickly looking weeds, others as if they had only just fallen down. The sun was high in the sky—Grave had allowed them to sleep through until lunchtime before rousing them.

It had been a little tense walking through the checkpoint. There had been no sign of the trolley of panels they had left there the night before. But they had not left it by their truck and the guards did not keep a close record of who had brought in what. Grave had warned them to keep their cool, and they had unloaded the salvage items left in the trailer from their previous foray into the Badlands and departed without incident.

The brakes squealed alarmingly as the truck pulled to a stop, jolting Silver out of her daydream. Looking around, she realised they were at the same spot they had searched the day before.

'Well, the dogs made short work of the bodies,' Sarge said, and it was only then that Silver noted that there was no sign left of their savage encounter with the mutes.

'Masks on,' Grave ordered as he pulled his breathing filter into place. With her mask firmly in place, Silver followed Rat and Asp out of the truck. The heat outside was oppressive, and Silver was relieved it would be a shorter day. They gathered round Grave and Sarge for briefing.

'Rat and Asp pair up and take the right side. Silver and I will pair up on the opposite side. Sarge, stay alert and warn of any danger. I don't want us getting caught out again like last time. Let's go.'

Silver groaned inwardly as Grave walked past her towards the building where they had found the panels. Why had he paired them together? The last thing she needed when she was already feeling like shit was his sullen moods and abrupt nature. She didn't know if she could be trusted to hold her tongue.

She nodded at Asp, and the dark skinned woman mouthed the words 'behave' at her, as if she had read her thoughts. Silver shook her head then hurried to catch up with Grave, who was studying the building before them.

'So this is the spot where you found the panels?'

'Yep, that's the one.'

'I want to climb to the top and take a look.'

Silver shrugged and pushed past him, moving quickly and quietly up the rubble until she had reached the sunken peak where they had taken their stand against the mutes. When she reached the top, she turned around with the beginnings of a smirk on her face. It disappeared, and she nearly stumbled from shock when she realised Grave was right behind her, having made his way up the slope as quickly as she and without a sound.

'Here's where we found them.'

Grave climbed into the space and immediately crouched down to look around. He spent a particular amount of time studying the wires protruding from the roof from inside a cracked piece of plastic piping. Silver recalled that it had been attached to the panels, and they had severed the wiring when they pulled the panels free two days before.

'What do the panels do?'

'That's what I'm trying to find out.'

Grave's answer was elusive, spoken without making eye contact. It frustrated Silver, adding to her anger at the way he had ignored her the previous day. However, knowing the Badlands was not the best place to instigate an argument, she bit her tongue and turned away from him, looking around from the elevated position for any sign of danger. The sun was hot, and the air was a hazy yellow colour, though clearer than usual. She could see no sign of movement nearby, other than Sarge standing on the roof of the truck and Rat preparing to crawl into a building nearby, while Asp played anchor for a change.

Silver returned her attention to Grave and the wires. She knew that electricity travelled along wires; she had seen people try to tap into them to get free access. One of these men had suffered a massive electric shock and died as a result. On two other occasions they had been successful in tapping into the power source. On both occasions, Silmac's man Meek had arrived with a squad of police within hours. Neither had been seen again, some saying they ended up in the mines, others claiming they were thrown out into the Badlands at night, left to the mercy of nature.

'So these panels need power to work? What do they do?'

Grave ignored her questions. 'Right, let's head back down. We need to find the power box for this house.'

Silver knew what Grave was talking about as she had come across them from time to time in the ruins, and many of the buildings in the Dome still had something similar—though mostly in disuse. It had something to do with regulating the electricity in and out of the building, back in the days when all households had access to power.

'What for?' Silver tried again. 'Will it give you some answers on the purpose of the panels?'

'Perhaps,' was Grave's only reply, as he rose and began descending the rubble pile to the house below. Silver clenched her fists and shook her head at another elusive answer, but followed him down nonetheless.

Back on the ground, the pair began picking their way around the borders of the house, sifting through the rubble, lifting larger pieces of debris together in order to search underneath. The house had been a large multi-storey structure, and it was hard work. Soon the pair were sweating profusely in the heat and humidity of the air. Silver found that Grave was a hard worker and strong, something she had not expected.

After almost an hour of sifting through the rubble, they shifted a section of bricks and Silver caught sight of a partially crushed box that resembled the power boxes she had seen in the past.

'There!' she called, pointing to the spot.

Grave nodded, and on the count of three they hauled the bricks to the right, kicking up a layer of dust as they did so. Grave crawled into the space they had uncovered and pulled the box free. Silver crouched down beside him as he pried the lid open, using a knife he carried on his belt.

Under the lip of the box, there was a tangle of wires, bent and broken fuses,and lifeless power switches. Grave studied the box intently, murmuring to himself something that Silver did not catch. Labels for various fuses could be spotted, but few indicated what was what.

After a few minutes, Grave looked over to her. 'Can you help me pull this out? We'll be taking it back with us.'

Silver nodded, and the two reached in and tested the box. It gave slightly, so they pulled it some way before being forced to cut away some wires at the back and pry off some anchoring brackets that had remained intact when the house collapsed. After ten minutes of work, they had pulled the box free; severed wires left dangling underneath like the trailing tentacles of a jellyfish. It looked a mess, and Silver still wondered what value it could possible offer.

'Won't fetch much at the markets,' she commented, hoping to prompt Grave into offering some more information about his interest in the box.

'I'm not interested in money,' Grave responded, his attention still on the box. It was not much, but finally a little more information in his answer.

'So how are you going to pay the crew?'

'Don't worry, you'll get paid if that's all you're concerned with.'

Silver bristled at the response, on the verge of dropping the box as they carried it together over to the truck. Again, she surprised herself at her restraint. Grave was infuriating, but she didn't know him well enough that she couldn't be sure he wouldn't leave her out in the Badlands if she pushed him too hard. Asp and the rest of the crew had faith in his loyalty to them, and she had seen glimpses of care and concern to support that, but she could not be certain that extended to her.

When they reached the truck, Silver unceremoniously dumped the box into the trailer. Grave glared at her briefly, but she met his gaze evenly. 'What now?' she inquired sweetly, sarcastically.

'We see what else we can find,' he replied evenly, turning and making his way back out into the ruins. With a sigh, Silver followed him out again.

The rest of the day passed relatively uneventfully. Working with

Grave was a little awkward and quiet, but Silver grudgingly found him to be a good anchor and hard worker. They found little in the way of metal, and no more panels, but Silver did uncover a number of items that would fetch some value at the markets; kitchenware, a beautiful picture frame, an old but well-kept wind-up clock—all the more valuable because it did not require battery power. Grave showed some genuine interest in the clock, but on the whole was largely unimpressed with the items they uncovered.

When it came time to head home, Silver was exhausted. Her hangover had improved as the day wore on, but she was physically sore and dehydrated from the half day's work. They piled back into the truck along with the assortment of items they had recovered from the ruins. The trip back to the Dome was a little livelier than the drive out that morning. Asp was more awake and Rat's mood had improved and the two chatted away, with Sarge even chiming here and there as he drove. Grave stayed quiet in the front, and Silver only gave cursory answers when the conversation was directed her way.

'The mutes kept a low profile today,' Rat commented. He had one of his homemade grenades in hand, and his tone was almost disappointed.

'Our encounter the other day left them pretty decimated,' Asp noted. 'They must be lying low.'

'Or perhaps they are just well-fed,' Silver added, causing Asp to grimace.

Back at the checkpoint, Silver helped the others unload the truck and walked home with the group but remained silent throughout the trip.

'You okay, girl?' Asp inquired as they neared the clubhouse.

'I just don't get it. What does he want with the black panels? What is it that they do?'

'Did you ask him?'

'Yep, he just avoided my questions.'

'The way I see it, it doesn't really matter what they are for. All that matters is that he has a buyer interested in them. Grave is a good boss and I trust him. You should too.'

'But what about with the Homeless?' Silver pressed. 'Don't you want to know what he promised to get us out of there?'

'I'm just glad he got us out of there,' Asp retorted, and Silver fell silent.

When they got in, Silver went straight upstairs to hit the showers, then into her room and crashed onto her bed without even stopping to get dressed. It felt like such a luxury to have a room to herself, something she had never had before. She figured she should put something on but it seemed like too much effort, and her naked body felt comfortable in the warm air. She was just beginning to doze off when there came a soft knock at the door, and before she could reply the door opened, revealing Muzzle's head and shoulders.

Silver quickly pulled the sheets up, suddenly regretting her decision. 'What do you want?' she inquired a little sharply, irritated at having been disturbed.

The smile on Muzzle's lips faltered, replaced by a look of hurt and uncertainty. 'Oh, um, sorry. I just thought you might want to hang out is all. I can go.'

Muzzle started to retract his head from the door and Silver was almost inclined to let him go, but she felt a moment of guilt at the disappointment painted over his face.

'How's your leg?' she blurted, causing him to pause. Some of the confidence returned to his face, and he came back into the room fully, closing the door gently behind him.

'Better. The wound is starting to scab up nicely. A couple more days and should be as good as new. How were the Badlands?'

Muzzle hobbled over to the bed as he talked, and sat down on the edge, close to Silver. She drew back from him slightly, pulling the sheet up higher, around her neck and shoulders.

'Exhausting. I'm kinda beat ...'

'Well, I've got loads of energy. I can give you a shoulder massage!'

'No, that's not necessary.'

Before Silver could finish her objection, Muzzle had manoeuvred onto the bed behind her and had begun working her shoulders with his hands. Despite her irritation, it did feel good, if a little heavy handed. She closed her eyes and relaxed.

After a minute or two, she felt his breath on her neck and his lips kissing down to her shoulders. She pulled away gently, turning to face him side on.

'Muzzle, not now. I'm stuffed and just want to rest.'

His face turned to disappointment once more. 'I just thought it might help relax you. And after yesterday ...'

'Yesterday was great, but now I need some sleep.'

For a second, a shadow seemed to pass across Muzzle's face. But then it was gone, replaced with an easy smile.

'Sure thing,' he said, rising from the bed and heading over to the door. 'Rest up.'

Before Silver had time to reply he was gone, shutting the door behind him. Silver sighed. She was alone again, but the sleep that had beckoned her so warmly earlier was nowhere to be found. It had been a mistake to drag Muzzle upstairs as she had, and she was convinced that somehow it was Grave's fault. Now it seemed Muzzle expected more, something she wasn't sure she was prepared to give. Recalling the look she had seen flash across his eyes, she decided she would need to talk to him about it, let him down gently.

Silver tried to put it all out of her mind and get back to sleep, but she found herself tossing and turning again. Eventually she got out of bed and retrieved the diary she had been reading. It had proven to have a therapeutic effect on her previously, helping her to find sleep. Not because it was boring—she was fascinated by the insights it provided into the world of the past. But it seemed to have a calming effect on her, settling her mind and guiding it into dreams of other places and times.

While she was up, she pulled on a singlet top and some underwear just in case Muzzle reappeared or someone else decided to drop by. She settled back down on the bed with the book and began to read. After a handful of pages, she was starting to feel drowsy once again and was just about ready to put the diary down. But a line in the book gave her pause.

*... including the solar panels we just had installed. Jess and I are more conscious than ever of trying to do our part for the environment. The panels will help reduce our energy costs longer term, which is a bonus.*

She read it again, then flipped to the next page and the pages prior, but no further reference to panels was made. Could there be a connection between the panels mentioned and the black panels Grave was interested in? She sat back against the wall, the diary on her lap and all thoughts of sleep gone. After a moment, she climbed out of bed, looking for some clean clothes. Reaching for an old faded pair of khaki jeans, she heard the front door closing. She hurried over to the window and peered out the crack. Below, she saw Grave walking briskly down the street away from the clubhouse. In his arms he held the box they had pulled from the Badlands that day. It was dark and getting late, not a great time to be out on the street alone.

'Oh no you don't,' she muttered. 'I'm getting answers out of you this time.'

Determined not to let him get away she quickly pulled on her jeans, threw on a jacket and hastily pulled on her boots. She grabbed her gun as she raced out the door and took the stairs two at a time, tucking it into the back of her pants and pulling her jacket down to conceal it. She hurried through the common room below, where only Rat remained, on guard duty. He eyed her, but didn't comment as she hurried out the door and onto the street.

There was no sign of Grave on the street and Silver grew concerned she had lost him already. She ran down Smith Street in the direction he had been heading, checking down side streets as she went but seeing no sign of him. She picked up her pace and at the following intersection caught a glimpse of him sixty metres ahead and disappearing around the next corner.

Casting her usual caution aside, she sprinted after him, slowing only when she reached the corner. Her haste was rewarded when she saw him striding up Commonwealth Street, heading towards the heart of the Dome. Having closed the gap between them, Silver rounded the corner much more slowly this time, concentrating now on avoiding detection.

Grave continued to wind through the streets, seemingly unaware of her presence. Silver became concerned when he turned onto Pitt Street, heading directly towards Silmac Tower. Lights appeared here and there in the surrounding buildings, and the debris on the streets lessened noticeably. Where previously the streets had been empty, there were others out and about. Further ahead she could see more light, with expensive restaurants and businesses open to cater for the wealthy.

Forced to abandon her efforts and remain hidden in the shadows, Silver adopted a casual gait, trying her best to not attract attention, while feeling intensely out of place. If Grave looked around, there was every chance he would spot her, but if she tried to remain hidden from him, she would attract scrutiny from others on the street. She bit her lip and hoped for the best.

*Where are you going?* she thought, as they continued up Pitt. Her eyes continually looked up to the looming presence of Silmac Tower, worried it was there Grave was headed.

However, as they neared Market Street, which bordered the mall from which the tower rose, Grave crossed the road and headed north towards George Street. Silver let out a breath of relief, crossing the road herself. She glanced briefly over at the main entrance to Silmac Tower as she rounded the bend onto Market. It was opulent and grand, with immaculate tiling on the floor and pillars, a high entrance and darkened glass panels, beyond which dimly glowing lights revealed an immaculate lobby. The doors opened and a group of men emerged, forcing her to duck her head and hurry on down the street.

Moving down Market Street, she passed a shopfront that had been converted into a huge hydroponic lab. Tomatoes, peas, lettuce, cucumber, celery and all manner of small vegetable plants filled the shop. The vibrant greens with flashes of reds and yellows were among the brightest colours she had ever seen, and the fruit caused her mouth to water. She had to tear her attention away from the window, just in time to see Grave crossing George and continuing west down Market Street. Knowing they were leaving the vibrant centre of the Dome and heading back into darker streets, Silver hurried to close the distance between them.

As she crossed George she saw him take a right onto York Street, and she hurried to the corner. Peering carefully around, she saw him a few doors up the street, fumbling with some keys while he held the fuse box under one arm. This area was still near enough to the city centre to be expensive and sought after by wealthy members of society. The buildings were in relatively good condition, with security maintained to keep out squatters and unwanted elements of society. A few lights here and there in the surrounding buildings demonstrated the affluence of their owners.

'Well, look who we have 'ere.'

Silver felt hands clamp down on her a split second before she recognised Coal's voice, and she cursed under her breath at letting her guard down. She had been so intent on following Grave's passage that she had not taken the proper care to check who else was about and might be following her. One of Coal's strong hands had grasped her tightly by the left upper arm, while the other had reached immediately to her belt, finding the gun she had stowed there.

'Ahh, my gun,' he said, pulling it free and pressing its nozzle into the small of her back. 'That's one thing of mine that I've been keen to retrieve.'

'You can take the gun. It's clear you feel inadequate without it. Understandable.'

Coal laughed and Silver felt other hands grabbing her arms as he released her, realising that he had some of his crew with him. Of course he did; he never travelled the streets alone. She looked left and right, hoping to see Lead or other former crew members whom she had been friendly with, but had no such luck. Tip held her left arm. He was young and impressionable, but also eager to please Coal and she could not see him disobeying orders. The man holding her right arm she did not recognise; presumably a new member of the crew. He was older, probably in his late twenties, and he looked rough, with a shaved head, bulging muscles and a mean face. She also noticed Slip hovering around the back and knew that after their last encounter she definitely wouldn't find any help there.

Meanwhile, Coal had circled round to face her, tucking the gun away as he went. He was surprisingly well dressed and groomed, as were the other crew members for that matter. They sported suits; slightly ill-fitting to their larger, muscled frames, but a far cry from the normal overalls and singlets she was used to seeing them in.

'A summons to Silmac's office is always a bit uncomfortable,' Coal commented. 'But seeing you strolling on by just as we were leaving brightened my day considerably.'

'What do you want, Coal? You made it clear you didn't want me in your crew, so I left.'

'Oh, but that's where you're wrong, Silver. It was not your decision to make. I say who comes and goes from the Silmac Ops crew, and I never said you could go.'

'You left me in the Badlands, Coal, 'cause you're a fucking coward. That story about getting separated from me was bullshit. You couldn't even spare me a warning that there was danger coming, just left me in the hole, rope still attached, to be dragged out by the mutes. Then, when I make it back I overhear you speaking with that whore, again too much of a fucking coward to come out and say it to my face.' She looked at the crew members with him. 'If he does that to the girl he's sleeping with, imagine how he'll repay *your* loyalty.'

Coal's face had grown more and more crimson as she spoke, until he was veritably shaking with rage. She expected him to lash out any second, but he restrained himself, instead reaching into his pocket and pulling out her flick-knife. He seemed to regain some control as he waved the knife, its blade still sheathed, in front of her face.

'Remember this? I gave it to you but you carelessly forgot it when you left. I want you to have it back. The only question is, where will I put it?'

The blade suddenly appeared with a violent click as he pressed the release button, and Silver flinched involuntarily. Coal smiled evilly at her reaction, twisting the glinting blade ever so slightly to emphasise its wicked point. Silver began to struggle but the grip on her arms tightened, holding her iron fast. Enjoying the moment, Coal teased her with the blade, bringing it close to her face, then down towards her breast, and down lower still, hovering it over her stomach, then her crotch. Silver closed her eyes. He was taking pleasure from the fear in her eyes, so she wanted to deny him that at least. She forced her face to remain blank, denying her inner panic.

She heard a sickening thwack, and was surprised when it was Coal's voice who yelled out in pain, not her own. Her eyes sprung open to see the knife on the ground, and Coal down on his knees, gripping his forearm, which was bent at a sickening angle. To her right was Grave, swinging a thin but dangerous looking metallic flick-mace in an arc towards the shaved-headed brute holding her right arm. The man started to pull back to avoid the blow, releasing Silver in the process. However, Silver grabbed him and pulled, enough to prevent him completely evading the hit, and he suffered a glancing blow to his temple, causing him to drop like a sack of bricks.

Slip, who had been hovering to Coal's right, had pulled out his knife and lunged in at Grave's mid-section. Grave twisted, sweeping the edge of his coat across in front of him to divert the blow. The manoeuvre left Slip off balance and head down, giving Grave the opportunity to bring his mace down on the back of his neck, and the heavy blow sent him sprawling onto the broken pavement.

Tip still had a half-grip on Silver's left arm, but had been slow to react. His face belied his shock, clearly unaccustomed to such a sudden and effective assault. His focus was on Grave, and Silver did not waste the opportunity. With her right arm now free, she swung around to face him, bringing her right knee up into his groin as she went. The air blew out of him in a great gasp and he wasted no time joining his companions on the footpath.

Silver turned back to find Coal pulling out a pistol left-handed from its holster and bringing it to bear on Grave's back.

'Grave!' she screamed, a fraction of a second before the gun fired, the discharge echoing loudly off the tall buildings surrounding them. Grave had been turning back to face them when the bullet struck him in the side, punching through his coat and sending him stumbling back towards the rock wall of the building behind him.

Silver aimed a kick at Coal's hand, sending the gun spinning away to clatter on the ground a few paces away. She then landed a second kick at his face, and with his right arm down by his side, he had nothing to block the blow. Her foot collected solidly with a sickening crunch of nose cartilage and he fell to the ground, out cold.

Silver scooped up the gun and flick-knife and rushed over to Grave, who was leaning heavily against the wall, gasping with each breath. Looking inside his loose coat, she could see a blossom of red spreading outward from his side. She moved over to his right side and ducked under his arm, forcing as much of his weight onto her as she could.

'We've gotta get moving before the cops get here. We need to get you back to the clubhouse.'

She started to lead him back up Park Street, but Grave resisted, shaking his head.

'Macquarie Street,' he wheezed.

Silver paused for a moment at the strange request, trying to think of what was on Macquarie that could help. Then it came to her.

'The hospital? They won't help you there. You'll die on the doorstep unattended.'

'Hospital. Macquarie Street,' Grave insisted.

Silver hesitated. Grave needed help, but the hospital was reserved for rich people who could afford to pay the extremely high cost of medical treatment. They would turn the pair of them away. The sound of police approaching eventually prompted her to move, forcing her down York in the direction Grave had indicated. The police were reluctant to get involved in street disputes, but once shots were fired they would generally respond, albeit slowly. They preferred to let the gangs have it out and then clean up the mess afterwards. It was easier dealing with dead bodies than live ones. Their imminent arrival, coming from down Park Street, ruled out returning the way she had come. York headed in the opposite direction to the clubhouse, but it would allow her to circle back and come up close to Macquarie.

The pair shuffled along the dark street as quickly as they could, Grave leaning heavily on her. As soon as they reached the corner, she swung East onto King Street, which would take them up towards Macquarie. By this time Silver was breathing heavily, Grave's extra weight taking its toll. He continued to stumble at her side, trying to take as much of his own weight as he could. She noticed with worry that his wheezing was getting worse, with the gurgle of fluid clearly audible at the end of each breath.

They crossed George and headed up towards Pitt, crossing over the mouth of the mall as quickly as possible. A couple of rich diners looked in their direction, but there were no security forces present, likely drawn to the other end of the mall by the sound of their fight with Coal. When they hit Elizabeth Street, Silver tried to direct them right, which would lead them on the long walk south towards the clubhouse, but Grave pulled the other way, his added weight dragging her to a stop. He indicated left, which would take them through a lane towards the hospital on Macquarie.

'You need rest', Silver insisted, angry at his stubborn insistence on the hospital. 'You'll die there.'

'Hospital. Trust me,' Grave gasped back, and started to pull away from her to head in that direction.

Frustrated, Silver swung around after him, taking up his weight again before he fell, and then a little more roughly than necessary pulling him along towards the hospital. She felt her eyes welling up, and she rubbed at them angrily with her free hand. What did she care if he wanted to get himself killed?

A few minutes more and the steps of the hospital were in sight. It was not a huge building, but given its limited number of patrons it was large enough. The gangs and common people of the Dome were forced to use street doctors, whose methods were just as likely to kill as heal.

Silver dragged Grave the last few metres to the entrance, which was cold and dark, and thumped on the door. A minute passed with no sound other than Grave's rattling breath, its intensity growing by the minute.

'See, nothing!' Silver hissed. 'We need to get you back to the …'

She didn't get a chance to finish the sentence as the doors before them abruptly opened. Two large men blocked the way, their arms folded over their chests. They didn't look like doctors.

'Push off.'

'We don't service your kind around here.'

'You mean, our kind,' Silver shot back. 'Don't kid yourself, buddy—if you were to get shot in the line of duty, you'd be told the same thing. Let's go, Grave.'

Silver started to turn, not sure she was going to be able to make it all the way back to the clubhouse supporting Grave, and even less certain he would make it back alive. Once again, Grave resisted. He reached into a pocket inside his coat and the guards tensed in anticipation, relaxing a little when he produced a thin black leather card book rather than a weapon.

He reached over and offered it to one of the guards, who reluctantly took it and flipped it open. Silver watched in growing amazement as the guard's eyes widened slightly, then he turned and motioned to someone inside the building.

'Help is right on the way, Mr Meldon.'

The two guards hurried forward and helped support Grave, taking his weight from Silver, who was too dumbfounded to resist. Within moments a male and female nurse had arrived behind the guards, bringing with them a bed on wheels. One either side, they helped him climb onto it and lie down.

Grave's eyes met Silver's as the nurses readied to wheel him inside. 'I will explain,' he said weakly, only just loud enough for Silver to hear.

He was gone before Silver could respond, wheeled inside at a brisk pace. Silver started to follow, but quickly found her way blocked by one of the security guards.

'You'll have to remain here, lady, unless you can produce some ID?'

Silver shook her head dumbly and stepped back. In the back of her mind she thought she should be angry with the guards for their smugness. But she was still too surprised by what she had just witnessed to give voice to her anger. As soon as she was clear of the doorway, the guards stepped back inside and the doors closed with a bang, leaving her alone on the dark street.

# CHAPTER 15

*From the diary of Benjamin Adams*
*July 21$^{st}$, 2012*

*I've been offered a promotion at work today, which is exciting. I'll be taking on leadership of another division in the company, on top of the one I'm already managing. It's going to be tricky to balance the workload, but it's nice to know that City Design have put their confidence in me. It's a pay rise, so that'll help with our home repayments, and probably bring the time line of a kitchen renovation a little forward.*

*In saying all that, we're in bad need of a holiday. It's proving to be a long winter, with the boys playing tag team with the flu so far. We've booked in a trip to Fiji in early November, which will be nice—something to look forward to. It'll be the first time the boys have been overseas, and the first big holiday as a family. The boys are getting big so fast, and it will be good to stop and take some time out with them.*

* * * * *

Silver sat alone in the common room at the clubhouse, everything dark around her. Thankfully, the trip back from the hospital had been quick and uneventful. When she had arrived home, Rat let her in.

'Your watch,' he'd said without preamble, and headed downstairs to the basement where he kept his room. She had not mentioned what had happened to Grave. Her instincts told her that he would not want them to know, at least not yet, and that she should give him a chance to explain. Everyone else had already gone to sleep, so Silver had been left alone with her thoughts.

Restless, she stood and paced back and forth across the common room, wringing her hands. Being accepted into the hospital had at least improved Grave's chances, but she still worried for him, particularly given how he had received the injury.

She still couldn't work him out. One minute he seemed to not want to know her, acting rude and evasive, and the next he was taking on four armed men in order to protect her. The behaviour was playing havoc with her emotions—she felt simultaneous disdain and gratitude towards him.

Meanwhile, her hatred and disgust at Coal had grown tenfold, and she felt self-loathing for ever having spent time with him. Street etiquette inside the Dome was that you didn't pull a gun. Everyone knew, and Coal was no exception. Beaten, he had done exactly that. She had been right; he was a coward to the bone, and she did not know how she had missed it for so long.

She ceased her pacing to do a round of the house, but her thoughts drifted back to Grave and the hospital. In order to be admitted, he must have some serious cash to his name. Was he some rich boy playing at slumming it? The thought fuelled her anger towards him. The crew was the livelihood of its members; without it they would likely be on the streets, starving and desperate. Assuming he even survived the injury, what then? Would he give it away, decide he'd had his fun and it was time to take on some other project? Her anger was even greater because she knew it was her fault. If she hadn't joined the crew, he probably would have never met Coal.

All around the house was quiet, and she returned to the common room. Her watch had passed surprisingly quickly, and it was almost time for her to finish up. As she waited out the last few minutes, her thoughts drifted back to the hospital. One of the guards there said his name. Meldrum? Meldron? No, it had been Meldon. The name had sounded familiar to Silver, but she couldn't place it.

The stairs behind her creaked gently, and she turned to see Blocka descending.

'Any trouble so far tonight?'

'Nope, everything quiet.' Not completely true, but true of the clubhouse.

'Go get some sleep. I'll take it from here.'

Silver nodded and made her way over to the stairs, but paused before heading up.

'Blocka, does the name 'Meldon' mean anything to you?'

'Meldon? They write the paper, don't they? Or used to, at least. Silmac bought it off the family a few years back.'

'Yep, that must be it. Thanks.'

Silver ascended the stairs, recalling the events from a few years before. Blocka was right; the Meldon family had run the only remaining newspaper in the Dome. Then, like most things, it had been sold to Silmac. Silver had read it from time to time before then, but had not bothered since. It had become little more than a propaganda newsletter for the Silmac empire.

She hadn't detected any indication that Blocka knew of any connection between Grave and the Meldon family. She had briefly considered the possibility that the rest of the crew might know Grave's true identity and she was the only one who didn't know who he was. But if that were the case, they were all better liars than she.

As she slipped into her room and prepared for bed, her mind continued to work overtime. She wondered if she should tell the crew about his injury; his death would affect them all, so they deserved to know. But that would lead to questions as to where he was and what he was doing, as well as how she had become involved. His admission into hospital would tell them straight away that he was not who he said he was.

Which led back to his agenda; what was he up to? Adventure seeker? Or something more noble, or sinister? Silver flopped down onto the bed and sighed. Ultimately, she would have to hold her tongue until she could talk to Grave. He had saved her from Coal twice now, so she owed him that much. She closed her eyes and tried to find sleep, though had a feeling it would be hard to come by.

* * * * *

Silver slipped out early the next morning and quietly got dressed, stifling yawn after yawn. She had awoken during the night to another quake. The room shook violently, her bed actually vibrating almost a metre out of position with her still in it. The tremors had lasted about twenty seconds before subsiding, at which point Sarge had done the rounds to ensure everyone was okay. Eventually, everything settled down and she had gone back to sleep.

The good thing about the quake was that the checkpoints would be closed and they would not be venturing out into the Badlands. This presented her with the opportunity to go and check on Grave. She grabbed the little money she had saved up, figuring she might need it. Once ready, she made her way quietly down the stairs, avoiding the spots she had learned elicited a loud creak every time they were stepped upon.

It was dark outside, black gradually turning to grey, and the rest of the crew were still in bed, no doubt using the quake as an opportunity to get a sleep in. However, Asp had taken the final watch of the night and she was up and about, preparing for breakfast. Silver waited until she was busy pulling some pots and pans from the cupboard under the stairs and hurried across to the door, quietly opening it and slipping out.

She waited a few moments until she was satisfied Asp had not heard her before heading onto the street and towards the hospital. The streets were relatively quiet for the time of day, the normal south and west flow of traffic towards the gatehouses absent. Those who were out and about were heading in her direction, down towards the north-east edge of the Dome where a crowd would be gathered. The tsunami that had no doubt followed the quake would be long gone, but that wouldn't stop people gathering and celebrating another day off.

Arriving at the closed and uninviting entrance to the hospital, she hesitated. Why would they answer her questions? They probably wouldn't even answer the door, let alone yield any information. She patted the pouch that contained her money—she would give it a try. Most people in this city could be bought; there was no reason why the guards on duty there would be any different.

She approached the door and knocked on it as she had the night before, waiting for a response. It came through a panel of tiny holes drilled through the door. The voice was muffled and bored.

'Go away. We do not serve your kind here.'

'I am only after information on a patient admitted last night. I would be very grateful for any information you can give me. Please.'

Silence followed, but eventually she heard the doors being unbolted.

'Step back, turn around and hands on the back of your head.'

Silver obeyed the command. If she were a guard, she would take similar precautions. The lure of coin was enough to get the guard to risk opening the door, but not enough to throw caution to the wind.

A moment later Silver felt hands on her, searching over her body for any hidden weapons. The hands were efficient and did not linger where they were not meant to. She had left her gun at the clubhouse, and the only weapon she carried was her newly retrieved flick-knife, hidden in the sheath within her cleavage.

Finally, she was allowed to turn around and found a guard of average height and build, but with gun in hand and a no-bullshit look on his face. He held out his other hand in expectation.

'Well, how much do you want this information you seek?'

Silver dug into her pouch and fished out a couple of coins, placing them into his palm. He looked at them disdainfully.

'Is the man, Meldon, admitted last night still alive?'

The guard looked at the coins and nodded, yes. Relief flowed through Silver's body, washing away worry she had not even realised was there. The guard had also confirmed her suspicions: Grave was definitely a Meldon.

'Is he going to be okay?'

The guard looked down at the coins in his hand before looking stony faced back at Silver. Getting the message, she fished in her pocket and pulled out a note, handing it to him.

'Yes, he'll live. We'll likely hold him today and he will be released tomorrow morning.'

'Can I see him?'

'Your purse isn't big enough for that, honey. Answers are all you get.'

Silver nodded, not having expected any other response. 'Thanks for your time.'

Without a word, the guard stepped back through the door and pulled it closed; their transaction, and thus his interest in her, over.

She stood outside the hospital for a few more moments, wondering what she should do next. She was relieved that Grave was stable and would be well, but frustrated she couldn't see him. A mighty yawn forced its way past her lips. She was tired and needed more rest. She decided to head back to the clubhouse.

When she arrived back, the others were preparing to leave, and she met them out the front. Asp walked over to her, the look in her eyes belying curiosity at where Silver had been.

'You were up early this morning.'

'Couldn't sleep, so decided to go for a walk and run some errands.'

Asp nodded slowly, clearly not buying the story.

'We're heading down to the gathering—you want to join us?'

'No thanks.' Silver smiled. 'I think I'll stay and try to get some of that sleep I missed out on.'

'Well, we'll probably be there a while if you change your mind.'

Silver nodded and smiled again, moving past them to make her way inside. As she passed Muzzle, she smiled up at him, but he avoided her gaze, busying himself with a bag of alcohol instead.

'Oh, Silver?' Asp called out. 'You haven't seen Grave around have you?'

'No,' Silver lied, pausing only ever so slightly before answering. Her eyes lingered on Muzzle for a moment, who pointedly ignored her. She opened her mouth to speak, but another yawn escaped her lips instead. Before she could recover, Muzzle pushed past her and made his way out the front door. Silver sighed, knowing she'd have to talk to him again, but was too tired to chase him down.

Resolved to have the discussion when he returned, she headed upstairs, stripped down and showered, the warm water soothing her body, a luxury she had rarely experienced. Throwing on a nightshirt to sleep in, she went to her room and jumped into bed. Unlike the previous night, it did not take her long to drift off to sleep.

* * * * *

Silver was awoken by a gentle knocking at her door. For a moment she was disoriented, not knowing where she was. Light filtered in through the window, bathing the room in a warm glow.

Before she could properly collect her thoughts to answer, the door opened and Grave entered. She was shocked to see him, not expecting him to have been released so early. She immediately looked at the spot where he had been wounded, but his shirt and coat covered the area and there was no evidence of his injury. He shut the door gently behind him.

'Grave, are you okay? I was worried you'd ...'

She wasn't able to finish that sentence as he crossed the room and before she could stop him, leant in and kissed her. His kiss was firm, his breath hot. He smelled good to her, like a man should. Shocked, she surrendered to his kiss, closing her eyes and kissing him back.

At last he pulled back for breath and she found herself staring into his gentle blue eyes. His touch had quickened her pulse, and though he was the one injured, she suddenly found herself breathless.

'I'm sorry. It's my fault you got injured.'

'It's fine, no injury could keep me from your side.'

He leant in once more and kissed her again, climbing onto the bed and pushing her backwards onto the pillow. She felt his hands exploring her body, and she returned the favour, pulling at his clothes and trying to free him from them. He leant away for a moment, dragging his coat off his shoulders while she worked the buttons on his shirt. Underneath she found a clean white bandage, wrapping under his arm on the side of the wound and both under his arm and over his shoulder on the opposite side. His body was well toned, the definition in his arms chest and torso obvious despite the bandage.

Silver pulled away from his lips. 'I have questions for you …' she started, but he leant in and kissed her again, silencing her. She vaguely thought she should argue with him, insist he stop. But her mind was sluggish and her body responding to his touch.

He reached up under her nightshirt, his smooth hands running up her stomach and over her breasts. She helped him get the shirt off over her head and then they were kissing again, as she fumbled at his belt, and he removed his pants. In a moment they were free of their clothes and he was pushing inside her, filling her. She arched her back to receive him, filled with pleasure by his gentle lovemaking.

She didn't realise at first that she was moaning in pleasure, but she didn't care as she drew nearer and nearer to climax. A knock at the door caused Grave to pause and look over at it. She reached up and pulled his face back down to hers, wanting him to ignore the knock and continue. But the thumping sounded again and suddenly, Grave was gone and she was in the room alone.

She sat up and looked around, still breathing heavily, her nipples were hard against her nightshirt. It had been a dream, but her body had reacted as if it were real.

The knock from the door came again.

'Come in,' she said, half expecting it to be Grave standing on the other side. But it was Muzzle who stepped into view, entering the room fully and closing the door behind him.

'I thought you were heading over with the others to the Dome edge?'

He shrugged. 'I went for a while but it was a bit lame. I wanted to see you.'

His eyes travelled down to her nightshirt where her nipples were visible through the fabric.

'I was asleep,' she replied bluntly. She struggled to keep the annoyance from her voice, reminding herself that she had led him on that night and couldn't blame him for looking to take things further. Even so, his behaviour was starting to irritate her.

Ignoring her reply, he moved over and sat down on the bed next to her. She could smell alcohol on his breath. She wondered how long she had been asleep. His left hand moved up to her breasts, and he leant in to try to kiss her. Resisting the urge to strike him away, Silver attempted a gentler approach, pulling back out of reach of his lips and taking his hand in hers.

'Muzzle, what are you doing?'

'I'm picking things up where we left off.'

'I'm not interested in that. Look, the night we had together was great, but it was nothing more than that. I don't want an ongoing relationship. I'm sorry if I led you to believe otherwise.'

Muzzle pulled his hand from hers, the hurt clear in his eyes. 'What's wrong with me? I'm a nice guy. The sex was good, right?'

'It's not about that,' Silver replied. 'You are a nice guy, and the sex was good, but I've done the whole relationship with someone you work with before and it didn't work out for me. I don't want to make that mistake again.'

'But I'm not like him. It'll be different with us!'

Silver fought to maintain her calm under his continued pressure. She knew it wouldn't be productive to shout at him, but she was losing patience. 'I'm sorry, Muzzle. I'm just not interested in a relationship with you.'

He stood up from the bed and this time made no effort to hide the anger, his nostrils flaring and brow furrowed.

'Oh, I get it. You're one of those girls who only get off from being with jerk-offs like Coal. You probably like it rough. I can do that.'

He lunged in at her, pushing her back onto the bed and bearing his weight down on top of her. She tried to strike out at him but he caught her arms and pinned them down. He leant in to kiss her but she head-butted him, her forehead connecting with his nose. It was not a clumsy blow, but it was partially effective, causing him to growl in rage, pull back and strike her a ringing blow across the cheek.

Her vision blurred momentarily, but she forced herself to move while her body was no longer pinned. She pulled her other hand free and dragged herself towards the opposite side of the bed where she kept her gun on the bedside table. As she reached for the weapon he lunged at her again, this time pushing one hand on the back of her neck, and bearing her face down into the sheets.

From this position, she could not get her hands around at him with sufficient power to cause him any real harm, but she kicked, screamed and writhed to break his hold. When that didn't work, she remembered the wound on his thigh and grabbed for it, pressing her fingers into the spot with as much strength as she could muster. It worked, as he howled in pain and his hand slipped off her neck to the bed beside her. She immediately pushed up and slammed her left elbow into his head with enough force to throw him off balance before dragging herself over to the edge of the bed and reaching for her gun.

When he came at her for a third time, Muzzle found himself looking down the barrel of her firearm.

'Get the fuck out of my room, before I blow your fucking head off!' Silver's voice was shrill, her hands trembling. An angry welt was growing on the side of her face from where he had struck her.

His eyes widened, and the anger flowed out of them, replaced by shame and regret. 'Silver, I'm sorry.'

'Save it. The fact that you're drunk is the only thing stopping me from pulling the trigger. I suggest you leave before I decide otherwise.'

Grabbing his pants to keep them from falling down he backed out of the room, nearly tripping over as he went. Silver kept the gun trained on the doorway as she heard the muffled footsteps flee down the stairs and across the floor below.

Her heart hammered loudly in her chest and as the door below slammed shut, her trembling hands began to shake more violently. She put the gun down on the bed and gingerly got to her feet, moving over to close the door. As an afterthought, she moved the chest that housed her few possessions in front of it as well. She then sat on the bed, her whole body trembling. A sob forced its way past her lips and soon her whole body was wracked with them, her face buried in her hands and the tears flowing.

After a moment, Silver got up from her bed clutching her stomach. She stumbled over to the door, dragging at the barriers she had put against them and running to the bathroom. She only just made it to the toilet in time, flipping up the lid and heaving into the bowl.

When the sickness in the pit of her stomach finally starting to ease, she rose slowly and moved over to the basin where she wiped away her tears and rinsed her mouth. She made her way back to her room and sat down on the edge of her bed. She was there for a long time, not sleeping, no longer crying, but her face pale and expressionless.

Finally she rose and started gathering her belongings. She moved lethargically at first, but her urgency increased with each item stuffed into her backpack. When the pitiful few things she owned were stowed in her pack, she got fully dressed and took her gun, tucking it in the back of her pants.

Her eyes still red-rimmed, Silver looked around the room one last time, not sure if she'd be back. She spied the diary she'd been given by the bedside and grabbed it, adding it to her pack. She hadn't yet finished it and didn't know if she would now, but was still curious to know how the author's life shaped out.

Downstairs she took up pen and paper, but stood there blankly for nearly two minutes, unsure of what to write. Eventually, she put the pen down, leaving the page blank. She left the house, ensuring the door locked shut behind her. Outside the building she paused, looking for and finding the ever-looming sentinel that was Silmac Tower. She stared at it for a while, her eyes hard, face grim. She took a deep breath and started off in its direction.

# CHAPTER 16

*From the diary of Benjamin Adams*
*February 24<sup>th</sup>, 2013*

*Jess has finally had enough of our car and looks like it's time to get a new one. The Corolla has seen better days and is starting to get a little small for us.Ideally I'd like to get an electric or hybrid car, but the cost and the lack of range is prohibitive. The electric cars are only available as small cars and they only do around 150km on a full charge. The hybrid cars are more practical, but are pretty pricey and still have limitations like no, or very low, towing limits. So looks like we are sticking with a petrol car for now.*

*Speaking of the environment, we've had a major energy company doing exploration in our area and proposing to start mining coal seam gas, virtually under our doorsteps. From all accounts, the technology is unproven and the potential environmental impact is high, especially in a highly populated area. The community and council have opposed the proposal and we've just had confirmation that it has been withdrawn, for now. But it is deeply concerning to me that this location would even be considered.*

* * * * *

'I need to see him!' Silver pressed.

'Look lady,' the guard at the hospital explained, her voice tinny through the drilled holes that served as an intercom. 'No matter what you need, you're not coming in.'

Silver ground her teeth in frustration, her fists clenched, knuckles white. She thought about pulling her gun and trying to force her way in, but quickly buried the idea. Getting herself shot would not achieve anything.

'Can you at least tell me when he'll be out?'

The guard sighed. 'Stay there, I'll see what I can do.'

Silver paced back and forth outside the entrance to the hospital, agitated and impatient for his return. Finally the voice rang through the intercom.

'Looks like he's as impatient as you. The doctor wishes to check him one more time and if all tests go well, he'll be discharged within the hour. Until then, you're going to have to wait. And you can't do it here, so push off.'

An hour. She felt like she couldn't wait, but knew she'd have to. 'Thank you,' she said to the guard before moving away from the door. She didn't go far, stopping about twenty metres down the street, within sight of the hospital entrance. She sat down against the wall and, needing something to pass the time, pulled out the diary. She was around two-thirds of the way through and guessed she could finish it in an hour. Besides, she was impatient and knew that reading would help the time pass.

* * * * *

'The guard told me an annoying woman had been asking after me. I figured it'd be you.'

Startled, Silver rose to find Grave standing behind her. She had unconsciously turned away from the hospital in order to better catch the fading light while she read the last few pages of the book. And she had been so absorbed in the story she had not heard him approach.

'You're okay?' she asked, scrutinising him.

Grave nodded. 'A bit tender but I'll live. What are you reading?' he asked, referring to the diary in her hands.

'Oh, this? Nothing.' She put the book back into her pack and stood. 'I'm relieved you're all right, 'cause we need to talk, and I won't take no for an answer this time.'

'And here I was thinking you were just concerned for my health. Let's … wait, what's that? What happened to your face?'

Silver raised a hand to her cheek, having forgotten about the raised welt. 'Oh, it's nothing,' she mumbled, looking away to hide the bruise from him.

'It's not nothing, Silver,' Grave said, moving around to get a better view of it. 'Tell me what happened.'

'I … he …' Silver felt the tears welling up again, did her best to hold them off, but lost the fight and broke down as she had earlier.

'Hey, it'll be all right.' Grave stepped in to her, trying to comfort her with a hug but she pulled away from him.

'Will it? Will it really be all right?' she responded, her voice shaky. 'Because I don't see it Grave. I can't see it.'

Grave tried again to take her in his arms and this time succeeded. Once she had stopped struggling she let him hold her, weeping into his chest. He stood there quietly, gently stroking her hair but otherwise still.

'Let's get off the street,' Grave suggested gently, once the worst of her tears had subsided. 'I owe you some answers, but I'm going to need some from you too, starting with who did this to you.'

'I can't go back to the clubhouse, Grave,' Silver objected.

'Good, 'cause that wasn't where I was planning to take you. Come.'

He took her hand and started leading her in the direction of where the fight had taken place two nights earlier. He walked well, showing little sign of the injury that had put him in hospital. His face looked a little more pale than usual and he wore the same clothes he had entered with. While they had been washed, the shirt still sported a hole in its side, showing a flash of white bandaging beneath.

'Should you be out of hospital yet? You look like shit.'

'Thanks,' came Grave's dry reply, yet a grin broke over his face, which Silver returned weakly. 'I'm not one for sitting idle. They wanted to keep me longer, but I managed to convince them otherwise.'

'Bribe?'

'Works every time.'

'Yeah, for those who have the means,' Silver replied pointedly.

They fell into silence, making their way slowly down Macquarie. When they crossed Pitt, Silver ventured slightly ahead and spent a moment scanning the arcade for any sign of Coal or his crew. There were a few people about, but no one who looked like they posed a threat so they proceeded. As they turned onto York Street and approached the spot where she had watched Grave stop the previous night, Silver found her apprehension growing as to what she might find upstairs.

'So, is this where the late night meetings with your secret lover take place?'

'What?' Grave asked. He looked genuinely confused.

'That's what the crew think—that you head off each night to meet up with your lover.'

'Ah yes. So they do.'

'Well, is it true?'

'What does it matter to you?'

Silver felt the heat rising to her cheeks as the image of Grave from her dream appeared, unbidden, in her mind. 'It doesn't, but if there's some naked chick waiting upstairs, I'd prefer to have some forewarning.'

Grave studied her face for a moment, and Silver resisted the urge to look away under his probing eyes.

'There's no secret lover. Asp and the others jumped to conclusions when I first founded the Ash Walkers. I didn't correct them.'

'Why not?'

'It saved them asking the uncomfortable questions you are about to ask me. Besides, I'm not interested in a relationship.'

He turned away from her as he added this last comment, fishing out a plain key from his jacket and fitting it into the lock of a heavy wooden door. A click signalled the opening of the door, and Silver found herself looking up a narrow set of stairs. The fuse box they had taken from the Badlands the day prior sat just inside the door. Grave picked it up then stood to the side and motioned for her to proceed. Silver started up the stairs while he locked the door behind them. It was dark inside and she needed the handrail to maintain her course up the steep incline. At a small landing at the top, another locked door blocked her way. Grave squeezed past her and produced a second key to open this door, moving deftly despite the darkness. Silver gasped in wonder as he opened the door and motioned her to enter.

Grave's home was bathed in a warm glow from lights in the ceiling, and a couple of lamps placed strategically around the room. The floors were wooden, but a large thick rug dominated a good portion of the floor, rich maroon in colour. The walls were dominated by wooden bookcases filled with books of all variety. Three comfortable antique armchairs in good repair were placed around the room, with matching wooden side tables next to them. A beautiful wood and glass coffee table sat in the centre of the room, atop the carpet.

Curtains were pulled closed on each of the room's windows and from what Silver recalled of the exterior of the building, the windows beyond were all boarded up. It was not a great idea to advertise that you could afford electricity to the world outside, so the boards and the thick maroon curtains would ensure that the light from within did not escape. Between the windows, classical works of art hung on the walls, framed in ornate carved wood and gilded in gold.

Two other doors led out of the room: one into a kitchen and dining space, and the other to a hallway down which Silver could see a couple of doors.

A gentle hand on Silver's arm startled her from the stunned stupor that had overcome her upon seeing the place.

'Please, take a seat,' he offered, putting the fuse box down inside before shutting the door and locking it. 'Can I get you a drink?'

Silver nodded, sinking into one of the armchairs and Grave disappeared into the kitchen. He returned a moment later holding two glasses, each half full of amber-coloured liquor. He passed one to Silver and lowered himself into the armchair opposite hers, sipping at his drink. Silver did the same and found it to be a strong but smooth taste, filling her belly with warmth. Used to the harsh homemade liquors that were available on the streets, this was incredibly smooth and rich in flavour.

'So please, tell me what happened to your eye? Did Coal do it to you?'

'No, it was Muzzle.'

'Muzzle?' Grave questioned, his expression sceptical, confused. 'But you slept with him. I thought you two were together?'

'What? So that gives him the right to beat me? Is that what you're saying?' Silver slammed the glass down on the side table, sloshing some liquor out and rising to her feet. 'If that's what you think then I'm outta here.'

'No, Silver, that's not what I'm saying,' Grave sighed. When Silver continued over to the door, he put his own drink down and hurried after her, placing a hand gently on the door to stop her opening it. 'That's not what I think. It took me by surprise, is all. Please come and sit down.'

Silver was shaking slightly, on the verge of tears again but determined this time to hold them back. She stared at Grave for a long while before eventually heading back over to the armchair and sitting back down.

'So did he … ?' Grave asked hesitantly.

Silver shook her head. 'No, I fought him off. He was drunk.'

'Silver, I'm sorry.' Grave's face had darkened, and his voice seemed genuine to her. 'I didn't think Muzzle was capable of that. He is no longer a member of the Ash Walkers—that behaviour will not be tolerated in my crew.'

The room descended into silence, and Silver sipped at her drink, somehow feeling guilty about Muzzle. Trying to distract herself from the feeling, her eyes explored the room. It was the most amazing and expensive place she had ever seen and reminded her of the reason she had come to see Grave again.

'You own all this?'

Grave nodded. 'It was given to me by my father.'

'Meldon?'

'Yes, that's right. His name is Rupert Meldon.'

'And he owned the newspaper business?'

'That's correct, until he sold it off to Silmac.'

Though Grave had kept his voice even, the pursing of his lips indicated to Silver that it was a sore point for him. Unperturbed by his discomfit, she continued with her questioning.

'What's your real name?'

This time, Grave's reluctance was obvious as he shifted in his chair. 'My real name is Lance.'

'Well, *Lance*, what are your motives for running a crew? Some hobby to pass the time?' Silver's voice was sarcastic, angry. 'You do realise that Asp, Blocka and the others rely on their jobs, right? Unlike you, they are screwed without it. You're messing with people's lives here and for what? A bit of excitement and adventure?'

Grave placed his cup down on the side table and locked eyes with Silver's.

'Boredom had nothing to do with my reason for founding the Ash Walkers. My motivation is breaking Silmac's power, once and for all. Yes, I have some wealth, for now. But I can't sit by and watch while the human race struggles and Silmac sits back, happy to keep it that way. I see the way people live on the streets and I feel pity for them …'

'So you do this out of pity then?' Silver interjected angrily, rising from her seat and pacing across the room. 'We don't need your pity, *Lance*.'

'No!' Grave retorted, the edge in his voice punctuated by the clunk of his glass on the table as he slammed it down. 'I do it for the desire to change things, to make a difference and improve the quality of life for everyone. I use my money while I've got it to try to find a solution. At least I'm trying to make a difference.'

'Solution? What solution? You're just a rich boy playing a hero.'

Grave rose from his chair again, moving over to Silver and holding out his hand. His eyes flashed dangerously and his cheeks were slightly flushed. 'Come on, I need to show you something.'

'What, you're going to show off more of your luxury apartment?'

'Will you give me a chance?' Grave exclaimed, exasperated. 'You came here looking for answers and I'm trying to give them to you but you're too busy making judgments to stop and listen. Since showing up unannounced, you've put my work at risk, you've put my crew at risk, and I've just about had enough. So either pipe down and listen, or get out.'

The outburst caused Silver to cease her pacing and stare open mouthed at Grave, who met her stare, steely eyed. Her hand clenched briefly, and she looked over to her bag and the door, then back to him. Eventually she extended her hand to him. 'All right, show me this solution.'

Grave shook his head, then snatched her hand and led her down the hall, where she caught fleeting glimpses of a well-kept bathroom and a comfortable looking bedroom. At the hall end he pulled her round the corner to the right and started up a second set of stairs. Arriving at the landing she caught a glimpse of a large open floor, cluttered with workbenches, tools, and all manner of metal and wiring. Among it all she noticed fragments of panelling like that they had pulled from the ruins a few days earlier. He didn't stop there though, and they continued upwards, turning another corner in the stairwell before arriving at a closed door. Grave used one of the keys he had pulled out earlier to unlock the door and open it.

The door led out onto the roof. It was a nondescript concrete roof, bordered by brick edges rising to waist height. Around them loomed tall skyscrapers, dwarfing the three-level building. The only thing of note on the roof was a trio of the black panels, fixed up on wooden brackets and facing the northern sky, or more specifically, a gap between buildings on the northern skyline. Grave gestured towards the panels.

'You might recognise these …'

'Yep, they're solar panels.' Silver pulled her hand free of his and moved over to the panels, her interest piqued. She ran her hand over the edge of one of them. 'Do they really work?'

When Grave didn't respond immediately, she looked over to him where he still stood by the door, mouth agape and looking shocked. 'You know what they are? How?' he asked incredulously.

'I read. So do they really work?'

'Yes.' Grave answered after looking skyward for a moment. 'Yes, I got them working. They generate enough power to provide light and water heating for the whole building, assuming I go easy on my usage. Inside the Dome is not the ideal place to be generating electricity from the sun.'

'They really generate electricity, just from the sun?'

'Yes, they do. This is no game I'm playing here, not some hobby to pass the time. These panels have the ability to be a game changer for life in the Dome.'

'And you're saying those who came before us knew about these? They had the technology to create power out of nothing?'

Grave nodded. 'Not nothing. The sun. But yes, I believe solar panels were relatively common.'

'So how did we get here? What happened?'

'Greed is what happened,' Grave responded. 'Greed and short-sightedness. Come, let's head back downstairs and I'll tell you what I know.'

He ushered Silver through the doorway, pulled it closed and locked it behind them. 'You see, from the discovery of electricity, human kind's usage of it grew exponentially. Fossil fuels were originally used to generate electricity, and as the demand for it grew, so too did the mining industry. These mining companies invested heavily but also became increasingly wealthy.

'As time went on and more and more coal and oil was required to keep up with demand, pollution started to become a problem. The power stations spewed out vast quantities of carbon into the air while motor vehicles vomited petrol fumes. Refill?' They had reached the living room, and Grave paused while he gathered his and Silver's empty glasses and moved into the kitchen to refresh them.

'It was around this time that our forebears started to get some understanding on the impact of all this pollution, with scientists coining the term "global warming", then moving to a more apt description of "climate change". Along with environmental impact there were very real health effects. With this understanding, the world started to take some greater interest in alternate energies, among them wind and solar power.'

'Wait, so you can also create energy from the wind?' Silver asked, bewildered.

'Yep, that's right, and from water. Humans have been using windmills and watermills for many, many years to help pump water or assist with processing. Technologies were developed to harness power from this and convert it into electricity.'

'So with all these other options, why did the world continue with fossil fuels?'

Grave paused to take a sip of his drink. 'Scale was part of it—the mining industry had built up over decades to cater for the volume of energy the world required, a demand that continued to grow. Alternate energies could not hope to produce the volume covered by fossil fuels, short term. But the main factor was the efforts of the mining companies to limit the growth of alternate energies.

'You see, by this time the mining companies were exceedingly profitable, with billions of dollars invested in them. Their owners and shareholders wanted to protect that, and they saw alternate energy sources as a major threat to them. They formed consortiums and industry bodies to tackle the problem and employed different tactics to thwart the growth of solar power and other industries. They produced experts to throw doubt on the validity of climate change science. They spent millions of dollars on media campaigns on mining, some feel-good, but many using scare tactics to indicate the negative impact on the economy and jobs that any change to the mining industry would do, or threaten on the significant rise of energy. Their campaigns toppled governments and halted legislation aimed to tax or regulate their industry.

'They employed more underhanded tactics as well: hiring top legal firms to threaten and intimidate those who would question them with legal action. They courted politicians, offering them god-knows-what to push their agendas and mining-friendly legislation through parliament. Eventually they started buying up shares in media companies themselves, or seeking roles in government. There are suggestions that at times they went even beyond these methods.

'All the while the impact on the environment continued to heighten. Increased seismic activity interfered with mining operations and caused demand to outweigh supply. This led to chaos, as nations scrambled to try to secure their energy sources, while reeling from natural disaster after natural disaster. Eventually it led to war.' Grave took another sip of his drink. His tone was sombre. 'War added to the chaos of climate change and society fell apart. There might be other outposts like ours, or we could be the only ones left.'

Silver sat in horrified silence as Grave finished his story. 'So we had the chance to avoid this and we didn't take it?' she asked eventually.

'Yes.'

'So why don't we know about it? How is it that no one except you knows what the panels do? They're rare, but I've seen them out in the Badlands before.'

'I'm not the only one—Silmac most definitely knows about them. There was a deliberate effort by the late Silmac Senior to destroy all evidence of them. Books were hunted down and destroyed, and soldiers were sent searching for panels in the Badlands. Without knowledge of what they are or what they do, they just become another nameless technology that the human race has lost.'

'So even after all that's happened, the Silmacs continue to try to suppress them?'

'Yes,' Grave answered, moving forward in his chair. 'Their family's wealth was built on the back of fossil fuel, and it is their monopoly over the Dome's power source that keeps them in power. They fear that knowledge of the panels will be their undoing.'

Silver shook her head, wanting to deny it, to fall back to the more commonly held belief that the events that led to the building of the Dome and the destruction of the city had been unavoidable, an act of nature and war. But Grave's description matched what she had read in the diary, making denial almost impossible.

'So the panels you have upstairs, Silmac doesn't know about them?'

'That's right. I would be dead if he knew, and all evidence would be disposed of. The energy I use in this apartment comes from it. These panels are used to charge battery cells, which I take to the clubhouse and use to power it. As far as he is concerned, the clubhouse has no power. He suspects someone is hunting solar panels though. He is looking for me.'

'All this is great, Grave, but what do you hope to achieve with this technology? Powering one building is hardly going to help the common person or challenge Silmac's power.'

The remark had a deflating effect on Grave, and his expression took on a wounded look, halfway between anger and hurt.

'It's a start,' he answered defensively. 'That's why I founded the Ash Walkers—to find other such panels so that I might increase the operation. And if we can get the panels in a more optimum position, then that will also help. We can clear a spot outside the Dome, hidden among the debris. The power generated out there in full sun would far exceed what I am currently producing.'

'Silmac is not about to let this happen under his nose. How do you propose to keep it from him?'

'I only have to keep it from him until I have a decent base of panels. Then, I'll print and distribute a newspaper to the entire Dome, so that knowledge of the panels becomes widespread. It'll include instructions on how to go about wiring up the panels. If people know of them and we can demonstrate they work, that will go a fair way to breaking Silmac's stranglehold. At least, that's the hope. It's not perfect, I know, but we have to try something.'

Silver studied Grave's face intently while he spoke. 'And you don't mean to charge for it? Assuming it all works and Silmac is thrown down? Do you intend to take his place?'

'What? No! I hate this—the way we live in fear, the decay of a once beautiful city, the mutes, the Homeless. I hate the dead bodies I walk past on the street, the starving orphans who have lost their parents in the Badlands,' he paused and pointed at Silver, 'the women with bruised cheeks who have had to fight for their bodies and lives. This is a chance to salvage something, to break our reliance on fossil fuels once and for all, and give the planet and the human race the opportunity to heal. We will only achieve that working together, not replacing one tyrant for another! Is that what you think? That I'm doing this for power?'

Silver smiled and shook her head. 'No, that's not what I think, but I had to be sure. I don't think your plan will work though. Silmac knows something is up. If he wasn't certain before, the panels we left in the checkpoint will have him clued in. It's a small miracle he hasn't found us already. To effectively break his hold we need to move quickly, and we need lots of panels—way more than we have to provide for the entire city.'

'I'll make it work!' Grave snapped, his voice rising for a moment, before softening. 'We'll hide, lie low for a while, start again. I have to make it work. There's no other way.'

'There is,' countered Silver. 'I know of another way.'

# CHAPTER 17

*From the diary of Benjamin Adams*
*September 17<sup>th</sup>, 2013*

*I'm actually feeling scared at the moment. Scared for the boys and scared for our new baby. Jess is pregnant and due in January, which is exciting. But the latest election was just won with the key promise to strip out all the environmental legislation that has been put through over the last six to seven years. And they won comprehensively. We'll come to our senses soon, but I just hope it's before irreparable damage has been done.*

*We're having the family over for Alex's birthday tomorrow. He's getting big and starts school next year, which he's ready for. The weather's meant to be good, so it should be a nice day.*

* * * * *

'What? How?' Grave asked, incredulous.

Silver rose from the lounge, moved over to her pack and drew from it the diary of Benjamin Adams. She held it out to him.

'That's the book you were reading earlier,' Grave noted curiously. 'What is it?'

'It's a diary I found out in the Badlands. I just finished reading it. I think you should take a look.'

Grave took the bound book and studied it, running his hand over the cover. He opened to the first page and scanned the text there.

'Benjamin Adams? Wasn't he the architect and project leader for the construction of the Dome?'

'That's what the diary suggests.'

'Is this genuine?'

Silver shrugged. 'Read and then you tell me. I certainly hope so. Can

I go and get cleaned in the meantime?'

Grave had already lowered himself into one of the armchairs, becoming quickly absorbed in the book. At her request he started to rise, but she motioned for him to stay. 'I can find my way. Just tell me where I can get a towel.'

'The cupboard in the hall has towels and washers. Try the wardrobe in my room for clothes if you need.'

Silver made her way down the hall, grabbed a towel and went into the bathroom. It was luxurious compared to any she had been in, with clean white tiles, a spacious shower cubicle and a clean white vanity. There was even a bar of scented soap in the shower, which she had never before had the chance to use.

She stripped out of her clothes and turned on the tap, moving under the spray when it turned warm. She winced in pain initially as the water stung her numerous cuts and scrapes. But after a few moments the pain eased and, feeling more relaxed than she had in a long time, she enjoyed the warm caress of the water, and the subtle vanilla scent of the soap. She washed every inch of her skin with it, feeling cleaner than she ever had before.

When she had finished washing, she reached towards the taps, but hesitated for a couple of minutes before eventually sighing and turning them off. She was tempted to stay in longer, but guilt got the better of her.

She towelled herself off, again enjoying the feel of the clean, fresh linen. Wiping the condensation away from the mirror, she looked at herself critically. Her right cheek was swollen, her lip slightly split, but she looked better with the grime washed away. Her hair was a mess, so she hunted in the cupboard under the vanity for something to tame it. Finding a comb, she spent the next fifteen minutes working the knots out of her hair. Once straight, she turned to her clothes, searching through her pack for something flattering to wear. Her lack of choice was depressing, and there was nothing in there that was clean and fresh.

Reluctant to get back into dirty clothes, she decided to take Grave up on his offer, though was dubious about what he would have that would fit her. Wrapping the towel around herself, she ventured back out into the hall. Looking up into the sitting room, she could see that Grave was still absorbed in the diary.

Heading into Grave's bedroom, she found a large, comfortable bed made up with beige coloured sheets and spread. An antique wooden side-table sat on the right side of the bed, a small reading lamp on top. More artworks graced the wall of the room, paintings of buildings in cities that Silver didn't recognise. A built-in wardrobe with glass sliding doors filled the entire wall opposite the bed. Sliding back one of the doors, she found it to be surprisingly full, with a fair selection of clothes from casual T-shirts and shorts, to work overalls and formal suits. They were all men's clothes and a little large for her. Eventually she selected a long blue striped button-up shirt, pulling it on and rolling up the sleeves.

Returning to the bathroom, she hung the wet towel on one of the racks before venturing back out into the sitting room. Grave had not moved from his chair and was engrossed in the diary laid on his lap. As she watched he turned the page, and she noted he was already close to halfway through.

Not wanting to disturb him, she moved on towards the kitchen, her stomach rumbling as it had been some time since she had last eaten. She stopped short upon entering the kitchen, her mouth agape at the sight before her. It was a stainless steel kitchen, with metal benches, a large metal oven, a metallic frame hanging from the ceiling with hooks for cooking implements to hang from. Had the kitchen been paved in gold it would not have elicited a more shocked response from her. The metal in this kitchen would be worth a small fortune. The fact that Grave owned this and hadn't chosen to sell off the metal confirmed, for now at least, that he had money to burn. She shook her head in amazement.

Another grumble from her stomach reminded her of her original purpose, and she began hunting for food. After checking a few cupboards and finding only pots, pans and plates, she found the pantry and her eyes were immediately drawn to a half-eaten loaf of fresh bread. Her mouth salivated at the sight; the loaf of bread was like a rare pearl when put next to her usual fare of manufactured gruel.

She grabbed the loaf, found a couple of plates and a knife to cut it into slices and spread them evenly across the two plates. Unable to resist any longer, she took a large bite from one of the slices, savouring the crunch of the crust and the fluffy texture of the centre. She took another large bite while she grabbed a couple of glasses and filled them with water. As she chewed on the bread, she balanced the cups on the edge of the plates and carried them out to the sitting room. She laid one down on the coffee table in front of Grave before taking her own to the chair opposite his and curling up with it. Grave remained absorbed in the diary, but she didn't care as she returned her attention to the bread. It didn't take her long to finish off the first slice and proceed to demolish the other two. She drank the glass of water in two gulps and then looked longingly over at the untouched bread on Grave's plate.

Grave glanced up at her. 'This account is incredible,' he said.

Silver pulled her eyes away from the bread and glanced at the book, noting he was three quarters of the way through.

'Not as incredible as the end,' she answered, her eyes drawn back to the bread. 'Are you going to eat that?'

Grave looked at the bread, grabbed one of the slices before pushing the plate, still laden with two generous slices, across the table in Silver's direction.

'Thanks,' he said as he took a bit of the bread himself. 'Better keep on reading then. Are you going to be okay while I finish this off?'

'I'm sure I'll manage.'

Grave returned his attention to the book, only occasionally remembering he held a piece of bread in his hand and absently taking a bite. Silver pulled the other two slices of bread towards her and tucked in.

* * * * *

Silver drifted along gently. She was out in the Badlands, but her passage was smooth, unhindered as she floated a metre above the rubble and debris. The wind howled around her, and she could see rain and ice—a terrible winter storm. But the cold and wet did not touch her, for she was protected inside a translucent cocoon that kept it all at bay.

She floated into a clearing among the rubble and there stood the elderly mute who had given her the diary. He was not protected by the same force that surrounded her, and his skin was turning blue from cold. Silver reached out to him, but he shook his head sadly, raising a hand in farewell. He turned and walked away into the rubble, disappearing into the rain. Silver tried to follow, but the cocoon was now like a prison, holding her within and refusing to follow the mute.

*Silver*, a voice called out to her, but she could not detect its source.

*Silver!* the voice came again, a little louder and edged with excitement. She felt a hand brush gently across her cheek.

'Silver!'

She sat bolt upright, forcing Grave to jerk backwards to avoid a head clash. He overbalanced and sat heavily on the coffee table behind him. She was curled up in the armchair, breadcrumbs covering her lap.

'Sorry, I didn't realise I had drifted off.'

'It's me who should apologise. I should have let you sleep.'

Silver shook her head and looked properly at Grave, noticing the diary in his hand. 'You've finished it?'

He nodded, an excited smile at the corners of his mouth.

'What it says about the Dome, could it be true?'

He nodded again, his smile growing. 'I think so.'

'So there's hope?'

'There's always hope, Silver. Without it we are truly doomed. But this,' he held up the diary, 'this gives us more than hope. It gives us a fighting chance to break Silmac's power once and for all. Where did you come across it?'

'A mute gave it to me, on the night I spent out on the Badlands.'

Grave raised his eyebrow in question, so Silver continued.

'I saved him from a couple of other mutes who were attacking him. In return he led me to his home and saved me from the storm that hit that night. It was surreal—a basement full of relics collected from the ruins—books, toys and all sorts of items. It would have been worth a fortune. And he had power—the lights in his basement worked perfectly.'

Grave shook his head at the story. 'Amazing, truly amazing.'

'Grave, you said something earlier about what we did to the mutes. They were human once, weren't they?'

He nodded. 'No different from you or I. They're what are left of the people not afforded a place in the Dome.'

Silver had to choke back her grief as her suspicions were confirmed. 'How did it happen?' she managed to ask.

'What is written in the diary pretty much confirms what I know of it,' Grave admitted. 'The Dome could never have housed the whole population of the city. There were plans to build other structures, but the government secretly delayed and abandoned them long before this one was complete. There were millions in Sydney who were not allowed a place, and millions more around Australia. They were deceived and abandoned, and many more killed as they tried to get in. It was all well planned and executed by the prime minister at the time—another Silmac. The design of the Dome was to keep undesirables out—weather, pollution and tidal waves—but it proved equally effective against humans.

'It was justified to those within as a necessary evil for the survival of the human race. As time went on, a new story was spun. The people left outside changed so drastically, from the effects of the increasingly caustic weather and from their return to savagery. It was easy to paint them as inhuman monsters, to eradicate any memory of wrongdoing against them.'

Tears were streaming down Silver's face by this time. 'I've killed them, Grave. I've murdered them and thought ill of them all my life. Really it is we who are the monsters.'

Grave leant forward and enfolded her in a hug. 'You weren't responsible for their betrayal, Silver. No one alive today is. And you have only acted to protect yourself against them. They are different to us today. Time and the environment has changed them, irreparably perhaps. But it is another reason why I am so determined to do something. Silmac remains in power, and the type of regime that abandoned the mutes into the Badlands continues to rule the Dome. It has to end. We are not responsible for the past, but we are for our actions here in the present.'

Grave released her from his hold and Silver could see the intensity in his eyes as he locked gazes with her. It filled her with courage and resolve.

'You're right, we have to do something.' She took up the diary and held it between them. 'Like you said, this gives us a fighting chance, but it doesn't guarantee success. We've got a lot of work to do.'

# Chapter 18



*From the diary of Benjamin Adams*
*December 1ˢᵗ, 2013*

*A project I've just completed has been nominated for a National Architecture Award, in the sustainability field! I'm pretty excited by it, because at last I've had the opportunity to work on something that might make a difference. I'm still a little annoyed though, as many of the really ground-breaking ideas I had for it got vetoed by the builder, based on cost. I tried to explain that he would make the money back in the mid-term but my arguments fell on deaf ears.*

*The boys are getting ever bigger. Alex had his preschool graduation last night, and Jayden is seven and finishing year one. His asthma remains a worry; we had a pretty rough winter again with constant breathing issues and night-time coughing, which takes its toll on Jess and I. Jess is getting big and very uncomfortable in the heat of summer. Not long left to go at least.*

* * * * *

Silver awoke to a wonderful aroma. Grave's bed was comfortable and luxurious, and while she had insisted that it wasn't necessary, she was glad that he had been adamant she use it. He had slept on the lounge.

She rolled over and found Grave entering the room, holding a steaming mug of something, the source of the aroma.

'I made you some coffee,' he said, smiling. He rounded the bed and brought it to her, as she sat up to take the offered cup. 'It's expensive to buy, but worth it. Careful, it's hot.'

She breathed in the smell of the coffee and then took a cautious sip. The taste was bitter, but good, and the warmth of the drink soothing. 'Thanks.'

'So last night I told you my real name,' Grave said casually, moving about the room, grabbing some clothes from his wardrobe and drawers. 'What's your given name? Where does "Silver" come from?'

Silver hesitated in answering the question. Very few people knew her real name. It was one of the few things she owned and had been reluctant to give it away.

'Forget about it,' Grave said quickly. 'A name is private. I shouldn't have asked.'

'No, it's okay,' Silver replied. 'You were honest and open with me last night, and if we are going to work together we need to be able to trust each other. The name my parents gave me is Silvana. Silvana O'Lachlan.'

'Silvana is nice. From the forest.'

'What?'

'The meaning of your name. Silvana means "from the forest", I think.'

'Really? How do you know that?'

'I had a book of names and meanings as a child. Silvana stuck because of its meaning. Forests fascinate me, a large part because I've never seen a real one and would love to experience it.'

Silver raised an eyebrow, reflecting on the name while she took another sip of coffee. 'I like the meaning, though I'm not sure if it was the most appropriate choice by my parents. Clearly I'm not "of the forest".'

'Maybe it is not literal but symbolic, like where your soul is from.'

Silver nodded thoughtfully, the hint of a smile on her face. 'So how did you come up with Grave for your street name?'

Grave gave a sheepish smile. 'I guess I thought it sounded cool and would fit in. I needed a name that would not arouse suspicion. Why do salvagers take on street names anyway?'

'Not sure really.' Silver shrugged. 'It's part of the persona you take on to survive out in the Badlands, I guess. You deal with some pretty messed up shit out there, something "Silver" can deal with so "Silvana" doesn't have to. It's also got something to do with protecting your family. Some salvagers come from a different breed, and you want to keep them right away from your family. I heard of a guy who was killed out in the Badlands not long ago, and his crew decided to take their sport with his wife and daughter before selling them to a brothel owner for a little extra cash. Other families get targeted for revenge attacks or over turf disputes. Keeping your name secret helps protect those close to you.'

Grave had stopped and was looking at her, horrified. 'Is that why you don't see children on the street much?'

'Yep. Anyone with half a brain knows to keep their kids out of sight and hidden as long as possible. They have a habit of going missing.'

Grave's look of horror deepened. 'I kind of knew this type of stuff happened, but not the regularity or brutality of it. It must have been tough for you growing up.'

She shrugged and refused to meet his eye. 'Tougher than some, easier than others. So have you had any more thoughts how we are going to get past Silmac's men?'

A clean shirt in hand, Grave's expression changed from sympathetic to stern. 'I was thinking about it last night. There's no "we". I do this alone.'

Silver's brow furrowed in anger and she put the mug down on the bedside table. 'Don't you dare try that one. I brought you the book and I'm just as capable as you. More so given that still-healing bullet wound. It's in both our interests to get this done. Besides, you're going to need help.'

Grave opened his mouth to protest, but Silver held his gaze unflinchingly and he closed it again without voicing his thoughts. He didn't look happy though.

'You're right,' he conceded eventually. 'It's not my place to keep you from this task. Probably couldn't even if I tried.'

'Damn right. We forest folk are a stubborn bunch,' Silver said with a smile, getting out of bed and reaching for her overalls. 'We should tell the crew as well.'

'No, I have to draw the line at them. We're taking on Silmac, which means our chances are slim at best. I can't ask them to join us in this!'

'They deserve the right to know, to choose. An opportunity to break Silmac's hold on the Dome affects everyone who lives within it. Like you said—our chances are slim at best, but they get a little better with each person willing to help out.'

Grave considered Silver's words carefully, before eventually nodding in agreement. 'Okay, okay. But there needs to be no pressure to join us. I've already endangered them more than I should have. They need to be given a chance to opt out.'

* * * * *

'Where have you been, Grave? We feared the worse,' Asp scolded as Grave entered the clubhouse. But when she saw Silver behind him her eyes widened and she moved forward to engulf her in a hug.

Silver was taken aback by the embrace and took a moment to return it. 'What was that for?'

'I thought you had taken off,' Asp explained. 'All your stuff was gone, and when we gleaned the truth out of Muzzle, I thought you had left us for good. Are you okay?'

Silver nodded, touched by Asp's concern for her.

'Where's Muzzle?' Grave asked as they moved into the clubhouse, his voice low and threatening.

'He's gone,' Asp explained. 'He was acting weird all day and when we got back from the wave and found you gone, we confronted him. Things got pretty heated, and he did the runner.'

'Okay, we need to get out on the streets to find him,' Grave started, his face dark again. 'I won't stand for what he tried.'

'Let it go, Grave,' Silver interjected, grabbing his arm before he could leave. 'We've got more urgent things to focus on.'

Grave's face remained dark, and he stood there in silence a little longer. Eventually he nodded and turned to the crew, who by this time had gathered down in the common room.

'It's time I filled you in on a few details. Take a seat. Silver, can you grab the rum? We might need it.'

* * * * *

'Count me in!' Sarge exclaimed, beaming as Grave finished telling them about who he was, and what they had planned. It was the most animated Silver had seen him in the short time she had known him. 'I owe Silmac some payback, and I'm not getting any younger.'

Rat was a little more reserved, merely shrugging. 'As long as I get to blow up stuff, I'm in. All the better if that includes Silmac.'

The concern on Asp's face told a different story. 'I can't, Grave. I want to help, but if we don't succeed, my involvement could lead back to the shop and my parents. I can't risk that. I won't put them in danger. I'm sorry.'

It was Silver's turn to step forward and offer Asp a hug. 'You are making the right decision, Asp. For us, the risk is only to ourselves, but for you it extends to your family and they have to come first.'

'Silver is right. There's no need to apologise Asp. Blocka, I guess that rules you out as well?'

Blocka looked just as torn as Asp had. 'My place is with Asp. Otherwise, I'd be right there with you, Boss.'

Grave nodded and reached into his pocket, pulling out a generous wad of cash. He held it out to Asp and Blocka. 'This should keep you going for a while, in case we don't make it.'

'It's too much!' Asp exclaimed. 'That's more than a year's wages you're holding there!'

'Take it, please. You've been loyal friends and I thank you for it.'

Reluctantly, Asp took the money and then wrapped Grave up in a fierce hug. When she finally released him, Blocka stepped up and extended his hand.

'Take care of her, and yourself,' Grave said, shaking the big man's hand. 'I have never felt safer than with you standing at my side.'

Blocka nodded his understanding and thanks.

'The sooner we get out of here, the better,' Grave said, turning to the others. 'Grab anything you need and we'll get moving.'

It took less than five minutes for everyone to pack their belongings and assemble downstairs. Goodbyes followed, with Asp saving Silver till last.

'Take care of yourself, Silver,' Asp whispered fiercely in her ear. 'Give Silmac hell.'

'I will,' was all Silver could manage in reply, finding herself too choked up for further words. When they finally pulled out of their embrace, Silver fished into her pack and pulled out the diary of Benjamin Adams. She handed it to Asp. 'Please, take this and hide it, keep it safe. If we don't make it, it can't fall into Silmac's hands.'

Asp nodded, taking the book and carefully stowing it in her own pack. Without further words, Asp and Blocka left the clubhouse, packs on their back. Rat and Sarge waited a few minutes before leaving. Silver and Grave, who had left all their stuff back at the unit, left last, locking the door of the clubhouse for perhaps the last time.

* * * * *

Muzzle lurked in a shadowy doorway as he watched Grave unlock the door on York Street and usher Sarge, Rat and Silver inside. His brow furrowed as he noticed Grave's hand briefly rest on Silver's back as she filed past him. Grave was the last in, shutting the door behind them and leaving the street empty.

From his position almost a block away, Muzzle ground his teeth and clenched his fists in agitation. After a moment, he left his hiding spot and started down the street towards the door his former crew mates had disappeared through. Crossing Market Street, he strode past the unmarked door, eyeing it suspiciously but not stopping.

He walked briskly around the next corner to ensure he was out of sight before he stopped and punched out at the crumbling brick wall. His hand came away bloody, but he barely noticed it. He closed his eyes and rubbed at his temples.

With a dangerous look in his eye, he returned to York and strode back the way he had come, toward the unit door. He stopped outside it, raising his hand to knock, but then paused. For a moment his hand moved to his gun, but again he stopped short of pulling it out. Eventually he pushed off, walking away from the unit.

Ten minutes later, he was back in Surry Hills outside the clubhouse. He had been there half an hour earlier, watching Grave lock it up. He had spent the night out on the streets and had returned home to beg forgiveness, only to see Asp and Blocka leaving the house, their gear in hand. He had jumped behind cover and watched as Rat and Sarge followed suit, and finally Grave and Silver had left together.

He had followed them at a safe distance, and they had taken a roundabout route, eventually meeting up with Sarge and Rat and heading to the unit in the wealthy section of the city.

Using his key to enter the clubhouse, he moved through the building, slowly at first but with growing urgency. Sarge's room was left orderly and tidy as usual, but the few personal effects he'd had were gone. Rat's basement was its usual mess, and some jars remained, but fewer than before. The same was true of the whole house, each room missing any personal effects, each wardrobe devoid of clothes.

Ending in Grave's room and finding another empty wardrobe he slammed the door roughly, causing it to crash closed and bounce open again, hanging slightly wonky on its hinges. He kicked at the door and his foot went through the thin wood, splintering it. He nearly tripped trying to tug his foot free and that sent him into a frenzy: punching, kicking and tearing at the door until at last it came off its hinges. He grabbed it and threw it across the room, where it crashed against the wall and fell to the ground in a heap of shattered wood.

Breathing heavily, Muzzle sat on the bed and lay back, staring up at the ceiling. He had not been there long when a crash from downstairs caused him to jerk upright once again. The crash was followed by voices, too muffled to make out words but clearly more than one. He rushed over to the door and peered out into the hall beyond. It was clear for the moment, but he could hear heavy footsteps moving about downstairs. Moving quietly but quickly, he slipped out of his room and made his way down the hall and into the bathroom. Below, he could hear footsteps ascending the stairway.

He ran his hands over the bathroom wall in a panic, searching for the tile that would spring open the concealed door beyond. Out in the hall the footsteps drew nearer.

'Where is it, Grave?' Muzzle whispered, his hands roving the wall in a panic. Grave had built the room, walling off what had once been a small toilet cavity and using tiles from the toilet area to cover over the doorway and conceal it. At last, Muzzle located the tile and pressed it, opening up the door. It was not a huge area, only enough for five or six people in a pinch, but ample room for Muzzle. He slipped inside and gently pulled the door closed, easing it back into position.

Listening intently, he made out the sounds of people moving down the hall and checking over the adjacent rooms. At least one person entered the bathroom area, but was gone in a few seconds, their footfalls moving on. After a few minutes, whoever was out there appeared to have finished their search and the footsteps receded back down the stairs.

Muzzle leant back against the wall and breathed a sigh of relief. He could still hear the muffled sounds of movement below, as well as voices. He lay down on the ground, trying to hear what was being said but could not make out the words. Climbing back to his feet, he hesitantly reached for the door, easing it open and moving lightly over to the bathroom door. The hall beyond was clear, so he slipped out of the room and edged down towards the stairs until he was close enough to make out the words.

'… place is empty. Looks like they've packed up and gone.'

'Not a chance. They've left too much good stuff behind. Besides, this place is in pretty good nick—why would they leave it?'

'Because they knew we'd be coming for them, idiot. Ain't that right, Coal?'

'Shut the fuck up, all of you. I don't give a fuck where they've gone or what they're doing. I want that slut found so I can fuck her up!'

A slow grin spread across Muzzle's face as he realised who it was and what they wanted. Straightening, he started down the stairs, keeping his hands wide and visible. In the living area below he found a group of eight assembled. He recognised a few of them from the day they had arrived at the clubhouse looking for Silver. It took him a moment to recognise their leader, Coal, whose right arm was supported by a splint and whose face had dark, purple-black bruising under both eyes and a nose swollen to twice its normal size.

Halfway down the stairs the group noticed his presence and seven guns were quickly levelled in his direction. He held his arms out further, making sure his empty hands were fully visible. A grin remained fixed on his face.

'I couldn't help but overhear your problem. I think I may be in a position to help you out.'

# CHAPTER 19

*From the diary of Benjamin Adams*
*July 19th, 2014*

*I've forgotten what a good night of sleep feels like. We had our third baby, Chloe, in January and she is beautiful and healthy but not sleeping well. It's the hardest part of having kids; dealing with the lack of sleep in those first six months. We are over the worst of it now, I think, but still getting one or two rough nights a week.*

*The boys have been great with a new baby in the house. They help Jess out during the week and love their little sister. Work remains challenging, which is good, and I am running another big, multi-storey project, which will take a lot of time and work over the next couple of years.*

* * * * *

'I know you said you were well off, but I didn't know you meant *this* well off!'

Upon entering Grave's apartment, Rat had spent the first ten minutes in stunned exploration of the riches it held. When shown around the workshop upstairs, his excitement had grown considerably at the resources available.

'I guess this explains the electricity, hot water and plentiful if bland food at the clubhouse. I thought you had been a fool, wasting money on us that way, but turns out we were the fools and you were holding out on us the whole time!'

Grave looked a little embarrassed. 'You understand that what I'm working on here would get me killed if the wrong people found out. If I had splashed out too much at the clubhouse, people would have started asking questions.'

'No need to apologise,' Rat replied with a grin. 'I wouldn't have trusted me either. Had I known about all this I might have ratted you out a long time ago!'

Sarge had taken it all in more stoically, mildly interested in the kitchen, but clearly impatient to get started on what they had come here for. It was clear to Silver that his motive was revenge.

Eventually, they coaxed Rat back downstairs and settled down on the lounges to discuss their next course of action.

'So let me get this straight,' Rat started. 'The Dome is actually one big solar thingy, capable of producing electricity from the sun? And the switch to turn it on is inside Silmac Tower?'

'Not quite,' Silver answered. 'The diary says the switch that will activate the solar panels is in the spire of Silmac Tower, so actually outside the tower and the Dome. It was put there to keep it hidden from the mining magnates in control at the time.'

'Forget the switch. How'd this Benjamin chap manage to build a solar panel the size of … well, that big, right under their noses?'

'He was the expert architect,' Grave took over. 'The framework and bottom layers of the Dome are purely functional, designed for the job they were intended, to keep us protected against pollution and the elements. The top layer is made from the panels, which he passed off as a layer to prevent against an excessive build-up of ice in the event of severe and sustained cold weather. Such a build-up could easily compromise the Dome by adding massive amounts of weight to the structure. By running a current under the top layer of the Dome he was able to insure against any such occurrence. What he hid from the magnates was that the final glass layer was also built from solar panels, and the same wires that could bring electricity to the surface of the Dome could be used to draw electricity away. If it proves to be true, it would make him a genius, truly remarkable.'

'So what happened to him?' Sarge asked this time. 'Why are we not all enjoying free sun-generated power already?'

'He never got the chance to reveal his secret, because of Silmac. Not the current one, but one of his ancestors, a great, great grandmother I think. She was prime minister of the country at the time and led a coup against her own people. The Dome was meant to be the first of many, built to protect the population of all Australians. But she cut a deal with the army and took it by force upon its completion, surprising everyone. The remaining Dome projects were abandoned, as was the vast majority of the population who were not offered a spot within.

'Benjamin Adams and the few colleagues who knew the secret of the Dome were among those not granted entry. The population attacked the Dome, trying to force their way in, but Great Grandma Silmac and the military were ready and used force to repel them. Everything turned into chaos from there. Millions died, and those who survived became animals, the mutes we know today.'

Though Silver already knew the story, she was left sickened again. She had cried the first time she read it, tears of sympathy for the thousands of people left outside the Dome, who had degenerated into the mutes they knew today. Sarge's frown had deepened, no doubt his already low regard for Silmac falling further.

'So, how do we go about taking this bastard down?' Rat asked eventually. 'It's not like we can just walk into Silmac Tower, grab a lift up to the top floor, have a quick drink with Silmac and then flip the switch. What's the plan?'

Grave looked at Silver. 'Actually, that's exactly what I've been thinking we should do. Silmac's office is on the top floor of the Silmac Tower, and there is an access point from there to the roof above. He has been known to take visitors in his office from time to time, and my status may be able to get me an audience. If we position the meeting as a chance to introduce Silmac to my new fiancée, I can probably get Silver in as well.' As he spoke, he reached into one of his pockets and pulled out a beautiful diamond studded platinum ring. It was delicate and intricate, with three interweaving bands, each inset with a row of diamonds.

It took Silver a second to realise what was happening, and when she did, she could feel the heat rising instantly to her cheeks. Grave got down on one knee in front of her, and she could feel the weight of all sets of eyes on her.

'How about it, Silver? Will you agree to marry me?'

'Married?' Silver croaked, choking in surprise. 'No one gets married these days!'

'It's still custom among the wealthy to offer a ring, have an engagement period and then a marriage ceremony. As head of state, it would

be normal to announce the engagement to Silmac, to seek his blessing.'
Grave remained on his knee, ring held towards her.

'It is a beautiful ring,' she ventured, gazing down at it. 'Is that a real
diamond?'

'It's my mother's ring,' Grave said softly. 'It's real.'

'Well in that case I definitely can't take it! What if I lose it?'

'I want you to have it, Silver. Besides, it won't be convincing if I give
you a shoddy, plain ring.'

'You're right. Well, I do, I guess.' She took the ring reverently and fit
it onto her left ring finger. It was a surprisingly good fit. 'Thank you.'

'Hate to interrupt this touching moment,' Rat spoke up, 'but where
does that leave us? Do you have another ring for me? You promised I'd
be able to blow things up!'

'And how do you plan to get past Meek?' Sarge added, his voice
gruff. 'No offence, but if I had to wager on an outcome of a fight with
him involved, I'd put my money on him.'

'That's where you both come in. We'll need a distraction, something
away from Silmac Tower, and enough of a security threat to draw Meek
away, but not serious enough to threaten Silmac. Maybe a feigned hit
on one of the greenhouses or something, which can easily be passed off
as hungry people trying to get some fresh food. Can you do it?'

'That we can do!' Rat answered enthusiastically, and Sarge nodded
his assent.

'Just make sure you don't linger. I'd bet on Meek too, and I don't want
him catching up with you.'

'Don't worry, I have no intention of taking on Meek,' Rat assured
Grave. 'Even Blocka would have a tough time against him. Time to
make some bombs—can I use your workshop upstairs?' Grave nodded
and Rat grabbed an old shabby sports bag he had brought with him and
started eagerly upstairs.

'So that's it?' Sarge asked.

'Essentially,' Grave answered. 'If we can get upstairs without Meek
present, together we should be able to overpower Silmac and gain
access to the roof above.'

'But how do you plan on getting out? And what's to stop Silmac just
having the power switched back off?'

'Sarge is right,' Silver said. 'We need some way to get word out about it, so that regardless of what happens to us, Silmac's monopoly can be broken.'

'I had always planned to publish information about the panels to distribute around the Dome. I've got the material pretty much ready to go. We'd need to sneak in to the old printing press, but that shouldn't be a problem, as I'm still technically employed there. The printing machines sit idle most of the time, with Silmac only using them occasionally since buying Dad out. If we can get in tonight, I'll be able to print out pamphlets to distribute through the streets.'

'That could work,' Sarge said. 'Not everyone reads, but there will be enough that can make sense of it to get word out. And as soon as they realise they should be getting energy for free, there will be some questions asked of old Silmac, for sure.'

'Right, so when do we get started?'

'If we get the pamphlets printed tonight, I can seek an audience with Silmac as early as tomorrow evening,' Grave reasoned. 'What about Rat?'

'We'll be back with the pamphlets before Rat even realises we're gone,' said Sarge. 'You know how he gets when he's in his workshop—he can go for hours without noticing anything around him. I'm sure he'll be fine here.'

'That's settled then,' said Silver, standing. 'Let's get moving.'

* * * * *

'Why don't we just break in there, Boss?' Slip asked, his toe tapping impatiently.

Coal ignored the question as it was not the first time it had been asked. He was starting to think the same thing, impatient with waiting and watching. Back at the abandoned clubhouse, he had allowed Muzzle to speak, and then followed the turn-cloak to York Street, where they had been watching a doorway for the past two hours. Coal was not a patient man, and the little he had was starting to wear thin. Only the location of the building, on the edge of the wealthy sector, had his interest piqued and caused him to operate with caution.

'You better not be yanking my chain, Muz,' Coal threatened. 'Cause if you are, you'll have hell to pay.'

'She's in there,' Muzzle assured him. 'I watched her enter with the three others. If we wait, we'll see them emerge eventually.'

'Can we get some food at least?' Slip whined.

'Shut it, Slip,' Coal growled, once again wondering what had possessed him to accept the weasel into the crew. He was still angry about Lead's disappearance from the crew and Slip was a poor substitute. His long-term friend and deputy had disappeared from the club following their argument over Silver. This had incensed him even more than Silver's departure, and his rage had grown further when no one had been able to uncover even a rumour as to his whereabouts.

Adding to his agitation, he was starting to come down off his last fix. He fingered the bag of white powder hidden in his pocket absently, pulled it out and looked at it, before stuffing it back out of sight and glancing around at his crew to see if anyone had noticed. The streets were not a great place to shoot up given you didn't know who could be watching, and it was not a good idea to let junkies know you had gear.

The crew was as restless as him, leaning back against the wall and fidgeting endlessly. He hadn't brought all of them along, but made certain all present were armed and ready for a fight.

Blade, a big brute with a shaved head and heavy swelling down the left side of his face cracked his knuckles loudly. 'Fuck, I wish they'd finish whatever they are doing in there,' he muttered to Arlia, who stood next to him.

'You're just still upset by that bruise he gave you. I heard you didn't even throw a punch,' she goaded him.

'Shut it, bitch,' he growled. 'He caught us unawares and had a baton. We'll see how he fares when I'm ready for him.'

'Whatever,' Arlia responded disinterestedly, inspecting her nails critically. As always, she was dressed to accentuate her assets. She wore bright pink lipstick, drawing eyes to her ample lips, a feature she knew how to use to full effect. Her nails were alternately painted pink and black. Her eyes were highlighted with dark eyeliner and her blond hair tied up in pigtails. She wore a pair of short, tight denim shorts to further draw attention to her long shapely legs, along with a slim-fitting, pink laced top, which ensured her breasts were not forgotten. She had twin knives sheathed on each hip. An astute observer would have noticed the faint outline of straps under her top, holding a concealed sheath and small pistol in place on her back between her shoulder blades. Growing bored with her nails, she absently grabbed one of her pigtails, wrapping it and unravelling it around her fingers in endless repetition.

The fifth and sixth crew members Coal had brought along were identical twin brothers who went by the names Brew and Mack. They were both big and strong, with big guts, shaven heads, meaty arms and necks that melted into their shoulders. Their skin was darker than average, suggesting some sort of Islander blood was responsible for their size and strength. Brew was named for the homebrewed beer he made, which tasted horrible but was strong enough to get both men drunk on just a couple of bottles. Mack had a large tattoo of a truck on his right bicep, which was what Coal used to distinguish one from the other. Both had worked with Silver when she was part of the crew but had no qualms about going after her now.

'Boss, they're coming out!'

Slip's whispered warning pulled Coal's attention back to the task at hand. He roughly pulled Slip out of the way so he could peer around the corner of the building. Sure enough, the street door was open and three figures had emerged from the doorway. As he watched, they pulled the door closed and began walking down Market Street, away from the city centre, towards the Pyrmont end of the Dome.

'Is that all of them?' Arlia asked, peering past Coal as he tracked their progress.

'All but one. The little one is still inside.'

'Then what are we waiting for?' Brew asked in his slurred, meaty voice. 'Let's get after them.'

He and his brother started forward, but Coal signalled for them to stop.

'I've got a better idea.' He motioned to Slip and Blade. 'You two follow them, but remain unseen. If they start heading back, come warn us. Muzzle, you're going to take us to pay the little one a visit. Let's see what they've got hidden in there.'

* * * * *

Silver looked nervously over her shoulder again, as the printing machines continued to clack and whir, spitting out the message they had mocked up. It seemed inevitable that the noise would draw attention and bring heat down on them.

'You shouldn't worry, Silver,' Grave assured her for perhaps the seventh time. 'This place is all but abandoned, since Silmac bought it from my dad nine years ago. It's been at least eight months since it was last used, to spit out some crap propaganda about a project Silmac was financing. An upgrade to the botanic gardens, I think? The only people to benefit from it were those wealthy enough to afford the fruit and vegetables grown there, which excludes at least ninety-five per cent of the Dome's population. Silmac didn't buy this place to make use of it; he bought it to stop others printing anything that might threaten him. I'm surprised he hasn't reduced it to scrap already. Besides, Sarge is watching the joint and will warn us of any danger.'

As with the other six times, the assurance did little to calm Silver's nerves. It had been easy enough breaking into the building. Grave's key had gained them entry, and they had seen nothing in the way of security. Grave had quickly gotten the machines working, and it had all been relatively simple getting the press up and going. She had helped here and there, following Grave's directions. It all seemed too simple.

At six pages, the paper they pulled together was short, but she hoped it would be extremely damning to Silmac. The first page was dominated by the title in big bold letters:

SUN SETS ON SILMAC'S SUPREMACY:
DOME TO PROVIDE FREE ENERGY FOR ALL

The rest of the paper gave details on the solar panels covering the Dome, taken directly from Benjamin Adams's diary. Grave had also pulled together detailed diagrams on how to wire solar panels, so that even if the Dome power failed, people would have the knowledge and skills to attempt setting up their own power generators.

Regardless of whether their attempt to get inside Silmac Tower and activate the panels was successful, the paper would shed light on the fallacies Silmac maintained. Which was why Silver couldn't shake the feeling that it couldn't be this easy, that at any moment Silmac himself, accompanied by a score of armed guards, would arrive to thwart their attempt before it had even begun.

'We're done,' Grave said, interrupting her thoughts of impending doom.

'What? Really?'

'Yes, really,' Grave answered, while pulling the stack of freshly printed papers into two piles. There were not heaps of them; only a hundred copies altogether. Word of mouth would do the rest.

Silver hurried over and grabbed one of the piles, while Grave took the other before switching off the lights in the warehouse and plunging them into darkness. Momentarily deprived of sight, Silver became acutely aware of the smell of the freshly printed papers, a not unpleasant aroma.

'You smell it, don't you?' Grave asked. At Silver's nod he smiled. 'I spent a lot of time in here when I was younger, learning how a paper was created, how to fix the machines when they got jammed or broken. I always loved the smell of the place. It brings back some good memories.

Though Silver could barely see Grave, she could sense him gazing around the warehouse as if for one last look. She reached out and rested her hand gently on his back. 'We should get moving. There's plenty still to do for tomorrow.'

Grave nodded and led the way out of the warehouse, Silver following his faint outline. Outside, she could not immediately spot Sarge, and Silver's concern started to grow once more. But a couple of breaths later he emerged from of a particularly dark patch of shadows to their right.

'No sign of activity tonight. But we'll take no risks on the way back— follow me closely and keep quiet.'

Without waiting for an answer, Sarge led them back through the gate, and then ran swiftly across the street and into the shadows of the next building. Silver wasn't convinced that their stealth would actually serve to avoid attention, but she stayed close to Grave and followed suit. She found her eyes drawn to Grave whenever they paused. He was moving well despite his injury and had worked efficiently to produce the papers.

Before long they had arrived unchallenged at the door to Grave's apartment. Grave already had his key in hand and wasted little time unlocking the door and moving inside the stairwell. Sarge held the door and ushered Silver to follow. Inside, Grave paused for a second, reaching out a hand to clasp Silver's, smiling down at her. Silver grinned back in relief.

'See, we made it,' Grave said. 'Thanks to you, the Dome is about to become a better place for most, and a lot worse for a deserved few.'

'I wouldn't be so sure about that,' a voice above said.

Silver looked up in horror to see Coal move out onto the landing, manhandling Rat before him with a gun pressed to the smaller man's head. Coal's right arm was strapped in a splint, but the injury didn't prevent him from using it to push Rat around like a rag-doll.

Grave whirled around, reaching for his pistol, but stopped as Coal pressed the muzzle of his gun even harder into Rat's right temple, causing him to wince. It was clear Coal and his crew had not been gentle—Rat sported a blackened eye that was swollen completely shut, a bruised and flattened nose that was clearly broken, and a nasty gash close to his hairline. Partially dried blood covered half his face, and his left arm hung limply at his side as he shuffled awkwardly forward when Coal prodded him.

'Hand over the gun, stumpy,' another voice said from behind them.

Silver twirled to find two men on the street below, effectively putting an end to any thought of escape. She recognised one of them as Slip, and the other as the man Grave had taken down with his mace a few days earlier. Both had guns trained on Sarge, who had been in the process of pulling out his weapon. The one-armed ex-soldier reluctantly handed his gun over. The two men below then moved in, pushing Sarge fully inside the stairwell and pulling the door closed behind them.

Guilt and anger simultaneously flooded through Silver. 'Your beef's with me, Coal. I'll come quietly if you let them go.'

'My beef *was* with you, you cock-sucking whore,' he shot back with a sneer. 'Now it's with all of you. You should have handed her over when you had the opportunity, Grave. I always take what's mine, only now I'll be claiming interest. And what's more, I'm thinking Silmac might be interested in taking a look at your workshop upstairs. I don't suppose your little excursion tonight to the old print house had anything to do with that?'

'I'm sorry, Grave,' Rat said weakly. 'The boy tricked me. I shouldn't have let him in.'

Silver was confused for a moment, until she realised that one of the figures on the stairwell behind Coal was Muzzle, looking down at the three of them with a hard expression on his face.

'How could you, Muzzle?' Silver protested. 'To me, maybe, but to your crew? Your friends?'

'My "friends" were quick enough to take sides with you and kick me out. And you? Well you should have considered this before you decided to dump me and shack up with Grave.'

Silver opened her mouth to protest but Grave cut her off, ignoring Muzzle and appealing to Coal. 'I'm worth more to you than the girl and the others. If you let them go, I'll hand over all the wealth to my name, and you can still take me to Silmac and claim the credit and any reward he might have for you.'

'Well isn't that just touching?' Coal sneered. 'So many fucking heroes. The only hero tonight will be me, when I hand you lot over to Silmac. He'll love to see what you've been up to, Grave. Or should I say Meldon? And I happen to know he has some interest in you too, Silver—another tick in my favour. It will also show up that snot-nosed fucker Meek, which is itself worth its weight in gold. No, tonight is proving pretty good for Coal, so you can save your breath. Now, we've got an appointment with Silmac I'd hate to miss. Hand over your weapons, and don't try nothing or the scrawny one here and the old one-armed guy will bleed.'

# Chapter 20

*From the diary of Benjamin Adams*
*April 3rd, 2016*

*Life is busy! Work and family keep us continually on the go. The boys are both playing footy, so lots of running around on the weekend. Chloe is two-and-a-half, super cheeky and running amuck. Jess is happy keeping busy with the kids, but finding some time to spend on herself as well.*

*I've started my own firm called Envirotectual Design, specialising in the integration of cool technological solutions with efficient and environmentally friendly design concepts. The business is going reasonably well. There is not much competition in this space, so while the market is relatively small, I'm getting enough work to stay busy, which is great.*

* * * * *

'What an extremely enlightening read, information that could prove very valuable indeed, in the right hands.' Silmac laid the freshly printed paper down on the desk in front of him and leant back in his chair. 'I especially like the title: "Sun Sets on Silmac Supremacy". Very creative.'

Silver, Grave, Sarge and Rat were seated on the lounges in Silmac's office at the top of the tower. Coal, Blade, Muzzle, Meek and five of Silmac's security force surrounded the couches, hands held close to their firearms to dissuade any escape attempt.

Anger and helplessness seethed within Silver. Next to her, Grave was bloody and bruised, with a gash across his right eye, a blackened left eye and heavily bruised cheek. His lower lip was split and swollen. More injuries were hidden by his clothes, which had not escaped unscathed and were now torn and dishevelled.

Sarge and Rat were on the lounge opposite her. Rat sat in a miserable heap, nursing his wounds and keeping his eyes downcast. Sarge sported similar, though slightly less severe injuries. The biggest hurt had been to his pride, and his head hung in shame. Grave had been given no chance by Coal and the crew, attacked en mass with fist and foot, but Sarge had been toyed with, taunted for the fact he was older and missing an arm.

Silver herself had not been touched. 'We've got to keep her pretty for Silmac,' Coal had said, much to Arlia's disappointment. She had been made to watch the beatings though, and had pleaded and begged them to stop. Now she was quiet, her expression hard-set, eyes red, and cheeks tear-streaked.

All this had occurred back in Grave's apartment. Afterwards, Coal had called in the rest of his crew to clean the place out of anything valuable. Finally, the four of them had been half marched, half dragged to Silmac Tower.

Meek looked on silently, a frown across his normally neutral features. Coal was brimming with glee, trying to keep his face straight when talking with Silmac, but taking every opportunity to grin gloatingly in Meek's direction.

'I am extremely disappointed in you, Lance,' Silmac said, talking now to Grave. 'Your father is a sensible man, and I would have thought he'd have imparted some of that onto you. Had you had the sense to come to me with these discoveries, you could be a very rich man by now. But instead you resort to this?' He again took up the paper, brandishing it in front of him with a look of chagrin on his face.

'If I had come to you with these discoveries earlier I'd be dead already, and nothing would have changed,' Grave shot back, though his voice was thick and slightly slurred from his swollen lower lip. 'My father is a foolish and weak man. Perhaps I don't have much more sense than he, but I'll not bend over to you the same way he has. Rat, Sarge and Silver have nothing to do with this. They did not know what they were doing, merely employees following my instruction. Let them go free.'

'Oh how very noble of you, but now you are taking me for a fool. These people knew exactly what they were doing, and even if they didn't, you know very well I wouldn't be able to let them go. But I am interested in taking a closer look at one of them—bring the girl to me.'

Meek moved forward to do Silmac's bidding, but Coal was quick to cut him off, reaching down to clasp Silver by her left arm and drag her to her feet. He marched her over to the side of the desk, in front of Silmac.

'Your reputation precedes you, Silver. You survived a night out in the Badlands, then you managed to evade Meek here. I was becoming ever more intrigued by you. Only now you disappoint me. You've become … tainted by your involvement with a group attempting to overthrow me. A failed attempt, one that will not see the light of day, an irony that I find quite delightful. Now I'm forced to send you out into the Badlands once again. Only this time, there will be no return. It will be a tragic accident, as happens from time to time to salvage teams. You and all the material you have gathered will disappear in the Badlands and this whole episode will be forgotten.'

'But we have a chance here at free power, that will make the Dome a better place for all,' Silver protested. 'Why not use it? It might allow us to rebuild much of the city, to prosper as our ancestors once did.'

'No, that does not serve my needs at all, and I am seriously starting to wonder what I ever saw in you. I am quite happy with the current state of affairs. When given too much freedom, humans make poor decisions. Our ancestors were plagued by self-inflicted problems; they smoked cigarettes, almost as bad for them as the air outside the Dome. They ate glutinously till there were more obese than there were healthy, bringing with it a whole other host of medical problems and diseases. They became fickle, greedy and intolerant of each other, and their leaders were so bogged down in the democratic process that they were helpless to avert the disasters that leave us where we are today. No, I am quite happy making the decisions on behalf of the Dome, and if I happen to prosper in the process all the better. Energy from the sun would indeed save me much time and money, but it will also lead people to presume to take their other liberties and freedoms back, and that I am unwilling to allow. Which is why you all must die. Now, what I need to know is if there are any others who were in on this plot.'

Silver tried to keep any emotion from her face, but she was sure Silmac sensed the panic in her eyes. He looked over at Coal and Meek.

'There were two other members to their crew,' Coal admitted.

'And where are they, prey tell?'

'Um, they weren't with them at the apartment, and weren't at their clubhouse neither.'

'Well, that is a problem, and puts an unfortunate dampener on your otherwise excellent work of bringing them to me.'

'Wait, I have someone who will be able to find them,' Coal exclaimed, desperate not to tarnish his moment of glory. 'Muzzle here worked with the crew and will help track down the missing members.'

Muzzle's expression flickered for a moment as he fought to maintain the stony face he had up until that point.

'Don't do it, Muzzle!' Silver pleaded with him, earning a stinging backhanded slap from Silmac, who lurched forward out of his chair.

'He will do it, or else he will be joining you on your little jaunt out to the Badlands.'

'Sure, I'll take you to them,' Muzzle weakly consented.

'No!' Silver lurched forward, swinging her fist at Silmac. However, Coal had a firm hold of her and was ready for it, pulling her back before she could connect. Silmac glared and struck her with a second back-hand, snapping her head to one side and leaving her vision blurred. Behind her Grave and Sarge tried to stand but were immediately restrained by the guards around them.

'Meek, you know what to do,' Silmac ordered.

The head of security nodded, motioning for Muzzle to follow him over to the lifts. Silver continued to struggle against Coal's hold, but the twins moved over to help restrain her and she could only watch as Muzzle and Meek disappeared from view.

Meanwhile, Silmac wandered over to the curved glass windows sur-rounding his office. 'Morning draws near. You have done excellent work today, Coal, but I have one more task for you. You must take these four out into the Badlands. Take their truck, and make sure they don't make it back. I want it to look like they were waylaid by mutes, so that no questions will be asked if they turn up missing. No one will worry much about the other three, but Lance here may attract some attention if he goes missing inside the Dome.'

'Yes, sir. We will ensure it is done.'

'Excellent. Now, everyone get out. It is high time we put this behind us.'

* * * * *

Silver fought to retain her balance as Arlia shoved her along. The streets were deserted, though dawn was not too far away. Coal led them towards the Silmac Ops clubhouse. Once they were taken down from their audience with Silmac, Coal ordered their hands to be tied behind them, and cable-ties were produced to cuff them at the wrists. This had presented a challenge for Sarge, who had eventually been allowed to walk without the cuff, but Slip followed close behind with a gun trained on his back. The twins had Grave in between them, while Blade half carried Rat, who could not keep up with the pace due to his injuries.

'You thought you were a fucking queen when you were with him, didn't you?' Arlia whispered in Silver's ear, before shoving her roughly again. 'Well, he used to come to me after being with you, because you couldn't satisfy him properly. We fucked for hours behind your back, princess, yet you thought you were so much better than me.'

'No, I didn't think about you at all,' Silver shot back.

'Bitch!' Arlia screeched, landing a kick in the small of Silver's back, causing her to pitch forward. With her hands behind her back, Silver's face struck the ground painfully, though she managed to turn her head to protect her nose and teeth. Before she could recover, a second kick caught her in the side, and the air exploded from her lungs. 'I always wanted to do that. It will be a joy watching the mutes eat you alive and … Argghhh!'

Arlia's enraged rant, and an intended third kick, was cut short as she was slammed bodily to the ground by Grave, who had torn free from the twins and shoulder charged her from the side.

'What the fuck?' Coal growled, arriving on the scene and landing a punch to Grave's face that knocked him to the ground. He glared at the twins. 'He's half your fucking size and has had the shit kicked out of him. Hold onto him!'

Shame-faced, the twins nodded and stopped to haul Grave to his feet, while Coal turned on Arlia who was in the process of picking herself off the pavement. He reached down, grabbed her by the hair and yanked her to her feet, eliciting another yelp.

'As for you, keep your fucking mouth shut and your hands off her, unless she tries to make a move. If I wanted your mouth open, I'd tell you, and by then you'd be on your fucking knees.'

Without another word, Coal released his hold on Arlia's hair, turned around and resumed the march. Meanwhile, Sarge had been allowed to help Silver to her feet and the Silmac Ops crew again prodded their captives along, this time in silence.

'Something troubling you, Coal?' Grave asked as they neared the clubhouse. 'Could it be that you're worried Silmac will do away with you once you're done with us? He doesn't want word getting out about the panels, and you and your whole crew know about them now. If I were Silmac, I'd be a little worried if that many people knew a secret that could destroy my power completely.'

Coal didn't answer, arriving at the clubhouse and pounding on the door until they were admitted. The rest of the crew was waiting around in the cluttered common room. Silver noted it was a little more cluttered now, filled with the items pilfered from Grave's apartment. The stack of papers they had printed along with the panels Grave had reconstructed were sitting by the door.

'My explosives!' Rat exclaimed, spotting the homemade bombs he had been working on amongst the loot. 'At least someone will get some use out of them.'

Coal headed over to the stairs and disappeared into his room. Silver, Grave, Sarge and Rat were herded over to one side of the common room, forced onto their knees and gagged. The Silmac Ops crew meanwhile gathered around, waiting for Coal.

Silver noticed that Arlia hung at the back of the group, her eyes redrimmed, lips pursed and sullen. She felt strangely sorry for the girl; no doubt Coal had fooled her in much the same way Silver had allowed herself to be fooled by him. She scanned the crew and could not find any sign of Lead among them. She wondered what had happened to him. Turning her attention back upstairs, she saw Coal exit his room, eyes wide and wiping at his nose vigorously.

'Right,' Coal's voice barked down from the balcony to those assembled, numbering fourteen strong. 'We've taken a good haul today, and we'll be eating well for a long time to come.'

A cheer went up among the crew, and Coal waited until it had died down. 'But we've got one more job to do before we can celebrate. This lot need to be taken out into the Badlands and left for the mutes. It needs to look like they were ambushed and killed so we'll take two of our trucks, and theirs. The papers and the panels go with us and are to be burned along with their truck. Blade will have command.'

'What about you, Boss?' Tip called out.

'I've got some business here I need to wrap up. Besides, taking out four trucks will attract attention, and there won't be enough seats to bring everyone back in two. Now, let's get moving.'

The crew sprung into life, hurrying around to make final preparations to head out. Coal descended the stairs back down into the common room, Silver noticed that as the twins were about to walk out the door laden with the two piles of papers, he stopped them and grabbed one off the top, folding it and tucking it into the back of his pants. Afterwards, he spent a few moments conversing quietly with Blade, away from the flurry of activity. Silver looked over to Grave, who had also noticed, and raised an eyebrow in question.

Before she could dwell on it further, she and her companions were pulled to their feet. But as they were escorted over to the door, Coal stepped over and grabbed Silver by the arm. 'She stays with me.'

'What?' Arlia exclaimed, her voice high pitched and shaky. 'But Silmac ordered …'

'Is that a leadership challenge you're voicing?' Coal growled, referencing the right of any crew member to make a challenge for the leadership of the crew. 'Cause you've been spouting your mouth off a bit lately and I'm getting sick of it. If you want to Make Challenge, then I suggest you declare. Otherwise, shut the fuck up before I rip your tongue out.'

Arlia turned and stormed out the front door, shoving past Silver roughly as she went.

Blade hesitantly approached Coal. 'Boss, do you think it's wise to keep her here? Only, if Silmac found out …'

'Silmac wants her dead and fed to the mutes, and that's what will happen. In the scheme of things, it won't be a big deal if it happens a day later than the others. Now fuck off and get the crew on the road before the sun comes up.'

At that moment, Grave lurched to his feet, lunging head first at Coal. Blade was quicker, stepping forward to intercept him. One hand grabbed him by the forearm and a knife appeared in the other, finding its way to Grave's throat.

With a snarl, Coal stepped up and struck Grave viciously, knocking him to the ground. 'Always trying to play the hero, but not so tough without your mace.'

Still gagged, Grave snarled in reply.

Coal knelt down in front of Grave, grabbing him roughly by the collar and pulled him face to face. 'Rest assured she will get what's coming to her. I'll give it to her good. And it will be all the more sweet knowing what that'll do to you.' He released Grave and stood. 'Get them out of my sight.'

Grave tried to charge at Coal again, but Blade dragged him backwards and pushed him out the door. The twins manhandled Rat and Sarge to their feet and similarly ushered them out of the clubhouse. The last of the crew filed out after them, leaving Silver alone with Coal.

# Chapter 21



*From the diary of Benjamin Adams*
*November 5th, 2018*

*It's been a rough few months internationally, following a chilling string of natural disasters. We've had a major drought and famine in large parts of Africa with thousands dead and tens of thousands starving. Aid is pouring in, but so far the drought is refusing to break.*

*A major earthquake struck Indonesia a month ago, which triggered a tsunami in the region. Like those in India and Japan, it has been devastating, with hundreds of thousands killed and the nation crippled. Even the top end of Australia saw some huge waves coming in, with two fatalities reported.*

*It's also been reported that the quake disrupted some major drilling projects in the oil-rich waters around Indonesia. There is speculation that it was the mining that triggered the quake. They still haven't contained the leak, so millions of litres of oil continue to spill out into the ocean.*

*The quake in Indonesia seems to have triggered off quakes all over the region; the Solomon Islands, New Zealand and Japan have all had tremors in the last month, though thankfully none as devastating as the first. And two days ago, Australia had another quake up the coast in Newcastle. It was not a large tremor by comparison, though enough that it could be felt here in Sydney.*

* * * * *

Once the rest of the crew had left, Coal pushed Silver down onto one of the old, dusty couches and without a word, busied himself in a number of mundane tasks. Still gagged and bound, and with Coal never actually leaving the room, she was helpless to do anything and was forced to wait. The taste of the gag was foul in her mouth—some greasy used rag that had been snatched up indiscriminately. The silence of the club-house was just as stifling, Coal's silence more terrifying than his blustering rage.

But the thing that filled her with the most fear was not thoughts of her own likely fate, but that of her friends. Asp and Blocka could even now be bleeding into the filthy streets, with Silmac's henchman Meek standing emotionless above them. Sarge and Rat had already suffered on behalf of her and were now en route to suffer a gruesome death at the hand of the savage mutes.

And Grave. Though he had frustrated and enraged her initially, the last couple of days had shown his true identity and she had warmed to him. It surprised her to realise that it was the thought of his loss that caused her the most grief.

'Just look at all the mess you've caused me, Silver.' She jumped at the words. Though they had been spoken softly, they crashed the silence like a deafening crack of thunder. Coal gazed at her from across the room, leaning against the stair banister, his over-sized pistol held in hand. His eyes were red rimmed, irises so wide that his eyes appeared black, alien.

'LOOK AT THE MESS YOU'VE CAUSED ME!' he exploded, violently smashing his left fist down onto the banister with so much force the wood cracked and splintered. His hand came away bloody, but he didn't notice, instead striding across the room towards her, his face contorted in rage. Silver couldn't help but recoil, his approach like the charge of a raging bull.

'Why couldn't you have just died out in the Badlands like you should have?' he fumed, his charge ending in a punch that smote the couch cushion just to the left side of her head, threatening to tip the whole lounge over backwards. 'I could've lived with that. But making it back and then walking out on me—you backed me into a fucking corner! Fuck it was hard when I saw you walk in that door! I realised I had made a mistake leaving you out there. But then Arlia was at me again, and before I could do anything about it you were gone. And what the fuck was I meant to do then—let you go? How would that look in front of the crew? Did you think about that when you were shacking up with that Meldon fuck?'

Coal was pacing now, looking like a giant from Silver's vantage. She wasn't sure if he was talking to her anymore or just to himself, arguing with his conscience. But in striking the lounge he had caused her to slide down, and she had also brought her legs up reflexively, which put her in a position to possibly slip her still cuffed arms under her butt and in front of her. It was not much, but it was something if she could pull it off without him noticing. She carefully began working her arms down while Coal, apparently oblivious, continued his rant.

'And Arlia—fucking hell! She's a good fuck, but now when I'm with her I can't stop thinking about you! I've had to put up with her shit, mindless crap about love and weddings for Christ's sake! That's what I miss about you, Sil; there was no baggage. But thinking of you with that fucker. If I can't have you, no one can. How could you do that too me, Sil? After all the time we spent together? I took care of you, took you with me as I rose up through the ranks and took over the crew, raised you up above all other crew members. And now this!'

He pulled the paper she and Grave had put together from where it was tucked into his pants and flung it down at her. She froze in case he noticed what she was doing. 'You had to go and get involved in some stupid shit-brained idea about taking on Silmac! Jesus Christ, what were you thinking? Now I have no fucking option but to kill you, because if I don't, Silmac will have my head. And even if I do there's no certainty I'm not dead anyway. Grave was right when he said Silmac won't let that type of secret remain known to so many people. You've fucking destroyed this crew, and I'll be lucky to keep my head when all this blows over. You've ruined me, Sil, and now I have to kill you, even though I don't want to. What do you have to say for yourself? Speak!'

Unable to speak, Silver was forced to make murmuring sounds to remind him that she was still gagged. He rounded on her just as she got her legs back down after finally squeezing them through her bindings. Given his frame of mind, and the fact that he had forgotten about the gag, she was hopeful he wouldn't notice what she had done. He strode over and roughly tore the gag out of her mouth.

'What did you expect me to do, Coal?' she spat. 'You left me to die out in the Badlands, and when I managed to make it back, I find out you had been cheating on me for God knows how long. Did you really expect me to forgive you, then drop to my knees and suck your cock?

Don't talk about what I've brought you. You've brought this on your fucking self!'

With a snarl, Coal grabbed her by the hair and yanked up, pulling her completely off the ground. Agonising fire erupted through her scalp. She reached up with her bound hands and grabbed his wrist, trying to take some of the pressure from her head. With his spare hand he tore at her clothes, ripping her shirt open and her pants off, and sending something clattering to the ground. He then flipped her around and pushed her face first onto the couch below. The agony in her head was replaced by sharp pain lancing up her legs as her knees struck the hard concrete floor. She tried to roll away, but he grabbed her hair again with his left hand, and with terrible strength shoved her face down into the cushions.

'You ungrateful bitch!' he yelled, spraying spit with every word. 'You deserve everything you're about to get. I was going to make this easy on you, but that was before. Now I'll take my pleasure and your life, and take as long as I like doing it. You'll be begging for death at the end.'

It seemed to Silver that death was not far off. With her face buried in the cushion, she couldn't breathe, and though she struggled, Coal's grip was like iron. As he knelt down behind her, tiny sparks ignited at the edge of her consciousness and her lungs burned for oxygen. Her hands scrabbled at the floor below, seeking purchase to help push her head clear to draw breath, and they landed on something cold, smooth and rectangular in shape. Her flick-knife! She had completely forgotten she had retrieved the blade and returned it to its customary sheath when she and Grave fought Coal on the street. It must have sprung free when he tore at her clothes.

With her lungs screaming for air and light now exploding before her eyes she flicked the blade and struck back blindly, between her own legs, the only place she could reach from her current position. A howl of pain suggested she had struck him and she stabbed again, and a third time before finally the pressure was gone from her head and she was able to draw a ragged breath.

Instinctively she rolled to one side, with Coal's fist pounding down onto the couch where her head had just been. On her back now, she struck out at him again with her feet, aiming for his bloodied groin region. It was a clumsy kick, with her feet tangled in her pants, but with

Coal on his knees it was effective enough, and he bellowed in pain once more.

Silver scrambled towards the front door of the clubhouse, desperately tugging at her pants as she went. The door was only three metres away, and she was halfway to her feet when he struck again, full force into her back. Air exploded from her lungs as his weight landed on her. She dimly felt the flick-knife go flying from her hands, spinning well out of reach.

Next thing Coal flipped her over effortlessly, and she stared up at his deranged face. Foam collected at the corners of his mouth like a rabid dog. His eyes were red, face contorted with rage. He was on his knees above her and before she could react his hands enclosed around her throat and began to squeeze.

'You bitch!' he spat onto her face. 'I'm going to fucking kill you.'

Black spots began forming in front of Silver's eyes, and she felt the strength leaving her arms as she feebly tried to break his grip. But he was too strong, and she was too tired. It would be easy to just close her eyes and sleep.

At the sound of a shot ringing out, Silver's eyes fluttered open, and she saw blood spurting from Coal's mouth. He looked past her, towards the doorway, a stunned expression painted on his face. Suddenly the pressure on her throat was gone, and with a gurgling sound Coal fell away from her.

As Silver struggled to draw in breath, she tilted her head towards the doorway and saw a dark figure standing there, pistol held in two hands, still pointed at where Coal had been kneeling.

'Lead!' she croaked, the word causing her to erupt into a fit of coughing and gasping. The big man tucked away his gun and hurried over to her, lifting her gently to her feet and awkwardly trying to pat her on the back to help her with the cough. She leant into him for support, and he enclosed her in a hug.

'You all right, Silver? He didn't … ?'

'Man it's good to see you, Lead. No he didn't, thanks to you,' she croaked once her coughing had subsided and her breath returned. 'I was worried for you, worried that you and Coal had fallen out and he had done away with you.'

'You were worried for *me*?' Lead responded, having a chuckle despite himself. 'Girl, you need to worry about yourself more, given the trouble you keep finding yourself in. No, once I would have done anything for Coal, stood by him no matter what. But the last couple of years he's been getting more and more messed up on drugs, making increasingly bad decisions. Leaving you in the Badlands was the worst of all, and since then he's been going downhill faster than a rabid mute to a corpse. Loyalty can only go so far, so I walked out on him and have been lying low for a while. I just came back to grab a few things I had left behind, thinking the whole crew had gone out. Lucky I did.'

He let go of her, pulled a knife from his belt and gently cut through the ties that held Silver's wrists together. Then he moved over to where Coal lay, blank eyes staring up at the ceiling. A small puncture in the near centre of his chest indicated the spot the bullet had struck. A pool of blood was spreading out from beneath his body. Kneeling, Lead reached out and shut his former friend's eyes. 'Goodbye old friend. I hope you make some better decisions wherever you are now.'

'Lead, I need your help,' Silver interrupted. 'Silmac is about to get my friends killed and I need to save them.'

'Whoa girl, why you messing with Silmac? That only has one ending and it ain't a good one. Besides, as much as I'd be happy to stare at those all day long, you need to find yourself a new shirt before you do anything else.' As he spoke, he took off his jacket and draped it over her shoulders.

'Thanks,' she said, pulling the jacket tight. 'But please, hear me out. The Ash Walkers took me in and they're about to get killed for that help. And there's more at stake.' She searched around until she found the paper Coal had kept, fallen behind the couch in their struggle. She held it out to Lead. 'Read this while I grab a few things.'

Silver ran upstairs, raiding the rooms of her former crew mates to find some clothes. She managed to find a reasonable fitting black singlet and a grey hoodie. As she was about to leave the room, she spotted an old pack lying in the corner behind the door. It was old and ragged, but it had a facemask and some other salvage gear inside, so she shouldered it.

She ran back down the stairs, taking three at a time and, noticing the explosives that Rat had made, she scooped them up and added them to her pack. She also spotted Coal's discarded gun and her flick-knife and grabbed those as well. She bent over Coal and went through his pockets, finding a couple of spare clips, a reasonably sized wad of cash, and a set of keys, all of which she pocketed.

'Is this for real?' Lead asked, having flicked through the contents of the paper.

Silver nodded, handing his jacket back to him. 'I think it's the real deal. You in?'

'Fuck. I don't know, Silver. This is serious shit and will likely get us all killed.'

'We're dead anyway, Lead. Living the life we live, death comes to all of us, and chances are it's going to be sooner rather than later. This is a chance to make a real change, make things better for everyone.'

Lead hesitated, pursing his lips, but eventually nodded. 'Where to?'

Silver couldn't answer the question immediately. They could go after Grave and possibly catch them before they left. But in the meantime, Asp and Blocka were being hunted by Meek, who'd had a substantial head start.

'We go after Asp and Blocka. You know the clothes shop on York, Smart Design? We'll look for them there. Meek's after them though, so we need to be careful.'

'Meek? Well we better get going then, 'cause if he hasn't caught up to them already, he'll do so soon.'

# CHAPTER 22



*From the diary of Benjamin Adams*
*October 16th, 2019*

*I've just won a large-scale tender, building a new stadium, which will keep me busy for the next two years. They loved the design and bought in to my proposal to make it fully sustainable, which means it will catch all its own water and harness all the energy it needs from the sun.*

*While we have been free from further natural disaster over the last year or so, fall-out from the Indonesian quake remains. Oil production was so disrupted that prices have soared and this has caused global panic and flared tensions, particularly in the Middle East. So far, all-out war has been avoided, but it feels like that could change at any time.*

* * * * *

'We've got to get in there!' Silver whispered urgently to Lead.

'I don't see how we're going to,' he replied, scanning the street ahead. 'It looks like they've got the place pretty well covered. I've counted twenty cops, though there could be more. I don't see Meek though.'

'The fact that they've got the place surrounded means we might not be too late. Someone's still alive in there.'

Lead nodded at the logic, unable to refute it. The cops stationed around the shop all had weapons out and had taken cover. A few were on the street, clinging to the cover offered by piles of debris. Others had taken up station in shopfronts opposite, or lurked in the shadows of doorways. A couple had even made their way to second level windows and had their guns trained down on the shop. Whoever was inside had already taken down at least one cop, judging from the uniformed figure that lay unmoving on the pavement just outside.

'What do you propose then? Whatever it is we'd better hurry. They'll have the Riot Breaker here soon. I'm surprised it's not here already.' The Riot Breaker was an armoured vehicle, which, as its name suggested, was primarily used by the police when crowds on the street started to get unruly, or a fight between rival crews got out of hand. Whenever a cop was seriously hurt or killed, it would inevitably come out of hiding and be put to use.

'Back door onto the lane?' Silver suggested.

'Not that shop—it was bricked up long ago, like many of the shops around this stretch. Too many robberies, too many escape routes.'

'But there was a door there once?' Silver asked.

'Most likely, with the lane there.'

'Let's go. I have an idea.'

Silver crept back from her position at the mouth of the street and jogged back down Erskine Street, intending to head into the lane that ran parallel to York, behind the shop. Lead grabbed her just before she entered the lane.

'Wait a second, they could have a cop stationed here just in case.' He took a moment to scan the lane from the corner and then nodded, pointing to Silver. 'There, in the shadows. He's got his back to us, but he looks pretty alert. It'll take a bit of luck to get to him before he sees us.'

'Wait here. If he's looking at me, he won't be looking at you. Are you okay to do this?'

Lead shrugged. 'I never could say no to you. I'll just take him down, but he'll live.'

Silver gave him a quick peck on the cheek, then took off at a run, down Erskine and left into Clarence. She ran fast but softly, her feet padding quietly on the pavement. Time was ticking for Asp and Blocka inside the shop, and for Grave and the others, who moved further away from the Dome with every minute wasted.

When she reached Barrack Street, she slowed to a jog, then to a fast walk as she rounded into the lane, approaching from the opposite end. Her hood was pulled low, and she strolled quickly and purposely down the street. She would be fully visible to the cop, but she acted as though she was unaware of him. She was also careful not to look in Lead's direction, who she now spotted making his way quietly but quickly up the street behind the cop.

As she neared the spot he was stationed, Silver swung the pack off her shoulder and knelt down. She slowly reached inside, making a show of searching through the contents. Eventually she grabbed one of Rat's homemade explosives and drew it out.

Chancing a look over, she spotted Lead standing where the cop had been stationed. He gave her a wave of confirmation and she rose to her feet, canister in hand. It didn't look like much: a piece of plastic tubing, plugged up at the end with a clay-like substance, a short fuse sticking out one end. Scanning the walls at the back of the building, she fervently hoped it would be enough.

The bricked up doorway that once led into the shop presented a logical place to try, given it was well away from the counter inside. Taking a box of matches from her pocket, she struck the match, lit the fuse and rolled it in towards the doorway. Turning tail, she ran like hell towards where Lead waited, behind some crates and rubble.

The canister exploded as she dove behind cover, sending a concussive wave of force up and down the lane. The crates fell down on top of Silver and Lead, and bits of brick and rubble rained down around them. Silver's ears ached from the volume of the blast, with a static-like noise echoing in her ears.

Looking up through the dust now thick in the air, she saw a gaping hole in the building where the bricked up doorway and surrounding wall had previously been.

'Gotta hurry!' she shouted, lurching to her feet and running towards the hole. Lead followed close behind her, gun in hand.

'Asp!' she shouted, peering in through the dust. 'It's me, Silver. Let's go!'

As her eyes adjusted to the gloom of the shop, she saw Asp over near the counter, squatting down next to Blocka, who was slumped on the ground, big legs out in front of him. Between them and the doorway there was a tangle of bodies, most dressed in police riot gear, but at least one in civilian clothes. Asp's eyes were red rimmed, with the smile erased from her normally jovial face.

'Come on!' Silver yelled from just inside the hole, standing on a pile of shattered bricks, and motioning for her to come. Asp shook her head. No. Silver looked again at Blocka and could see he was sitting in a pool of blood. A gunshot broke the silence, causing all of them to duck down instinctively.

'Silver, we've gotta go,' Lead cautioned behind her, gun out, watching the street. Silver knew he was right, but couldn't leave her friends. She took off her pack and passed it to Lead, before moving into the shop, keeping low and making her way over broken and twisted racks that once held clothes for sale. The clothes themselves were strewn over the ground, the blast reducing them to little more than rags.

'Come on, we'll help him,' Silver said, arriving at Blocka's side. The big man shook his head sadly. His face was pale white, and up close Silver could see he had multiple wounds blossoming from his torso. Around him lay the bodies of the police who had likely inflicted the wounds. Nearest was a man she recognised—Meek, whose head had been twisted around, his face just as expressionless in death as it had been in life. Silver also spotted two dark-skinned bodies near the entrance of the shop, conspicuous among the cops in their civilian clothes.

'Go,' Blocka said to Asp, using his one functioning arm to try to push her away from him. 'Go.'

Asp shook her head again, tears falling silently down her face as she clung to him. Guilt and grief washed over Silver as she knew she was responsible for this. Her own tears started to fall, and she reached out a hand to Blocka's, squeezing it.

'Go,' Blocka said again. 'Please. I love you.'

His head began to slump, and Asp broke down into violent sobs, clinging to him desperately, as if trying to physically stop him from departing. Another shot rang out, this one coming dangerously close to them. Silver ducked down once again. Dimly, through the ringing in her ears, she heard a rumbling sound that seemed to be getting steadily louder.

'Silver, Riot Breaker!' Lead called out. 'We need to go now!'

Silver leant forwards and grabbed Asp's arm. 'Asp please, he's gone. There's nothing we can do for him now. Don't stay to die with him; live and get revenge on the bastard responsible!'

Asp looked at her for a minute and Silver momentarily wondered if she was going to do exactly that. It would be deserved and she wouldn't stop it. But Asp nodded, laying Blocka's head down gently. Silver was already ducking back to the hole at the back of the shop, keeping low to the ground but moving quickly. Asp scooped up her gun and followed, the roar of engines growing louder by the second. Just as they reached the hole, the front of the shop exploded inwards in a second spray of rock and debris, as a metal vehicle with a bulldozer plough attached crashed into the shopfront. Silver and Asp threw themselves clear into the street at the back, where Lead awaited. He had in hand another of Rat's homemade bombs.

'This way, quickly!' He helped the women to their feet, and the three sprinted down the lane towards Erskine Street, back the way they had come. As Lead approached the street mouth, he slowed, lighting the bomb and hurling it ahead of them so that it bounced out onto Erskine in the direction of York. The trio heard a few cries of distress before a second concussion ripped through the Dome. Throwing their hands up to protect their faces and eyes, the three plunged into the dust cloud, Silver now in front. They took a left onto Erskine under the cover of dust. A couple of shots rang out, but they had been fired wildly and didn't come close to hitting.

Silver pulled ahead, leading them straight down Erskine, crossing Sussex and heading under an old, crumbling motorway suspended above on concrete pillars. Rounding a bend, she slowed her run to a jog and then stopped completely, breathing heavily and waiting for Asp and Lead to catch up.

When Asp rounded the bend, she slowed to a walk but stalked straight up to Silver, grabbing her by the throat and pushing her violently back against a concrete support of the bridge.

'Why? Why did they come for us? We opted out! We opted out, and they still came.' Her eyes were hard as rock, the tears gone. She was trembling noticeably, her face twisted in anger and grief.

Lead started to intervene, but Silver held up a hand to warn him off, and then motioned back the way they had come. He nodded reluctantly, moving over to the corner they had rounded and peering cautiously around, gun in hand.

'I'm so sorry Asp,' Silver gasped, her throat partially constricted from the pressure of Asp's grip. 'It was Muzzle. He went to Silmac Ops and brought Coal down on us. They took us out before we even had a chance to get started. Once Silmac had us, Coal filled him in on you and Blocka, and Muzzle confirmed. It should have been me. None of you deserved this. I'm so sorry.'

'But how is it that you are still here?' Her trembling was increasing, her grip on Silver's throat tightening. 'Blocka and my parents are gone, but you're still here.'

'I wouldn't be if not for Lead. We came straight to you but were too late.'

'Too late,' she repeated distantly, her eyes starting to glaze over as if she were staring into some other world. The pressure eased on Silver's throat as Asp's hand fell away. 'If I had come with you in the first place, maybe this wouldn't have happened. Now everyone's gone.'

Asp broke down into tears of grief, sobbing loudly onto Silver's shoulder. Silver wrapped her in a hug, stroking her hair gently.

'Not everyone's gone,' she whispered into Asp's ear. 'Grave, Rat and Sarge are being driven out to the Badlands as we speak, and will be thrown to the mutes unless we stop them. We can do it, but we need your help. They need it.'

'What does it matter now?' Asp sobbed. 'My family is gone. I should be with them.'

'But while Silmac is in power, more families will die!' Silver exclaimed, grabbing Asp by the arms as if to shake her out of her daze. 'Blocka's death, your parents', will be in vain if we don't try to stop him. He killed them even though they weren't involved. He does whatever the fuck he likes, hurts whoever the fuck he likes. Together, with Grave, Rat and Sarge, we have a chance to take him down, to get revenge.'

Asp's eyes started to regain focus, and she looked at Silver, wiping at her eyes. 'Silmac will die for what he did to my family.' Her voice was still shaky and choked, but there was a hard edge to it now, a simmering undertone.

'Then let's get to the checkpoint. Hopefully we can still catch them before they go.'

Asp nodded, and the three started running again, heading south and west towards the checkpoint. Outside the Dome, the sky was starting to lighten as dawn approached.

# Chapter 23



*From the diary of Benjamin Adams*
*April 8th, 2022*

*It's hard to believe I'm in my forties now. Even more staggering are the kids: Jayden is nearly sixteen, and in year ten. Alex is thirteen and in his second year of high school, and Chloe is eight years old, and halfway through primary! They are all good kids—smart, healthy and happy, which is great.*

*Jess is talking about going on a big overseas trip now that the kids are all old enough. I'd like to go and things have settled down and are relatively stable overseas, though we'd have to avoid anywhere near major fault lines as quakes continue to hit with seeming regularity. We also have to wait until the house sells—the coal seam gas project that was proposed years ago recently got approval from the government. It's quite literally under the suburb where we live. I'm not expecting to get a lot for the house, but luckily business has been going fairly well and we are doing okay. Many will be stuck there though, with their property value dropped due to the project and unable to afford other areas.*

* * * * *

The truck bumped and skidded along violently, Lead pushing it to speeds beyond any Silver had ever experienced. Under normal circumstances it did not pay to push the trucks this hard and risk breaking something. At best, it would leave you out of action and out of pocket while the truck was fixed. At worst you could be left stranded in the Badlands. But these were far from normal circumstances, and they needed to make up ground. The sun was edging ever higher in the sky and Grave and the others were running out of time. After the heartbreak of arriving to Asp and Blocka too late, Silver was determined to get to them.

Her hope wavered when, upon reaching the checkpoint, they found two of the Silmac trucks already gone. 'We're too late! How will we find them now?' she gasped.

'There's a way,' Lead insisted, spotting the third unused Silmac truck. 'You took the keys from Coal, right?'

Silver nodded, pulling the keys from her pocket and handing them to him. 'Follow me,' he instructed.

It had been surprisingly easy getting into the truck and out the gates. With Lead and her being former members of the Silmac Ops crew, and in possession of the keys to the truck, it had only taken a little cash to get the guards on duty to turn a blind eye. Clearly they had not yet been informed of the fighting on York Street and were not particularly vigilant. Once they were out of the Dome, Lead switched on a small monitor to the side of the dashboard.

'Coal had the trucks installed with these trackers so we'd have the chance to find each other in the Badlands. He ordered them months ago, but they only just came in the night you were left outside the Dome.' The screen was quartered, and featured a series of circles radiating out from the centre. A green blip was located at the centre of the screen and another two blips were located in the south-west quadrant of the screen, slowly heading away from them. 'That's them, looks like they are heading south-west, and are still on the move.'

Asp sat quietly in the back, gun in hand. A breathing filter was secured tightly over her face, masking her expression. There had been no tears, no more words of anger, just unresponsive silence. It was like finding yourself in the eye of a storm, when everything has suddenly become calm and quiet, but you know that soon you'll come out the other side and be plunged into violence and chaos once again. Silver had tried to talk with her, to console her, or to find out exactly what had happened but Asp had ignored all the questions, her gaze directed out the window of the truck.

Unable to help Asp, Silver turned her thoughts to the fight ahead, while closely monitoring the screen to check their progress on the other trucks. Searching through her pack, she found two more of Rat's home-made bombs, which she stashed carefully in the glove box so they'd be within reach.

'So how do you want to play this, Sil?' Lead asked, eyes remaining on the rough terrain ahead as he took the truck over a section of road that had dropped away, leaving them airborne for a gut-wrenching second. The engine roared, and then the truck crashed back to the ground, the big shock absorbers taking much of the impact and causing them to bounce once before regaining full control. 'It's one truck against three, and there's about fifteen of them.'

'We'll have to hit them hard and fast,' Silver answered, checking the clip in her gun to ensure it was full before clicking it back into place. 'Try to get the other trucks off the road. Get in close and force them into the rubble. Asp and I can help lay down some fire, but we'll need to be careful 'cause we don't want to hit Grave, Sarge or Rat. Whatever happens, don't stop. If they can immobilise us, they'll be able to use their numbers to full advantage and we'll be done for.'

'They've slowed,' Lead commented, motioning to the tracking display. 'They've seen us on screen.'

Silver looked down at the screen and confirmed what Lead had said. The twin blips ahead seemed to have slowed down and the gap between the two groups was closing much more quickly. 'We can still take them by surprise. With a bit of luck they'll assume its Coal behind the wheel. Remember, hard and fast. Asp, get ready!'

'He was my hero, and I loved him,' Asp said suddenly, breaking her silence. 'They burst into the shop without warning. Blocka and me were asleep in the back; Mum and Dad were out getting some work done for the day ahead. I heard the commotion and woke to find Dad arguing. I peeked out of the room and saw Meek cut his throat. It was so quick, so mechanical, so casual. Dad fell and Mum went hysterical, striking one of the guards, knocking him to the ground. They shot her. I had my gun by that time and opened fire. I took down a couple, but Meek was gone. Then the return fire came, and Blocka took it all, protected me with his body. The guards charged him, but he took them down with his bare hands. Meek came in, moving quick, struck him a dozen blows, but he kept his feet. Once he got a hand on him, Meek didn't stand a chance. Blocka just held him and squeezed, absorbing all the hits and scratches until Meek stopped moving. Then he smiled at me, sat down and told me to go. I couldn't leave him. I want him back, Silver. I want him back!'

The pure grief in Asp's voice, the tears brimming in her eyes was heart wrenching. 'We can't bring him back, Asp. His strength and bravery will never be matched. You're right, he was a hero. All we can do now is remember and avenge him.'

'You'll have that chance sooner than you think,' Lead cut in. 'We're almost on top of them!'

Silver glanced around and looked at the screen. The gap between the blips had closed considerably. 'Are you sure you are right to do this?' she asked Asp.

Asp nodded, pulling out her gun. Silver checked hers one last time. 'Filters on. Asp, you take the right side, I'll take the left. Don't open fire till we're close, and watch your shot. Lead, remember: no matter what happens, don't stop.'

* * * * *

'What's going on, Corbett?' Gavin demanded, an edge of uneasiness to his voice.

'Just some fighting on the streets,' Silmac replied from behind his desk. 'Nothing to be concerned about. No different from what we've dealt with in the past.'

'I saw the Riot Breaker heading out, and felt two explosions!' Gavin countered. 'You can see smoke rising not far from here! Sounds pretty bloody serious to me! Where is Meek?'

'Meek is out doing his job, dealing with the issue,' Silmac replied evenly, suppressing the agitation he felt at his sibling. 'The situation is even now being brought under control.'

'It's to do with Meldon and these solar panels, isn't it?' Gavin pressed, his voice shaky. 'We should have just done away with him here. Word's gotten out, and the Dome is rebelling. They'll be knocking on our door next.'

'Gavin, get a grip!' Silmac demanded sharply. He rose, walked around the desk to the bench that held his liquor, and poured two generous glasses of whiskey, passing one to Gavin. 'Drink this.'

Hand shaking a little, Gavin took a large gulp, squeezing his eyes shut as he swallowed. Silmac sipped at his, the malt flavour of the whiskey lingering in his mouth even after he had swallowed. Comforting warmth spread from his throat down to his chest.

'I assure you, Lance Meldon and his lackeys are being thrown to the mutes as we speak, some thirty kilometres from where we stand. All the materials he produced, all the contents of his workshop will be burned with him. Now if you don't mind, I have some work to attend to, so please relax and return to whatever it is you were doing before clamouring up here. There is nothing to be concerned about.'

'Right,' said Gavin, swilling the rest of the contents of his glass and helping himself to another. He offered Silmac a top up but was waved away.

'Why don't you take the bottle with you?' Silmac prompted. He walked over to the lift and pressed the button. The doors slid open quietly, and he motioned for Gavin to enter. He didn't wait for the doors to close, turning and making his way back to his desk, where he pressed a button on the phone to activate the intercom.

'Do we have confirmation?' he inquired.

'Yes, sir,' the voice responded. 'We've found his body. Meek is dead.'

Silmac pursed his lips. 'How?'

'It appears his throat was crushed, sir.'

'And the targets?'

'The shop owners are dead, as is a large man who we believe to be a member of the Ash Walkers crew,' the voice responded. 'At this time we have not found the female crew member.'

'What about Coal and his crew? Have you tracked them down?'

'I've received confirmation that Silmac Ops departed with prisoners from Checkpoint E, approximately one hour ago. However, Coal was not with them. We've since located him, back at his clubhouse. He is also dead.'

'What! How?'

'He had sustained some stab wounds, but we believe a bullet wound to the chest was what killed him.'

Silmac fell silent as he considered his options.

'Sir? What do you command?'

'What's your name?' Silmac asked.

'Johnson, sir.'

'Johnson. As of now, you are my head of security. I want you to find whoever was responsible for killing Coal, and track down the missing crew member. Take adequate men to ensure it is done. All other police members should be pulled back to Silmac Tower. Keep them out of sight, but ready. Do you understand?'

'Yes, sir,' the officer stammered, unable to keep the tremor from his voice.

'And Johnson?'

'Yes, sir?'

'Don't fuck it up, else you might find yourself to be the shortest serving head of security in the history of the Dome.'

'Yes, sir.'

Silmac killed the line and sat down in his chair. He swivelled it around to face the west, gazing out at the Badlands.

* * * * *

Muzzle leant forward over the steering wheel, tapping agitatedly and wondering for perhaps the twentieth time why the two trucks ahead of him were going so slowly. After taking Meek to Smart Design, he had started for the Silmac Ops clubhouse, but had met the crew on their way down to the check point and joined them.

The trip out into the Badlands had been a laborious one, not like he was used to. Arlia sat next to him in the truck, and she had been sullen and quiet the whole trip, fuming at what had transpired that morning. In the back sat Tip, Slip, and two others whose names he didn't even know. They had grumbled at the start of the trip about being relegated to the Ash Walkers truck, and eventually had started talking about the sport it would be to watch mutes fall on their prisoners. They had made no effort to include Muzzle in the conversation, and the topic had made him feel more uncomfortable than ever, given they were discussing his former companions.

'The little one'll be the funniest,' one of the men in the back said. 'I bet he'll squeal when they get their claws into 'im.'

'No way, it'll be over too quick with 'im,' the other countered. 'I reckon the leader, Grave, will put on the best show. He'll fight back and last longer.'

Muzzle ran a hand through his hair and it fell to his mouth, then he began absently biting at his nails.

'I'm not sure who's got it worse though: this lot having to face the mutes, or the ones that Meek is dealing with. That guy scares me.'

Muzzle's hand fell back to the wheel, his knuckles turning white. One of his nails was bloody where he had bitten away too deeply. 'Where the hell are we?' he asked suddenly.

They were driving through some type of suburban city centre, which was more intact than many areas of the Badlands. Some taller buildings remained standing, though they appeared to be decaying at a rapid pace. The streets were fairly tight, narrowed by the rubble spilling onto them.

The trucks ahead took a left hand fork in the road and finally started to accelerate. Muzzle followed, gazing around at the surroundings as he sped up. The Ash Walkers had not ventured this far from the Dome, so he not seen this area before.

'We're in the old Liverpool area,' one of the men in the back said. 'The mutes are thickest in these parts. Will make for better sport.'

'Why don't you give it a fucking rest?' Muzzle exclaimed, throwing a dark look over his shoulder. Their laughter subsided suddenly. He turned back to the road and only then did he notice the truck, identical to the two he was following, coming in fast at them from the right hand fork. For the briefest of seconds his eyes locked with Silver's, sitting in the passenger seat of the truck. Then his world exploded into violence and chaos before descending into darkness.

* * * * *

'He's right behind us now. We should see him soon,' Trax said, his eyes alternating from the road to the screen above the wheel. On screen he could see their own truck, and the one behind them as a blip on screen. A third blip was rapidly approaching. With no tracking unit on board, he could not see the Ash Walkers truck on screen, but a quick glance in the rear-view mirror showed it was still there.

'Good timing. We're in the thick of mute country now. Speed up, but keep an eye out for somewhere suitable to stop,' instructed Blade, next to him in the front passenger seat. He turned to gaze out the back window, past the three figures in the back, to try to catch sight of the fourth truck. The twins, Brew and Mack, were asleep, snoring contently. Sandwiched in between them was Grave, slouched down uncomfortably, and unconscious. The twins had handled him roughly and knocked him out while getting him into the truck. Blade scrutinised him a little longer before turning to face the front.

'The screen says he's moving pretty quick,' Trax noted as he increased his speed. 'Should be coming into view any second now.'

Blade slouched down in his seat to look out the passenger side mirror. He spotted the second Silmac Ops truck following close behind them, and the dented and run-down Ash Walkers truck third in line. They drove alongside a row of half-intact buildings, blocking view to the left or right. But behind them the road was relatively straight and clear and there was no sign of the fourth truck.

He sat up straight and grabbed the rear-view mirror, angling it so he could get a better view of the road behind. As he shifted it, he at last caught sight of the pursuing truck, coming up alongside them from a side road.

'Oh, there he is. He's coming down pretty fast. If he's not careful, he'll ... FUCK!'

As he watched, the fourth truck smashed directly into the side of the Ash Walkers truck, causing it to career violently to the left, mount the gutter and plough headlong into a partially collapsed shopfront on the side of the road. The other truck bounced away from the impact, swerving for a second and then straightening until it was following the first two. The heavy bull bar mounted on the front, along with its higher driving position, had protected it from any crippling damage in the collision, and it now began to accelerate towards them.

'That's not Coal driving the truck,' Blade growled. 'Step on it, Trax. Try to work your way back around to this spot. Brew! Mack! Wake the fuck up and start laying some fire down on those mutha-fukkas behind us.'

The big men started awake and after a second to orient themselves, they grabbed their masks from the floor in front of them, jostling Grave roughly in the process. Fixing his mask in place, Brew reached for the gun holstered at his belt and failed to notice that the knife sheath next to it was empty of its blade, or that the captive between them was not as oblivious to his surroundings as he appeared.

# Chapter 24

*From the diary of Benjamin Adams*
*March 1st, 2023*

*An earthquake shook Sydney last night, measuring 7.2. Not huge, but bad enough. It struck around 1:30am, which was lucky because it meant I was home with Jess and the kids, who were pretty scared. No one was hurt and the damage to our house was pretty minimal. But we were lucky. The centre of the quake was a couple of kilometres out to sea, and it triggered some six-metre waves, which hit the coastline. Forty-two fatalities have been reported so far, and many more are missing. The damage bill will reach into the multi-millions.*

*I imagine this will spark a fairly rigorous review of building standards and structural integrity, particularly in the city. Quakes like this have never happened here before, so there will be a lot of concern about the ability of our infrastructure to cope with it.*

* * * * *

'That was Muzzle we hit!' Silver exclaimed, once the truck had recovered from the collision.

'Good, that bastard deserves what he gets,' Asp responded coldly from the back seat.

While Muzzle had shown little concern for his former companions, Silver couldn't help but feel a little guilty. Had she not allowed herself to get so worked up by Grave, she would have never slept with Muzzle and perhaps all of this would never have eventuated. Even so, it was he who had given them away, and he had then stood by impassively as his former friends and companions got sentenced to death along with her.

'I think they've clued in that we're not friends,' Lead said, drawing

Silver's attention away from the smashed truck behind them and back towards the other two ahead. 'It's about to get a whole lot hotter.'

'I didn't see Grave, Rat or Sarge in the truck. They must be in the front two. Keep with them, Lead,' Silver instructed.

The trucks ahead were both accelerating and Lead had responded in kind, closing the gap between them while swerving through the ruined terrain. The closest truck clipped an out-jutting pillar of concrete and lurched up precariously onto two wheels for a second before bouncing back down onto four. Lead avoided the obstacle cleanly and in doing so closed the gap between them.

Up ahead, the first truck reached a T-junction, and swerved right around the corner, while the truck in front of them swerved left.

'Left or right?' Lead yelled.

'Stay on this one!' Silver directed. 'Whoever's driving is shaky and may be easier to take down.'

Lead banked hard into the corner, the truck drifting for a second before regaining traction and accelerating out of the curve. The truck ahead of them took another left turn, and again Lead took it more cleanly, closing the gap between them to just three or four truck lengths.

The front passenger door of the truck swung open, and a figure half climbed out, looking backwards and levelling a gun at them.

'Company!' Lead yelled, and pulled the wheel to the right, as the first shot was fired at them, going wide. 'We need some heat on this guy or we're toast!'

'Let's go,' Silver said to Asp, and opened her door. Warm wind ripped into the car, buffeting her as she steadied a foot on the step that ran along the side of the high position vehicle. Behind her, Asp climbed fully out of her seat, swinging into the tray behind the cab. Another shot from the car in front of them struck Silver's door, causing her to flinch backwards for a moment, fighting to maintain her balance.

Asp fired of two shots of her own, which travelled wide but forced the man in front to duck down lower, buying Silver time to recover and take up position in the 'V' formed by the open door and the truck's front windshield. Fighting for stability against the wind and the swerving of the truck, she took aim and fired off a shot of her own. It struck the roof less than half a metre from their assailant's position. He slouched down again, but just at that moment, the truck hit a brick on the road ahead and lurched violently, and the already off-balance gunman lost his footing. He managed to catch himself with one arm over the top edge of the open door, but as his weight fell onto the door, it swung fully open, flinging him out sideways and leaving him dangling helplessly over the road. Adding to his woes, the driver then banked into another left-hand turn, and as the centrifugal force flung him even further outwards, he lost his precarious grip and flew away to the side, landing heavily among the debris.

Silver gripped the handrail above the door opening tightly as Lead banked into the same turn, and she lost sight of the fallen gunman as they passed his position. The truck ahead took the turn too wide, clipping the gutter again and swerving wildly as the driver over-corrected. Lead took the turn much more smoothly, accelerating out of the corner and drawing still nearer to the truck ahead.

'You've got him rattled, Lead,' Silver shouted. 'Keep on them!'

The truck banked into a right-hand turn this time, taking the corner wide and then correcting back onto the right-hand side of the road. Lead also took the curve wide, but stayed left, accelerating to draw up alongside the back end of the truck. Silver ducked back inside the cab, unable to get a clear shot. A shot rang out and a bullet hole appeared just behind the wheel as Asp took another shot at it.

'Look out!' Silver yelled as she saw the crashed Ash Walkers truck on the road ahead and realised they had driven in a large circle.

Lead braked and pulled the wheel right, forcing their truck in behind their quarry while they passed the wrecked truck. One of the crewmen who had crawled from it was forced to dive aside as the two trucks tore past. Once they had passed the vehicle, Lead accelerated again and pulled back out alongside the Silmac Ops truck.

Silver glanced at the tracking display and noticed their blip and that of the other truck stuck together on screen. But the third blip was incredibly close as well, coming in at them from the left. As they entered an intersection, she spotted it bearing down at their exposed side like a big black metal bulldog.

'Lead, look out on your left!' Silver yelled, just as another shot rang out from above. The truck to their right shuddered as its tyre blew out. At the same moment, Lead braked and pulled right, clipping the back edge of the other truck and causing it to skid around in front of them before spinning away to the left. A moment later they were hit on the left side by the third truck. Lead's manoeuvre softened the impact to a degree, but the hit sent a violent jolt through the truck and caught Asp unawares. Silver heard her yelp and when she looked back, Asp was no longer in the tray behind them.

'Asp!' Silver yelled, as Lead fought the steering wheel to regain control of the vehicle. Silver looked back out the window, but recoiled as it shattered, raining glass down around her. The third truck, now behind them, had both back doors open, with a gunman on either side, firing off shots at them. Lead pulled hard on the wheel, swerving the truck back and forth across the road to try to evade the shots as best as possible. Another shot struck them, taking out a rear side window.

'We can't last long under this, Sil!' Lead exclaimed.

'I know! I know. I'm working on it.'

* * * * *

Blade yelled in triumph as their truck crashed into the rogue utility, throwing the passenger riding in the tray out onto the road. From the back seat, Grave caught momentary sight of the falling figure and recognised Asp. His heart leapt simultaneously in hope and fear. He was relieved that she had somehow managed to evade Meek, but worried that the fall from the truck would have equally lethal consequences.

'Trax, stay on their hammer, we've got 'em! Brew, Mack, keep the heat comin'!' Blade yelled, his voice slightly tinny and muffled through the filter. The big men had their doors open and were perched on the steps either side of the truck. Forgotten on the back seat, Grave felt the noxious air of the Badlands fill the truck and, filterless, was forced to breathe the befouled air. It had a chemical tang to it, tasting of petrol and ash and strong cleaning chemicals all at once. Almost immediately his throat began to tickle from it, and each breath felt as though he didn't quite get enough oxygen.

Behind him, his hands were slick with blood as he continued to saw away at his bonds with the knife he had managed to slip from Brew's belt while they slept. Squashed between and not wanting to alert them, he had been limited in his efforts to free himself and had numerous cuts and nicks on his wrist and back. But with a little more freedom and his captors' attention focused on the truck ahead, he began sawing in earnest, finally getting the blade fully between his wrists and against the zip-tie binding him.

While the twins continued to lay down fire on the truck ahead, at last Grave's bonds snapped open and he had his chance. Turning sideways in the seat, he kicked out hard with both legs at Brew. Caught unawares, the big man fell from the truck with a grunt, his gun spinning away in the process. Without wasting time, Grave stabbed out with his dagger at Mack on his right side, catching the second twin in the upper thigh, and then again in the gut.

The man yelled out in pain and, in his efforts to pull away, he too lost his balance and tumbled from the truck. Blade and Trax simultaneously looked around, their eyes wide at seeing Grave free on the back seat.

'You're fucking dead, Meldon,' Blade growled, reaching for the gun on his right hip.

Grave lunged forward with his knife, hampered by the position of the seats. Blade was able to evade the blow, but in doing so dropped his gun under the seat as he pulled it free of its holster. Grave reached for it, but Blade twisted and lunged at him between the two seats, grabbing his wrist where he held the knife. Grave tried to wrench his arm free, but Blade was strong and he held on, pushing all the while with his legs to force himself fully over the seat and down on top of Grave.

Grave struck at him with his free hand, but in the restricted space the blow was ineffective and Blade caught it. Now holding both of Grave's wrists, Blade lashed out with his forehead. Grave evaded the worst of the impact, but Blade's mask still caught him on the side of the head painfully. He continued to grapple with Blade, but his opponent was stronger, and his breathing was becoming ever more a struggle without a filter.

Above him, Blade grinned evilly through his mask, letting go of Grave's left wrist and instead clamping down on his throat.

* * * * *

'Wait a second, one of the gunmen has fallen. There goes the other one!' Silver exclaimed as she saw the second gunman tumble away from the truck. 'Whoever they've got in there is fighting back. Lead, can you get down beside them so we can help?'

Silver climbed onto the back seat of the cab and then took advantage of the missing back window to climb through onto the tray where Asp had been stationed earlier. Lead took a right-hand turn, going in a little sharper this time and easing back on the accelerator. The pursuing truck followed him into the curve but took it wider, bringing it up alongside Silver's position. She could see two men wrestling in the back of the cab. Blade was on top, and appeared to be in a stronger position, but she could not be sure who was underneath.

Lead eased back a little more, but as he did so the other truck veered into them. Silver braced herself against the impact, gripping the roll bar tightly but still fell to her knees as the trucks ground together. By now the trucks were almost fully side by side, but after the bump the gap between the two trucks had opened up to over three metres, too far for her to jump. She waited for the truck to come in for a second hit, and just before they clashed she leapt out over the gap and landed on all fours in the other truck. The impact followed, causing her to pitch forward and nearly go over the opposite side of the tray. She caught herself, banging her shoulder painfully in the process.

Shrugging off the pain, Silver steadied and got to her feet, pulling her gun as she arose, and then swinging her way down to the ledge on the side of the cab. She wrenched the door open, pointing the gun in at Blade, who looked up in surprise. Grave was beneath him, struggling for breath with one of Blade's hands held tightly around his throat.

'Let him go, now!' Silver ordered.

Blade reluctantly released Grave and moved off him towards the other side of the cab. Grave drew in a ragged gasp of air, coughing violently. Silver wondered if it was the suffocation or the lack of a filtered mask that caused the racking cough. Looking at Blade, she saw his eyes dart to the driver of the truck, and she quickly moved the gun to the back of his head, pressing it in for emphasis.

'Keep your hands on the wheel, cowboy. I want them where I can see them.' The driver eased his right hand, which had been drifting down towards the holster at his side, back up to the steering wheel. 'Good, now bring this truck to a stop up ahead. Nice and easy now.'

Out of the corner of her eye, Silver noticed some movement in Blade's direction, and as she turned to him, he lunged for the gun that was sticking out from under the seat in front. He had the gun halfway towards them when the first bullet took him in the chest. The gun tumbled from his fingers as the second bullet struck him. Blood sprayed the window and seat of the cab, splashing over Grave in the process. Blade keeled over backwards and out the still open door of the truck.

Silver's hand shook badly at the sight. She had never shot a man from such a close range, and while she had been given little choice, her stomach rebelled over what she had done. Grave reached out a bloodied hand and grabbed her, so she didn't lose her legs and tumble backwards out of the still moving truck.

'Try anything and that's what will happen,' Grave said to the driver, Trax. His voice was raw and croaky. 'Cooperate and no harm will come to you. Stop up here.'

'No! Take us back to the spot where the other truck crashed,' Silver ordered. 'We've got to get Asp, Sarge and Rat and make sure they are okay. This is mute territory.' Silver leant back out of the cab and gave a wave to Lead to let him know everything was under control.

* * * * *

Muzzle's consciousness returned in stages. Pain was first, his body aching from head to foot, with a more acute pain in the region of his hip. Next was smell. He could smell blood, with its distinct metallic tang, thick and coppery. It mixed in with another metallic smell, this one of heated metal and oil, the smell of the truck's engine after returning from a long drive in the Badlands. There was also fumes and smoke, the smell of the Badlands itself. With it came the realisation that he was not wearing his air filter.

Muzzle's hearing was the next to return, noticing a ticking, creaking noise coming from somewhere nearby, a sound he associated with a cooling engine.

He ventured to open his eyes, and was greeted by a bright blur, which slowly focused into images he could begin to decipher. He was inside the truck, but its shape had been altered, which confused him for a moment. The driver's seat was in the middle of the car, with the door panelling bent in obscenely. The steering wheel was twisted badly out of shape and the front windscreen was gone. The truck's bonnet was badly crumpled, sticking upwards on the right side at a sharp angle. Weirdly, he could see the front right-hand tyre through a tear that had opened up in the floor.

He lay across the front seat, his head half out the open passenger door. He was covered in blood that he guessed to be his own. He tried to pull himself up into a sitting position, but gave up as intense pain exploded through his body. Judging from the new shape of the truck, he had borne much of the impact on his right hip, which was now blue and black in colour, the skin stretched and swollen.

He looked out the open door and could see the others—Tip, Arlia, Slip, and another whose name he didn't know, gathered on the road nearby. They sported cuts and bruises, and Slip lay on the ground, clearly in pain.

Some movement further down the street caught his eye, and he shifted his head slightly to try to work out what it was. At first he couldn't see anything until another movement drew his attention— something pale ducking from a broken building to behind a pile of rubble. Another followed soon after and, horrified, Muzzle realised they were mutes, sneaking out of buildings and making their way towards the truck.

'Mutes!' he croaked out, causing his companions to look questioningly in his direction for the first time. 'Mutes,' he said again, more clearly this time, pointing.

They spun around and, spotting the advancing mutes, immediately pulled out weapons and started backing away. Tip pulled Slip up to his feet, and the group moved back towards Muzzle and the truck.

'Help me,' Muzzle appealed to them, pulling himself across the seat towards them. Tip was the only one who looked his way, throwing him a quick, pitiful glance, but making no move to assist. Arlia fired off a shot at the approaching mutes, and Muzzle could see it gave them pause, but only for a moment. There were more of them now, streaming out of the buildings and loping down the road towards the truck.

'Help me, please!' Muzzle screamed this time, sliding out of the truck and falling onto the ground. His hip ignited in pain and he screamed from the intensity. Arlia and the others continued to back away, firing more shots and ignoring Muzzle as they moved past the truck.. A couple of the mutes fell, and a few more dropped to feast on those that had. But others bypassed these and continued on towards the group.

Slip was the first to break and run, and as soon as he did, the others followed suit, abandoning Muzzle beside the truck.

'Help me,' he whimpered, watching the mutes drawing ever closer.

# Chapter 25



*From the diary of Benjamin Adams*
*August 22<sup>nd</sup>, 2029*

*Global tensions are rising and I have a feeling we are all in trouble. Oil prices have skyrocketed again, to the point where the roads are becoming emptier than I have ever seen them. Prices of groceries and most other things are also rising dramatically. People are getting desperate here, and from all reports it is much worse overseas. War is a very real possibility.*

*It's not just the threat of war that has me deeply concerned though. We've now had five quakes here in Australia in the past six years, each of them above seven on the Richter Scale. Floods are now an annual event and in ever widening areas. We're getting more thunderstorms than ever, and we've had snow in Sydney four times in the last three winters. It shouldn't be snowing in Sydney! The same thing is happening all around the world. I don't know what's happening, but I am scared for the kids and the future.*

* * * * *

Asp hit the ground hard and fell into an uncontrolled roll until the momentum was absorbed by the cracked and potted tarmac below. There was a crash nearby as the truck they had been pursuing spun into a building on the side of the road. The roar of the other two trucks receded as they continued on down the road, locked in battle.

When Asp tried to get up, she found her left elbow hurt like hell. She lifted it and flexed it experimentally, causing pain but giving some assurance it wasn't broken. Favouring her right side, she pushed herself up to her feet. Her clothes had protected her from some of the damage, but even so she sported more scrapes than their old truck had dents. She also had a bleeding gash on the back of her head, but her hair seemed to be helping somewhat to staunch the flow. Scanning around, she spotted her gun nearby and gingerly walked over to retrieve it before crossing the street to head towards the crashed truck.

As she went, she eyed the buildings warily. It appeared they were in what was once a suburban centre, more than likely the region once known as Liverpool. The buildings were on average five or six storeys high and, miraculously, many of them still looked intact, though far from safe. This far in from the coast, the buildings were still affected by tremors, but generally escaped tsunami damage, and didn't get the same frequency of storms. The apartments made her uneasy, the threat of their cracked and worn façades hiding a possible horde of mutes, feral dogs, or both, within.

The truck was immobilised, but more on account of the tyre Asp had shot out than from the final crash. They had struck the building almost completely side-on, which had distributed the impact more evenly than it otherwise may have. The tyre marks on the road also indicated that the truck had spun a couple of times before actually hitting anything.

A groan prompted Asp to raise her gun. The driver had blood dripping down his forehead and appeared a little groggy but looked otherwise okay. The front passenger seat was empty, and Asp recalled that the gunman had lost his balance and tumbled from the truck a couple of blocks back. The back seat housed Sarge, Rat and a mean-looking woman, who had clearly seen plenty of fights in her time. She was out cold, and Rat was not moving, but Sarge was in the process of using his one arm to pull himself over the woman and out of the truck. Asp noticed he had a gun tucked into his belt.

'Asp! It sure is good to see you, though you've looked better. Where's Blocka?'

She couldn't bring herself to answer the question, but the look she must have given him explained all. He came over to her and gripped her forearm somewhat awkwardly.

'Asp, I'm sorry.'

'Yeah, well, sorry won't bring him back,' she responded, wiping her eyes angrily at the moisture forming there. 'Anyway, we've got other things to worry about at the moment. Is Rat okay? What are we doing with these two?'

Sarge released her arm then looked back at the truck. The driver was conscious and watching them, though had not made a move for his gun or to get out of the truck. He seemed to be in shock. The woman was now stirring, having been jostled by Sarge as he climbed past her. His gaze flickered briefly over their surroundings, evaluating the ruins looming over them.

'We need to get moving, I think, and should take these two with us. I don't like the look of this place, and I don't want to be here when the mutes come out to investigate what all the banging and screeching of tyres was about. Much as I hate to say it, we might need 'em if it comes to that, though not sure if this one will be much good.' He indicated the driver.

'You two, out of the truck, now,' Asp ordered, motioning with her gun. 'You won't be harmed if you don't try anything funny.'

The Silmac Ops crew members slowly climbed out of the vehicle and stood before them. Apart from a few cuts and bruises, they looked in reasonable shape.

'You, hand your gun over.' Sarge indicated the still-holstered gun at the driver's side. 'And you, get back in and pull out Rat for us. Nice and gentle like. Free his hands too, and pass out two breathing filters.'

Without a word, the driver handed his gun over to Asp, and the woman climbed back into the truck and started dragging Rat across the seat so she could pull him out. He stirred as she moved him, allaying Sarge's concern that he might be dead.

A gunshot rang out, the sound echoing from one abandoned building to the next. It had come from somewhere down the road, in the direction of where the Ash Walkers truck had crashed.

'Time to get moving,' Sarge commanded, to which there were no arguments. Asp could see mutes pouring from a building in between the two crashed trucks and already some were looking in their direction.

'Help me, please … please … .ease … ease.' The shouted words echoed up the street, the desperation of them evident even in the ghostly echo that followed.

'Sounds like Muzzle,' Rat murmured, conscious now but sporting a gash on his forehead and limping a little. Sarge began herding everyone down the street, away from the truck and the mutes, staying in close to the buildings to try to make themselves less visible. The Silmac

Ops crew members were first, supporting each other and moving at a limping run. Asp and Rat were next, and Sarge followed up the rear, constantly looking over his shoulder to check for any mutes in pursuit.

'Well, I guess he'll find out if his new companions come to his aid, or whether they'll prove as loyal as he,' Asp answered coldly. 'Even if he deserved help, there's nothing we can do for him now.'

'They're on to us,' Sarge called softly from the back. 'Asp, we need to get off the road, find somewhere to defend ourselves.'

Asp picked up the pace a little and scanned the street ahead, looking for viable options. Many of the shopfronts were gaping black holes, the glass that had once opened up onto the street long shattered and gone. Finally, she spotted one that looked promising and made for it. The window of the old shop had been boarded up, and while it was missing a door, the narrow entrance was something they might be able to defend. It was an older, two-storey brick building, with a balcony above, facing the street.

She entered the shop carefully, wary of what might be hiding in the black hole that was its entrance. As her eyes adjusted, she could see the interior was relatively clear and empty. It was rundown and shabby inside, the interior walls having been ripped out long ago and thrown into a corner, no doubt in search of metal inside the walls. There was a small, equally empty room in the back, with the rear exit having been securely boarded up at some point long ago, and a rickety looking staircase leading up.

The rest of the group piled into the room, with Sarge lingering at the door a moment, peering back on their pursuit. 'We have about a minute before they reach us.'

'Did they see where we went?' Asp asked.

'Not sure.'

'Let's head upstairs. Maybe they'll pass us by. Careful on the stairs, stay close to the wall.'

Rat led the way upstairs, then Asp and the two Silmac Ops crew members, and finally Sarge. The stairs groaned and protested under the weight, but held. Above, the scene was similar to below, the room having been stripped bare. Light filtered in from the street via the door that led onto the balcony. The floor creaked with every movement, so the group gathered in the centre of the room, out of sight from the bottom of the stairwell, and far enough away from the door to the balcony that they would not be seen from the street.

Sarge offered the gun he had confiscated to the Silmac Ops members, and the woman reached out and took it. 'What names do you go by?' he whispered to them.

'I'm Hawk, and this is Schmidt,' the woman said, her voice gruff.

'Well, Hawk, if they come at us, you, me and Asp take the front and stop them getting up the stairs. Use bullets sparingly and call your targets. Rat and Schmidt, stay out of the way, but be ready to jump in once the bullets are spent. In the meantime, no one moves. We make a sound, they will find us.'

'If only I had my grenades with me,' Rat lamented, before being shushed by Asp as the sound of approaching mutes filtered in from outside. Their breathing could be heard, a rattling, wheezing sound emitting from their ruined throats and damaged lungs.

The group upstairs fell deathly quiet, not daring to move lest they elicit a groan of protest from the floor below and give themselves away. Asp scanned the faces around the group. Sarge had his eyes on the staircase, looking relaxed and only concerned with being ready to act if needed. Rat looked down at the floor, clearly fearful but managing to keep his emotions in check. The woman, Hawk, looked much like Sarge, eyes focused on the stairway. Only the white knuckles on the hand gripping her gun gave away her nervousness. The driver, Schmidt, was the risk, his eyes wide with fear, darting back and forth between the staircase and the balcony. His body trembled with barely contained terror. If he could not control his fear, there was a real risk he would give them all away.

The skip of a stone on concrete sounded from downstairs, indicating that at least one of the mutes had entered the building. The five barely breathed for fear of making a sound. Asp imagined she could hear their five heartbeats drumming out a rapid rhythm in anticipation.

And then Schmidt moved. It was not a big movement, merely a shift of weight from one foot to the other. But the creak it elicited from the floor below might have been a clap of thunder to Asp's ears. The reaction downstairs was immediate, with soft footfalls padding over to the stairs, and then more creaks and groans as a mute began to ascend the stairs.

Asp looked to Sarge and met his eye, a silent communication passing between them. They moved almost in unison, tucking their guns into their pants and charging down the stairs at the mute, trying to get to it before it could draw others down on them, and hoping there was only one in the building.

The mute widened its eyes in shock as the two barrelled down the stairs towards it. Sarge got there first and punched out at it, throwing his momentum behind the blow. The mute tried to get its hands up but was a fraction of a second too slow. Sarge's fist struck its face with the crunch of shattered cartilage. It fell to the floor, out before it hit the ground. Asp rushed the rest of the way down the stairs, scanning for other mutes in the room, and finding it clear. Wasting no time, she grabbed the mute's arms, and Sarge grabbed its legs, hoisting it and backing up the stairs. Its skin was rough to touch, dry and cracked, covered in sores. It was surprisingly heavy despite its wiry frame.

They were halfway up the stairs when Asp heard a strangled cry and saw another mute staring in at them, signalling to others beyond the doorway. She immediately dropped the body, pulled her gun and fired off a shot at the mute, striking it cleanly in the chest and turning its cry into a gurgle of blood as it fell to the ground. The shot rang out loudly, but their cover was blown, so the time for stealth was over. She then rushed up the stairs after Sarge, who was already issuing orders. The stairway shifted noticeably as she ran up, its supports clearly in poor condition.

'We stop them at the stairs. Hawk, Asp, you're with me. Alternate shots—me, Asp then Hawk—so we don't waste ammunition. Rat, find something in that pile we can use as weapons once we're out of bullets. Schmidt, keep an eye on the balcony in case they try to come up that way, and stay out of the way for Christ's sake!'

He had barely finished speaking when the first of the mutes came into view at the bottom of the stairs, starting up them in a frenzy. Sarge lifted his gun, but Asp put a steadying hand on his shoulder. 'Let him come. Enough weight on the staircase might cause it to collapse.'

Sarge nodded, allowing the mute to charge almost to the top before discharging the weapon into the degenerated creature's chest. It went down instantly, tumbling back halfway until it came to a stop against the body of the mute they had knocked out earlier. More mutes were pouring into the building to take their place on the stairs. Asp fired off her round, taking down the second, and Hawk fired at the third, sending it sprawling down the stairs, impeding the progress of those behind it.

The creatures kept coming, their eyes wild, faces contorted in frenzied grimaces of rage. Male, female, young and not so young, all had pale, cracked skin covered in sores, all were wiry thin, with straggly, thin hair and bulging eyes. The slaughter sickened Asp, but the alternative left her little choice.

The pile on the stairs grew, though bodies twisted and tumbled down to the bottom as other mutes swarmed over those who had fallen. Despite the weight, the stairway held. Asp was the first to run out of ammunition, having fired off a few shots earlier on the back of the truck. She turned, and Rat handed her a length of wood he had dug out of the pile. It was a little lighter than ideal, but it added length to her arm and was better than fighting with her bare hands. Hawk was the next to fire her last bullet, so she pulled out a knife from a sheath on the inside of her left boot.

Sarge held his gun level at the nearest mute, struggling up over the bodies of its fallen comrades, unfazed by the fate of those who had come before it. A scream from behind them caused him to turn. In the doorway that led to the balcony, a mute had grabbed hold of Schmidt from behind and was biting down on his neck. Sarge steadied and fired his shot, hitting the mute in the head and flinging it away, back through the doorway. Schmidt fell to his knees, clutching at the bloody wound and whimpering.

The distraction was all the mutes on the stairs needed. As Sarge turned back towards them, one grabbed his leg and yanked hard, pulling him off balance. He dropped his gun as he fell hard onto the stairway and was immediately grabbed by a second mute. Together, they began dragging him down.

'No!' Asp yelled, lunging forward to grab hold of his one arm and try to pull him back up. She pulled hard, but a third mute had now joined the first two, and they had gravity on their side. Sarge grunted in pain as one of them bit into his leg. All the while Asp was being dragged closer to the stairs and her grip on his wrist becoming more and more tenuous.

'Sarge, hold on!' she cried out through gritted teeth.

He met her eye and slowly shook his head, slackening his own grip on her. His fingers slipped through her hand and he came free. Unprepared for the sudden release, the mutes fell backwards on the stair and with a final creak of protest the staircase gave way. Asp's cry of distress was lost in the crash of the stairs and the din of splintering wood.

A scream from Sarge confirmed he had survived the fall, but when Asp scrambled to the edge she saw a swarm of mutes descending on him. 'He's still alive. We have to help him!'

A gunshot cut off any thought of action, and Sarge's body went limp, a blossom of blood appearing in his chest. Asp looked around to see Hawk standing next to her, her face grim. Sarge's fallen gun was in her hand.

'It was a mercy,' the hard woman defended.

Asp opened her mouth to protest, but then nodded her thanks. 'I couldn't have done it.'

A yell from the other side of the room drew their attention. Schmidt was locked in a grapple with another mute who had climbed up to the balcony. Blood streamed from the wound on his neck. He had produced a knife from somewhere and was stabbing at the mute, who tore at him with its fingers and kicked at him with its bare feet. Asp and Hawk rushed over, dragging it from him and moving out onto the balcony to hurl it to the ground below.

The sight that greeted them from the balcony was straight out of a nightmare. At least two score of mutes were milling around the base of the building. Three were in the process of climbing up the wall towards them and more were inside, fighting over Sarge's remains.

A collective howl rose from the gathered mutes as they saw the two women above. Mutes began charging at the building, leaping up at the walls in a frenzied effort to get at them. A finger of ice shot up Asp's spine; she found herself rooted to the spot, paralysed with fear and unable to look away. Beside her, Hawk was similarly still.

At the back of the pack, a mute suddenly paused in its growling, looking away from the balcony down the street. Soon another followed suit, and then a third. A moment later Asp heard it too: the distant sound of engines grumbling over the din of the mutes and slowly growing in volume.

The sound galvanised Asp into action and she ran back inside, retrieving her makeshift club. She raced back to the balcony, swinging at a mute just cresting the rail on the balcony, sending it sprawling back to the ground below. She leant out over the rail, looking up the road. Two trucks tore down the road towards them, some way off but moving fast. A figure stood on the back of the first truck.

'Rat, Schmidt, get out here now. We're going,' she yelled through the doorway, swinging her club down on a hand that had just caught grip of the rail. With a strangled howl, the mute fell to the ground. Hawk did the same thing on the other side of the balcony, having stowed her knife in favour of another length of wood. At Asp's words, she looked down the street and the closest thing Asp had seen to a smile cracked her lips.

'We're going to need to be quick and time the jump right,' Asp said to Hawk. 'Schmidt goes first, then you. Rat and I will take the second truck. When you hit the tray, get up and fight off the mutes, or they'll overrun us all.'

Hawk nodded and swung her club at another mute mounting the rail while the trucks drew closer to their position.

# CHAPTER 26

*From the diary of Benjamin Adams*
*June 7th, 2031*

*Jayden got married yesterday. I think he and Amber decided to move it forward because of everything going on. It was not like the weddings we grew up with, but it was a welcome respite from everything else. They had a happy day and I am pleased for them.*

*The design I have been working on is almost complete. It is a dome big enough and strong enough to shield a city, and has been a long project. Everything needs to be considered: structural integrity, power, water, air, food. It seems crazy that we may need to resort to this, but every day that passes affirms the need of such a structure. We continue to get quakes, tsunamis and volatile weather and the air quality is getting poorer and poorer.*

*The government is calling for tenders for the project, so I will be presenting to them in the next month. My design includes the capacity for the dome to create its own energy from the sun; effectively it is one big solar panel. But with the volume of mining influence present in parliament, I am concerned this will work against me. I must find a way.*

* * * * *

The wind whipped through Silver's hair as the truck tore along the road, heading back to the crash site. Her pack rested open beside her, with Rat's remaining grenades in easy reach. She had grabbed them from the glove box, and now stood in the tray of the truck driven by Lead. Behind them followed the other truck, driven by Trax under the watchful eye of Grave.

'Faster, Lead,' she shouted, tapping her foot impatiently as the truck sped along. They had heard distant gunfire, but the moment had come when a single, final shot rang out, and no more had followed. The absence of sound was deafening, and she feared the worst.

At last, they rounded a bend in the road and saw a pack of mutes up ahead, milling around the base of a building. Silver leant forward over the cab and saw that some were scaling the shopfront. One tumbled to the tarmac, and she saw a couple of figures on the balcony, doing their best to repel the mutes.

'Get under that balcony!' she yelled to Lead through the now glass-less back window of the truck. She squatted down and grabbed one of the grenades and a match, striking it down low out of the wind. The match took on the second attempt, but she did not immediately light the fuse, recalling the speed at which it had burned down last time.

Lead continued to accelerate, and they closed rapidly; a hundred metres, eighty, sixty. At about fifty metres, Silver lit the fuse and stood. Forty metres. Thirty. The fuse burned down rapidly and when they were about twenty-five metres from the pack, she pitched it forward, gripping the rollbar one-handed to steady herself.

The grenade spun through the air towards the pack of mutes, who by this time had seen the truck bearing down on them and had started to scatter. The grenade hit the ground once before exploding in a brief but spectacular flash of heat and light. Some mutes were lost in the blast; others were hurled away by its concussive force. Silver felt the wave of heat wash over her as the truck screeched to a halt in the space the blast had just cleared.

'Asp! Sarge! Rat! Hurry, jump down!'

Silver could almost reach the balcony from her position in the truck, though could not see over it. Mutes were already starting to pick them-selves up, and she caught sight of movement within the shop. Behind her, Grave's truck pulled up beside them, close enough to easily step across onto his tray.

Asp's face appeared, followed by Hawk and Schmidt, both crew members she had worked with at Silmac Ops. Lastly they were joined by Rat, but there was no sign of Sarge. Schmidt was already climbing up onto the rail. He hesitated a moment when it came to jump, and Hawk gave him a shove, sending him kicking out towards the tray. He landed heavily and Silver grabbed his arm to stop him pitching over the other side. When she looked back up, Hawk had already leapt down, landing a little more gracefully next to Schmidt.

A handful of mutes were now converging on the stationary truck. 'Jump across to the other truck, quickly!' Silver yelled at the two, and Hawk wasted no time helping Schmidt across and following suit. As soon as they were in, the engine roared and Grave's truck lurched forward, pulling away so Lead would be able to follow once Asp, Rat and Sarge were on board.

Asp was helping Rat up onto the railing as two mutes reached the truck and started trying to scramble up into the tray. Silver fired a shot at one, blasting it away.

'Quickly!' she yelled to Rat, who cried out as he jumped and landed heavily on his wounded leg. Silver fired off another shot at a mute who had gotten one leg up into the tray and then bent to drag Rat aside and allow room for Asp. As soon as a spot was clear, Asp leapt down, landing smoothly..

'Where's Sarge?' Silver yelled to her, looking to the balcony for their one-armed companion.

Asp gave a small shake of her head and thumped her hand on the top of the cab. 'Go, Lead!' she yelled.

The tyres squealed as Lead put his foot down, and the truck lurched forward, throwing Silver off her feet as they hit the pothole the grenade had torn into the tarmac. The gun slipped from her grasp as she fell heavily against one side of the tray and came face to face with a mute that had grabbed hold of the side. With a hiss, it reached for her, its wiry but powerful fingers grasping her hair. At the same time it let go of the truck, yanking her head painfully forward in an attempt to drag her off.

Silver's scalp erupted in pain as the weight of the mute drew her head over the edge of the truck. She scrambled for a hold on the tray's rim, catching a glimpse of the tarmac rushing past below, too quickly for her eyes to pick out detail as Lead accelerated away from the shopfront. Despite the mute's legs dragging on the road, it would not relinquish its hold on her hair, and the pain on her scalp was excruciating.

She felt a hand grab her by the shirt collar and heard a sickening thwack. Finally the pressure on her scalp was gone, and the mute was left rolling across the tarmac behind them as the truck sped away. She pulled herself up to see Asp standing above her, makeshift club in hand.

Her relief was short lived as, beyond Asp, she spied another mute pulling itself fully up onto the tray.

'Look out!' she yelled as the mute barrelled into Asp's side, knocking her from her feet. Silver was about to jump to her aid when a third mute appeared on the far side of the tray, scrambling in and over at Rat, who was huddled in the corner.

Up front, a gunshot sounded as Lead tried to rid the bonnet of two more mutes who had jumped on and were pulling themselves around to get at the side doors.

As Asp grappled with her attacker, Silver launched herself at the one attacking Rat. She shoulder charged it, hoping her momentum would throw it from the truck. But another gunshot up front preceded a sudden lurch of the truck, causing Silver to stumble as she connected with the mute. The impact knocked the mute off Rat and into the side of the tray, but failed to knock it out. It lashed at her with filthy, broken nails, drawing lines of blood across her bicep that stung painfully. She punched out in retaliation, striking it in the face and stunning it for a second. Sitting up, Rat grabbed one of its legs and she grabbed the other, pitching it up and over the rim of the tray and sending it tumbling out of the truck.

Silver was breathing hard through her filter, but she spun around to where Asp continued to wrestle with the final mute on the left side of the truck. The mute was on top of her, snapping in at her neck like a rabid dog. Asp had hold of its wrists and was desperately writhing and kicking to keep her neck clear of its yellowed, jagged teeth.

Silver lurched over at the pair, throwing her shoulder in at its exposed side and trying to get her arm in under its torso to pull it from her friend. The impact knocked the wind out of the creature, and while it attempted to regain its breath, Asp and Silver were able to push it up and throw it over the rim of the truck.

Lead had managed to rid himself of the two on the bonnet. Exhausted from the sustained assault, both women slumped back into the tray.

'Everyone all right back there?' Lead called out.

'We'll live,' Silver managed. 'Just get us the hell away from this place.'

* * * * *

'Report.'

Johnson, Silmac's new head of security, stood in front of Silmac, doing remarkably well to keep his trembling in check. He was tall, muscular, clean-shaven and dressed impeccably in uniform, standing rigidly at attention. He reminded Silmac of photos he had seen of decorated army men from the past.

'Sir, I believe we have uncovered who was responsible for shooting Coal, and where the missing crew member is.'

'Well? Who, and where?' Silmac asked impatiently, irritated not for the first time by Meek's death. His former head of security had been efficient and to the point, knowing when to speak and when to await orders. It was an inconvenience to have lost him.

'Some witnesses saw a dark-skinned man, street name Lead, arrive at the Silmac Ops crew house in the early hours of the morning, followed shortly by a gunshot. Lead was a previous, long-term member of the crew, who had recently been stood down by Coal.'

'Why was Coal there alone? Where was the rest of his crew?'

'The rest of the crew had departed for the Badlands, but Coal was not among them. And he was not there alone; the witness spotted Lead leaving the scene with a woman in tow. We believe it was Silver, one of the women ordered to be executed. Checkpoint guards confirm that they did not see Silver leaving with the rest of the crew.'

'Fuck!' Silmac exclaimed, striking his still half full whiskey glass from the table in a rare loss of control. The glass flew across the room, shattering when it struck the wall some five metres from the desk. 'This woman is turning into a major headache.'

'There's more,' the head of security ventured, somewhat nervously. 'Police forces believe they spotted these two at the shop on York, fleeing with a dark-skinned woman in tow; street name Asp. She was one of the two Ash Walkers crew members that Meek had been targeting for retrieval.'

'And your police force let them get away?'

'Affirmative. Police on the scene took up pursuit, but were hampered by explosives carried by the trio. However,' he added quickly, to try to pre-empt a further outburst, 'I have found what happened to the three. They departed the Dome in a Silmac Ops truck not long after their escape from the police. I've contacted each of the operating checkpoints and am confident that they remain out in the Badlands.'

Silmac squeezed his eyes shut and pinched the bridge of his nose against the dull ache forming there. 'And what of the other crew member Meek was hunting?'

'Street name Blocka. His body was found among the ruins of the shop, along with the bodies of the female's parents.'

'What is the status on the streets?'

'It is tense, sir. All officers other than those assisting in my investigation have been pulled back to Silmac Tower. There are not many reports of violence at this stage, but the streets are restless. We are getting a steady stream of wealthier subjects coming and wanting answers and protection. Your brother is below, seeking an audience with you.'

Silmac massaged his temple, weighing up all he had been told. 'The odds of these three in taking out the Silmac Ops team are not high, but I will not take any more risks. Seal off all but one gate out of the Dome. Post a sizable force at that gate and ensure that every truck that comes through is thoroughly screened. Any members of the Ash Walkers crew or the Silmac Ops crew are to be taken into custody and held in isolation. The contents of their trucks must also be confiscated and placed in secure lockdown. The Ash Walkers are dangerous criminals who are trying to spread propaganda to start a rebellion within the Dome. And since this Lead character, ex-Silmac Ops, has been seen with them, I cannot afford to have any Silmac Ops crew members loose within the Dome either, until we know who we can trust.'

'Yes, sir. All you have said will be carried out.'

'Good. Leave me now.'

'Should I send up your brother?'

'No, I can't stand to listen to his incessant panic and whining. Tell him I am indisposed and will call for him later.'

# Chapter 27



*From the diary of Benjamin Adams*
*February 6<sup>th</sup>, 2034*

*Construction of the Dome began officially today. It has been a long and exceedingly busy two-and-a-half years since the initial presentation. I omitted the solar panels from the design I presented to the board and have spent much time since working on a way that I can still incorporate the panels without giving away my deception.*

*It was the right choice to omit the panels from the presentation. The lead panellist, Jenny Silmac, is one of Australia's wealthiest mine owners, and three other panel members have family interests in different mining ventures. It is rumoured some of the other submissions were vetoed because of their clean energy recommendations.*

*My plan is a risky one. I have worked with a contact to develop a new, partially transparent panel design that lets some light through but is efficient enough to harness considerable power. It is much darker than clear glass, which I have disguised as a feature to protect the Dome against extreme heat conditions, a legitimate condition that the Dome will need to cope with. The panels will darken when energy production needs to be increased, and lighten when it needs to slow, effectively meaning that the Dome will manage its own energy levels, and reduce the need for major energy storage solutions.*

*The wiring to the panels serves a dual purpose. It brings energy to the Dome surface as protection against frost and ice build-up. This is a very real threat for such an immense structure. However, the wiring is also capable of taking generated energy away, directing it to the energy grid. The switch to turn the panels on and off will be hidden in the spire of Centrepoint Tower, which I have designed to sit in the direct centre of the structure and poke through the top of the Dome. It is not an ideal place to put it, but will ensure it is not uncovered prematurely.*

*The weather is becoming ever more extreme and the quakes are increasing in regularity and severity. I am pushing on with the project as hard as I can.*

* * * * *

Up ahead, Grave's truck came to a stop in a relatively clear, open section of ground and Lead pulled his truck up next to it. They had gained some distance from the mutes and were once again much closer to the Dome. Asp and Silver were both in reasonable shape physically, with numerous scrapes, bruises and small scratches, but nothing too serious. Rat was in the worst shape, having suffered first at the hands of the Silmac Ops crew back at the Dome, then when the truck crashed, and again when jumping from the balcony. Silver suspected he had broken ribs, a dislocated shoulder and a badly sprained ankle—nothing life threatening at this stage, but enough to take him out of action.

Silver, Lead and Grave were the first out of the trucks. 'I owe you both a big thanks. It's Lead, right?' Grave extended his hand.

'That's right,' Lead replied, shaking hands firmly. 'You got Trax and Hawk in the truck? What happened to Schmidt?'

'We had a couple of mutes grab hold of the truck. They dragged Schmidt over before Hawk or I could stop them.' He glanced over at the Silmac Ops crew members in the truck. 'Can they be trusted?'

Lead nodded. 'They should be okay. I'll go lay it out for them.' He took his leave, heading over to Grave's truck and jumping in. Grave and Silver were left in an awkward silence.

'You okay?' Grave asked her eventually.

'Exhausted, but I'll live. You?'

'Likewise.' More silence. 'What happened to Coal?'

'Dead. Lead chanced by and took him down.'

'Did he hurt you?'

She shook her head, but felt tears threatening anyway. 'I'm so fucking tired, Grave,' she said, her voice quivering.

Grave stepped forward and wrapped her in a hug. His grip was strong and gave her a measure of comfort as the tears began to fall. 'I don't blame you, Silver. But take some strength from the fact that you saved us today. Without you we'd all be dead. We owe you big time; I owe you big time. You can't know how relieved I am that you got away from Coal.'

He stroked her hair gently, which had a soothing effect. After a few moments she extracted herself from his arms.

'Thank you. I'm relieved you're all right as well.' Their eyes met and locked for a few seconds, before Grave turned away, looking towards the truck.

'Where's Blocka and Sarge?' he asked, sudden concern on his face.

'Blocka didn't make it,' Silver replied. 'Meek got to the shop before Lead and me. When we arrived, the place was under siege, Asp's parents were dead, Meek was dead by Blocka's hands, and Blocka was dying from multiple gunshot wounds.'

Grave closed his eyes, rubbing his forehead wearily. 'And Sarge?'

'The mutes got Sarge,' Silver said. 'Asp says he fought well, but they got him. Hawk made sure he didn't suffer though.'

Grave's face was dark, unreadable. 'How is Asp doing?'

'Not good. Only a sense of duty toward you, Sarge and Rat, and the chance at revenge convinced her to come out with us. The only time she's come close to her old self since then is while we were fighting the mutes on the back of the truck.'

'I feel terrible—it's my fault that they are dead. I should have never dragged others into my plans against Silmac,' Grave said.

'No, it's my fault,' Silver countered. 'Had I not come to the Ash Walkers, you never would have got involved with Silmac Ops, and ended up Coal's prisoner in front of Silmac.'

'Then it's Coal's fault, or Silmacs', or our ancestors for fucking up the world so badly,' Asp cut in, having opened the door and overheard their conversation. 'Or it's my fault, for opting out. Had Blocka and I been with you, maybe Silmac Ops wouldn't have taken you all.'

'It's not your fault, don't blame yourself!' Silver objected.

'I think what she's trying to say is there's nothing to be gained by playing the blame game,' Lead interjected, having also reappeared, Trax and Hawk with him. 'The past can't be changed, only the future. So what I want to know is, what are we going to do next?'

Grave nodded, though his gaze lingered on Asp for a while longer and he stepped forward to engulf her in a hug. 'I'm so sorry for your loss, Asp, and for whatever part, large or small I played in it.'

Asp returned the hug, gripping him tightly. When at last Grave and Asp came apart, Grave looked slowly around at the others in the circle. 'What we do next is up to you. I can't ask more of you.'

'We take down Silmac,' Asp responded immediately.

'I agree, we can't stop now,' Silver affirmed.

'The way I see it, we don't have much choice,' Lead reasoned. 'To stop now would be pointless—either we take down Silmac, or he us. The Dome is too small a place to hide from him for long. But even if I had a choice, I think I'd say we continue. Silver filled me in on the situation and if it turns out to be true, then we gotta give it a go.'

Hawk shrugged. 'Count me in. I'm guessing I wouldn't be welcome back in the Dome anyway. Silmac'd just as soon take me out as you, just to be safe. Trax feels the same.' Next to her, Trax nodded, though not with much enthusiasm.

'Okay, so we're all in,' Grave said. 'Now we've just got to find a way to continue with the plan. Have we got the panels and the papers we printed?'

'The papers are in the back of this truck,' Hawk said, patting the roof. 'The panels were in your truck, the old one that is. It got taken down not far from where we did, and last we saw there were a whole lot of mutes swarming that way. I don't like your chances of getting them back.'

Grave nodded in agreement. 'The panels are less important for the time being, the papers are what we need. If we can get back in and start distributing them, that will help. Getting into Silmac Tower will be tougher though. Silmac will be wary and I can no longer draw on my name to get inside.'

'You're getting a bit ahead of yourself—getting back inside the Dome is going to be the first challenge,' Lead commented.

'We've got Silmac Ops trucks with us,' Silver objected. 'We should be able to drive in as usual, pretend like nothing's amiss.'

'Maybe,' Grave conceded. 'But Lead could be right. It wouldn't surprise me if Silmac has a welcoming committee waiting for us, whether we return as the Ash Walkers or Silmac Ops. This is a sensitive secret that he didn't want getting out, and the fewer people that know about a secret, the safer it is. It's likely his intention is to do away with Silmac Ops on their return.'

'Sil, Asp and I were also seen leaving the scene of the shop,' Lead added. 'Someone would have pieced the puzzle together now and knows that we drove out into the Badlands soon after. So pretty safe to say the gates will be watched.'

'Okay, so the gates are out,' Silver agreed. 'What about the old ventilation tunnels?'

'I'd prefer to make it back into the Dome *not* chopped up into tiny pieces,' Hawk noted dryly.

'Don't they lead back up into the checkpoint buildings?' Lead asked. 'We might not be any better off than trying to drive in. And like Hawk says, we'd still need to get past the huge fan blades.'

'I've got one more of Rat's bombs, which should do the trick on the fans. And like Grave, Asp and I found out the other day, the checkpoint buildings also have access to the sewer systems. We could find our way into those and come up onto the street beyond the building.'

'What about the Homeless?' Hawk recoiled in horror. 'We'll never make it back up to the street. They'll take us captive and eat us alive!'

'No they won't,' Grave cut in. 'It's a good plan and our only real option. Let's go.'

* * * * *

'You assured me everything was under control, Corbett,' Gavin complained. 'Unrest on the streets and a flock of wealthy citizens seeking shelter is not what I call under control. A few have already had their property raided by mobs. Anna's beside herself with worry, and the kids are scared.'

'I've told you, this is nothing we haven't seen before,' Silmac replied smoothly, his calm voice belying his impatience. After delaying another couple of hours, he had been unable to put his brother off any longer. Gavin was extremely agitated. 'Necessary steps have been taken to protect us here until the mob grows weary and decides to go home. Accommodation is being found for the wealthy seeking asylum, for peace of mind. Any who lose property can be compensated when things settle down.'

'What news of Meldon and that girl? Are they dead yet?'

Silmac's eyes flashed but otherwise his face belied calm. 'Silmac Ops has not yet returned from the Badlands, but these things take time. In all likelihood, they will be back soon with word that everything has gone to plan. And in the event they are not, precautions have been taken as extra insurance.'

'I don't like it, Corbett. I've got a bad feeling about this,' Gavin said.

Silmac's eye twitched involuntarily. 'Your bad feeling is probably indigestion from stuffing your face with food day in day out,' Silmac replied.

'You think this is funny?' Gavin asked, his voice sounding shrill. 'You think you can make jokes about it?'

'I think I can do whatever the hell I want,' Silmac said, his voice rising in volume as he stood up from his desk. His eye twitched again, this time more noticeably and Gavin recoiled. 'Too long have I carried you, Gavin. I've given you a position and tasks to make you feel useful and important. I've provided for you, included you in discussions I didn't need to, coddled and babied you. But all you do is bring your problems to me to solve. You don't know half of what it takes to run this operation, and so you overstep yourself. I rule the Dome, not you, not us. Everything you have I gave to you. My decision is final and it will not be questioned. Do you understand?'

'You can't …' Gavin began to object, but Silmac rounded the table and backhanded him across the cheek.

'I can and I will!' he shouted down at him, the veins in his forehead standing out. 'Get out. I don't want to hear so much as a peep from you, or you'll be taking a long walk in the Badlands without an escort. You'll be praying for the feral dogs to get you before the mutes do. DO YOU UNDERSTAND?'

Gavin held his bruised cheek with one hand and stared silently up at his brother with wide eyes. Slowly, he rose from his chair and headed over to the lift.

Silmac watched him go, breathing heavily. When the lift doors closed, he straightened his tie and ran his hands through his hair, as he walked around the desk towards his chair. Halfway there, he changed direction, yanked his tie off, and strode across the office towards the door to his private apartment. He wrenched the door open and slammed it shut behind him, throwing the tie to the floor, then tearing off his jacket. He checked his watch. It was not time for his scheduled workout, but he continued on towards the gym anyway, a trail of discarded clothes behind him.

# CHAPTER 28

*From the diary of Benjamin Adams*
*July 21ˢᵗ, 2034*

*I am now a grandfather and feeling much older for it. Jayden and Amber named their baby boy Jack, and he is gorgeous. It was good taking some time out from the project to spend with the family and see everyone together. Alex is also getting fairly serious with his girlfriend, Tracey. Chloe is twenty-one now, which is hard to believe. Jess and I are so proud of them all.*

*Work on the project goes well. Silmac is heavily visible around the site, and I suspect she is the one throwing lots of money at it to smooth over any problems and delays. I heard a rumour last week that she is considering running for prime minister at the next election.*

* * * * *

Silmac felt wearier than he had in a long time, but it wasn't physical fatigue. He had spent two hours in the gym, and it had been enough to calm him down, but not enough to settle him completely. He paced the room, as he had found himself doing most of the day, waiting for an update that hadn't come. It was dark beyond the windows of his office now. Finally, Johnson arrived in person.

'Sir, the checkpoint gates have now been closed and there is still no sign of the Ash Walkers or any of the Silmac Ops trucks. We've searched every truck that came through and I'm confident that they are not back inside the Dome.'

'Any word of them from other teams out there today?'

'Negative. There were a couple of reports of gunfire heard by crews working the south-west district. But no sightings of the Silmac Ops or Ash Walkers trucks.'

Silmac clenched his fists in frustration. 'That's no good to me, Johnson. I need to know. Are they alive? Are they dead? I need certainty!'

'I'm sorry, sir. I will get some recon units out in the morning, assuming there is still no sign of them.'

'Morning? What happens in the meantime?'

'I've briefed the checkpoint guard that under no circumstances are they to open the doors to anyone during the night,' Johnson replied. 'I'd advise to continue with just one gate in operation for the next couple of days to be sure.'

'Yes. Good. What of the streets?'

'The streets remain restless, night has not dispersed the crowds.'

'Do you think a display of force would produce the desired effect?'

'Unsure, sir. It could escalate the situation for some, but if we are able to act quickly and efficiently for those, I think we would discourage further unrest.'

'Begin arming your men in full riot gear and make sure it is a visible display. However, do not act yet, other than to sound the curfew sirens. I don't want to escalate issues, nor can we be seen as showing any weakness. If they are still out on the streets by midnight, we go out in force with no mercy shown. I will shut down all power outside of Silmac buildings until then. When you are ready to attack, we will flood the city with light, so that there is no place for them to hide.'

'Yes, sir.'

'Oh, and make sure all your men are equipped with breathing filters.'

'Will do, sir.'

'What of the rich seeking shelter?'

'We have housed them all within the Silmac Tower building downstairs. It is cramped but all who have come are in. Many are asking after you.'

'They are cowards, all of them. I will speak to them, but on my terms, before the attack. Brief me again half an hour before time.'

'Yes, sir.' Johnson turned and disappeared into the lifts. Once the lift had descended, Silmac pulled a key from his pocket and inserted it in the desk to reveal a hidden map of the city. As the panels rose, he moved over to the map and one by one began pressing the buildings on screen that were alight. With each tap a building faded slowly to dull lifelessness, until only a handful of buildings, all of them his, still had power.

Once he had switched off all the non-essential areas of the grid, his hand hovered over a virtual dial labelled 'vents'. It operated the air filters and vents that kept the air in the Dome free of the poisoned air of the Badlands, and was currently hovering in a low green level, indicating moderate power. One flick of his finger could easily swing the dial to reverse, sucking bad air into the Dome and pushing clean air out. He would be fine within the tower itself, and his forces were equipped with breathing filters so they would be protected. But for the rest of the populace, they would be subject to the poisoned air, which would make them think twice about continuing with their unrest. The salvage teams would have access to filters, but many of their families and friends would not.

His hand lingered over the switch, but eventually he pulled it back. He would wait a little longer; give them time to respond to the curfew before taking that next step. His father had always told him that a demonstration of power only had the desired effect if timed right. If timing was not considered, it could foster anger, jealousy and further discontent, solving an immediate problem but creating a bigger, longer-term challenge. But the thought of using the fans thrilled him, and his eyes lingered on the switch even after his hand had moved away.

* * * * *

Very little could be seen in the tunnel other than the flashing glint of light as the rotating blades of the giant fan caught the faint light filtering in from outside. But while their eyes were starved of stimulus, Silver's and Grave's other senses were suffering sensory overload inside the tunnel. The sound of the rotating fans was intense, forcing them to shout at each other to be heard over the rhythmic whooshing. It was an effort just approaching the vent mouth, with Silver having to lean heavily forward to combat the gale force winds. She was leaning so far forward that if the fans were to suddenly stop, she'd end up falling flat on her face.

Only a couple of metres into the tunnel, their way was blocked by a heavy, metal grate, with bars the thickness of Silver's wrist deeply embedded in the curved sides of the tunnel. The bars formed a grid that would keep out anything bigger than a cat. Roughly five metres beyond the grate was the fan itself. A little over three metres in diameter, and filling the entire tunnel from ceiling to floor, the fan could barely be seen in the gloom. There was a square rectangular gate set into the grate, with thick strong hinges and a heavy padlock holding it firmly in place.

'Will the bomb get us through these bars?' Grave shouted, his voice being snatched away the moment the words left his mouth.

'It has to. We're kind of out of options if it doesn't. You saw the checkpoints.'

Grave nodded. They had driven within site of the gates, seen the snaking line of trucks waiting to get in through a single checkpoint and the lack of activity at the others.

'Assuming it does work, what then? How do we get through the fan? The blast will be hard pressed to take out both.'

Silver peered into the darkness of the tunnel, and after a moment spotted what she was looking for. 'There, you can only just make it out, the panel on the wall. They have crews that come out here to maintain the vents from time to time, and I've heard that they occasionally come in from the outside. I'm hoping there will be a panel inside the gate that might allow us to turn off the fan.'

'It's a big if,' Grave said, 'but I don't suppose we have much choice, unless you have another one of Rat's bombs stashed away in your pack?'

Silver shook her head. 'We're going to need some sort of windbreak in order to light the fuse and ensure it stays lit. Some debris we can work up along the inside of the bars.'

Grave nodded, and the two retreated from the windswept tunnel mouth, where the trucks were parked and the others waited. They discussed their needs, and a sweep of the area soon produced an assortment of small but heavy debris, enough to slip through the bars of the gate and set up a small and temporary windbreak.

Silver ushered everyone back and knelt down by the spot, still having to lean forward into the wind to maintain her balance. It took a few attempts to light a match for long enough to hold it to the fuse but eventually she struck one that stayed lit, holding it close to the ground, behind their windbreak. She had already positioned the grenade half through the bars of the gate among the debris. As soon as the fuse caught, Silver scrambled away, allowing the wind to propel her along.

She only just made it out of the tunnel and to one side when the bomb exploded, sending a great gout of flame out the vent's mouth, and peppering the area with shrapnel.

* * * * *

Silmac was reaching for the button that would retract his map of the Dome when a beeping gave him pause. A survey of the map soon revealed a flashing red warning in one of the segments on the northwest edge of the Dome, not far from Checkpoint B.

Frowning, he hurried over to his desk and started tapping away at the keyboard, bringing up security footage from the checkpoint onto the screen. He scanned the multiple images on screen, looking for any disturbances but finding nothing. The warehouse-style building was lifeless, feeling almost empty with fewer trucks than normal parked there. The checkpoint gate itself was closed and secure, as were the doors and gates leading out into the city streets. A flash of movement caught his eye in the bottom right-hand corner of the screen, an image lit green indicating a night vision camera. It showed the vent tunnel, looking down onto one of the big fans.

To the left of the screen, a gap in the wall led to a staircase that he knew ascended to the checkpoint itself, and was used to maintain the fans. A panel on the wall nearby controlled the fan, which was shut down from time to time for maintenance. It also operated two safety doors, which could be dropped down in the tunnel on either side of the fan to secure the way while the fan was out of action, ensuring bad air did not find its way inside. Behind the camera, Silmac knew another metal grate blocked the tunnel, as the vents led into the sewer system, and there remained much stigma and fear of the Homeless.

He watched the screen closely, trying to see what it was that had drawn his eye. Then he saw it; a flash of movement from beyond the fan. Something or someone was inside the tunnel mouth and looked to have gotten past the protective grate there. He immediately picked up the phone.

'Are you seeing this alarm at Checkpoint B? They are trying to get in through the vents. I want a team there immediately. Send one via the access stair, and another group from outside. I want them stopped. Use whatever force is necessary.' Satisfied, he hung up the phone and settled in to watch the screen.

* * * * *

Grave waited a moment for the dust to settle from the blast before venturing out into the tunnel mouth. 'It worked! There's not much of the grate left.'

'Of course it worked!' Rat called out from his perch in one of the trucks, his tone indignant.

Silver followed Grave into the tunnel and indeed, while still clinging to two of its anchors, the tangled mess of metal that was once the grate had been blasted flush against the tunnel wall.

Grave and Silver made their way past the blasted gate and over to the fan access point, buffeted by the wind and sound from the fan. The panel was small, with a numbered keypad and a single lined digital display above for brief messages. When Grave touched the panel, it lit up a green colour and a message appeared on the display: ENTER FAN DISABLE CODE.

Silver shook her head in annoyance. 'I was hoping for a simple switch!' she shouted over the noise of the fan. 'We'll never guess this code.'

'We could give it a try,' Grave shouted back. 'Maybe I could look at rewiring it?'

'No time,' Silver shouted, shaking her head. 'The blast will not have gone unnoticed. We have to hurry. Come on.' She grabbed Grave's hand and pulled him from the panel and out of the tunnel.

'No luck?' Lead asked.

'Nope,' Silver replied. 'On to plan B.' She moved over to the trucks, selecting the one already missing windows, and jumped in. Gunning the engines, she drove the truck over to the tunnel mouth so that the nose and front wheels were inside the tunnel, but the door was not obstructed.

Grave grabbed her arm. 'I can't let you drive down there, Silver. We don't know what the fan will do to the truck, or to you.'

'I may be brave but I'm not that brave,' Silver responded, opening the door to the truck but leaving the engine running. 'I need a large rock, or a couple of bricks.'

'Oh, right, good thinking,' Grave said, as Lead, Hawk and Trax moved to follow Silver's request. Finding themselves alone, Grave's expression suddenly turned serious, his voice earnest. 'Silver, we might not make it through this. I just wanted to let you know that I'm glad that Asp found you and brought you into the Ash Walkers.'

Silver felt the heat rising to her cheeks. 'You're only saying that because of the diary. Otherwise I'd just be a pain in your arse.'

Grave shook his head vigorously, stepping forward and taking her hand. 'You're wrong. Forget the diary, forget Silmac. The more I see of you, the more I see how remarkable you are.'

Silver felt the blush in her cheeks deepen, but before she could reply, Lead returned bearing a rock roughly the size of Silver's thigh.

'Good,' she said, turning from Grave and putting the truck in gear, but keeping her foot down on the brake. 'Put it here, on the accelerator.'

Lead manoeuvred the rock into position, causing the engine to roar as the accelerator was forced down.

'I'm going to release the brake then jump free,' Silver said. 'Everyone ready?'

Grave stepped forward again. 'Give me your hand. I'll help pull you free.'

Silver extended her arm and Grave gripped it tightly, clasping her wrist with his right hand and taking hold of her forearm with his left. Silver released the handbrake before turning to face Grave.

'On three. One. Two. Three! Go!'

She let her foot off the brake, and the truck lurched forward. Grave pulled at her arm, tugging her free of the cab just before it disappeared into the tunnel mouth. He fell backwards into the dirt, with Silver sprawled on top of him.

The rhythmic thumping coming from the tunnel mouth was replaced by a loud crunch and an ear-splitting shriek of metal on metal. Silver started to rise, but stopped as her eyes met Grave's. The look was intense, and she felt simultaneously embarrassed and comfortable on top of him.

The moment was interrupted by Lead, who pulled Silver to her feet by the back of her overalls, before offering his hand to Grave and helping him up. The three of them, joined by Asp and Hawk moved into the tunnel mouth to see what had happened. Rat remained in the second truck, still too sore to move about, and Trax stayed with him, lighting a cigarette.

The absence of wind was the immediate indication that the plan had worked. The fan and truck had both come to a stop; the latter lodged in the former. Silence had fallen over the tunnel mouth, sounding eerie after the cacophony of sound that had previously spewed from it. The five made their way down towards the fan, passing the twisted metal of the grate and arriving at the truck itself.

The truck had careened into the fan and had its cab all but torn off from the force of the blades. The centre of the fan had busted through the front windshield of the truck, and one of the four blades was bent back out of shape. The next blade had torn into the side of the truck, carving through the driver's side window, down through where the driver's feet would have been, eventually grinding to a halt in the rough centre of the passenger side seat. A narrow space remained on each side of the truck to squeeze past. The smell of petrol was strong in the air, and Silver ducked down to see fluid dripping from the bottom of the truck.

A tapping noise caused her to rise, and she turned to find Grave tapping the tunnel wall with a piece of the metal grate. Tap. Pause. Tap, Tap, Tap. Pause. Tap, Tap, Tap.

'Grave, what the hell are you …' The rest of Silver's question was cut short by the chatter of gunfire from out in the Badlands.

'Lead, Hawk. Get to the door and hold it,' Grave ordered. 'Silver, Asp, we'll go back for Rat and Trax.'

Silver had already pulled her gun and started running to the tunnel mouth, followed closely by Grave and Asp. She peeked around the corner, and immediately had to pull her head back as bullets thudded into the tunnel side nearby, chipping bits of concrete away. The brief glimpse into the night had shown a number of dark figures making their way towards the tunnel, as well as Trax's form, slumped down next to the truck. She stuck her gun out around the tunnel and fired off a couple of shots, then chanced another look. Again, she was forced back behind cover as bullets and concrete exploded around her.

'How many?' Grave asked from behind.

'I don't know, but more than we can handle.'

'Rat?'

'Not sure. Last I saw he was in the truck, but can't see him now. Trax is down and isn't moving.'

More gunfire, this time from within the tunnel, caused the three to look around. Hawk and Lead were on opposite sides of the tunnel, in the narrow spaces between the truck and the curved wall. Both had their guns out and were firing at targets, obscured by the bulk of the truck.

'Fuck! We're surrounded and sitting ducks where we are,' Silver cursed.

'We've got to get down the tunnel and behind the truck. If we stay here, we've got no hope,' Grave said. 'The tunnel won't offer any cover from a frontal approach.'

'What about Rat?' Silver countered.

'They've either got him already, like they got Trax, or he's kept low in the truck and escaped detection,' Asp said. 'Either way, there's too much heat out there to get to him. If he's still alive, then drawing them this way may be his best chance at survival.'

Silver nodded reluctantly. She fired off a few more shots blindly and pulled back as more retaliatory fire exploded around her. Asp and Grave broke and ran down the tunnel towards the truck, Silver following them.

Grave ushered Silver down the left side of the truck where Hawk had taken up position, and continued to trade shots with the police beyond. Grave moved down beside her, turning to cover the tunnel mouth. On the other side, Asp edged down beside Lead.

Peeking past Hawk, Silver could see that a door on the right side of the tunnel was open, and two police bodies lay unmoving in front of it. Another couple crouched in the cover of the doorway, firing off semi-automatic weapons towards the truck. Hawk pushed up to fire some more shots over the mangled bonnet of the truck, then pitched backwards, letting out a scream of pain as she was struck. Silver helped pull her behind cover as more bullets exploded against the tunnel wall above. A patch of blood was rapidly blossoming from her left shoulder, while concrete chips rained down on them from above.

Lead and Asp opened fire, giving them a brief respite from the assault, but doing no real damage as the open door and poor angle protected their assailants from harm.

'I can't get at them, Sil,' Lead yelled out.

'You all right, Hawk?' Silver asked.

Hawk grimaced. 'This one hurts like hell, but won't kill me. Not sure I'll be much use shooting though.

Silver nodded, and squeezed past the wounded woman, rising to fire off a couple of shots. A grunt indicated she had hit one of her targets. There was no time to celebrate though as gunfire opened up from the tunnel mouth, the police there moving into position. Grave returned fire, resulting in a pause in the barrage.

'It's getting hot here, Silver!' Grave called over his shoulder. 'We've got thirty seconds before we're toast. A minute max. We need to get moving!'

Knowing his words were true, Silver edged out to take a look around the corner, but had to pull back immediately as bullets thudded into the front end of the truck.

'They've got us pinned down here,' Silver called back, firing off a blind shot as she spoke. 'There's too much heat to move. It'd take a miracle to move them from their position.'

'Then we better pray for a miracle,' Grave answered, also taking cover as more fire came in from the police at the tunnel mouth.

* * * * *

Silmac watched the screen intently, a smile spreading across his face as his confidence returned with each passing moment. The assailants, Silver among them, were clearly pinned down beside the truck as his troops tightened the noose around them.

He leant forward eagerly in his chair as Silver got off another shot, which took down one of his men, only to have her duck back behind cover under a rain of bullets.

'It's like a modern day Ned Kelly,' he muttered to himself. His father had told him stories of the infamous Kelly Gang. They were bushrangers, criminals, but had been romanticised in the telling and retelling of their tale. 'You've proved courageous to the end, but like Kelly you'll eventually yield to justice.'

He lifted his phone and dialled a number.

'Johnson. Yes, I'm watching from the camera ... Send your team in now … I don't care, I want you to send the team in and take them down. And Johnson, try to keep the girl alive if you can. No, the short one. Take down the others but keep her alive. I've a mind to bring back public hangings as a deterrent against those who would attempt to challenge me.'

He hung up the phone and leant in even closer to watch the action unfold. It was disappointing there was no sound to fill out the picture, but at least he had a clear view of the screen, with Silver in the forefront. As he watched, his police squad swarmed out the door to the left, firing wildly at the front of the truck.

'Yes!' he whispered as his men pushed forward, swooping in for the kill. Silver got off a shot and took one down, and another fell on the other side, before all were forced to hug the cover of the truck under the barrage of bullets.

More figures appeared at the bottom of the screen, coming out from under the camera, from further within the tunnel. Silmac frowned, then stood in rage as the newly arrived figures swarmed in at the backs of his men, falling on them with clubs and sticks, taking them down with the advantage of surprise and weight of numbers.

'No!' he shouted at the screen, fists slamming down onto the desk. 'No, no, no!'

# CHAPTER 29


*From the diary of Benjamin Adams*
*August 11<sup>th</sup>, 2035*

*The Dome Project as it has become known is progressing well. The government, now under the leadership of our new prime minister, Mrs Silmac, is accepting no delays. The money they are throwing into the project to keep moving to an aggressive schedule is remarkable. I am pleased though; the quicker I can get finished and get my family inside, the better.*

*My life is now about the Dome and my family. During the day I work on the project from dawn till dusk. In the evenings I spend all the time I can with Jess and the family. We take Jack overnight once a week, which is nice, and gives Jayden and Amber a break. We try to get the whole family around for lunch or dinner on the weekends as well. Occasionally I just sit back and watch them all, feeling amazed and blessed at what Jess and I have produced.*

* * * * *

With bullets exploding around her, Silver thought it was the end. The sound was deafening, and all she had been able to do was cower down behind the truck's wheel. Hawk's body was pressed in next to hers. She looked towards Grave, who was huddled in a similar position at the other end of the truck. His eyes met hers and they were sad but strangely comforting. The gunfire seemed to melt away, the truck, the Dome, everything else gone except the two of them.

It took a second for her to realise that the gunfire *had* died away, replaced by yells of surprise and grunts of pain. She pulled her gaze away from Grave's and turned to look down the tunnel, finding a cha-otic scene unfolding in front of her, one sweet to her eyes. Men and women, pale of skin and dressed in filthy rags, swarmed over the police, having already taken down most of them and in the process of pulling down the last few still struggling. She spotted one she recognised among them—John, the Homeless patrol leader. They bore no guns other than the ones they had just pulled from their opponents. Most were armed with an assortment of clubs and rocks.

'It's the Homeless, Grave!' Silver called out, jubilation evident in her voice.

'I know, but we're not out of trouble yet!' Grave yelled back, scrambling up towards them as bullets peppered the wall where he had just been sitting. Beyond, framed by the end of the tunnel, Silver could see a line of police taking up position to rain down more firepower at them. She scrambled around to the front end of the truck, dragging Hawk with her. On the opposite side of the truck, Lead and Asp followed.

Silver scooped up a semi-automatic rifle that one of the police had dropped, but as she turned to return fire, there was an abrupt pause in the gunfire and the last remaining Silmac Ops trucks suddenly tore past the tunnel entrance, striking at least two police as it went and scattering the others.

'It must be Rat!' Silver gasped. 'They didn't get him!'

'He should have had more sense and gotten out of there,' Grave replied, picking himself up. 'The surprise of the drive-by will wear off pretty quick. What was he thinking?'

Even as he spoke, shooting once again broke out, but this time not pointed down the tunnel.

'He's bought us some time, so let's not waste it,' Asp cut in. One arm was held down by her side, her shoulder sporting a growing patch of blood similar to Hawk. 'Rat's no fool; he'll be driving off into the night by now.'

'Asp, you're hit. Are you okay?' Silver asked, moving over to inspect the wound.

Asp waved her away. 'It's nothing. Merely a scratch.'

The leader of the Homeless band, John, joined them.

'You came,' Grave said.

'You remembered the signal,' he replied. 'It's time?'

'Yes, it's time,' Grave confirmed.

'We'd best be moving then. The police are regrouping.' He indicated down the tunnel mouth where police were again taking up position at the tunnel entrance.

The Homeless band began to withdraw, soundlessly pulling those police still alive, who had been bound and blindfolded, to their feet and melting away into the shadows deeper into the tunnel systems. The dead they left as they lay.

Grave helped Hawk to her feet, and the five began to follow the Homeless away from the truck. But just before going through the gate, Silver paused and turned back towards it. She was still carrying the semi-automatic rifle, and she aimed it back at the truck, pointing down towards the ground and letting off a burst of fire. As hoped, a fan of flames sprung up from under the truck as the bullets struck the pool of leaked petrol that had formed underneath.

'That should slow down any pursuit,' she said as she pushed back through the gate and joined the others. A moment later the sound of the explosion reverberated through the tunnel, briefly expelling the darkness around them.

Silver caught up with Grave and fell into step beside him. 'So, when you say "it's time", what does that mean?'

John, walking just ahead, answered before Grave could. 'It means it's time for the Homeless to come home. We have dwelt in the darkness too long now. Tonight we take our place in the Dome that was denied us many years ago.'

'A place that is well deserved,' Grave added, stopping by a ladder. 'Here we part ways, though I will look for you above. Will you take Hawk and Asp with you? I'm afraid their fighting this night is done.'

Hawk did not protest, but Asp stepped forward, her brow furrowed in anger. 'I'm staying with you! I can still shoot a gun.'

Grave stared at her, concerned. 'You've lost colour, Asp. You need medical aid and rest.'

'I've also lost Blocka,' Asp countered. 'I don't care about me, I'm in this for him now, and for Sarge, and all the others Silmac has casually discarded in his time.'

Grave nodded, seeing the determination in her eyes. 'Very well, but with your arm like that you won't be able to get into the tower the way we intend to go. There is another role you can play though. And you, Lead, if you're willing?'

'Count me in,' Lead said.

'I'm listening,' Asp added, wary.

'Only two of us can get into the tower by the route we mean to take. That's going to leave us vulnerable up there and potentially outnumbered. We need pressure down here on the ground to keep Silmac's attention and his troops away from us. The Homeless will provide that pressure, but they will be severely out-gunned by Silmac's forces. You two are known faces among the crews. Lead, you've worked for a long time and Asp, what happened at your parents' shop will be common knowledge on the streets by now. Together you can rally more to the cause. Give the chaos on the street some structure and throw it Silmac's way. The crews are better equipped than most and have the potential to even up the odds a little.'

'I think I'll be able to get some together,' Lead agreed. 'There will be a crowd waiting for you both when you come on down, Silmac in tow.'

Asp opened her mouth to protest, but eventually nodded.

'Well then, we don't have time to waste.' Grave shook hands with Lead and then hugged Asp.

Lead moved over to Silver and the two embraced.

'Back at the clubhouse, those things I said,' Silver began. 'I was upset, and it was unfair to you. I'm sorry. You've been a true friend to me, Lead—the best.'

'All good, Sil. I could have handled things differently. Better. Just don't go and fuck things up by getting yourself killed up there, all right? I want to see you on the other side.'

'You too, Lead. Buy us time but not with your life. Oh, here, take these.' She shrugged off her pack, reached inside, and pulled out the somewhat crumpled stack of papers they had made. 'I retrieved them from the truck but almost forgot about them. Make sure they get spread around.'

Lead nodded, taking the stack of papers from her.

Asp was next in line to say goodbye and Silver stepped over and hugged her.

'Make him pay, Silver,' Asp whispered fiercely in her ear, holding her tightly. 'Someone needs to make him pay, and I know you can do it. This is goodbye for us, so I'm relying on you to do this for me. That way I can let Blocka, Mum and Dad know when I see them.'

Silver felt the tears coming. 'You can get through this, Asp.'

'I'm tired, Silver, and I don't want to go on without Blocka. Once Silmac is down, I'm free to go to him. Promise me.'

'I promise, Asp. I promise.'

With a final squeeze, Asp released her. Lead was already halfway up the ladder, and Asp followed him, while Silver wiped the moisture from her eyes.

With a few final words to John and a farewell to Hawk, Grave and Silver made their way up the ladder, reaching the dark streets above and replacing the cover over the vent. Lead and Asp had already disappeared and the streets directly around them were empty.

'Are you still sure you're okay to do this?' Grave asked her. 'It's not too late to back out. I'll continue on alone.'

'If you think I'd let you go in there alone, you're sadly mistaken,' Silver responded. 'Blocka and Sarge have already died for this cause. Rat could be dead. I owe it to them, at least, to keep going. Besides, I've always wanted to climb the tower and finally I'll get a chance. I'd be a fool to turn it down.'

Despite her cavalier façade, Grave maintained a serious expression. 'Silver, whatever happens I just want you to know that I ...'

'Please don't say anything that is going to make this harder,' Silver cut in before he could finish. When Grave's face fell, she took his hand. 'What I mean is, tell me afterwards. I think I know what you are going to say, and I think I feel the same. But if I hear the words now, my resolve could weaken, and I need to stay focused.'

The hurt look disappeared from Grave's face and he nodded, his expression serious. 'You're right. We'd better get going. It could take a bit of time to get the stuff we need, depending on what exactly Coal took. We'll hit the clubhouse first, then stop in at my place if needed. Let's go.'

* * * * *

Silmac stared vacantly at the image of the burning truck on the screen. The fire was starting to die down, and he could see a few police on the opposite side, still trying to get past. On the nearside of the truck there were only dead bodies, the intruders having departed from the screen minutes ago. He couldn't be sure, but he thought one of the unmoving bodies might be Johnson. He picked up the phone once again and dialled, but no one answered.

He rose from the desk and began pacing the room. A hand crept up to his chest, massaging the tightness that had once more formed there. What would his father have done? Or his grandfather? They had held this same position before him and kept firm control of the Dome. He could see that control slipping away as Meek and Coal had fallen; his brother had turned into a blithering imbecile, more hindrance than help; and the status quo of the Dome had started to tip dangerously against him. The richer members of the Dome were no good to him—they were all holed up in the building below, scared and seeking protection. He needed something that would crush the current unrest, send the common man of the Dome running back to the hole from which he crawled.

'If they want to see what life is like without everything the Silmacs have provided them, perhaps I should show them,' he muttered. A smile crept along his face and he strode back over to his desk, reaching under to press the button that would display the map of the city. The panels rose, and he moved over to the screen, a mad gleam in his eye.

* * * * *

Silver tried not to look at Coal's body, unmoved from where she and Lead had left it half a day earlier. Already the air in the clubhouse was starting to take on an unsavoury smell as his body went through the early stages of decomposition. She and Grave had arrived at the Silmac Ops clubhouse and began rummaging through the pile of loot they had taken from Grave's apartment, looking for the items they would need to get into Silmac Tower.

Grave had already found a chunky looking rifle along with some coils of thin metal cabling. He was still looking for a pair of glass cutters he had been using to cut the solar panels, but hadn't had any luck locating them. Silver finally tore her eyes away from Coal, heading into the kitchen to grab some food for them, along with some extra ammunition. Her stomach grumbled as she grabbed the nutrient bars.

'Found them,' Grave said eventually. 'I think that's it—we're good to go.'

Silver handed him a protein bar, which he accepted gratefully. 'How do you think Asp and Lead are faring?'

Grave shrugged, while he chewed and swallowed. 'Only time will tell. But the activity out on the streets suggests they will find some support. What happened at the shop this morning has stirred up the Dome.'

'Better get going,' Silver suggested, grabbing up some of the things they had collected. Grave nodded, stuffing the rest of the bar in his mouth and grabbing the remaining items. They were halfway out the door when a long, loud wail sounded across the Dome, much like the tsunami warning siren.

'I didn't feel any quakes,' Silver said, confused. Everything was dark and quiet. It was as if a sound, which she had not previously been aware of, was missing and she was now only noticing it for its absence.

'Before Grave could comment, a familiar, amplified voice echoed across the Dome.

'Citizens of the Dome, this is Corbett Silmac speaking. The Dome is currently under curfew. As many have chosen to break the laws of curfew I have been left with no choice but to shut down the fans. If you abide by the laws of curfew, these services will be restored in exactly one hour. If, at this time, any have chosen to continue to ignore the curfew, the checkpoint gates will also be opened, and they will remain so until all citizens are off the streets. The choice is yours and a simple one: return to your homes and all will be restored to normal.'

'He's mad!' Grave exclaimed. 'He'd let mutes in to run riot within the Dome?'

'No, he's not mad, but getting desperate, and we're wasting time chatting about it. Let's go!' Silver took off at a run, Grave close on her heels.

# Chapter 30

*From the diary of Benjamin Adams*
*October 14ᵗʰ, 2036*

*The world is at war. This is not like the wars we have seen in the past. This is long-range warfare with devastating bombs being dropped on major populations. Jess and I watched the news all night in disbelief. Details were in short supply, but images were not and they were horrific. Apparently a conflict in the Middle East over oil triggered it, but it escalated quickly, like a match to a fuel-covered bonfire. Asia, Europe, America—they have all become involved, as targets and in retaliation. The Pacific region seems to be spared for now, but it is early days and who knows what will happen? Either way, the world as we know it has changed.*

*The Dome is progressing at a breakneck speed, and now more than ever it needs to. The environment can only suffer further from the amount of devastating munitions being dropped even as we speak. There are reports of nuclear strikes and chemical warfare being employed by multiple parties. Assuming we do not become a target of the war, we need to get this project finished.*

* * * * *

'Are you sure about this?' Silver asked, not for the first time.

'The theory is sound. This is the type of thing these guns are designed for, used by elite armed forces in the past.'

'So you've tried them out?'

'Yes, but not over such a long distance. You're not scared of heights are you?'

Silver glared at Grave, then peered down once more into the void below them. The height was dizzying, with darkness all but obscuring the ground below. 'Heights don't bother me. But climbing out over them and onto a cable thinner than my middle finger does.'

The pair stood on the rooftop of the largest building they could find in close proximity to Silmac Tower. The roof of the Dome felt strangely close and Silver began to feel slightly claustrophobic, though it was still well above them. Being up here brought back memories from her younger years. Some of them were pleasant, feeling elation and excitement at being so high up. Most were not, overwhelmingly lonely and hungry, fearful of being discovered by someone who might harm her, and on occasion considering leaping from the heights to put an end to the loneliness and fear.

Getting into the building and up to the top had been a challenge. Crowds were gathered around the base of Silmac Tower, and they were agitated. The police held a presence around the building, having taken up positions around barricades and dressed in full riot gear. There had been much indecision among the crowds, and they lacked leadership. Silver and Grave heard one man urging people to call Silmac's bluff, to stay and protest. Another woman had been imploring the crowds to heed Silmac's threats and return to their homes. A few were agitating for a fight, taunting the police, trying to provoke them into starting something. Thus far it appeared the guns were having the desired effect, and none had yet had the courage to overtly threaten the police line.

Keeping a low profile, they skirted around the crowds where possible, forcing their way through at the fringes when there was no clear way. Eventually they had made it past the crowds and into the building. The hike to the top floor was excruciating, particularly under the weight of their equipment. Both were out of breath by the time they reached the summit, and Silver's legs felt weak and wobbly. With time ticking away, there had been no opportunity for rest, and Grave begun unpacking his gear, preparing the rifle and ensuring they had enough cable length. Silver helped out where she could, her apprehension on what was to come growing all the while.

When all was ready, Grave stood, lifting the gun into position against his shoulder and moving over towards the edge.

Silver moved up beside him. 'Won't we be sitting ducks up on the wire?' she asked, glancing down once more.

'The darkness will obscure us,' Grave answered, taking aim. 'Besides, very few people look up unless they are looking for something specific.'

'I'm more worried about being spotted by someone looking down. The tower is mostly windows.'

Grave shrugged. 'If they have their lights on or curtains drawn, then we should be okay. If not, then you're right, we'll be sitting ducks. The lower levels of the tower are mostly used for storage though, and that's where we're headed. So hopefully we'll be a little low for anyone gazing out the window. It's not too late to back out though, if you're having second thoughts.'

'Not a chance. Let's just get this over with.'

Grave shifted the gun, putting his eye to the telescopic sight on top. He took a few moments to find a mark and then with a click and a whoosh, the bolt shot out across the empty expanse between the buildings, the thin metal cable trailing behind it. It hung in mid-air for a moment and then struck a point on the bottom edge of the building, below the level of the glass. Grave gave a good tug on it and the cable held, so he set about securing it at their end, wrapping the excess cable around a solid vent.

Silver pulled on a pair of black gloves, then sat next to the cable on the low wall surrounding the building top and swung her legs out over the gap. Careful not to look down, she gripped the cable tightly in both hands. It curved up and away from her, the lower edge of Silmac Tower still at least twenty metres above their current position. Over fifty metres of cable lay between her and their destination.

'What are you doing? Grave asked as he finished securing the line. 'I'll go first.'

'Sorry, if I don't go now I might not have the courage.' Gripping the cable tightly and clenching her eyes shut, she slipped off the ledge and swung down so that her back was to the tower and she was facing Grave. Straining, she walked her legs up the wall of the building and then hooked them up over the cable, taking the pressure off her arms. With a steadying breath, hand over hand she began pulling herself along the cable. It swayed under her movement and a layer of perspiration covered her brow.

Grave shook his head, but couldn't fully keep the smile from his face, impressed by her determination. Once she had moved far enough along, he followed her lead, sitting on the building edge, swinging himself down and getting his legs up and crossed over the cable.

A gunshot sounded from somewhere below, echoing back and forth half a dozen times against the Dome and the surrounding buildings. Silver paused to look down, still swaying disconcertingly from side to side. She spotted a brief flash a moment before she heard the second shot, with a third and fourth following quick on its heels. Within moments the Dome was alive with gunfire. It was too dark to spot any detail, but she could imagine the police down there, standing off against the civilians, Asp and Lead among them.

'It's started,' Grave called. 'We have to hurry.'

*Promise me.* Asp's parting words echoed through her mind, and her gaze returned to the cable stretching out ahead of her. Silently and methodically, she continued her climb.

* * * * *

A group of nearly five hundred men and women marched down Pitt Street towards Silmac Tower. They were a motley crew, dressed in singlets, jeans, overalls, muscle shirts, belts, jackets, hats and other adornments. A huge assortment of tattoos and piercings could be found among them, along with a kaleidoscope of hair colours and styles. Skinheads, mo-hawks, braids and beards walked side by side. Dark-skinned men and women of Aboriginal and African descent marched shoulder to shoulder with the lighter tones of Asians, and the pale skin of those with European heritage.

There were two things that the entire group had in common. All were armed, though like their clothes, skin and hair, their weapons varied. All had handguns of some sort, but plenty also sported knives, bats, knuckle-dusters, even a sword or two. Crude shields were also in abundance, mostly pieces of wood with makeshift straps or handles for carrying. A few held canisters of homemade explosives. The second thing that formed them into a coherent group was that they all wore breathing filters, ready for Silmac's threat of opening the gates.

At their head marched Lead and Asp. Both had spent the last hour gathering the group, visiting multiple crew houses and calling in favours.

'More than I expected, though not as many as I had hoped,' Lead commented to Ash as they walked. The dark-skinned woman had her shoulder bandaged, but it had not completely stopped the bleeding, with a crimson flower marring the white gauze.

'We were never going to get everyone,' Asp answered without looking at him. 'The Silmacs are ruthless. It's how they've stayed in power for so long.'

'Let's hope the Homeless keep their end of the bargain. Without them this could be a short and bloody affair.'

'They'll come. They could have left us in the ventilation tunnel if they weren't interested in helping. '

As they neared their destination, Lead could see that the crowd gathered around the base of the building was looking pitifully small. It had been much larger earlier, from all accounts, but even as he watched a few more started to slip away. Beyond the crowd, the police had made a show of force, armed in riot gear and carrying automatic weapons, arrayed behind barricades.

'At least eighty, maybe ninety,' Lead estimated. 'They are well equipped and hold a strong position. We don't have enough to break through.'

'We don't need to break through. We just need to keep them occupied down here to buy Grave and Silver time.'

Lead nodded, straightened his shoulders and held his head high. Those civilians who had stayed at the barricades joined the marching ranks, adding to their numbers slightly. It was unlikely to be enough, but it would help.

The tinny, amplified voice of an officer speaking into a megaphone rang out across the otherwise quiet plaza. 'Curfew is under operation. Return to your homes immediately. Force will be used on any who fail to do so.'

The group came to a halt some fifty yards from the nearest barricade. Those with shields came to the front, forming a patchwork wall that would offer some protection against the guns.

Lead waited for a moment, watching the police who faced them. 'They aren't confident,' he noted to Asp, sensing their unease in the nervous shifting of their feet, the sideways glances to their comrades.

'They know that even if they can hold us off, many of them will die tonight,' Asp agreed.

'We have our own offer,' Lead shouted at the police line. His voice was clear in the still evening despite the lack of amplification, and he held aloft a copy of the paper they had produced. 'Silmac's reign will soon be over. Copies of his lies are even now spreading through the Dome. If you hand over your guns and disperse, you will not be harmed. We plan to enter the building, whether you stand before it or not.'

Beside him, Asp raised her gun and her voice in a battle cry. Her voice was clear and high, and in a second it was joined by hundreds of others.

There was no answer from the police. They looked on impassively, guns in hand and fully prepared to open fire if the signal was given. As the cheers died down, Lead noticed another crowd enter the mall from the other end of Pitt Street. They were an even more ragged group than the one he led, and it took him a second to work out who they were.

'They're here,' Asp said, noticing them at the same time.

A ripple of nervous uncertainty expanded through the crew at the sight of the near mythological group who had been feared for so long. Lead and Asp turned and called for quiet. The murmured comments and whispers eased to silence.

Asp spoke in a clear voice. 'Like you, I feared the Homeless. But I have met them and they are human like you and me. And like us, they have had enough of Silmac's oppression.' She paused and gazed around at the sea of faces looking towards her. She pointed behind her to the line of armoured police waiting for them and cried, 'Today, any enemy of Silmac is a friend of mine!'

A cheer erupted from the group and it was louder this time, echoing off the tall buildings around them and steadily growing in volume. Soon it was taken up at the other end of the street by the Homeless and it felt as though the whole Dome was joining in. The nervous shifting and uncertainty in the police ranks amplified with the sound.

'See you on the other side,' Asp said calmly to Lead, before breaking rank and charging at the police line. Lead took off after her, and five hundred salvagers and Homeless followed hot on his heels.

* * * * *

Silmac could not hear the gunfire from up in his office, but he could see the images on the screens before him. Since his warning, the crowds had grown, rather than dispersed. He had seen figures climbing out of manholes in the street—what appeared to be the Homeless spilling forth. Salvage teams had poured out onto the streets, guns in hand, calling for his blood.

For the first time in his life, he didn't know what to do. Meek had failed him, and Johnson had been killed in the vents. Now when he picked up the phone, it often went unanswered, or he found himself talking to someone with no authority or any clue what was going on.

For the moment, the barricades the police had set up were holding, resulting in a temporary standoff. Temporary, because Silmac had no allusions that the large crowds gathered would be satisfied with a couple of dead policemen. No, they wanted his blood.

Well, they wouldn't get it! He tapped at the keypad furiously, bringing up the security control program that gave him remote override access to pretty much anything within the Dome. He tapped into the area that would open the gates, his hand hovering over the button, hesitating. Silmac Tower was well protected and well supplied. It would be easy enough, once this was over, to shut the gates and then round up any feral dogs and mutes that had made their way inside. Those who survived would think twice about messing with him in the future.

His hand descended towards the button, but before he could press it, the building began to shake, and a low threatening grumble accompanied it. The shaking continued, worsening until it felt like the whole building was rocking from side to side. The grumbling evolved into a pounding, then a roar of sound, assaulting him almost physically. Silmac sat back, his hands gripping the chair arms until his knuckles turned white.

When at last the quake subsided, and the roar had faded away into silence, Silmac could still feel his body trembling. The quake had been longer and more intense than any he had ever experienced.

Belatedly, he released his grip on the chair and looked on the screen to find the command to open the gates still waiting for him. An evil grin spread slowly across his face. Silmac leant forward and hit the button. On the screen before him he watched the gates at their various locations opening up to the Badlands.

# Chapter 31

*From the diary of Benjamin Adams*
*May 5th, 2037*

*The world is dying. There is little other way to describe it. Entire cities in the east and west no longer exist. War and disaster have wiped them away. We are hearing less and less on the news because there is no one left to report it. Australia is barely holding together. Disease is rife, aeroplanes have been grounded and the roads are unused wastelands only driven on by the government and the military. Poverty has risen dramatically and there is a heavy strain on the health system. There have been riots in the streets, particularly in the poorer areas.*

*A few months' more work and the Dome is in sight of being completed. I can barely keep up with the workload at the pace we are moving. No one has questioned my design at this stage and the panels are going in. A ballot will determine who gets a place within the Dome, though I negotiated positions for me and my family right at the start of the project.*

*For those who miss out, other Dome projects have been announced for other cities and areas, though I fear it will be too late. I'm also not sure how they will be able to afford the construction of more.*

* * * * *

Silver was roughly two-thirds of the way across the cable when the quake hit. Her shoulders burned, and her whole body ached from the strain of the climb. She was covered in sweat, and without the gloves she would have slipped and fallen long before. Behind her, Grave was in similar shape, a grimace of effort painted across his face. Below, the drop was dizzying, an abyss over two hundred metres to the pavement below.

When the shaking started, her legs slipped from the cable and she yelped as she found herself hanging by only her hands. The tremors intensified, and she was tossed back and forth like a ragdoll, as if the building above had realised they were there and was trying to shake them off. The tremors continued for what felt like an eternity; Silver's arms weakened and she had started to lose feeling in her tightly clenched hands.

A series of concussions somewhere to the north signalled the collapse of another skyscraper. Silver caught view of it from between two buildings as its top descended into an ever-expanding cloud of dust and debris. It tilted dangerously sideways as it fell, triggering the collapse of a second high-rise building nearby.

'Hold on!' Grave shouted, the strain Silver was feeling and the horror of the collapses reflected on his face. It felt as if the world was ending. She shut her eyes and tightened her grip, and at last the tremors eased, then faded altogether. The cable continued to sway and the deafening grumble of the quake lingered in her ears. Below, a dust cloud rolled through the city streets.

'Come on! Let's get moving before we are struck again.' With a grunt, Grave swung his legs up and managed to get one, then the other back over the cable.

Silver tried to follow suit, but she felt she had no strength left in her body. 'I can't do it,' she cried.

'You can,' Grave insisted, and he shuffled along the cable closer to her. 'You must! I'll help.'

He released a hand from the cable and reached out for her as she swung her leg up towards him. It made it three quarters of the way to the cable, but he caught her by the ankle and between the two of them she got her leg back over. Once both her legs were up, the intense pain in her shoulders eased.

'You can do it,' Grave insisted again. 'We're almost there.'

Silver clenched her jaw and started to pull herself along, her arms feeling weak but the movement helping to ease the burn. Agonising minutes later she made it to the building. The bolt of the cable had punched through the gold coloured metal panelling the exterior of the tower, roughly a metre above the bottom edge of the building top. Half a metre above, the bottom-most ring of windows sat within reach.

Using her thighs, Silver carefully levered herself up so that she lay on top of the cable rather than dangling under it. Carefully, she pulled herself forward and, reaching out to the building for support, managed a sitting position, one leg either side of the cable. It was not the most comfortable of positions, but with her toes against the wall and one hand still gripping the cable, she felt relatively stable. Above them, the underside of the Dome was closer than ever, as it arced into the edge of the building a handful of storeys up.

'Can you pass the cutters?' Silver asked.

Grave sidled up as close to her as he could get, then carefully reached into a pouch on his belt. Moving slowly, he extracted the cutters and passed them up to her. 'Anchor a spot in the centre of the window and work the cutter in an arc from the middle,' he instructed breathlessly.

The cutter consisted of a black, cone-shaped centre with a suction cup at the large end and a handle at the small end. Midway up the cone, a round metal shaft jutted out, along which a smaller black handle and cutting blade was set. The position of the blade could be adapted by loosening it and moving it up or down the shaft. Once set, the blade was gripped and worked around in a circular motion to cut out the glass.

Silver took the blade and after a quick inspection carefully set the suction, extending the arm to around thirty centimetres, and began to cut. The glass was thick, and she had to swap hands a couple of times. She felt the glass start to give, and she grabbed the handle of the suction, pushing onto it as she cut the final few rotations. Finally the glass panel came free, and she set it inside, fed through her pack, and then climbed in herself. Behind her, Grave had managed to get up on top of the cable in much the same way she had, and she was able to take his pack and help pull him inside.

The two collapsed on the floor, exhausted from the climb. It was Grave who eventually broke the silence, sitting up and looking around the room.

'What is this place?'

Silver had only done a cursory scan for danger when she first climbed into the room, but had taken in a few details. Looking around, she found what appeared to be a storage room. Plastic crates were stacked around the outer edges of the large space, with neat rows of crates also filling the centre of the room. The crates were stacked four high and had labels on the sides. She peered more closely at one of them, trying to make out the words in the dark.

'This stack is titled "Keyboards". I've seen these out in the Badlands from time to time.' She looked at the other stacks nearby. '"Laptops", "Smart Phones"—it appears to be a collection of electronic relics from the past. I wonder why he keeps them all here?'

'For someone with access to electricity, these items can be extremely valuable tools, and ones that we have likely lost the skills to produce ourselves. Keeping a collection could be assurance that he will never run out, or it could be that he intends to employ people to use them down the track.' Grave was fascinated by the collection, looking into boxes, studying the contents within.

'Either way, we don't have time to worry about them just now. We've got to get moving!'

'Right. We need to find stairs, or lift access, that will take us to the top.'

Silver led the way across the room to the entrance, moving quickly and quietly, peering out before entering the corridor beyond. The other rooms around them seemed to contain similar crates of tech. It didn't take them long to find the central point of the building that housed the lifts. Above the lift doors was an electronic display showing what floor the lifts were on. Grave was about to press the button to call a lift to them when Silver grabbed his hand.

'Won't the lifts be monitored? Calling one could alert Silmac to our presence and bring the guards down onto us.'

'You're right.' Grave looked around and found a door marked 'Emergency Stairs' in faded red letters. He moved over to it and tried the handle but it wouldn't turn. 'It's locked.'

'Here, let me have a look,' Silver said, grabbing her pack off her shoulders and digging into one of the compartments. 'I've gotten through a few locked doors in my time.' Pulling out some tools she had stashed within, she knelt down and began working on the lock of the door.

Behind them, Grave watched the display on one of the lifts rising steadily. He signalled a warning to Silver, who stopped her work and pulled her gun free. But the lift passed their level by, the display indicating it was headed right to the top.

* * * * *

The doors opened to a darkened room, causing Gavin to pause midway out of the lift and look around nervously. He had never known his brother to turn off the lights. He was starting to think Corbett must be next door in his private suite when he spotted him, standing quietly at the window. He was gazing out into the darkness beyond, his back to Gavin. A flash of lightning signalled a storm approaching, coming in from the west, perhaps the object of Corbett's scrutiny. The only light within the room came from the backlit screen showing the map of the city. Gavin could see that the checkpoint gates were all flashing red, indicating they were open. He turned back towards Silmac, starting towards him hesitantly.

'Are you all right, Corbett? Security was having some trouble getting through to you, so they approached me to check on you.'

'As you can see, I am perfectly fine.'

'So you know the state of affairs below in the Dome?'

'Yes, I have been watching on the screens and listening to the updates security have offered. All is going as planned.'

'How can you say that? Things are completely out of control!'

'It may appear that way to you, but all will shortly be set right. Nature will take care of it for us. Morning approaches.' Silmac remained facing out the window.

Gavin took another couple of steps towards him, hesitantly, unsettled by his brother's behaviour. 'Corbett, you've opened the gates to the bad air, the mutes and god knows what else. The quake we just had has caused two high-rise buildings to collapse, and the air in the Dome is thick with dust and debris. What's worse, we could be hit by a tsunami any minute, and you've got the gates to the Dome wide open!'

'Exactly! The tsunami waters will enter the Dome, washing away the dust and filth and sweeping away any mutes that have entered, along with all those who remain on the street in defiance. It's perfect.'

'It's madness!' Gavin shot back.

'Then what do you propose, Gavin?' Silmac's voice was quiet, dangerous.

'Maybe we need to talk with them, come to some sort of compromise?' he suggested. 'This will not just all go away, Corbett. Things have turned ugly and violent, and with the gates open and a tsunami on the way there is no good outcome in this. Not for us, or them. All the leading families agree.'

Silmac turned suddenly from the window to face them, though his frame was silhouetted by the lightening sky behind him and his features remained hidden in the darkness of the office.

'So you would listen to those pathetic excuses for human beings? They have no power or authority here. They have money only because I have chosen to allow them to keep it. I have bought their businesses one by one, paying for them handsomely and allowing them a life of comfort and luxury, above what they could otherwise hope for. And now they would have me bow and scrape to the masses, the very people they loathe, the people they would have become if not for me? This is typical of you, Gavin. It's why I rule and you are nothing.'

'No, you rule because you were born first, Corbett,' Gavin replied. 'You need to be reasonable. Thousands of lives are at risk, ours included. We don't know what impact leaving the gates open during a tsunami will have!'

'Reasonable?' Silmac screeched, with such venom and malice that Gavin retreated a step. 'You think they will be reasonable with us when we back down to them? You want to see what will happen? That can easily be arranged, for you and your family.'

He strode over to his desk, hitting the button that would open the line to security. 'Yes, get up here immediately. I have an intruder in the building that I need removed. Yes, on this floor.'

Gavin turned white as Silmac slammed down the phone. 'You wouldn't?'

'Watch me.'

'Corbett, please. See reason.'

'Oh, no you don't,' he countered, a gleam of malevolence in his eye. 'I'm giving you what you want: a chance to be reconciled with the people of the streets. It's time to back up your words with actions and prove me wrong. If you successfully negotiate a peaceful resolution, I will hand over Silmac Corp to you.'

'I'll go, but don't send my family down. They're your blood too, Silmac. Don't do that to them!'

'I'm not doing anything to them, Gavin. I have faith that you are right and that the people of the streets will welcome them with open arms.'

Gavin's face twisted in anger and he took a threatening step towards his brother. Faster than the eye could register, a gun appeared in Silmac's hand, pointed at Gavin's chest.

'Or maybe I should just kill you now so I can concentrate on more important things.' Silmac gripped the gun tightly, his hand trembling ever so slightly.

'Please, no!' Gavin implored, the anger replaced with a look of fear.

'Pathetic,' Silmac responded, his face hardened and his index finger tightened further on the trigger.

A siren interrupted the showdown, its long drawn-out wailing causing Gavin to jump and Corbett to glance at his computer screen. A wave was coming.

# CHAPTER 32



*From the diary of Benjamin Adams*
*December 19<sup>th</sup>, 2037*

*We have been betrayed, and I have failed my family. The military moved in under cover of dark and took control of the Dome. It was due to be officially opened tomorrow. Millions were expelled, and reports that those who resisted were shot and killed. Silmac is inside and I'm not sure who else.*

*Those left outside attacked the gates and were met with lethal force. Thousands were massacred. Then panic spread right through the city, with looting, pillaging and violence. My family is here in the bunker I had built almost five years ago. There is food and supplies and we are safe for now. But the food and water will only last so long. What then, I don't know. I don't know.*

* * * * *

The wail of the tsunami caused a brief pause in the fighting. Asp was slick with blood, much of it her own. She had been hit twice by bullets already: one a grazing shot across her left shoulder, which burned like a line of fire; the other a puncture to her right quadriceps, which was bleeding heavily and had just forced her down onto one knee. She had pushed on through the pain for a few minutes already, whispering 'Blocka, Mum, Dad' with each opponent she brought down. Then came a moment when there were no immediate targets left to shoot at, and her leg and weakening body forced her to stop.

The mall outside Silmac Tower was a mess of bodies: police, Homeless and salvagers. Much of it was obscured in the dust cloud that painted everything grey, hiding the blood. The gunfire had died down now, with many either having spent their ammunition or made it into close quarters, abandoning their guns for knives, clubs and batons. The quake and dust cloud had aided the attackers, throwing the more organised defence of the police into disarray and buying some time to close the gap and limit the casualties to machinegun fire. The moans of the wounded and dying were deafening though, a cacophony of death and human folly. The sight sickened Asp, causing her to retch, though her stomach had little in it to empty. How had it come to this? Why did it always seem to lead to this with humans?

A flash of movement in her peripheral vision drew her attention, and she turned to see a shape race out from the cover of one of the buildings nearby and start tearing at a corpse on the edge of the mall. It was hazy in the dust, but another followed, and then another. Asp's brow furrowed as she realised they were dogs. Within seconds a fifteen-strong pack of mangy hounds could be seen on the fringes of the mall, tearing into the fresh meat there.

Asp grimaced at the sight. She raised her gun to try to fire a bullet in their direction and scare them off, but she was out of ammunition.

'Ha! Get out!' she yelled at them. A few raised their heads in her direction before returning their attention back to the meat before them. One kept its eye on her, letting out a threatening snarl. It was a big black dog, a Rottweiler with a patchy coat and only one ear. It took a step in her direction, crouching low and snarling again.

With an aggressive bark, it bounded across the plaza towards her. She tried to regain her footing, but her leg wouldn't respond, so she dropped her gun and pulled out a knife. She held it out to the side, keeping her free hand out before her. The hound closed to within ten metres, moving fast and readying to leap. Before it could do so, a shot rang out, and it tumbled onto the pavement, rolled twice and came to a stop less than a metre away. Asp stared at the hound for a moment in shock, before turning to find Lead nearby, struggling forwards. He had a bloodied shoulder and a messy gash along his scalp, which had caused blood to run down his face and over half his chest.

'Last bullet.' He grimaced weakly, tossing the gun aside and offering Asp his good arm to help her to her feet.

'I don't understand. How did they get in?' Asp asked.

'There's only one possibility I can think of. Silmac must have made good on his threat and opened the gates.'

Asp's eyes widened. 'But the tsunami siren. If the gates are open …'

Lead nodded. 'Come on, we don't have long. We have to keep trying. Fighting has moved inside the building, but they've got some defensive lines set up in there.'

'I'm so tired, Lead.'

'I know, I feel it. But we're almost done.'

* * * * *

Grave and Silver took the stairs two at a time, puffing from exertion. Reaching yet another landing, they were about to head up the next flight of stairs when Silver pulled up, signalling Grave to a halt. She moved over to the closed door that opened onto the landing and placed her ear against the door.

*Someone's in there talking*, she mouthed to Grave, who shook his head and pointed onwards up the stairs. Silver held up her index finger and tried to steady her breathing so she could listen to the voices beyond. Reluctantly, Grave moved over as well, also placing his ear to the door.

The voices were muffled and it was difficult to make out exact words. She could tell there were at least two voices. At least one of the voices sounded agitated or distressed. She leant in closer, pressing her ear gently to the door in an effort to make out the words.

'… waters will enter the Dome, washing away the dust and filth and sweeping away any mutes that have entered, along with all those who remain on the street in defiance. It is perfect.'

Silver's eyes widened at the implications of the words she had overheard. She pulled back from the door.

'Did you hear that?' she whispered. 'They're talking about opening the gates to the Badlands, or the gates have already been opened. There'll be a tsunami on its way after that quake for sure. We have to get those gates closed.'

Grave's eyes darted to the stairway behind Silver, leading upwards. 'If this is Silmac's office, which I think it is, the entrance to the roof must be just up those stairs. We're so close to switching on the panels!'

'The panels can wait—they will still be there. If we do that first, and then don't make it back down in time, there may be no one left to benefit from our efforts! Asp and Grave are down there, fighting to buy us time. We can't abandon them.'

'You're right, of course,' Grave conceded, pulling his gun and aiming it at the door. 'Step back.'

Silver pulled out her own gun and moved back from the door, but before Grave could pull the trigger a long, wailing siren rang out—the sound of the tsunami warning. Grave and Silver shared a glance and, without a word, Grave fired off two quick shots at the door lock. Silver grabbed the handle and pulled, tugging the door open for Grave to enter the room and then following in close on his heels.

'Give it up, Silmac,' Grave yelled, having taken a left and rounded the interior wall that divided the lifts and emergency stairwell from the office. 'Drop your gun.'

Silver could see Grave, gun held out at arm's length pointed at someone beyond the screen. Rather than following Grave out the way he had gone, she quietly made her way right, creeping to the opposite end of the screen. When she had reached the corner, she carefully peered around it into the room.

Silmac's back was to her, his gun held out at Grave at the ready. Roughly halfway between Grave and Silmac stood a tall, overweight man, looking back and forth from Grave to Silmac and doing his best to shuffle backwards out of the direct line of the two guns.

'You've proved a thorn in my side, Lance,' Silmac growled. 'You and that girl. I don't suppose you left her downstairs in safety? Chivalrous of you, but when the tsunami hits you'll wish you had brought her along. She'll be washed away with the rest of them.'

'Close the gates, Silmac. All your money and wealth will mean nothing if there is no one left in the Dome for you to rule.'

'It'll all mean nothing if I back down. It'll be taken from me. Everything my family has earned and worked for will be taken away. I won't allow that.'

'You think you deserve all this?' Grave asked, incredulous. 'Everything you own was given to you, dirty money inherited from an industry that has to take much of the responsibility for the mess of a world we live in!'

'Mining made this country great. For years we pandered to governments on whose wealth we created. We deserve to be the rulers of the civilisation we funded and built! I will not hand that back to the rabble!' Silmac's face was a mask of scorn and spite as he spat out the words.

'I agree, Silmac. Mining did help build this nation and make it wealthy and great. But if you looked around you you'd notice the civilisation of which you speak is a decaying waste, barely clinging to existence. Mining may have helped build it, but it has since taken back everything it offered, and much more.'

'You fucking hypocrite!' Silmac spat back. 'You heap these wrongs upon an industry that your forebears gave voice to and colluded with. Oh yes, your family business was instrumental in shaping popular opinion in the direction my family wanted. And you've enjoyed the spoils of it ever since. You dare preach moral rights and wrongs with me?'

'Again you are right. The media industry and my family have much to blame for what has happened. Which is why I'm here, why we need to put an end to it, for good. I can't change what was done in the past and nor can you. But it is not too late to change the future.'

'So what happens now? You shoot me or I shoot you and whoever dies takes all?'

'No, you'll hand over your gun and we'll shut the gates to the Dome.'

'And what makes you think I'm going to do that?'

'This does,' Silver said, pushing the muzzle of her gun hard up against the base of his skull. She had slunk out from her cover while the two had talked and now stood directly behind him. 'Hand over your gun, Silmac. That's it, nice and slow.'

Silmac tensed and slowly lowered his gun to the table, where Silver immediately snatched it up. Just as she did so, a ping sounded from the direction of the lift. The otherwise mundane sound caused the room to explode into action. For a split second, Silver looked over towards the door, and Silmac immediately dove forward. She swung her gun towards him and fired a shot but narrowly missed as he disappeared from view behind the opposite end of the desk. Grave turned his gun towards the lift doors and fired off a warning shot as Silmac's security started to emerge. Gunfire finally uprooted Gavin from his spot and he clumsily flopped down in the direction of the desk.

'Find cover, Silver, now!' Grave yelled as he fired another shot and started backtracking towards the lounges at the southern end of the office.

Caught out in the open, Silver took a step towards the desk, but then looked towards the lifts and changed direction, running over towards Grave and the couches. She reached cover at the same time as Grave, and not a moment too soon as the security returned fire. Bullets exploded into the lounges, launching pieces of leather and foam up into the air. Behind them, bullets thudded into the windows, shattering one panel completely and causing a spider web of cracks to appear in another two.

Immediately, noxious fumes from outside began to fill the room, accompanied by wind and rain. Within moments Grave and Silver were soaked, lashed by the icy rain driven into the room. Grave fired a couple of shots blindly towards the security team while Silver fished in her backpack for the two facemasks stashed within. She handed one to Grave and pulled on her own, sucking in the filtered air.

Peering out from behind the couch, Silver scanned the room for assailants. She spotted the man who had been in the room with Silmac when they entered, huddled by the desk and in no real cover. He had pulled his shirt up over his mouth and nose and was coughing into it. Two cops, dressed in full riot gear, were stationed by the lift and another two had moved over to the desk and taken up positions there. She could not see Silmac initially, until she heard more coughing coming from the vicinity of the desk and realised he was huddling behind the chair, using it as cover as he tapped at something on the screen. She fired off a handful of shots in his direction, hoping to at least force him back down and stop him doing whatever he was doing. The shots had the desired effect: he and the police shrunk back behind cover. One of the glass panels beyond Silmac cracked and shattered under the impact of multiple bullets, increasing the wind and rain driving into the office.

A hail of return bullets forced Silver back behind the cover of the lounge.

'Hold fire!' Grave yelled out and held his gun nozzle-first up over the couch.

'What are you doing?' Silver hissed at him. 'They'll kill you!'

'Time is running out, and we are stuck here. I have to try something,' he replied. When no gunfire came from the police, he gingerly stood to his feet, throwing his gun forward and holding his hands out wide.

'Silmac has opened the gates to the Badlands,' Grave said, speaking loudly over the howl of the wind. 'You all heard the siren. A tsunami is on its way. Your families and friends will all be gone if the gates are left open. Close them, for your sake and ours. No more lives need be lost.'

'Liar!' Silmac screeched back, standing up from behind the desk. 'They are traitors and the instigators of the rebellion below. Kill them!'

None of the cops moved to carry out his orders. Peeking out from behind the couch, Silver could see them looking at one another, uncertain.

'Well? What are you waiting for?' Silmac asked, before peering a little more closely at one nearby. 'Is that you, Johnson?'

'Yes, sir,' the officer replied.

'Huh, I figured you were dead. Well, here's your chance to clean up the mess you left when you failed to do your job properly down in the vents. Take them down.'

Johnson didn't move. 'I'll take them into custody when you close the gates. I've got family down there.' He turned his gun towards Silmac.

'You have just earned your family and yourself a painful and torturous death for that treason!' Silmac spat back after his initial shock at being disobeyed had passed. He motioned to the other officers nearby. 'Whoever seizes this man will earn himself a promotion.'

Again, none of them responded to carry out his orders. Johnson raised his gun a little more threateningly at Silmac. 'They have family down there too. Now close the gates.'

Silmac looked at each of the cops present, his face cold. 'It seems I have little choice then,' he said at last, and leant forward over the computer and began tapping the keyboard intensely.

Still down behind the cover of the couches, Silver watched from her vantage point, fidgeting nervously. She looked over at the police, but two of them still had their guns trained over at her and Grave and were looking nervously back and forth between them and Silmac. Outside the wind continued to howl and the rain to drive in. Silver started to shiver as the water soaked through her outer layers and into her undergarments until her entire body was soaked.

Suddenly, something changed. The low hum of the air conditioning came to an abrupt halt. A moment later, the light from the digital map of the city on the wall panel faded to darkness. The policemen looked over at it, and at the moment of distraction Silmac grabbed the key from the desk and took a couple of steps backwards. Behind him, wind and rain drove in through the shattered window panel.

'I have disabled power to the city, and this key is the only thing that will restore it.' He held the key aloft behind him. 'Without power, the gates of the Dome will remain open. I suggest you carry out my command or this key goes over the edge.'

A shot rang out and Silmac suddenly lurched over, letting out a screech as the bullet tore through his right knee. Silver, who had fired the shot, rose from cover and started running towards him. 'The key. Grab the key!'

Johnson lunged towards Silmac, who was still a few metres away from the window and had fallen to the ground, his face contorted in rage and pain. Just before Johnson reached him, he hurled the key towards the shattered screen. Silver traced its flight through the air as it tumbled end over end towards the window. It bounced once, just before the sill, then was gone, disappearing in the wind and the rain. In the Dome below, the tsunami warning siren continued to wail.

# Chapter 33



*From the diary of Benjamin Adams*
*July 10ᵗʰ, 2041*

*I am dying. I have tried to remain strong, for the family, but I no longer have the strength to struggle on. Alex and Jess are gone, and without Jess, I am nothing. She got the cough about a year ago. The air is more toxic than ever since the Dome Dwellers shelled large parts of the city with god-knows-what in order to exterminate those banding together to try to fight their way in. Alex was among them and was killed in the fighting. I begged him not to go, warned him of the outcome. He told me simply that he had to try. He said that if more people had tried harder when things were still good, we wouldn't be in this hopeless situation. He was right, but now he is dead.*

*Jess held on for a long time, but slipped away a month ago. We burned her body, away from here so that we didn't draw unwanted attention towards us. People have resorted to cannibalism to stay alive, and I would not risk that happening to Jess. I couldn't bear it.*

*Our humanity has been taken away from us, but ultimately we are responsible for it. Those of us left outside the Dome are no longer human, but savage animals, becoming more so every day. All the good things of humanity have been stripped away and all that is left is anger, desperation and brutality.*

*My lungs hurt from the fumes and talking is getting harder. The spark and smile has gone from the eyes of those around me: Jayden, Amber, Chloe and her companion Andy, even little Jack. Chloe is pregnant, but I will not live to meet her child for I can feel Jess calling me from beyond. The secrets of the Dome are recorded in the pages that follow. No one inside the Dome knows its true capabilities. To my beautiful children, to my grandchildren, and to their children, I'm sorry. I could have done more to prevent this. I should have done more.*

* * * * *

Having reached him too late, Johnson struck Silmac a blow to the head, causing him to flop limply to the carpet, out cold. Silver arrived at the shattered window a second later, peering out for any sign of the key. Rain drove into her facemask, making it difficult to see. The Dome curved away below her, torrents of water washing over its faceted surface towards the Badlands. There was no sign of it. To the north she could see the Harbour Bridge and the shattered remains of what was once North Sydney. The light was strange outside; above a storm raged, but having blown up out of the south-west, the sky to the north and east remained clear. It was still early morning and light from the rapidly approaching dawn was visible, casting a yellow-green glow across the dark storm clouds.

'Any sign of the key, Silver?' Grave called from behind her.

'I can't see it—there's too much rain and wind,' she shouted back.

'If it's not somewhere immediately visible, you're not going to find it,' Johnson said from behind her. 'It could have washed down to the Badlands by now, or down into one of the tanks that harvest water from the Dome.'

Silver turned back towards the room to see Grave over at the computer on Silmac's desk. He tapped at the keyboard in a vain effort to get it started, but the monitor remained dark and lifeless. Between them, Johnson and a second guard were on their knees, in the process of cuffing Silmac, still senseless. Beyond the desk, the other two police stood, guns still raised uncertainly. Johnson rose and he and Silver joined Grave at the desk.

'At ease, men, the time for guns is over,' Johnson said to the two policemen. Grave made way for him at the keyboard as he tried another few combinations to get the screen working.

'Looks like he wasn't bluffing. He's cut power and master access to the system. Without the key, we are done for.' There was a slight tremble of panic in his voice.

While the two men looked at the screen, Silver started rifling through the drawers of the desk. 'Here!' she exclaimed suddenly, holding another key aloft that was tucked in the back corner of one of the second drawers. She shoved it in the hole and turned it. The map of the city on the wall before them came to life, bathing them in a blue-green glow. The image was also displayed on the smaller screen on the desk before them. Johnson tapped on one of the checkpoint sectors. A message flashed up on screen.

ERROR, CITY POWER DISABLED. RESTART.

He growled at the screen in frustration, tapping another point of the map showing a pipe entering the outskirts of the Dome. Another message appeared on screen.

RESTARTING POWER, PLEASE WAIT …

'How long is that going to take?' Grave asked, an edge of impatience in his voice.

'Too long,' Gavin piped up, picking himself up from the floor behind the desk. Silver had almost forgotten about him. 'Last time we shut down power completely it took an hour for everything to come back online.'

'But if we could get some power, you could get the gates closed?' Grave asked.

'Sure—if.'

'Right then, stay here and watch the screen. If the power comes on, get those gates closed and then turn on power to the whole city! Silver, we've gotta get to the switch.'

Silver nodded, racing for the stair doors with Grave.

'What if it doesn't work?' Johnson shouted at their backs.

'Then pray for a miracle and think of your family,' Grave replied over his shoulder, disappearing through the stairwell door.

Sprinting up another flight of stairs, they arrived at an airlock door. Silver grabbed the heavy metal wheel and started to turn it, Grave adding his weight a second later. Together, they shoved the door open and Grave ran to the next, opening it while Silver secured the first one. As the seal on the second door was broken, they were greeted by more rain, wind and cold. The door faced west, and the view was limited to dark grey clouds tinged a sickly green from the sunlight hitting them. The Badlands were obscured by the haze of the rain.

'Where is the switch again?' Grave had to yell to be heard over the wind and rain.

'It's hidden in a panel on the eastern side of the spire above us. Let's go.'

A thin platform surrounded by a rail ran around the tower, slick with rain. Silver edged out to her left, making her way around to the eastern side, Grave close behind. Looking up she could see a slight rim, above which the spire thrust up towards the clouds. There was no ladder and no space to stand above. She tested the rail strength with her hand, frowning at the way it wobbled. The further they went around, the colder she became, her hands trembling and turning white. Before them, out to the east, the sun had now risen above the horizon like a beacon pointing at the eastern side of the tower. When she judged them to be at the right spot, she stopped, looking dubiously upwards.

'I'll lift you,' Grave said into her ear. 'I won't let you fall.'

Silver nodded, given it was the only way she could get up higher. Grave sidled in behind her, took a firm grip of her hips and on the count of three she jumped while he hoisted her up towards the rim above. Her trembling hand slipped when she tried to grab hold and for a moment the pair of them teetered backwards, with only the rail stopping them from tumbling over. With a grunt, Grave recovered, pushing her forward and up to have another grab at the ledge. This time she got an arm up onto it, enough to keep her in place. She hoisted herself up a little further, getting her feet onto Grave shoulders where he gripped them tightly.

As stable as she was going to get, she looked around the ledge and despaired when she was greeted by a smooth, flat surface, slick and dark from the water on it.

'There's nothing here!' she shouted down to Grave, her voice cracking under the emotion. How could they have come all this way only to find the whole diary was a hoax?

'Are you sure?' Grave shouted. 'It has to be there!'

Silver rubbed her hand over the surface, back and forward, feeling for a crack or anything that could be an opening. She reached out to either side as far as she could, but still found nothing. 'It's not here, there's nothing!'

'Keep looking,' Grave shouted up. 'Don't rush, I've got you.'

She forced her trembling hand under control, running it over the surface once more, slowly. This time she felt something, the slightest of cracks. She still couldn't see anything, but her fingers returned to the spot, tracing up along the edge before losing it again. With a growl, she let go of the ledge and used both hands to search for the crack, trusting fully in Grave to hold her up. Identifying a corner, she worked her hands both ways, tracing the outline of a square. She tried to get her nails under it, but the gap was too fine. She felt within the square but could find no mechanism or keyhole to indicate how the panel would open. In frustration she struck it with her palm and felt the tiniest movement.

When she took her hand away, as if by magic the lines she had been feeling but struggling to see appeared, and a small door popped open revealing a shallow indentation in the spire underneath. Within, there was a single switch in the middle of the depression. Beyond was a package, sealed in clear plastic.

'We've got it!' Silver exclaimed, flicking the switch without hesitation. The button remained depressed when she took her hand away, but otherwise nothing else happened.

'Well?' Grave called from below. 'Anything?'

Silver grabbed the package and checked for anything else she had missed within the depression. When she found nothing, she pushed herself downwards, and Grave guided her feet safely back down to the ledge. The rain had eased somewhat, turning into more of a drizzle, while the wind also died down, but it remained bitterly cold. Grave's lips were blue through the mask and, like her, he was shivering visibly from the chill. He looked into her eyes, questioningly.

'I found a hidden panel and flicked the switch, but nothing seemed to happen. Will the panels work in a storm if they are drawing energy from the sun?'

'They should do. The panels I pulled together generated some energy even on overcast days, through the glass of the Dome. And the Dome as one big solar panel would be ten thousand times the potential of my panels. What's in the package?'

'Looks like a manual,' Silver said, handing it to Grave.

Using his body to shield it from the rain, he tore at the plastic packaging. Meanwhile, Silver leant out over the rail to look down at the

Dome below, searching for any sign of artificial light from below, refusing to give up. Only the slick, dark edge of the Dome greeted her.

* * * * *

Lead carried Asp back from the fighting, towards the entrance to the
building, which had long since been breached. The lobby of Silmac
Tower, once an elegant, marbled space, was a tangle of blood, bodies,
broken marble and shattered tiles. The doors had been ripped off their
hinges, chunks had been blown out of the walls and floor, glass had
been shattered and bodies left to breathe their last breaths.

Asp and Lead had fought side by side, but Asp had eventually fallen,
a stray bullet catching her in the stomach. With the wounds she had
already taken, Lead knew her time was limited. In a fury, he had smashed
down his nearest opponent and then gently lifted Asp and carried her
away from the continued violence. It was dark within the building, the
lights having blinked out some time before, so Lead moved towards
where there was more light near the building entrance. Finding a relatively clear area, he gently lay her down, propped up against the wall.
There he held her hand tightly.

'I wish I had a chance to know you longer, Lead,' Asp spoke weakly.

'You will, if you stay strong,' Lead replied, though he could hear the
lack of conviction in his voice. It was miraculous that she had fought on
as long as she had, but now Asp was deathly pale. Lead could feel tears
welling up inside, but he fought them with all his might, trying to stay
strong before her.

'Do you think they'll make it? Do you think all this is worth it?'

'They'll make it, Asp. Silver is the most determined person I know.'

'At least I'll get to be with Blocka soon.'

She had barely finished speaking the words when the lights flickered
back on, dispelling the dark and gloom from the building. Lead gazed
up at them, then looked outside and could see that the lights in the
plaza and those in the building opposite were coming on as well. It was
more light than he had ever seen, as if the Dome itself was aglow from
an internal light within.

'Look, Asp, they did it! The lights are coming on! We did it!'

He turned back to her, and she had a small smile on her face, but her eyes were closed and she was no longer moving. Lead's tears came freely now, and he leant down and kissed her forehead gently.

* * * * *

'Look!' Silver exclaimed, pointing at the Dome below. 'Lights are coming on in the Dome! It's working!'

Grave leant out next to her, following the line to where she was pointing. It was hard to make out but, sure enough, within the Dome she could see lights coming on everywhere, in places she had never seen them lit before. It was a beautiful, magical sight.

Grave turned to her and enfolded her in a fierce hug. She gripped him back tightly, tears falling down her face, just a few more drops in the flood of rain that continued to fall around them. Grave's body felt warm against hers, fighting away some of the chill from her soaked clothes. She felt the sun breaking through the storm clouds on her neck and opened her eyes to it, looking out east over Grave's shoulder.

'This is all thanks to you, Silver. You did this.'

'Grave.'

'Don't deny it. You found the diary, you brought it to me, you inspired others to help and kept fighting when hope was fading. You got us here.'

'Grave!

Finally, Grave let her go and looked at her, his eyes widening when he saw the dread in her eyes. 'What is it?'

She pointed past him, out to the east. He turned slowly and saw the sight that had alarmed her. Despite all the rain, the harbour looked almost empty. In truth there was water in it, just far less than there should be. But out past the desolate heads, a monstrous line approached them. The tsunami had arrived, and it looked huge.

'Jesus,' Grave breathed, pulling Silver into him tightly.

The wall of water drew closer, smashing into the headlands and rolling over them as if they were little more than speed humps. Once in the harbour, Silver could see that the approaching wave was truly massive, maybe forty to fifty metres high. There seemed a very real possibility it could tear through the Dome, regardless of the checkpoint gates being opened or closed.

'Will the Dome stand against it?' she asked, unable to drag her eyes away. She felt strangely calm, though dimly aware she was probably in shock.

'I don't know,' Grave answered. 'It has to, it must!' He faced Silver and pulled her into a tight embrace once more, finally dragging her eyes from the water.

'This is either the new beginning we dreamed of, or the end,' she whispered to him.

Grave pulled back from Silver, ignoring the approaching wave and lifting the filter up off his face. 'Either way, I'm glad I'm spending it with you.' Silver lifted her mask, and he leant in and kissed her, gently, passionately. She returned the kiss, her worries, the wave, everything falling away. They came apart, turning to watch as it sped towards them. Silver's head rested on Grave's shoulder and his arm gripped her waist tightly, pulling her into him.

# Acknowledgements

I have been truly blessed to be surrounded by so many wonderful people over many years who have all contributed in some way to the release of *Salvage*.

First and foremost, thanks to Cara for your support, belief and feedback. I love you and am honoured to have you beside me in this journey we call life.

To Mum and Dad, thanks for your love and for instilling a love of books in me from day one. Thanks to Clinton and Suzette for the valuable feedback you provided. To Luke, Clinton and Michael, for providing inspiration and balance over many years of gaming and friendship. To Sue, for your love and generous support in getting the ball rolling!

Thanks to Michelle, Jenna, Isobel and the Odyssey Books authors for sharing your experience and helping get *Salvage* to where it is. Thanks also to Brian, Emily, Jono, Mel and Julie for your generosity in supporting the release of *Salvage*.

To all our incredible family and friends: your friendship, support and encouragement mean the world to me.

# About the Author

Martin Rodoreda is a Sydney born and based media professional and writer with a love of speculative fiction and ancient history. Martin's writing draws on contemporary themes and seeks to combine action, fiction and social comment into worlds that are simultaneously familiar and foreign, realistic and extraordinary.

Martin's debut novel *Salvage* does just that. Set in Sydney in the near future, Salvage projects current political and environmental trends into a dark and dangerous future world. His second novel will transport the reader backwards in history by nearly 2,500 years to the ancient Greek civilisation of Sparta, where a young boy must find a way to grow and thrive in Sparta's militaristic culture.

Martin has many and varied interests. He loves to read all manner of books, though his first love remains the Speculative Fiction genre. He grew up playing table-top miniature games and role-playing games, and still enjoys these when he gets the chance. He loves Australian Rules Football and, while he hung up the boots a few years ago now, he enjoys keeping fit and healthy. He is passionate about the environment and strives to do his part to ensure a healthy world for future generations.

Above all these things, Martin is a dedicated husband, father of three boys and loves spending time with his family.